WHEN FALCONS FALL

WHEN FALCONS FALL

A Sebastian St. Cyr Mystery

C. S. HARRIS

AN OBSIDIAN MYSTERY

OBSIDIAN
Published by New American Library,
an imprint of Penguin Random House LLC
375 Hudson Street, New York, New York 10014

This book is an original publication of New American Library.

First Printing, March 2016

Copyright © The Two Talers, LLC, 2016
Penguin Random House supports copyright. Copyright fuels creativity, encourages diverse voices, promotes free speech, and creates a vibrant culture. Thank you for buying an authorized edition of this book and for complying with copyright laws by not reproducing, scanning, or distributing any part of it in any form without permission. You are supporting writers and allowing Penguin Random House to continue to publish books for every reader.

Obsidian and the Obsidian colophon are trademarks of Penguin Random House LLC.

For more information about Penguin Random House, visit penguin.com.

LIBRARY OF CONGRESS CATALOGING-IN-PUBLICATION DATA:

Names: Harris, C. S., author.
Title: When falcons fall: a Sebastian St. Cyr mystery/C. S. Harris.
Description: New York, New York: New American Library, [2016] I Series:
Sebastian St. Cyr mystery; 11
Identifiers: LCCN 2015041045 I ISBN 9780451471161 (hardback)
Subjects: LCSH: Saint Cyr, Sebastian (Fictitious character)—Fiction. I Great
Britain—History—George III, 1760–1820—Fiction. I BISAC: FICTION/Mystery &
Detective/Historical. I FICTION/Mystery & Detective/General.
I GSAFD: Regency fiction. I Mystery fiction.
Classification: LCC PS3566.R5877 W474 2016 I DDC 813/.54—dc23
LC record available at http://lccn.loc.gov/2015041045

Printed in the United States of America
10 9 8 7 6 5 4 3 2 1

Penguin
Random
House

In memory of Banjo, Scout, and Indie,
my three forever-kittens

Acknowledgments

*M*y profound and heartfelt thanks, first of all, to my agent, Helen Breitwieser, who has stuck with me through thick and thin for twenty years now. And to my amazingly insightful editor Ellen Edwards, who guided this series through its first eleven books; you have taught me so much, and you will be missed more than you'll ever know.

Thank you, Danielle Perez, who has enthusiastically picked up where Ellen left off. Thank you, Gene Mollica, for your wonderful cover art, and for so generously permitting me to use your images on my Web site. Thanks to publicists extraordinaire Loren Jaggers and Danielle Dill. Thank you, Claire Zion, Kara Welsh, Sharon Gamboa, Adam Auerbach, Daniel Walsh, and the rest of the great crew at NAL/Berkley. And a huge shout-out to the wonderful folks at Garden District Book Shop in New Orleans, Murder by the Book in Houston, Poisoned Pen in Phoenix, Powell's in Portland, and Seattle's Mystery Bookshop; thank you for everything you do.

Thank you to my daughters, Samantha and Danielle, for putting up with my bouncing plot ideas off you since before most children know what a plot is. Thank you to the Monday-night Wordsmiths—Pam

Ahearn, Rexanne Becnel, Elora Fink, Charles Gramlich, Steven Harris, Farrah Rochon, and Laura Joh Rolland—for years of friendship, conversation, laughter, advice, encouragement, and commiseration.

And finally, thank you again to my husband, Steven Harris, for being you.

Say, will the falcon, stooping from above,

Smit with her varying plumage, spare the dove?

. . .

Admires the jay the insect's gilded wings?

Or hears the hawk when Philomela sings?

—ALEXANDER POPE

WHEN FALCONS FALL

Chapter 1

Ayleswick-on-Teme, Shropshire
Tuesday, 3 August 1813

*I*t was the fly that got to him.

In the misty light of early morning, the dead woman looked as if she might be sleeping, her dusky lashes resting against cheeks of pale eggshell, her lips faintly parted. She lay at the edge of a clover-strewn meadow near the river, the back of her head nestled against a mossy log, her slim hands folded at the high waist of her fashionable dove gray mourning gown.

Then that fly came crawling out of her mouth.

Archie barely made it behind the nearest furze bush before losing the bread and cheese he'd grabbed for breakfast.

"There, there, now, lad," said Constable Webster Nash, the beefy middle-aged man who also served as the village's sexton and bell ringer. "No need to be feeling queasy. Ain't like there's a mess o' blood."

"I'm all right." Archie's guts heaved again and his thin body shuddered, but he swallowed hard and forced himself to straighten. "I'm all right." Not that it made any difference, of course; he could say it a hundred times, and word would still be all around the village by noon, about how the young Squire had cast up his accounts at the mere sight of the dead woman.

Archie swiped the back of one trembling hand across his lips. Archibald Rawlins had been Squire of Ayleswick for just five months. It was an honor accorded his father, and his father before him, on back through the ages to that battle-hardened esquire who'd built the Grange near the banks of the River Teme and successfully defended it against all comers. One of the acknowledged duties of the squire was to serve as his village's justice of the peace or magistrate, which was how Archie came to be standing in the river meadow on that misty morning and staring at the dead body of a beautiful young widow who had arrived in the village less than a week before.

"'Tis a sinful thing," said Nash, tsking through the gap left by a missing incisor. "Sinful, for a woman to take her own life like this. The Good Book says, 'If any man defile the temple of God, him shall God destroy; for the temple of God is holy, which temple ye are.' And I reckon that's as true for a woman as for any man."

Archie cleared his throat. "I don't think we can say that yet—that she took her own life, I mean."

Constable Nash let out a sound somewhere between a grunt and a derisive laugh as he bent to pick up the brown glass bottle that nestled in the grass at her side. "Laudanum," he said, turning the bottle so that the POISON label faced Archie. "Emptied it, she did."

"Yes, I noticed it."

Archie stared down at the woman's neatly folded spencer. It lay to one side with her broad-brimmed, velvet-trimmed straw hat, as if she had taken them off and carefully set them aside before stretching out to—what? Drink a massive dose of an opium tincture that in small measures could ease pain but in excess brought death?

It was the obvious conclusion. And yet . . .

Archie let his gaze drift around the clearing. The meadow was eerily hushed and still, as if the mist drifting up from the river had deadened all sound. The young lad who had stumbled upon the dead woman's body at dawn and led them here was now gone; the creatures of forest and field had all fled or hidden themselves. Even the unseen birds in the tree canopy above seemed loath to break the silence with their usual chorus of cheerful morning song. Archie felt a chill dance up his spine, as if he could somehow sense a lingering malevolence in this place, an evil, a disturbance in the way things ought to be that was no less real for being inexplicable.

But he had no intention of uttering such fanciful sentiments to the gruff, no-nonsense constable beside him. So he simply said, "I think you should put the bottle back where it was, Nash."

"What?" The constable's jaw sagged, his full, ruddy cheeks darkening.

Archie tried hard to infuse his voice with a note of authority. "Put it back exactly as you found it, Constable. Until we know for certain otherwise, I think we should consider this a murder."

Constable Nash's face crimped. His small, dark eyes had a way of disappearing into the flesh of his face when he was amused or angry, and they disappeared now. But he didn't say anything.

"There's a viscount staying in the village," said Archie. "Arrived just yesterday evening. I've heard of him; his name is Devlin, and he works with Bow Street sometimes, solving murders. I'm going to ask for his advice in this."

"Ain't no need to go troublin' no grand London lord. I tell ye, she killed herself."

"Perhaps. But I'd like to be certain."

Archie readjusted the tilt of his hat and smoothed the front of his simple brown corduroy coat. Standing up to the village's loud, bullying constable was one thing; Archie had only to call upon some six hundred years of Rawlins tradition and heritage.

But approaching the son and heir of the mighty Earl of Hendon and asking him to help a simple village squire investigate the death of a stranger was considerably more daunting.

Chapter 2

A picturesque cluster of half-timbered and stone cottages huddled in the shadow of a squat, timeworn Norman church, the Shropshire village of Ayleswick lay just to the southwest of Ludlow, near the banks of the River Teme. Once, it had been the site of the Benedictine priory of St. Hilary, famous along the Welsh Marches as a pilgrimage destination thanks to its possession of an ancient wooden statue of the Virgin, said to work miracles.

But the priory was long gone, its famous statue consigned to the flames and many of the stones from its sprawling monastic complex sold or hauled up the hill to build a grand Tudor estate known as Northcott Abbey. The once-bustling village had sunk into obscurity and now boasted only one decent inn, the Blue Boar, a rambling, half-timbered relic that fronted both the village green and the narrow, winding high street.

Sebastian St. Cyr, Viscount Devlin, stood at the window of his chamber at the inn, his view of the misty green below rippled by the casement's ancient leaded glass. The impression was one of bucolic peace, of innocence and harmony and timeless grace. But Sebastian knew that all is often not as it seems, just as he knew that those who probe the secrets of the past risk hearing truths they might wish they'd never learned.

He dropped his gaze to the mechanical nightingale he held in his hands. It had been purchased for an old woman Sebastian had never met, by a man who was now dead. And so Sebastian had come here, to the old woman's village, to deliver her dead grandson's gift.

He heard the soft whisper of fine muslin skirts as Hero came to slide her arms around his waist and rest her dark head against his. Tall, statuesque, and striking, she'd been his wife for a year now. Their infant son slept peacefully in his nearby cradle, and Sebastian loved both mother and child with a passionate tenderness that awed, humbled, and terrified him.

She shifted to take the nightingale from his hands, wound the key cleverly concealed in its tail feathers, and set the bird on the deep windowsill before them. The nightingale's gilded wings beat slowly up and down, the jewels in its collar sparkling in the early-morning sunlight as a cascade of melodious notes filled the air.

She said, "Shall I come with you?"

He hesitated, his attention caught by a young country gentleman in an unfashionable corduroy coat who was striding toward the inn's door. "You don't think a simple, aged countrywoman might find a visit from the two of us a bit overwhelming?"

"Probably," she said, although he saw the faint frown that pinched her forehead. She knew that the nightingale was only part of what had brought him to this small Shropshire village, just as she knew that what quickened his pulse and tore at his gut was the possibility that the unknown elderly woman might possess the answer to a question that had shattered his world and forever altered his understanding of who—and what—he was.

An unexpected knock at the chamber door brought his head around. "Yes?"

A spry middle-aged chambermaid with a leprechaun's face and wild iron gray hair imperfectly contained by a mobcap opened the door and bobbed a quick curtsy. "It's young Squire Rawlins, milord. He says t' beg yer lordship's pardon, but he's most anxious to meet with you, he is." She dropped her voice and leaned forward as she added, "I'm thinkin' it's on account of the lady, milord. Heard Constable Nash tellin' Cook about it, I did."

"What lady?"

"Why, the one they done found down in the water meadows, just this mornin'. Dead, she is!"

He and Hero exchanged silent glances.

On the windowsill, the mechanical nightingale wound down and stopped.

"The young Squire's a tad new to being justice of the peace, I'm afraid," confided the chambermaid as she escorted Sebastian down the stairs. "Took over from his father just a few months back, he did. A real tragedy, that; the old Squire died on the lad's twenty-first birthday."

"Tragic indeed," said Sebastian.

The chambermaid nodded. "Drank three bottles of port and then tried to jump his best hunter over the stone wall by the pond. The horse made it, but not the old Squire. Broke his neck."

"At least the horse survived."

"Aye. Would've been a shame to lose Black Jack. He's a grand hunter, that Black Jack. Best in the Squire's stables." She tut-tutted and shook her head as they reached the inn's old flagged entrance hall and turned toward the small parlor to the left of the stairs. "Here ye go, milord."

He found the new Squire Rawlins standing before the parlor's empty hearth, his hat twisting in his hands. He had a smooth, boyish face reddened across the tops of his cheeks and the bridge of his nose by the summer sun, and looked more like sixteen than twenty-one. Of medium height only, he was thin and bony, with a jerky way of moving, as if he'd yet to grow accustomed to the length of his own arms and legs.

"Lord Devlin," he said, surging forward as the chambermaid dropped a curtsy and withdrew. "I'm Archibald—Archie—Rawlins, Ayleswick's justice of the peace. I beg your pardon for intruding on you without a proper introduction, but there's been a rather peculiar death in the village, and since I know you have experience dealing with these matters I was hoping you might be willing to advise me on how best to go about things. My constable thinks it's suicide, but I . . . I . . ."

The young man's rushing tumble of words suddenly dried up.

"You find the death suspicious?" suggested Sebastian.

Archie Rawlins swallowed hard enough to bob his Adam's apple up and down, and nodded. But Sebastian noticed he didn't say *why* he thought it suspicious.

Sebastian knew the urge to tell Squire Rawlins that what he asked was impossible, that Sebastian was in town for a few days only and would soon be gone. The last thing he wanted was to get involved in some village murder.

But then he saw the mingled uncertainty and earnestness in the young man's eyes and remembered the good-humored derision in the chambermaid's assessment of the village's new justice of the peace. Which was how he found himself saying, "Hang on while I fetch my hat and gloves."

Chapter 3

"Her name is—or I suppose I should say *was*—Emma Chance," explained the Squire as they followed a shady path that led from the far end of the high street, down through a thick wood of oak and beech, to the river. "She's a young widow—only arrived in the village last Friday."

"She has family here?" asked Sebastian, treading carefully along a slippery stretch of the footpath deep in the shadow of the trees and still muddy from a recent rain.

Rawlins shook his head. "She was on a sketching expedition through Shropshire. You should see her drawings and watercolors; they're quite out of the common."

"How old did you say she was?"

"She told me she met Captain Chance when she was twenty, and was married seven years. So I suppose that would make her twenty-seven or twenty-eight. He died of fever in an American prison just six months ago."

"Tragic. Who is traveling with her?"

"Well, she had her maid with her."

"That's it?"

"Yes."

It was highly unusual for a gentlewoman—even a widow—to travel without a male relative. Sebastian said, "I take it you spoke with her?"

"Several times. She asked if she could sketch the Grange and I said yes. The original part of the house dates back to the thirteenth century, you know."

"And did she sketch it?"

"She did, yes. On Saturday."

"When was the last time anyone saw her?"

Rawlins drew up at the edge of the water meadow and turned to give him a blank look. "I don't rightly know. I suppose that's one of the first things I should find out, isn't it?"

Sebastian narrowed his eyes against the strengthening morning sun as he studied the clump of trees on the far side of the meadow. "It would help."

A broad, flat area of grassland that lay beside the river, the water meadow was kept irrigated when necessary by a carefully controlled series of sluice gates, channels, and field ridges. The latest crop of hay had recently been harvested, leaving the grass shorn close and the air smelling sweetly of new growth and the cool waters of the slow-moving river. Only a loud buzzing of flies near a far stand of alders hinted at the presence of death.

They crossed the clearing to where a belligerent-looking middle-aged man introduced by Rawlins as Constable Nash stood beside the young widow's body, his massive arms crossed at his chest. Sebastian remembered what Rawlins had said, that the constable was convinced the woman had killed herself. Constable Nash obviously did not appreciate having his judgment questioned by the new justice of the peace.

What was left of Emma Chance lay at his feet, her head propped against a low log, her bare hands folded at her heart as if she were already in her tomb. Even in death, she was beautiful, her features dainty, her skin flawless, her neck long and graceful, her hair a rich dark brown. A fashionable spencer and hat rested nearby, the fingers of one fine gray glove peeking out from beneath its brim. An empty bottle of laudanum, its cork stopper carefully replaced, was at her side.

"It's suicide, I tell ye," said the constable. "Plain as plain can be. She done took off her hat and that fancy little coat thing, laid down, drank the laudanum, and killed herself."

Rather than answer, Sebastian hunkered down beside the woman's small, delicate body. Her gown was plain but of good quality and fashionable, its soft, subdued gray appropriate for a widow who'd been in mourning for more than six months. He could see no signs of violence of any kind, although that didn't mean there were none.

Yanking off one of his gloves, he touched the back of his hand to her cheek. She was utterly cold.

"When was she found?" he asked.

The young Squire cast one quick look at the dead woman, then stared pointedly away, toward the slowly moving waters of the river. "Just after dawn. One of the lads staying at Northcott Abbey was out early looking for birds and happened upon her."

Sebastian shifted his gaze to the surrounding grass. The close-cropped stalks were visibly crushed in places, but the ground was slightly elevated here and too hard and dry to show the footprints of those who had trod it. And he found himself staring at the dead woman's feet, just visible beneath the hem of her gown. She wore half boots made of fine soft kid, relatively clean except for some dust on the toes.

He rested one forearm on his thigh as he felt a slow, familiar anger begin to build within him. For a beautiful young widow to be so overcome by a vortex of grief, desperation, or guilt as to take her own life was tragic. But for someone to steal that life away without her consent was an abomination.

He said, "Is there another path she could have taken to get here besides the one we followed?"

"Well . . . I suppose she could have come along the riverbank. But it's awfully muddy at the moment."

"Then you were right," said Sebastian. "She was murdered."

"What?" bellowed the constable, his features twisting with outraged incredulity. "What're ye talkin' about? Why, the laudanum she took is right there."

Sebastian shook his head. "Easy enough to kill a woman and leave an empty bottle of laudanum at her side."

Rawlins swatted at a fly crawling across his eyes. "But how can you tell she was murdered?"

"Look at her feet."

"I don't understand."

"Look at your own feet."

The Squire stared down at his serviceable brown-topped boots, their soles heavily caked with muck from the path through the woods. "There's no mud on her shoes! That means she couldn't have walked down here by herself. Is that what you're saying?"

Sebastian nodded. Judging from the stiffness of the body, he suspected she'd been dead a good twelve hours or more, but he was no expert. If they'd been in London, he'd have asked to have her remains sent to Paul Gibson, a former regimental surgeon who was a genius at teasing out the secrets of the dead.

But they weren't in London.

"Do you have a doctor capable of performing an autopsy?" he asked.

The Squire swiped at the fly again. "Dr. Higginbottom's done them in the past. I'll get one of the men from the village to help Nash carry her there."

"Is he any good?"

"I suppose so. Although I don't actually know for certain." The younger man's lips parted, his eyes widening as a new thought seemed to hit him. "Oh, Lord, I can't believe this. Why would anyone from around here want to kill a stranger?"

"Where was she from?"

Rawlins shook his head. "I don't believe I ever heard her say."

"I take it she was staying at the Blue Boar?"

Rawlins nodded. "It's the only place hereabouts suitable for a woman of quality."

Sebastian rose to his feet. "Perhaps the innkeeper will be able to tell us more about her."

The keeper of the Blue Boar was a gnarled little man named Martin McBroom. He had bushy side-whiskers and a full head of ginger hair that curled exuberantly and was slowly fading to white. Peering over the top rim of a pair of thick spectacles perched on the end of a bulbous nose, he shifted his watery gaze from Sebastian to the young Squire and back again.

"You're saying it was Mrs. Chance they found down by the river?" His voice rose to a high-pitched squeak. "Oh, bless us. The poor lady. The poor, poor lady."

"Where was she from, Mr. McBroom?" asked Rawlins, resting both forearms on the carefully polished counter between them. "Do you know?"

The innkeeper scratched his side-whiskers. "Said she was from London, though I don't think she came from there direct. You'll need to be asking that girl she brought with her—Peg is her name. And a sly, worthless thing she is, if you ask me."

"Is Peg here now?" asked Sebastian.

"Haven't seen her about, although I suppose she could be in the lady's chamber."

"We'll need to take a look at it, Mr. McBroom," said Rawlins. "Her room, I mean."

"Oh, I don't think I can let you do that." The innkeeper drew his chin back against his neck and shook his head. "Wouldn't be proper, it wouldn't."

Rawlins leaned into his forearms. "Mr. McBroom, she's dead. Not only that, but we don't know anything about her. Unless we find something in

her room to tell us, we won't even know whom to notify about what's happened."

"Well . . ." The innkeeper pursed his lips and made a sucking sound.
"I suppose you are justice of the peace now."

The red in Archie Rawlins's cheeks deepened considerably. "I am, yes."

"Still don't seem right, to be letting strange men go through her
room. Put their hands on her things."

The Squire straightened with a jerk. "Mr. McBroom!"

"If it would make you feel better," said Sebastian, volunteering his
absent wife without a second thought, "we could ask Lady Devlin for her
assistance."

The young justice of the peace looked horrified at the thought of
involving a real viscountess in a murder investigation. But the innkeeper
peeled off his glasses to rub his eyes and said, "That would be better—
her being a gentlewoman herself and all. But it still don't seem right, us
poking about in her things."

"It's not right," said Sebastian. "But the fault for that lies with whoever murdered her."

Chapter 4

*H*ero Devlin sat on a rustic stone bench at the edge of the broad village green, an open notebook balanced on one knee, her six-month-old son, Simon, on a rug spread on the grass at her feet.

The strengthening sun had burned off the morning mist, and she was grateful for the dappled shade cast by the spreading chestnut tree beside them. The air was sweet and clean and filled with cheerful bird-song, and she found herself smiling. For the moment, Simon was content to play with his toes and chatter happily at these fascinating append-ages, which left his mother free to draw up the outline for a new article she was planning.

She'd been born Miss Hero Jarvis, daughter of Charles, Lord Jarvis, the ruthlessly brilliant King's cousin who loomed as the acknowledged power behind the Hanovers' wobbly dynasty. Standing nearly six feet tall and possessing an education typically given only to sons, Hero was in her own way as ruthless as her father. But her radical philosophies were of the kind that gave Jarvis fits.

There'd been a time not so long ago when she'd been determined never to become any man's wife, determined to dedicate her life to chal-lenging the brutal social injustices that characterized their society. A chance encounter with a certain handsome, dangerous viscount had altered her attitudes toward marriage. But her passionate dedication to her cause had never wavered.

For the past year she had made the study of London's poor her special project. Now, a summer spent traveling between Devlin's manor down in Hampshire and several of Jarvis's estates had stimulated an interest in the effects of the enclosure movement on England's poor. She was focused on scribbling a series of questions to investigate when she became aware of Devlin walking toward her, the morning sun glazing his fine-boned face with a rich golden light.

"That didn't take long," she said as he drew nearer.

He shook his head. "It's only just begun, I'm afraid."

She felt the earlier surge of carefree joy seeping out of the day. "So the young Squire was right? It was murder?"

"Yes."

"Dear God."

He bent to pick up their son, the somber lines of his face relaxing into a smile as Simon squealed with delight. For a moment, he held the child close. Then he looked over at her. "You're working?"

It was one of the things she loved about him, that he respected the work she did. That he respected *her*—her mind, her talents, her opinions. "Just jotting down ideas." She closed her notebook. "Why?"

"I need your help."

Emma Chance had occupied a corner chamber overlooking both the village green and the high street. Low ceilinged, with walls papered in a cheery floral pattern, it was furnished with a heavy, old-fashioned oak-framed bed hung with blue linen; a single chair; a washstand and night-stool behind a carved screen; and a clothespress so ancient it looked as if it might be original to the inn. At the foot of the bed rested a new-looking trunk and a pair of tapestry slippers; a lightweight hooded cloak and a sprigged dressing gown hung from hooks near the door.

Although he knew it was something that had to be done, Sebastian still found himself hesitating at the chamber door. The sense of intruding on a private space was strong, and he couldn't help thinking that just yesterday, Emma Chance had left this room expecting to return to it in a few minutes or at most a few hours. She could never have imagined strangers coming here after her death to inspect her most private possessions, to analyze everything in a desperate search for clues as to exactly who she was and who could have wanted to kill her. And he found himself grateful that Hero had been able to leave Simon with his nurse, Claire, and come here with them. McBroom was right; her presence did, somehow, make what they were doing feel like less of a violation . . . although he acknowledged that could simply be a sop to his own conscience.

"How long was she planning to stay?" Hero asked the glowering innkeeper as she went to throw open the doors of the clothespress.

Rather than come into the room, Mr. McBroom stayed in the hall, his hands tucked up under his armpits. "Said she wanted the room for a week—maybe a bit more."

"She wasn't traveling with much," said Hero, studying the two spare dresses in the clothespress: a sturdy gray carriage dress trimmed with black piping, and a simple black morning gown. The drawers below held two nightdresses, a pair of soft leather shoes, clean undergarments, and several pairs of black stockings.

"And?" asked Sebastian. This was the other reason he was glad to have Hero with them: As a woman, she could evaluate Emma Chance's possessions in a way he never could.

"The carriage dress is nicely made and looks quite new—as if it's only been worn once or twice. The other things are also nice, but with the exception of the black stockings they're not new. The morning gown is an older muslin dress she probably dyed black when her husband died. How long did you say she'd been widowed?"

"Six months," said Rawlins. He'd positioned himself just inside the door, his hands thrust into the pockets of his coat and his shoulders hunched. He was obviously feeling as awkward and out of place as Sebastian.

"How sad," said Hero. She moved to study the array of objects spread across the top of the bedside table and washstand: a small embroidered silk sewing kit that opened to reveal dainty scissors, a thimble, thread, and buttons; a simple wood-and-silk fan painted with blowsy pink roses; a silver hairbrush and comb; a toothbrush and tooth powder; a half-empty bottle of rose water; a bar of rose-scented soap. . . .

"She obviously liked roses," said Hero, studying the rose-encircled initials on the back of the hairbrush: EC. "This is new too."

"So is the trunk," said Sebastian. He watched his wife walk to the center of the room, then frown and turn in a slow circle. "What is it?"

"You said you found a spencer, a hat, and gloves lying beside her. What about her reticule?"

Sebastian looked at Archie Rawlins.

Both men shook their heads.

"So where is it?" said Hero.

"Perhaps it's in the trunk," suggested the Squire, going to throw open the lid. But the trunk was empty except for an assortment of pencils and charcoals, a small paint box, and a sketchbook.

"Ah," said Rawlins. "I wondered where that was."

He laid the sketchbook on the counterpane and opened it to reveal a pencil sketch of Mr. Martin McBroom hunched behind his counter, his spectacles perched on the end of his nose, his chin pulled back in a heavy scowl.

"Why, it's me!" said the innkeeper, venturing closer. "It's good. Don't you think it's good?" he asked, glancing around at the others.

"It is. Very." Sebastian flipped the page. The next portrait was of

Archie Rawlins, looking wide-eyed and eager but a touch unsure of himself. Emma Chance had been more than simply adept at capturing her subjects' likenesses; she'd also possessed a rare gift for discerning and conveying the subtle nuances of personality and character.

"And that's me," said Rawlins with a soft, breathy laugh. "When did she do it?" He began turning the pages. "Look; there's the vicar. And that's Reuben Dickie and . . ." He broke off, his hand stilling at the sight of a full-length drawing of a man.

Most of the other portraits had been sketches only, usually showing a head and shoulders or, at most, the upper torso. But this was a full-length, careful rendering in charcoal of a man turned as if to look back at the artist, his wavy dark hair cut low across his forehead, his nose long and slightly arched, his gently molded lips and cleft chin painfully familiar.

"Good heavens," said Hero. "It's Napoléon."

Chapter 5

*A*rchie Rawlins shook his head. "No. But it is his younger brother Lucien—Lucien Bonaparte. He's here, you know; he and his family are staying out at Northcott Abbey."

Hero stared at him. "Napoléon's brother is *here?*"

Rawlins nodded. "Has been for more than two years now. Well, not in Ayleswick-on-Teme all that time, but in the area."

Sebastian studied the Corsican's swarthy, handsome features, so much like those of his more famous brother in his prime. Lucien Bonaparte had been captured with his entire family off the coast of Italy in late 1810. He claimed to have been fleeing from his brother's wrath, although there were those in London who suspected that Lucien's planned voyage to America had less to do with fraternal rivalries and more to do with the Emperor's desire to fan the flames of war between Britain and the fledgling United States. They could never quite get over the fact that, as president of the Council of Five Hundred, Lucien had played a vital role in elevating Napoléon to power.

"They were in Ludlow at first," Rawlins was saying. "Then Bonaparte bought an estate just to the east of here, near Worcester. I've heard they're having some repairs done on the house this summer, which is why they're staying with Lady Seaton." The Squire hesitated. "It was Bonaparte's son Charles who found Emma Chance's body this morning."

"How old is he?"

"Ten, I believe." Rawlins turned the page to reveal another sketch, this one of an open-faced, half-grown boy, his expression rapt as he watched an oriole take flight from a nearby tree branch. "That's him. Crazy about birds, he is. That's what he was doing down at the river this morning—looking for birds."

"Poor lad. Must have been a shock," said Hero.

Martin McBroom crinkled his nose and let out his breath in a harsh expulsion of air. "*Pssssh.* He's a Bonaparte—nephew to the Beast himself. Ain't no cause to go feeling sorry for him, my lady. Save your pity for the millions who've died because of that lot."

Sebastian flipped quickly through the remaining pages. The book contained nothing except portraits, followed by blank pages.

He looked up. "You said Emma Chance was on a sketching trip through Shropshire?"

Rawlins nodded. "That's right. She was drawing all the historic buildings around here—the church, the priory ruins, old houses—everything."

"So why are there only portraits in this book?"

"I can't imagine. I know for a fact she drew the Grange—she showed me. She must have had another sketchbook."

Sebastian's gaze met Hero's. "Where is it?"

They searched the room again, so thoroughly this time that Martin McBroom finally wandered off muttering beneath his breath. After a while, Hero heard Simon howling and went to see what he was fussing about. And still Sebastian and the young justice of the peace searched.

But neither the dead woman's second sketchbook nor her reticule was anywhere to be found.

"She must have had them with her when she was killed," said the young justice of the peace, slumping into the worn, ladder-backed chair and scrubbing his hands down over his face.

"Probably," agreed Sebastian. "So then the question becomes, why didn't the killer leave them to be found with her body?"

A step in the hall brought Sebastian's head around. A mousy, painfully thin woman appeared in the doorway, her hands twisting in her apron. She looked to be in her late twenties or early thirties, her face sharp boned, her pale gray gaze shifting uncertainly from Sebastian to Archie Rawlins and back again.

"Mr. McBroom says there's a justice of the peace who's wishful of speakin' to me about Mrs. Chance?"

Rawlins scrambled to his feet. "I'm the justice of the peace. You're Peg? Emma Chance's abigail?"

"Yes, sir." The abigail dropped a quick curtsy. "Peg Fletcher, sir. Only, I don't rightly know how much I can tell you about the lady. Haven't been with her above a week, I haven't. She hired me in Ludlow, right before she come here."

The young Squire glanced at Sebastian, who said, "Who recommended you to her?"

"I suppose you could say I recommended myself. I mean, I was working at the Feathers, where she was staying. Offered me a whole five pounds to come here with her and be her lady's maid, she did. Said it was only to be for a week or two, though I wasn't supposed to let on to nobody that she'd only just hired me." The abigail sucked her lower lip between her teeth. "Now that she's dead, I reckon it's all right to tell. Ain't it?"

"You must tell us everything you know about her," said Rawlins.

Peg stared at him, her eyes wide in a plain, colorless face. "But I don't know nothin' about her. Truly, I don't."

Archie Rawlins threw Sebastian a helpless glance.

Sebastian said, "Did she ever talk to you about her life? Where she came from? Her family? That sort of thing?"

Peg screwed up her face in thought for a moment, then shook her head. "No, sir. I don't recollect ever hearing her talk about nothing like that. She weren't one to chatter the way most ladies do."

"When did you see her last?"

"Yesterday afternoon, sir. She said she was going out sketching and probably wouldn't be back till near sunset."

Rawlins looked horrified. "Yet you didn't become concerned when she never reappeared?"

The abigail took an uncertain step back. "Well, I suppose I did, a bit. I mean, I thought it peculiar. But how was I to know what was usual for her and what wasn't? When it started gettin' dark and she still hadn't come back, I went to bed. I reckoned if she wanted me, she'd get me up."

"And this morning?" said Sebastian.

Peg shrugged. "I figured she must be having a bit of a lie-in. I mean, stands to reason, don't it, if she'd been out late?" Again she glanced from Sebastian to Archie, as if seeking approval or at least understanding for her behavior.

Sebastian studied the woman's pale, frightened face. "You said she went out sketching yesterday afternoon. Do you know what she did yesterday morning?"

"Well, she said she was gonna draw the church. But whether she did or not, I can't rightly say. She was always sketching." Peg sucked in a deep breath and set her jaw. "The thing I wants to know is, now that she's dead, how'm I to get back to Ludlow?"

"I'm afraid you won't be able to go anywhere for a few days," said Rawlins. "At least not until after the inquest."

She stared at him. "But . . . how'm I to eat? Who's gonna pay my reckoning here at the inn?" Her voice rose to a panicked pitch. "How'm I to get the five pounds what's owed me?"

It was obvious from the expression on Archie's face that he had never given a moment's thought to the predicament faced by a servant left destitute and far from home by the unexpected death of a mistress. "Well . . . I suppose we can consider your claims against Mrs. Chance's estate after the inquest. In the meanwhile, I'll have a talk with Mr. McBroom."

Peg looked doubtful.

Sebastian said, "Can you tell us anything at all about Emma Chance— anything that might help make sense of what happened to her?"

Peg's eyebrows drew together in a wary frown. "I don't know what you mean."

"What was she like as a mistress, for instance? Was she harsh? Demanding?"

"Oh, no, she was right kind, she was. Always saying please and thank you whenever I did anything for her. And she was never one for putting on grand airs, the way some do."

"Yet you've no idea where she came from?" asked Archie.

The abigail shook her head. "She was more'n a bit secretive, if you know what I mean?"

"Secretive about—what?"

"About everything. If you ask me, there was something havey-cavey about her, for all she was so nice. There's more'n once I've found myself wondering if I made a mistake, agreeing to come here with her."

"Why's that?" asked Sebastian.

"Well, for one thing, I wouldn't be surprised if her real name ain't something other than what she claimed it was."

"Good Lord," said Archie. "What makes you think that?"

"She didn't answer to it natural-like—I mean, not the way a body does with their own name. And there was one time I asked her somethin' about Captain Chance, and she acted like she didn't know who I was talking about. Weren't till I said, 'I mean your late husband, ma'am,' that she twigged what I was sayin'. Acted right peculiar, she did. Mind you, I've no notion what her real name was. But it's pounds to a penny that it wasn't Emma Chance!"

"Do you think it's possible the abigail could be right?" Rawlins asked Sebastian some half an hour later over a pint in the Blue Boar's public room. "That Emma Chance wasn't actually that unfortunate woman's real name?"

Sebastian leaned forward on his bench, one hand cradling the tankard on the table before him. "It seems rather far-fetched. Yet at the same time . . . it's an odd thing for the woman to have imagined if it weren't true. And Peg Fletcher doesn't strike me as particularly fanciful or imaginative."

"No, but . . . why would anyone do that? I mean, why claim to be someone she wasn't? The name 'Chance' means nothing to us here."

"I suspect that if Peg is correct—which is still only an if, after all—then the woman's main concern was to conceal her real name rather than to claim to be someone she was not."

The young Squire's cheeks darkened. "Oh, yes, of course. I should have thought of that." He drank long and deep from his ale, then swiped the back of one hand across his foamy lips as his eyes widened with a sudden thought. "If it is true—that her name isn't really Emma Chance—then maybe the killer knew who she really was. Maybe that's why he murdered her. I mean, for whatever reason she was using a false name."

Sebastian looked at him in some amusement. "Such as?"

"I don't know."

They drank together in thoughtful silence for a time. Then Archie said, "So how do we go about finding out if Chance is—was—her real name?"

Sebastian drained the last of his ale. "I haven't the slightest idea."

Archie Rawlins looked startled for a moment, then gave a soft laugh. "So what do we do?"

"You might begin by asking around town. Try to discover who saw Emma Chance yesterday afternoon, and when. In the meanwhile, I think I'll go have a talk with the vicar."

"Reverend Underwood? But . . . why him?"

"Because according to Peg Fletcher, her mistress spent yesterday morning sketching the church. Which means it's a place to start."

The young justice of the peace chewed his lip. "What if no one saw her?"

"In a village this small? Someone will have seen her—and they'll remember it."

Chapter 6

The aged, golden-hued sandstone church of St. Thomas was nestled into the side of the hill overlooking the village green and high street. Reached by way of a narrow lane that climbed past the Blue Boar and a rambling vicarage, the church boasted a bulky western tower pierced by twin round-topped windows almost as small as arrow slits, and a side porch with a gabled roof and a strong, nail-studded door that suggested the church had been built as much for defense as for worship.

The vicar of St. Thomas's was a tall, lanky man in his late forties, his straight black hair thinning with the passage of the years, his sky blue eyes fanned by laugh lines. He had a way of wincing when he touched upon painful subjects, and he winced as he spoke of Emma Chance, his breath easing out in a long sigh.

"She was in the churchyard when I first saw her, studying one of the old family crypts near the apse. You know what she said when I went to ask if I could help her? She said, 'Oh, thank you, but I'm not looking for anyone in particular. I simply enjoy reading old tombstones. I like to imagine the lives of the people whose names are engraved there, and think about the love they must have had for each other—husbands for wives, mothers and fathers for children.'" The Reverend Benedict

Underwood sighed again and shook his head. "That poor woman. The poor, poor woman."

Sebastian had come upon the vicar planting sprigs of rosemary near the lych-gate. He'd apologized for his dirty hands and pushed quickly to his feet when Sebastian introduced himself. But Sebastian found he had no need to explain the reason for his visit; news of both Emma Chance's death and the young Squire's request for Sebastian's assistance was all over town.

"What day was this?" asked Sebastian.

"Friday, I believe. She'd only just come to the village."

"Could you show me which tomb she was looking at?"

"Yes, of course. It's this way."

They turned toward the sunken path that ran along the side of the nave. The churchyard was surprisingly vast and crowded, given the small size of the village. But then Sebastian reminded himself that Ayleswick had once been a much larger place.

"Did she come here again yesterday, to sketch the church?"

The Reverend walked with his dirty hands held awkwardly out at his sides. "She did, yes. In the morning."

"You saw her?"

"I did. When I was on my way to visit old Jeff Cook. He's not well, I'm afraid."

"What time did she finish? Do you know?"

"Sorry, no. She was gone by the time I returned."

"And when was that?"

"About half past eleven, I should think."

"Did you speak to her at all?"

"Yesterday morning, you mean? Only briefly. I believe I called out, 'Lovely day now that the rain has cleared!' and she looked up and smiled." The Reverend shook his head and let loose another of his soulful sighs. "She was such a charming, polite young woman. Not at all forward or fast in the way one might expect, given the somewhat unorthodox nature of her reason for visiting the village."

"Her sketching expedition, you mean?"

Underwood pulled a face. "Yes. Not the sort of thing I'd care to see one of my own daughters doing—if I had daughters, which unfortunately I do not."

"Did she ever say anything to you about her family?"

The Reverend looked thoughtful. "Not that I recall, no. Although she may've said something to Mrs. Underwood."

"Your wife spoke to her?"

"Oh, yes. She came to the vicarage for tea."

"Did she happen to mention where in London she lived?"

"Was she from London? I don't believe she ever said, actually. We mainly spoke of the village. She was most interested in the history of the place. It makes sense, I suppose, given her interest in our historic structures."

Sebastian stared up at the heavy stonework of the church's ancient Norman tower. "Did this used to be part of the old monastery?"

"Oh, no, St. Thomas's has always been a simple parish church. What's left of the old Benedictine priory lies to the west of the village, beside the stream that now feeds the millpond. It was quite a magnificent place in its time, and the ruins are well worth a visit, if you've the chance." The Reverend hesitated. "You're certain . . . I mean, you're quite certain it's murder?"

"I'm afraid so."

The vicar sucked in a pained breath. "Well, for the sake of Emma Chance's soul I must be grateful to know that she did not take her own life. But the realization that someone living amongst us—one of our own—killed her . . . Well, I can't deny it's disturbing. Most disturbing. Although I suppose it's always possible she was killed by someone passing through?"

Sebastian doubted it, given the elaborate way Emma Chance's body had been arranged to give the impression of suicide. But all he said was, "I suppose it's possible."

"Here we are," said the vicar as they paused beside a weathered mausoleum engraved with the name BALDWYN. "It was the Baldwyns who built Maplethorpe Hall, to the east of the village. They died out toward the end the last century."

Sebastian studied the lichen-covered, neglected tomb. According to the inscription, the last burial was of a middle-aged man, John Baldwyn, who died just three weeks after his wife, Alice, in 1788. Their daughter, Marie, had died six months earlier at the age of eighteen. Was it simple curiosity that had drawn Emma Chance to this tomb? Sebastian wondered. Or something more telling?

He glanced over at the vicar, who was now surreptitiously wiping his dirt-covered hands on a handkerchief. "Do you know an elderly woman named Heddie Kincaid?"

The vicar's eyes widened slightly. "Yes, of course; she's one of my parishioners. Although not," he added ruefully, "as devout as one might wish."

"Where does she live?"

"She has a cottage up the road from the Blue Boar—right before you come to the millstream and the footpath that leads to the priory ruins. She's blind, you know—has been for years. Although until this spring I'd have said she was in fairly good health."

"What happened in the spring?"

"Her grandson died down in London. He was something of a favorite with her, and his death hit her right hard." The vicar tucked away his handkerchief. "Surely you don't think Heddie could have something to do with this killing?"

"No, not at all. My interest in her is purely personal. I knew her grandson, and I've brought her something he wanted her to have."

"Ah. Well, she'll be glad to receive it, no doubt. She's had a hard life, I'm afraid. Buried three husbands and a good half dozen children—not to mention a shocking number of grandchildren." The vicar paused, his lower lip bunching and protruding as he stared thoughtfully at Sebastian. "You say you knew Jamie Knox?"

"Yes. Why?"

The vicar gave a nervous laugh. "I didn't know him well myself, mind you—he took the King's shilling as a lad not long after I was given the living here in Ayleswick. But . . ." He broke off and colored faintly.

"Yes?" prompted Sebastian.

"Oh, nothing, nothing," said the vicar, nervously clearing his throat as he looked pointedly away.

Sebastian suspected he knew exactly what was suddenly troubling the vicar. But there weren't many with the courage to tell an earl's son that he bore an uncanny resemblance to a Bishopsgate tavern owner who had begun life as the illegitimate offspring of a Shropshire barmaid.

Chapter 7

Carrying a small box with the mechanical nightingale under one arm, Sebastian followed the narrow, rutted road that wound westward from the village toward the wild, purple-hazed mountains of the Welsh border. The hedgerows here were a fragrant tangle of sun-warmed dog roses, bryony, and traveler's-joy; the sky above a fierce, clear blue; the fields golden with ripening wheat.

He could have driven the short distance to Heddie Kincaid's cottage, for a gentleman who journeys with his wife and infant son does not travel lightly. But he had no desire to order out either his crested chaise and four or the light, fast curricle that was his preferred means of transportation. He walked, listened to the bees buzz in the clover, and thought about the past.

Growing up, Sebastian had always known he was different from his siblings even if he'd never understood why. Born the fourth child and third son of the Earl of Hendon and his countess, Sophia, Sebastian had instinctively felt himself to be an outlier, utterly unlike the Earl in looks, temperament, interests, and talents. Whereas his sister and older brothers had eyes of the famous St. Cyr blue, Sebastian's were a feral yellow, with a strange, animalistic ability to see clearly both in the dark and over great distances. And it didn't take Sebastian long to realize that his hearing was abnormally acute as well.

Yet somehow he'd never questioned his parentage, never questioned that he was a St. Cyr—until two years ago, when he'd learned the truth: that Hendon's beautiful, fun-loving, rebellious Countess had played her lord false; that Sebastian was not, in fact, a son of Alistair St. Cyr but the bastard offspring of one of the Countess's many nameless lovers.

It was a secret Hendon had always known, although he'd kept it hidden from both Sebastian and the world. Even when Hendon's first and second sons died, leaving Sebastian as the only heir, he hid it still, which was why Sebastian was known as Sebastian St. Cyr, Viscount Devlin, son and heir of the Earl of Hendon.

When in truth he was none of these things.

The discovery had helped send Sebastian into a downward spiral and very nearly destroyed him. He'd somehow managed to pull himself out of it—largely, he suspected, thanks to the appearance in his life of Hero and Simon. But the painful sense of being a stranger to himself, and the questions, remained. For if he wasn't who he'd always thought he was, then who was he?

And then he had encountered Jamie Knox, the tall, lean ex-rifleman who looked enough like Sebastian to be his brother.

Or at least a half brother.

He came upon Heddie Kincaid's cottage a quarter mile or so beyond the Blue Boar, beside a clear, small stream that flowed through a ferny glade shaded by towering beech and elm. The cottage was small, with only a single dormer, a lean-to shed, and a few chickens scratching in the yard. But the thatch was new, the casement windows freshly painted a cheery blue, and the vegetables, herbs, and flowers in the garden well tended.

Sebastian hesitated just a shade too long, then turned up the lavender-and rosemary-edged path to the cottage's front door.

The information that Heddie Kincaid was blind had eased one of his major concerns: that the old woman would see the resemblance between Sebastian and her grandson and be troubled and confused by it. Except that it was not Heddie Kincaid who opened the door to Sebastian's knock, but a willowy, striking woman who looked to be in her mid-thirties. Jamie Knox had been dark and yellow eyed, whereas this woman had reddish blond hair and eyes of a light, crystal-like blue. But her resemblance to the ex-rifleman was startling enough that for a moment Sebastian could only stare at her—as she stared at him, one hand tightening around the edge of the door.

"The Lord preserve us," she said at last, her chest jerking on a quickly indrawn breath. "Who are you?"

He removed his hat and held it in one hand against his thigh. "My apologies for the intrusion, madam. I am Devlin."

"You're the London lord the young Squire asked to help him with this murder?"

"Yes, but that's not why I'm here. I'm looking for Heddie Kincaid. I knew her grandson, Jamie Knox."

"Jamie's dead."

"I know."

Sebastian studied the unknown woman's flaring high cheekbones and square chin. He had always assumed that Knox must resemble the unknown man who had fathered him—who had perhaps fathered them both. But now, looking at this woman, he found that assumption called into doubt. And the implications had him reeling.

Somehow, he managed to say, "I was with him when he died. I've brought something he wanted his grandmother to have."

"Och, and look at me," she said, taking a step back as she opened the door wide. "Leaving you standing on the step. I beg your pardon, my lord. Please, come in."

Ducking through the low doorway, he found himself in a small room that served as a combination living area, dining room, and kitchen. A curtain half hid a bed in a small alcove, while steep stairs led up to an attic loft above. The ceiling was low, the room cramped. But the uneven, flagged floor was cleanly swept, the walls newly whitewashed. And it occurred to Sebastian that Knox must have been sending money back to Shropshire, to help the family he'd left behind.

An elderly woman sat on one of the old-fashioned high-backed benches at a trestle table drawn up before the smoke-blackened stone hearth. Her hair was snow-white, her weathered, aged face crisscrossed with deeply etched lines. But her frame was still robust, and though she stared straight ahead with milky white eyes, she was busy snapping peas in a bowl she balanced on her lap, her fingers moving easily with a lifetime of practice.

"Nana," said the younger woman, raising her voice slightly as she went to crouch beside her grandmother and lay a hand on her arm. "Here's a Lord Devlin to see you, from London. He knew Jamie."

The woman's fingers stilled at their task, her head turning toward Sebastian even though she could not see him. And he watched a breath of sadness waft across her features at the mere mention of her grandson's name.

Once, Sebastian thought, she must have been a handsome woman. He could trace quite clearly in her strong-boned face and faintly cleft chin the image of her dead grandson. And it occurred to him that the ways in which Jamie Knox had differed from Sebastian, he had resembled these two women.

"You knew Jamie?" she said, her voice still strong and unquavering. And he found himself wondering how old she was, this woman who had buried three husbands and countless children and grandchildren.

"I did, yes," said Sebastian, coming to take the seat indicated by the younger woman. "I have something he bought for you the very day he died."

The younger woman lifted the bowl of peas from her grandmother's lap so that Sebastian could place the box in her gnarled, work-roughened hands.

"For me?" she said in wonder as she lifted the box's lid and reached inside.

He watched her fingers move deftly over the bird's beak, its jeweled collar and gilded wings. "There's a key hidden in the tail feathers," he explained. "It's mechanical."

She lifted the nightingale clumsily from its box, feeling for the key as her granddaughter moved to help her.

"Here," said the younger woman. She wound the key and set the bird on the table beside them. The familiar, joyous melody filled the small cottage. "It's beautiful, Nana. And it looks just like a nightingale."

The old woman sat motionless, listening to the gracefully flowing notes, moisture glistening in her sightless eyes as the bird slowly wound down. "I've always loved nightingales," she said, her voice cracking as she reached up one bent knuckle to wipe away a tear that threatened to fall. "Did he truly buy it for me?"

"He did, yes."

She nodded and swallowed, hard. "He was an amazing lad. So bright and quick. Had the eyesight of a hawk and the hearing of a bat. Never seen anything like it."

Sebastian was aware of the younger woman's gaze upon him but said nothing. The abnormal acuteness of their senses was something else he and Knox had had in common.

"He was a rifleman, you know," said Heddie Kincaid proudly. "Best shot the army ever had, I reckon."

"Yes," said Sebastian. He cleared his throat, but his voice was still husky as he asked one of the questions he had come here hoping to have answered. "Did he get his eyesight and hearing from your daughter?"

"Och, no. No one else in our family has such gifts—not even Jenny here, and she's his twin."

Sebastian looked at the younger woman and felt the skin stretch oddly taut against the bones of his face. For if Jamie Knox had, in truth, been Sebastian's half brother, then that would make this self-possessed, vaguely hostile woman Sebastian's half sister.

"—must've come from his da, I always figured," the old woman was saying. "Whoever he was. My girl Eleanor—his mama—she died not long after the babies was born, poor child. Was too much for her, carryin' the two of 'em. Maybe if she'd lived, she could've said who their da was. But that weren't the way it turned out."

It fit with what Knox had once told Sebastian. But the disappointment was still intense. He said, "Jamie told me his mother worked at the Crown and Thorn, in Ludlow."

"Aye. She had a row with her stepda and took off after he found out she was in the family way." The old woman's face tightened as if with pain. "Maybe if she'd 've stayed, she wouldn't 've died."

He watched Heddie's fingers slide slowly over the now-silent bird, her face quivering with emotion. She said, "I've always loved nightingales. But I didn't realize Jamie knew it. And to think he remembered it all these years."

"He was planning to come see you," said Sebastian. "He wanted to bring it to you himself."

The old woman turned her face to the warm afternoon breeze gusting through the low, open windows. They could hear the scratching of the chickens in the yard, smell the fecund odor of the recently hoed garden mingling with the stale peat smoke from the cold hearth beside them. She said, "All them years he was in the army, I worried. Worried he was gonna die of fever in some godforsaken foreign outpost or get blown to bits in battle and lie forever in an unmarked grave. Never thought he'd get himself shot in London."

"He died quickly," said Sebastian, although it was a lie. The sucking wound in Knox's chest had taken nearly an hour to kill him. "He didn't suffer."

The old woman nodded, her fingers finding the mechanical bird's key. She wound it wordlessly, and the nightingale's gilded wings lifted up and down again as it poured forth its sweetly haunting melody.

Sebastian drew an envelope from his pocket and laid it beside her. "He also wanted you to have this." He pushed to his feet as her hand shifted to the envelope and the banknotes it contained. "If there's anything else I can do," he said, "please don't hesitate to let me know."

Jenny walked with him to the door but stopped him on the threshold by saying quietly, "Is it true? Did Jamie die quickly?"

He met her frank, level gaze. But all he said was, "Quick enough."

She blinked. "Why did you come here? Truly?"

He glanced back at the old woman, who now sat unmoving, staring blindly into space. "The man who shot your brother mistook him for me. He died because he looked like me."

Jenny's nostrils flared on a quickly indrawn breath. "That's why you gave my grandmother money? You think in some way it makes up for the death of my brother? Well, it doesn't."

"No," agreed Sebastian.

The hostility emanating from her was as stark and powerful as it was inexplicable. And he wondered if her antagonism was provoked by him personally, or by everything he represented—socially, economically, and culturally.

He said, "Miss Knox—"

She shook her head. "It's Jenny Dalyrimple. My husband's Alex Dalyrimple." She said it as if the name should mean something to him, although it did not.

She tipped her head to one side. "Jamie wrote to me about you. Said he'd met a grand lord who looked enough like him to be his brother. He thought maybe your father—the Earl of Hendon himself— might be our father. Only, then he got a look at Lord Hendon. And you know what he said? He said the Earl looked nothing like us. Or you."

Sebastian studied her fine-boned face, flushed golden by the hours she spent working hard beneath the sun. He traced with fascination the ways in which she resembled her twin—and him—and the ways she did not. But all he said was, "I mean it; if there is anything else I can do, you've only to let me know."

Her eyes flared. "We don't need your help."

"I didn't intend to suggest that you do." He ducked beneath the low lintel, then paused to settle his hat on his head. The day was bright and warm, the flox, lavender, and mulleins in her garden blooming a riot of yellow, pink, blue, and purple. He knew now that she was the one who tended them, just as she fed the chickens and milked the cow he could hear lowing in the shed. She was slender with a hard-muscled leanness that spoke of a life spent hoeing fields and kneading bread dough and hauling firewood. Yet there was a mental quickness about her, an instinctive intelligence that was impossible to miss. And she had, one way or another, managed to acquire something of an education, for her brother had regularly sent her letters, and she could read them.

"I saw her, you know," she said, one hand coming up to brush the hair from her forehead as he started to leave. "That widow they're saying someone killed."

Sebastian turned to face her again. "When was this?"

"Early yesterday afternoon. I'd taken the cow to graze in the grass along the side of the road and that's when I saw her, coming up from the village. She climbed over the stile by the stream and took the footpath that runs up to the old priory ruins."

"Did you happen to notice if she was carrying a reticule?"

The question obviously puzzled her, but Jenny answered readily enough. "I don't remember it. But she did have a canvas satchel with a leather strap over one shoulder."

"Did you see her come back?"

"No. But then, I spent the rest of the day weeding the kitchen garden on the other side of the cottage."

"She was alone?"

"She was, yes." Her face lifted to his, her unusual, faceted blue eyes dark now with some emotion he could not name. "I hear Constable Nash is saying she killed herself."

"She didn't."

"So certain?"

"Yes."

"She was a stranger. Why would anyone from around here want to kill her?"

"I haven't figured that out yet. Who do you think could have done it?"

She gave him a wary look, as if she suspected him of trying to lead her into a trap. "Me? What do I know of such things?"

"You know the people around here."

He thought she might deny that anyone in the village could be a killer. Instead, she looked thoughtful a moment, then said, "If anybody did it, I'd say it was probably Reuben—the Widow Dickie's simpleminded son."

Sebastian recalled one of Emma Chance's portraits, of a round-faced, vacuous-looking man with small, wide-set eyes and a mouthful of oddly spaced teeth. "What makes you suspect him?"

"He's always creeping about, peeping in folks' windows—particularly if it's a house with women living alone. He ain't right in the head."

"Where would I find him?"

"He hangs about the village green most of the time. Likes to sit on the step of the pump house—although the truth is, you never know where he's gonna pop up."

Sebastian doubted that anyone simpleminded could be either cunning or resourceful enough to carefully stage a murder to look like suicide. But he knew that people often treated the simpleminded as if they weren't there—as if they couldn't hear what was said or see what was done, or remember it.

Which meant that Reuben Dickie sounded like someone Sebastian ought to speak to.

Chapter 8

Roofed with lichen-encrusted slate, its paving stones worn shiny by centuries of passing feet, Ayleswick's pump house stood near one corner of the village green. Its sides were open, the roof supported by dark old beams that rested on weathered columns of large, square-cut stone blocks.

A short, squat-looking man sat on the pump house's single step and whistled tunelessly as he carved a piece of wood into a quadruped of an as yet indeterminate species. The man had lank, greasy brown hair and a wide, flat face that remained emotionless as he watched Sebastian walk toward him.

"I know who you are," said Reuben Dickie as Sebastian drew up before him.

"Do you?"

"Aye. Yer that grand London lord come to town with the pretty lady—the tall one with the baby. Heard about you, I did."

"Did you hear I'm helping Squire Rawlins with this recent murder?"

Reuben's tongue darted out to lick his lips as his gaze slid sideways. He said nothing.

Sebastian studied the man's small, oddly shaped eyes and flat nose.

He looked to be somewhere in his late thirties or early forties, although the hands wielding the knife with expert care were as small and short fingered as those of a child.

After a moment, Reuben thrust out his lower lip and said, "Heard Constable Nash tell the smith she killed herself."

Sebastian squinted off across the green, toward the gentle hill that rose above the village to the north. He was becoming seriously annoyed with the village's talkative constable. "She didn't, actually."

Reuben nodded and kept whittling. "Constable Nash ain't near as smart as he thinks he is."

"The lady drew your picture, didn't she?"

Reuben slanted a wary look up at him. "How'd you know that?"

"I saw it, in the sketchbook she left in her room. It was a picture of you sitting here, at the pump house."

He gave a quick, unexpected smile. "She drew it last Saturday. I was sittin' here whittling, and she said, 'Do you mind if I sketch you?' And I said, 'No.' So she did."

"Did you happen to see her yesterday?"

Again, that vague shadow of wariness darkened the man's eyes. "I s'pose I did."

"Where was that?"

"Well, it must've been when I was sittin' here, don't ye think? Saw her go in and out the Blue Boar a time or two. She was sketchin' all the old buildings hereabouts—the church and Maplethorpe Hall and the Grange."

That caught Sebastian's attention. "She drew Maplethorpe Hall?" According to the vicar, Maplethorpe was the ancestral home of the Baldwyns, the family whose tomb she'd been studying when he first came upon her in the churchyard.

Reuben looked up and blinked, as if puzzled by Sebastian's interest. "Aye. Why?"

"When was this?"

"I dunno. But Major Weston could tell ye. He lives in the old Dower House, ye know."

"And who lives at Maplethorpe?"

Reuben Dickie gave an odd, breathy giggle. "Ain't nobody lives there now. Not since it burned."

"It's a ruin?"

"Aye. Ain't nothing left but a few blackened walls." He tipped his head to one side. "Didn't ye know?"

"No, I did not." Sebastian propped one boot on the low step and leaned an elbow on his bent knee. "I'm afraid there's a great deal about Ayleswick that I don't know. Perhaps you can help me with that. I would imagine you know everyone around here."

"Pretty much," said Reuben, grinning with pride.

"What do you think happened to Emma Chance?"

The smile slid away from the man's broad, childlike face. "How would I know?"

"I imagine you must see and hear a great deal, sitting here all the time, watching people. I suspect most of the villagers don't realize just how much you see."

"They think I'm an idiot."

"I don't think you're an idiot." Reuben Dickie looked much like certain other mentally deficient men and women Sebastian had known in the past. But in Sebastian's experience, the intellectual capabilities of those so afflicted could vary widely, and he suspected Reuben Dickie's abilities were better than most. "Do you live with your mother, Reuben?"

"Aye." He nodded to the picturesque row of half-timbered houses that ranged along the eastern side of the village green. "Our cottage is the one on the end."

Sebastian studied the ancient house's fanciful facade, its timbers enlivened with quatrefoils and cusps and carved faces. "You and your mother live alone?"

"Oh, no. I got a brother, Jeb. He's not like me; he's real smart, he is. Works as a carter. Hauling a load of timber to Wales, he is. He's my little brother, but he takes care of me. Looks out for me, he does."

Sebastian straightened. "If you think of anything you saw or heard that might be helpful, you will tell me, won't you?"

Reuben grinned up at him. "I can do that."

As Sebastian walked back across the green toward the Blue Boar, he was aware of Reuben watching him, the knife and block of wood held slack in his hands. There was something about the man that unsettled Sebastian, although he could not have articulated it. Reuben Dickie had grown up an outcast in his own village. Mentally slow and physically different, he would have been the butt of children's pranks and a target for the taunts of the cruel his entire life. There were some who managed to retain their equanimity and good humor in the face of such relentless torment. But most grew sullen and resentful, and he suspected Reuben fell squarely into the latter category.

Yet there was something else about the man that troubled Sebastian, and he realized now it had something to do with the sly gleam in Reuben Dickie's eyes when he spoke of the tall, pretty lady with the baby.

Hero.

"You can't seriously think that poor, slow-witted man killed Emma Chance?" said Hero.

She was sitting at the table in their private parlor, thumbing through Emma's sketchbook while Simon played with a stuffed lamb on the nearby hearthrug.

"I think it's a possibility, yes," said Sebastian. "And not simply because Jenny Dalyrimple suspects him. I think he's hiding something."

"But . . . He could never have come up with the idea of carrying Emma's body down to the water meadow and leaving a bottle of laudanum at her side."

"No. But his clever brother, Jeb, might have done it. He 'takes care of' Reuben, remember?"

Hero sat back in her chair. "You don't think it's possible that Emma could have reached the water meadows by a different path than the one you and Rawlins followed? One that wasn't muddy?"

Sebastian shook his head. "According to Archie, there's a path that runs along the river, but it's muddy in both directions."

She went back to turning the sketchbook's pages, studying the various portraits.

He saw her forehead crease with a frown. "What is it?"

"Have you noticed that almost all these portraits are of men? There are a few women, but not many."

"No, I hadn't noticed." He moved to look over her shoulder. "But you're right. Maybe she simply found men more interesting to draw."

Hero grunted and flipped back to the beginning of the notebook. "She also wrote the names of some of the people she drew—but not others. She named Archie Rawlins and Reuben Dickie, but not Martin McBroom . . ." She paused at one of the rare sketches of a woman: a young woman with thick wavy hair framing a strong-boned, familiar face. He wasn't surprised to read the neatly printed caption. *Jenny Dalrymple.*

Hero looked up at him. "Did she tell you Emma Chance had drawn her portrait?"

"No. No, she didn't. But then, perhaps she didn't know it. Neither McBroom nor Rawlins did."

Hero studied the sketch in silence for a moment. "She looks a lot like Jamie Knox."

Sebastian walked over to the bottle of surprisingly fine French brandy from Martin McBroom's cellars and poured himself a glass. "Which is to say, she looks a lot like me."

"Yes." Hero set the sketchbook aside, her gaze on his face. "I assume Jenny also noticed the resemblance?"

"How could she not?" Sebastian took a slow swallow of his brandy and felt it burn all the way down. "She said Knox had written to her about me. He told her he thought Hendon might be their father—until he got a good look at the Earl."

"And she doesn't know any more about their father than Jamie did?"

"If she does, she's not talking. About a lot of things, actually."

"What are you going to do next?"

"Pay a visit to this Dr. Higginbottom. Hopefully he can tell us something about how and where Emma Chance actually died. Although I have my doubts."

"Not all country physicians are incompetent."

"No. But few have much experience with postmortems. And I've never needed Gibson's rare genius more than I do with this one."

"Perhaps Higginbottom will surprise you."

Sebastian drained his brandy with a grunt and set the glass aside.

Chapter 9

*S*ebastian hated looking at the victims of violent death.

He'd spent six years in the army, fighting King George III's wars from Italy and Portugal to the West Indies. He'd seen men blown into unidentifiable bloody strips of flesh by cannon fire and disemboweled by the swift, hot rush of lead. He'd decapitated men with the singing slash of his own cavalry sword and ridden through villages filled with nothing but bloating, blackened, fly-ridden corpses. Yet the sight of the cold, waxy corpse of a murder victim still hit his gut, still left him feeling sick and shaky and filled with a crusader's rage.

Someone had once told him that he was locked in a war with death— a useless vendetta that he could never win. But while he acknowledged that possibility, it hadn't changed anything.

Dr. Hiram Higginbottom lived in an old farmhouse just off the road that stretched northeast toward Ludlow. As was the case for most country doctors, the practice of medicine was something he did on the side. He also ran a large herd of sheep and hired cottagers to tend his orchards and milk his cows and plant, hoe, and harvest his fields.

The distance was not far, but this time Sebastian chose to drive himself in his curricle, an elegant, lightly sprung chaise drawn by a pair of white-socked chestnuts.

"Word round about the stables is that she killed 'erself," said Tom, the sharp-faced, half-grown lad who served as Sebastian's tiger, or young groom. "They're sayin' that if somebody'd murdered 'er, there'd 'ave been blood, and there weren't no blood."

"No, no blood." Sebastian swung the curricle in between two drunken brick gateposts and ran up a long drive flanked by rolling green pastures dotted with sheep. "I do trust you haven't felt inclined to try to change their minds with your fists."

Tom clung to his perch at the rear of the curricle and remained silent.

Sebastian ducked his head to hide his smile. "While I appreciate the impulse, I somewhat doubt your pugnacious approach will have its desired effect."

"My pug-what?"

"Pugnacious approach," said Sebastian, drawing up before a two-story square brick farmhouse that looked as if it had been built early in the previous century. "In other words, focus more on listening to what the locals are saying and give over attempting to protect my reputation. Understood?"

"Aye, gov'nor."

Sebastian handed Tom the reins and hopped down to the rutted, weed-choked sweep.

Once, the house must have been gracious; he could still follow the ghostly outlines of a pleasure garden long since vanished beneath what had now been turned into more pastureland. All that remained of the once extensive borders and beds was a stand of gnarled, overgrown yews that must throw the house into a sepulchral gloom, and a broken sundial marooned in a patch of thistles. The front step was cracked; only faint traces of paint showed on window frames weathered gray, and crows nested in the eaves. It occurred to Sebastian that if Dr. Hiram

Higginbottom conducted his autopsies with the same care he showed the upkeep of his house, then the chances of finding out exactly how Emma Chance had died were slim.

A breeze kicked up, bringing him the smell of manure from the nearby barns and the pungent pinch of burning tobacco.

"You're him, aren't you?" said a gravelly voice from behind him. "That grand London lord with all the nonsensical notions."

Sebastian was getting more than a bit tired of hearing himself described as "that grand London lord." He turned slowly to find a man seated on a rusty bench buried in the depths of the yews.

"I'm Devlin, yes. I take it you're Hiram Higginbottom?"

The doctor straightened and shuffled forward with a peculiar, splayfooted gait. He held the bowl of a burl wood pipe in one hand; the hem of his old-fashioned, bottle green frock coat flared as he walked. He was a small man, his frame solid and compact. But his head was huge, as if it should by rights have belonged to a much larger man, and it looked as if it had been stuck onto his body without a neck. In age, he could have been anywhere between forty and sixty, his sagging jaw gray with several days' growth of beard, his shoulders rounded and already tending to stoop.

"Young Archie Rawlins said you might be coming by. Said I was to give you my findings if you did. Well, here they are: She committed suicide."

He started to turn away toward the barns.

Sebastian said, "You've already completed the autopsy?"

Higginbottom kept walking. "There's no need for an autopsy, and it wouldn't show nothing anyway. It's obvious how she died: opium poisoning."

"I'm told it's impossible to detect an opium overdose in a postmortem."

Higginbottom swung around to jab one pointed finger into the air at him. "No need to detect it when you've got an empty laudanum bottle lying right there, and a suicide note in her hand."

"Suicide note? What suicide note?"

Higginbottom jerked his head toward the farm outbuildings. "I'll show you."

He led the way to a lean-to shed attached to one end of the cow barn. He'd left the door open, and Sebastian could hear the buzzing of flies as they approached, smell the sickly sweet scent of insipient decay. Instead of a stone slab like the one used by Paul Gibson for his official autopsies and surreptitious dissections, Higginbottom had only a stained wooden table. Emma Chance lay upon it still fully clothed. As far as Sebastian could see, the only thing the doctor had done was to lay her arms straight down at her sides before the rigor rendered her completely stiff.

"Here," said Higginbottom, plucking a small slip of paper from a shelf near the door. "See? Suicide."

Sebastian found himself staring at a narrow strip of heavy, aged paper that looked as if it had been sliced from an old book. It contained only four words, printed in an elegant Baroque typeface.

The rest is silence.

Sebastian looked up at him. "You call this a suicide note?"

"Well, what would you call it, then? Hmmm?"

"Actually, I'd call it one more deliberate misdirection by the killer— just like the empty laudanum bottle."

The other man's nostrils quivered, his gray eyes narrowing with annoyance. "This is ridiculous. It's as if you're determined to make this out to be a murder. Why can't you simply accept that it is what it is? A suicide!"

"How the bloody hell do you know? You didn't even look."

"Of course I looked. She hasn't been strangled. And if she'd been stabbed or shot, there'd be stains on her clothing. Well, there are none—except for the usual seepages of body fluids that are to be expected after death."

Sebastian shifted his gaze to the pale, slack face of the murdered woman on the table. She looked so very young—younger by far than twenty-seven or twenty-eight. Her nose was small and delicately molded, the tender flesh of her eyelids nearly translucent, her lips brown and dry now in death. And he suddenly felt swamped by a tide of inexplicable, useless fury. *How did you die?* he wanted to rage at her. *How did he kill you? How?*

And then Sebastian saw it: the faintest blur of purpling, almost like a shadow along the lower edge of her jaw.

He stared at it, then walked around to examine the other side of her face. It took a moment to find it, but it was there: a small, faint, elliptical bruise just to the left of her mouth, exactly the size of a man's fingertip.

Thoughtfully, he reached out to lay his right hand over Emma Chance's lower face, positioning it just so.

"What are you doing?" demanded Higginbottom.

Sebastian looked up at him. "I know how she was killed."

"What the devil are you talking about?"

"She was smothered." He lifted his hand, then carefully placed it back in position. "The killer put his palm over her mouth like this. He used the heel of his hand to shove up her jaw and hold her mouth closed while he pinched her nostrils together with his thumb and first finger. You can see the hint of a bruise here, on her cheek, where his little finger dug into her face as he applied the pressure."

Sebastian took his hand away and shifted to study the dead woman's wrists. Higginbottom was right; there was no sign of bruising. And any marks on her arms were hidden by the sleeves of her dress. Although . . .

"If he sat on her chest and held her arms down with his weight," Sebastian said aloud, "she might not even have any bruises on her arms. But the weight on her chest would have made it that much harder for her to breathe."

"You're mad. There are no bruises on her face. I had a good look at her before I had her brought in here, and I tell you there are no bruises. And you couldn't possibly see 'em in this light even if there were!"

"Get a lantern."

Higginbottom stared at him a moment, then turned away, grumbling, to light a lantern that rested on a nearby shelf. He was clumsy with the tinderbox, so that it was a moment before he swung back around, the lantern held high, his face twisted into a sneer.

"There. See? No bru—"

He broke off, his lips twitching as he leaned in close to peer at the edge of the dead woman's jaw. "Well, I'll be go to Ludlow," he said after a long, heavy silence. "How the blazes did you see that—especially in this light?"

"I see unusually well in the dark."

"Huh. You must be part owl." The doctor shifted around to shine the light on her left cheek. "Yes, there it is." He shifted the lantern back and forth. "There might also be the vaguest hint of a bruise from the killer's third finger, just here."

He set down the lantern, then rubbed his hand across his beard-stubbled face. "There could be some bruising other places on the body," he said almost to himself. "And sometimes with smothering you'll see changes in the heart and lungs—but not always."

He turned abruptly and walked out of the shed into the warm golden sunshine of the morning. Sebastian followed him.

The two men stood together in silence for a moment. Then Higginbottom shook his head and pushed out a painful sigh. "It's a nasty way to die—trying desperately to suck in air but not being able to breathe. Feeling your lungs burn, mad with panic for a good two or three minutes before everything goes dim and you finally lose consciousness. And then you've still got another two minutes till death finally comes. That poor girl. And to think her killer was sitting on her the whole time with his hand over her face, looking into her terrified eyes and watching her die." Higginbottom glanced over at him. "What kind of man could do something like that?"

The depths of compassion revealed by the old doctor's words took Sebastian by surprise. He stared off across the sunlit field, where sheep grazed lazily in a tableau of bucolic peace that was so cruelly misleading. "A very cold, dangerous one."

Chapter 10

$\mathcal{S}$ebastian drove back toward the village through pastures scattered with wild scarlet poppies, past a sunlit field of ripe grain where a half dozen or more men moved in a line, their sickles rising and falling in rhythmic sweeps. Behind them came their women, backs bent as they tied the stalks into sheaves, while the youngest children ran across the stubble, laughing and shrieking as they chased rabbits and rats disturbed by the reaping.

It was a timeless scene, repeated every summer on down through the ages. And the attempt to reconcile this image of cooperation and tradition with the brutal reality of Emma Chance's last desperate moments left Sebastian feeling oddly disconcerted.

In his experience, most murders were messy things, usually spur-of-the-moment and born of rage, fear, or greed. But Emma Chance's murder hadn't been messy. Sebastian didn't know yet what had motivated it, or if her death had been carefully planned. He didn't even know where she had actually died. But he did know that whoever took her life had deliberately chosen a method that would be easy to conceal even though it required her killer to hold her down for five long, agonizing minutes while he patiently, coldly watched her die. He'd then acted with stunning calculation to conceal his act by staging the body in such a way that her death should by rights have been deemed a suicide.

Taken all together, those actions suggested a killer with a degree of steady calm that was both rare and chilling. The fact that Emma Chance was a stranger to this small, quiet village only served to make her death all the more inexplicable.

Still lost in thought, Sebastian left the curricle in the stable yard with Tom and was headed toward the Blue Boar when he heard himself hailed by a gentlewoman's carefully modulated voice.

"Lord Devlin? It is Lord Devlin, is it not?"

He looked around to find an elegant little whiskey drawn by a glossy bay pulling up beside him. The small carriage's body and the spokes of its two wheels were painted bright yellow and, as if in careful coordination with her carriage, the slender, attractive gentlewoman seated on the single padded bench and handling the reins wore a blue-and-yellow-striped spencer and a yellow chip hat tied beneath her chin with a saucy blue satin bow. The only off note came from the shaggy, overgrown mutt seated beside her, its tongue lolling out happily, its curly brown fur shimmering in the late-afternoon sunshine.

"I do hope you'll pardon my forwardness, my lord," she said, smiling sweetly as she shifted both reins to her left hand so she could hold the right out to him. "I'm Lady Seaton, of Northcott Abbey."

He knew who she was. An ethereal woman with fine, fair hair and pretty features, she'd been born Grace Middleton, the daughter of a prosperous Yorkshire baronet. Married at seventeen to Leopold, Lord Seaton, she'd managed to present her lord with a son and two daughters before he died, leaving her a widow before the age of twenty-five.

Seaton had been dead some fifteen years now, which meant his widow must be close to forty. But her carefully guarded complexion still glowed with the dewy softness of a new rose petal, and her form was as slender and supple as a young girl's.

"How do you do?" said Sebastian, taking the tiny gloved hand she offered him. "Won't you come in and meet my wife? Perhaps join us for a cup of tea?"

She gave him another of those radiant smiles and wrapped an arm around the shoulders of the dog at her side. "Why, thank you. And I truly wish I could. But I daren't leave Barney out here alone to get into mischief. My daughter Georgina left him to his own devices a few weeks ago, and I'm afraid he stole a link of sausages from the butcher's and then 'christened' some half dozen tombstones in the churchyard before the vicar managed to collar him. The truth is, his origins are shockingly plebeian, and he's no notion of how to behave in polite society."

Sebastian laughed. "I understand entirely."

She gave the dog an affectionate shake. "My purpose in hailing you in such a shamefully vulgar fashion is because I would like to invite you and Lady Devlin to dinner at Northcott Abbey—shall we say, tomorrow evening?" She leaned forward. "Oh, do say you'll be able to come."

The truth was that Sebastian had his own reasons for wishing to visit Northcott Abbey and study a certain seventeenth-century painting hanging in its portrait gallery. He bowed and said, "We should be delighted."

"Wonderful. I have some houseguests I believe you'll find most interesting: Senator and Madame Lucien Bonaparte, the estranged brother of the Emperor Napoléon himself."

"I'd heard he's staying with you this summer."

"Yes; I fear the noise from the repairs on his estate in Worcester was interfering with his poetical composition. He's writing an epic about Charlemagne, you see."

"Is he? I understand he's already published a novel."

"He has, yes—*La tribu indienne*." She pulled a wry face. "Although I must confess I've yet to read it."

"Has he allowed you to see his epic?"

"No. But he spends every morning at the Roman temple by the lake working on it. He's very dedicated."

"I look forward to meeting him."

Her smile flashed wide. "Excellent!" Then she assumed a more somber expression and said, "I would also like to thank you for agreeing to help our young Squire deal with that unfortunate woman's death."

"Did you ever meet her?"

"I did, yes. She came to tea at Northcott just last Saturday. She was such a lovely young woman, neither painfully shy nor too forward. I suggested she might be interested in visiting the priory ruins, and she said she was eager to do so." Lady Seaton hesitated. "Was it truly a murder, do you think?"

"I'm afraid so."

A quiver of what looked very much like fear convulsed her delicate features, then was gone, carefully hidden away. "How absolutely ghastly. I keep thinking . . . I mean, if I'd known when I saw her at the ruins yesterday, could I perhaps have said something—done something—to prevent it?"

"You saw her?"

"I did, yes. I was taking Barney for a walk and came upon her by chance. She was sketching the west wall of the old priory church. It's quite beautiful, you know."

"What time was this?" he asked, more sharply than he'd intended.

"Around two, I suppose. Perhaps a tad later."

"Did you speak with her?"

"I did, yes. I complimented her work. She truly was an exceptionally talented artist. She thanked me for suggesting she visit the ruins and said something about how lovely they were."

"Anything else?"

"Well, let's see. . . . We discussed some of the other picturesque sites in the area. I asked if she'd visited Northcott Gorge yet, and she said she'd arranged to have a guide take her there in a day or two. And then she said something about hoping it wouldn't come on to rain again, because she wanted to sketch the river at sunset."

Sebastian found his interest quickening. "You're saying she was planning to go down to the river that very evening?"

Lady Seaton gave an exaggerated grimace. "I *think* she meant later that evening. But I wouldn't swear to it." She paused, her gaze steady and intent, her head tilted slightly to one side as if she were puzzling out a problem that troubled her. "You're quite certain the young woman didn't take her own life?"

Sebastian was beginning to realize just how intense was the village's need to believe that Emma Chance had killed herself. A comfortable verdict of suicide would mean no need to be afraid; no need for anyone to cast suspicious glances at their neighbors.

No need to confront the unpleasant truth that evil dwelt amongst them.

"She was smothered," he said, perhaps more abruptly than he should have.

Lady Seaton pressed the fingers of one gloved hand to her mouth, her eyes going wide in a way that made him regret his harshness. "Oh, no. It's too horrible to even think about."

"I'm sorry."

She nodded, her lips flattened into a painfully straight line. Then she gathered the reins and shrugged off her unpleasant thoughts with the ease of a hostess changing an uncomfortable conversation topic over dessert. "We keep country hours, so I fear dinner may be earlier than what you're accustomed to: a most unfashionable six o'clock."

"We'll be there," he said with a bow as he stepped back.

She drove off smartly up the street, the incorrigible mongrel at her side giving a happy woof as he lifted his muzzle to the breeze.

Sebastian stood for a moment, the sun warm on his face as he watched her nod pleasantly to Reuben Dickie by the pump house.

She had the careless charm and unthinking confidence of a woman born into wealth and privilege; a woman who had never known want or uncertainty and who had probably never questioned or even reflected on the brutal realities of the society of which she was a part. She showed the

world a cheerful, complacent face, and so successful was her assumption
of equanimity and goodwill that Sebastian could not have said with any
certainty what true sentiments lay behind her pretty smile.

But he had a strong suspicion that she was neither as naive nor as
uncalculating as she was at pains to appear.

Chapter 11

$\mathcal{A}$n hour later, Sebastian stood at the edge of the water meadows and watched as the dozen or so men organized by Archie Rawlins spread out along the banks of the Teme. The air was still hot despite the approach of evening and alive with the throbbing buzz of insects; the late-afternoon sun filtering down through the leafy canopy of willows and alders lining the river glinted off the slow-moving water in quick, bright flashes.

The men ranged from farmers and cottagers to stable hands and day laborers. Yet all wore the same vaguely disbelieving expression as they splashed through the shallows and beat thickets of gorse and stands of tall reeds. They were looking for Emma Chance's sketchbook and the canvas satchel in which she had carried it. But so far they weren't having any luck, and it was obvious that many of them were more than half-inclined to believe they were on a fool's errand, that the beautiful widow had killed herself, after all.

"I suppose the killer could have thrown her things in the river," said Rawlins, batting at a fly hovering around his face.

"Yes," said Sebastian, his gaze on the darkly swirling waters in the center of the river.

He'd assumed that Emma Chance had been killed elsewhere and

her body brought here, to the river, by her killer. But Lady Seaton's information suggested that she might have been killed on her way to the river. And that meant that her sketchbook and anything else she'd carried might be here too.

"I've been asking around the village," said the young justice of the peace, "trying to find people who saw her yesterday evening."

"And?"

"So far the last person known to have seen her was Alice Gibbs, the miller's wife. Says she saw Mrs. Chance climb back over the stile from the priory and turn toward the village."

"When was this?"

"Just after five. She remembers the time because she'd just been talking to Daray Flanagan—that's the village schoolmaster—about her oldest boy."

Sebastian watched thoughtfully as one of the men poking at the brush beneath a beech tree suddenly jumped back, startled by the whirl of a flushed partridge; the man's companions all laughed.

He said, "What time does the sun set these days?"

"About half past nine." Rawlins drew a quick breath as he caught the implications of Sebastian's question, for the old mill lay on the same stream that ran past the priory. "I hadn't thought about that; five o'clock is a long time before sunset. Surely she couldn't have been on her way here that early? Unless perhaps she wanted to give herself time to find the best angle—perhaps even sketch out the basics of the scene before the sun started going down? I don't really know how artists work."

"I suppose it's possible." Sebastian studied the rolling, daisy-strewn green pasture on the opposite bank. The river made a slow, lazy bend here. The view was pleasant and peaceful, but he wouldn't have thought it in any way remarkable or striking. "Would you say this is a particularly scenic stretch of the river?"

"It's all right, I suppose. Although I must say there are places I'd think would be more appealing to an artist."

"Such as?"

"Well, there's the old brick pack bridge down past Maplethorpe Hall, for one. Folks are always saying how pretty it is."

"Might not hurt to ask the men to search down there too. Just because she said she was planning to sketch the river doesn't necessarily mean she was coming to this part of it."

Rawlins turned to look at him. "You think she could have been killed at the bridge and her body brought up here? But . . . why? Why bring her up the river to the water meadows? Why not simply leave her there?"

"I haven't the slightest idea. But I think it's worth a look."

Rawlins nodded, his hands propped on his hips as he chewed his lower lip. "I stopped by Dr. Higginbottom's. He says you figured out Emma Chance was smothered." The young justice of the peace squinted up at the hard blue sky, a gleam of amusement lighting his eyes. "Can't say he's happy about it—you being the one to figure it out, I mean."

"Had he finished the autopsy?"

"Not yet, although I warned him I've contacted the coroner in Ludlow, and he says he wants to hold the inquest on Friday." Inquests were supposed to be held within forty-eight hours of an unexpected death, but that was sometimes difficult in the more sparsely inhabited country parishes. Rawlins swiped at another fly. "Higginbottom showed me that paper he found in her hand—*The rest is silence*. Seems odd, doesn't it? I mean, I assume that whoever put it in her hand wanted us to see it as some sort of suicide note. So why not pick something more to the point?"

"You don't recognize it?"

"Should I?"

"Only if you're fond of Shakespeare."

Rawlins gave a quick, unaffected laugh. "Well, that explains it, then. Never cared much for him myself—although my mother was always reading him when she was alive. It's from one of his plays, I take it?"

"It's the last line of *Hamlet*."

"Ah. Wasn't he that 'To be or not to be' fellow?"

"He was."

Rawlins watched one of the cottagers wade out into the river, the water rippling and lapping around his thighs. "The thing I don't get is, if the murderer wanted us to think she'd killed herself, why didn't he leave whatever book he cut that out of right there beside her?"

"Perhaps the book would have incriminated him in some way."

"I suppose."

The cottager who'd waded out into the river shook his head and surged back toward the bank. The men were coming together now in groups of three and four. The search had been futile.

Sebastian said, "As it is, in his attempt to be clever, the killer left us a valuable clue."

Rawlins swung his head to look at him. "He did? What?"

A breeze kicked up, shifting the feathery branches of the willows and bringing Sebastian the scent of damp earth and fish as they turned away from the river. "We now know that not only is our killer literate; he's also literary."

Chapter 12

After Archie and his band of volunteers had gone off to search the area around the old pack bridge, Sebastian lingered at the banks of the river, his gaze on the turgid, slow-moving water before him as he ran through everything they knew about Emma Chance and her death.

It wasn't much.

The woman herself was an enigma. Young, beautiful, and wealthy enough to outfit herself with fine new clothes and a silver-backed hairbrush, she'd embarked on a sketching expedition through one of the more remote areas of the county, accompanied only by her abigail. An abigail she'd employed just days before arriving in Ayleswick.

It told them something of the kind of woman she was: independent minded, eccentric, and courageous enough to do what she wanted even if it meant braving the conventions of their day. Yet beyond that her identity remained essentially a mystery. Was she actually from London? Or had she simply claimed London as her residence because the capital's enormous size made it a safe lie?

As he watched the pond skaters and water boatmen scuttling through the shallows at his feet, Sebastian couldn't get past Peg Fletcher's suggestion that Emma Chance might not even be the dead woman's real name.

If so, was it a ruse intended simply to protect her reputation from those who might be outraged at the idea of a young woman traveling alone? Or was it something more serious, more . . . nefarious in purpose?

Turning his back on the river, he walked to the stand of alders at the edge of the meadow where they'd found Emma's body. *Why here?* he asked himself again. She obviously hadn't walked all the way down to the river, and they'd found no evidence to suggest that she'd been attacked on the path through the wood. So why bring her body here?

Why?

What they'd learned thus far of her movements the day of her death helped little in their efforts to understand what had happened to her. After sketching Ayleswick's ancient Norman church in the morning, she'd walked out to the old priory and spent several hours drawing the ruins. Then, shortly after five, she'd climbed back over the stile and disappeared toward the village.

As far as they knew, that was the last time anyone had seen her alive.

Listening to the hum of the insects hidden in the drying grass, Sebastian knew a rising sense of frustration. They still had no idea where she had been killed, or why, or by whom. All they knew was that her death had been brutally slow, her killer physically strong and ferociously cold-blooded.

And *educated*, Sebastian reminded himself. Her killer was obviously well educated. Which eliminated not only Reuben Dickie and his brother, Jeb, but also a considerable portion of the village population.

A glint of sunlight on glass in the grass at Sebastian's feet caught his attention. Reaching down, he picked up the small laudanum bottle from where it must have fallen when Constable Nash removed Emma's body. The bottle was too common to tell them anything about the killer. But the fact that it had simply been abandoned here disturbed Sebastian enough that he spent the next half hour crisscrossing the meadow, looking for anything else that might have been missed.

He found nothing.

That evening, as the sun slipped toward the western hills and the sky faded from a hard blue to a pink-tinged aquamarine, Hero left Simon with Claire and climbed the lane that wound gently past the ancient Norman church, to the top of the low, round hill that overlooked the village of Ayleswick. The air smelled fresh and clean, a cool breeze rippled through the long grass, and a hawk circled effortlessly overhead.

At the crest of the hill she came upon the crumbling remains of what looked like a medieval watchtower, the upper reaches of its once-massive sandstone walls now broken and tumbled across the daisy-strewn grass. She sat on a large block still warm from the heat of the dying day and let her gaze rove over the surrounding countryside.

From here she could see the ruins of the Priory of St. Hilary nestled in a green dale threaded by a sparkling stream. Beyond that stretched the extensive, carefully cultivated park of the vast estate known as Northcott Abbey, its grand Tudor house built by whichever ambitious nobleman had managed to acquire the monastery after the Dissolution. The Grange, home of the young Squire, lay at the base of the hill to the east. Half-timbered except for a single stone tower and still partially encircled by a moat, the Grange was both several centuries older and considerably more modest than the Seatons' vast estate.

She had thought those the only two grand houses in the area. Now, as she gazed toward the river, she spotted the brick chimneys of another large house soaring above a clump of trees near the crossroads and closer to the river. Then she realized the chimneys were blackened, the brick walls broken; the house was a ruin.

Once, the fields surrounding the village would have been owned and worked in common, with common meadows for hay and livestock, and wasteland used by the villagers for collecting everything from furze and turf to berries and nuts. But the enclosure movement that had been under way in fits and starts for centuries had vastly accelerated in the past thirty or forty years. Now she could see only ghosts of the old medieval ridges and furrows, lost mementos of a past long since vanished. And she felt a wave of nostalgia sweep over her, as useless as it was sad.

The rattle of a dislodged pebble brought Hero's head around, and she found that she was no longer alone. A boy stood near the entrance to the old watchtower. He looked to be about ten years old, dark haired and handsome beneath the fine layer of fresh dust that coated his face. He wore a brimmed hat, sturdy trousers, and a short coat, all of which were obviously both new and expensive, although the collar of his white shirt was awry and grimy, his stockings were falling down, and a large rent showed in one knee of his trousers. And even if she had not seen Emma Chance's sketch, Hero would have guessed who he was, for the resemblance to his famous, feared uncle was inescapable.

"Hullo," she said with a smile.

He came forward, leaping gracefully from one fallen stone to the next until he came to a halt some ten feet away. "You're the Viscountess, aren't you? The one whose lord is looking into that gentlewoman's murder?"

"I am, yes. You've heard about that, have you?"

"I found her."

He said it matter-of-factly, as if stumbling upon dead bodies were an everyday occurrence—although she noticed a muscle twitch along the side of his jaw.

"Ah," she said. "Then I think I know who you are. Monsieur Charles Bonaparte, yes?"

He hopped off his stone and landed in a crouch before straightening slowly, his head tilted, his large brown eyes solemn as he regarded her fixedly. "It doesn't bother you? That he's my uncle, I mean." There was no need to specify which *he* they were talking about.

"Of course not. Why should it? I hope no one would think to hold me responsible for the actions of all my relatives." *Especially my father,* she thought.

He gave a delighted laugh. "Are they infamous?"

"Some. It's inevitable, you know. We all have them." *Some more than others.*

He came to sit on one of the stones beside her, his dangling feet swinging back and forth, his gaze sweeping the skies. There was an alertness, a watchfulness about him that intrigued her.

She said, "Do you come here often?"

He nodded toward the peregrine circling overhead, its long, pointed wings blue-black now in the gloaming of the day. "It's a grand place to see birds at sunset."

"You're interested in birds?"

"Oh, yes." He tipped back his head, his expression rapt as he followed the falcon's soaring flight. "It's a female, I think. They're bigger than the males, you know. I've read they can go over two hundred miles an hour when they dive. Can you imagine? Two hundred miles an hour!"

"However did anyone manage to time them?"

The boy laughed. "I haven't the slightest idea." Then he sat forward eagerly. "Look! There she goes."

Together they watched as the falcon folded back its tail and wings, its yellow feet tucked up as it launched into its stoop. At first, Hero couldn't see what it was after. Then she spied a single hapless dove flapping desperately toward the clump of birch on the side of the hill.

Oh, hurry, hurry, she thought, even though she knew it was already too late.

The falcon hit the dove in midair, striking its prey with clenched feet and then neatly turning to catch the dove as it tumbled, dead, toward the earth.

"Amazing, isn't it?" said Napoléon Bonaparte's precocious nephew. "Although . . ." He hesitated. "I know the peregrine needs to eat, but I can't help feeling sorry for the dove."

They sat together in silence for a moment, contemplating the necessary cruelty of nature.

Then the boy went very still and nodded carefully toward one of the tower's crumbling walls, "Look! It's a pied flycatcher. Did you know you can tell an insectivore by its broad, pointed bill?"

"You know a lot about birds," said Hero, watching him with a smile.

"I want to be an ornithologist when I grow up. I want to travel all over the world and discover new species no one has ever identified before."

Hero studied his sun-browned, eager face. It was an endearing and oddly compelling ambition for a boy whose uncle dreamt of his family ruling the world.

"I don't see any reason why you shouldn't be able to," she said.

He pulled a face. "My uncle says princes don't become ornithologists."

"I don't know about that. Peter the Great of Russia was fascinated by everything from shipbuilding to clock making. And George III was always passionately interested in farming."

"Yes. But he went mad," said Charles Bonaparte.

"True."

A flicker of movement near the stand of birch caught the boy's attention. She saw his eyes narrow and thought at first he must have spied another bird; then she looked closer and saw the angular line of a top hat silhouetted against the shrubbery.

"*Bah,*" said the boy under his breath. "It's him again."

The man's face was still obscured by shadows cast by the overhead branches, but she could easily discern the fashionable, military-like cut of his coat and his carefully tied snowy white cravat. "Who is it?"

"He calls himself Hannibal Pierce. He followed us here from Thorngrove—our house in Worcestershire. He watches us. Mainly he watches my father, but sometimes he watches me. Follows me. Papa says he works for your government."

"Was he following you this morning?" asked Hero as the man stepped out of the copse of trees into the fading light.

"I don't think so. But I don't always see him. Sometimes I throw rocks at him and tell him to go away, but Mama says I shouldn't do that."

The man called Hannibal Pierce paused, one hand coming up to adjust his hat. He was making no attempt to keep out of sight or to conceal his interest in his subject. Just quietly waiting.

Then he turned his head to stare directly at them, and Hero sucked in a quick breath.

She didn't say anything. But the boy was watching her now, and Charles Bonaparte was a very observant young man.

He said, "You know him?"

"I believe I may have seen him before." She hesitated, then added, "In London."

What she didn't say was, *He works for my father.*

Half an hour later, Hero was in their private parlor at the Blue Boar, a branch of candles at her elbow and Emma Chance's sketchbook open on the table before her, when Devlin walked in, bringing with him the scent of meadows and mud and country mist.

"Find what you were looking for?" she asked.

"No. Not a bloody thing." He took off his hat and whacked at the leaves and twigs still clinging to his breeches. "What are you studying there?"

She turned the sketchbook around to face him. "This."

He came to lean his outstretched arms on the table, his features intent as he gazed at the portrait of a man wearing a beaver hat and fashionably tied cravat. The face was rugged and big-boned, with a prominent jawline and a long, aquiline nose. Hero had seen the portrait before, when she first glanced at the sketchbook. But she hadn't thought to associate this sketch with the man she'd occasionally seen in London. Now she realized that either Emma Chance had been an incredibly intuitive portraitist or she'd known the man. He was drawn as if staring at the viewer, yet there was something about his demeanor that struck one as secretive, almost furtive.

"Who is he?" asked Devlin.

Hero leaned back in her chair. "His name is Hannibal Pierce and he used to be a captain in the dragoons. He now works for my father—doing the sort of things men like Pierce do for Jarvis." Jarvis was famous for his network of spies and informants.

Devlin frowned. "Pierce is here? In Ayleswick?"

"He is. I saw him. According to young Charles Bonaparte—who is quite the clever and engaging young chap, by the way—he's here to keep an eye on their family."

"Interesting." Devlin pushed away from the table to walk over to the chest near the door that held glasses and a bottle of Bordeaux. "Although I'm not surprised to hear that Jarvis is keeping an eye on Lucien. He is Napoléon's little brother, after all."

Hero said, "Hannibal Pierce is one of the few people whose portraits Emma Chance didn't identify by name."

Devlin poured himself a glass of wine. "Perhaps she didn't know it." He went to stand with one arm resting along the mantel, his gaze on the cold hearth.

"What?" she asked, watching him.

He looked over at her. "We keep asking why anyone would want to kill a young widow who came to their small, rural village simply to sketch. But what if her interest in Ayleswick's charming old buildings and landscape vistas was merely a ruse? What if she was here for a different reason entirely? Something that has to do with Lucien Bonaparte."

Hero closed the sketchbook and set it aside. "It fits with what the abigail, Peg Fletcher, told you—that she didn't think her mistress's name was actually Emma Chance."

"Your father has women working for him, I assume?"

"He does, yes—although I doubt I'd recognize any of them." She hesitated, then said, "Of course, she could also have been sent by Napoléon. He must surely have someone here as well, watching his brother."

"More than one, I should think. He must be nervous, having a brother under English control." Napoléon's popularity, like his rise to power, had always depended on his brilliance as a general. But after two brutal decades of nearly endless war, France was running out of soldiers. The loss of some half a million men in his disastrous invasion of Russia had reduced the Emperor to filling his ranks with schoolboys and old men. And with all of Europe turning against him, it was surely only a matter of time before the Allies reached the frontiers of France itself.

Hero said, "I have heard . . ."

"Yes?"

"There are whispers on the streets of Paris that the only way for Napoléon to save France is to abdicate in favor of his infant son. Some are suggesting the Allies are grooming Lucien to act as the child's regent."

"Good God. Did you get that from Jarvis?"

Hero smiled. "Not directly."

Hero's mother, Annabelle, Lady Jarvis, had always been considered more pretty and vivacious than clever, even before she suffered a severe apoplectic fit in the wake of her last, disastrous pregnancy. The incident had left her ill and incapacitated and easily dismissed by her husband as an imbecile—which she was not. It had always struck Hero as odd that her father—normally the most wise and insightful of men—had never understood or appreciated the complexities of his own wife.

Hero said, "If Napoléon has heard the rumors—which I've no doubt he has—and if he thinks Lucien is behind them . . ."

Their gazes met.

Devlin said, "You're suggesting Napoléon could have sent Emma Chance here to kill his own brother?"

"It's possible, isn't it?"

"Oh, yes, it's possible." He drained his wine and set the glass aside. "I think I need to have a talk with Captain Hannibal Pierce."

Chapter 13

$\mathcal{T}$he taproom of the Blue Boar had changed little from the days when devout pilgrims made the dangerous trek through the wilds of the Welsh Marches to pray at the feet of the priory's miraculous Virgin. Heavy beams darkened by centuries of smoke supported a low ceiling; oak wainscoting covered time-bowed walls, and patrons jostled one another on crowded benches pulled up to ancient trestle-and-board tables. The air was blue with tobacco smoke and heavy with the malty-sweet scent of ale. Men's voices and laughter rang loud.

But at Sebastian's entry, the room hushed and faces went slack as men turned to stare at him. The conversations started up again almost at once, but voices were noticeably quieter, more circumspect than before.

After some twenty-four hours in the village, Sebastian recognized many of the Blue Boar's patrons—burly Constable Nash and sharp-faced Alan the Ratcatcher and some of the other men who'd volunteered for that afternoon's search along the river. But even without Emma Chance's sketch, Hannibal Pierce would have been easy enough to identify.

He stood alone at the counter, a tall, broad-shouldered man in pol-ished Hessians and a well-cut coat that could only have come from the hands of a London tailor. He was half turned away, seemingly focused on his own thoughts and the drink he nursed. But Sebastian knew he was alive to every conversation and interaction, every subtle nuance in the room. It was, after all, the reason Pierce was here.

Several dozen men's gazes followed Sebastian's progress as he crossed the room to Pierce's side and ordered a brandy. Pierce stiffened but said nothing. Anyone who worked for Jarvis would know who Sebastian was.

Sebastian rested his forearms on the scarred old countertop. "Tell me about Emma Chance."

Pierce paused with his glass halfway to his lips. "What makes you think I know anything about her?"

"Your portrait is in her sketchbook."

Pierce took a slow swallow of his drink, his lips pressing into a tight wet line as he shrugged. "I'm not surprised; she was drawing everything and everyone around here."

"Why?"

"What do you mean, why?"

Sebastian turned his glass in his hand, the tawny liquid glowing gold in the flickering light. "I would think you'd know. After all, you do observe people for a living."

Pierce cast a quick glance at the crowded room behind them and drained his drink. "Let's go for a walk."

Outside, the night was white with swirling mist, the air throbbing with the strange, almost metallic whine of mating frogs. The cool, moist air smelled of manure and warm horseflesh from the nearby stables and peat smoke from the chimneys of the surrounding cottages. An unnatural hush lay over the village, as if those not in the Blue Boar's taproom were huddled behind closed doors, quiet and afraid.

"I take it Lady Devlin recognized me this afternoon?" said Pierce as they turned their steps toward the dark bulk of the old Norman church up the lane.

"You weren't exactly making an effort to stay out of sight."

Pierce twitched one shoulder. "In London—or even someplace like Ludlow—one can be discreet. Not in a village the size of Ayleswick. The Bonapartes know exactly why I'm here. So why play games and attempt to pretend otherwise?"

"I would think a servant placed within the Bonaparte household would be in a better position to watch them."

Pierce hesitated an instant too long before answering, a delay that told Sebastian he was right—that Jarvis had at least one more agent in place, someone posing as a servant. "In some ways, yes," said Pierce. "But servants' movements are constrained by the requirements of their duties, are they not?"

"True."

The vicarage loomed beside them out of the fog, its slate roof slick with moisture, its windows dark. Beyond it stretched the churchyard, the aged tombstones ghostly in the mist. Sebastian said, "So what about Emma Chance? Was she sent here from London? Or Paris?"

Pierce stared straight ahead. Neither his face nor his voice gave anything away. "She wasn't working with us, I can tell you that. But could she have been sent by Paris? I honestly don't know."

"Yet surely Napoléon has someone here watching his brother."

"Undoubtedly. I even have a few suspicions as to whom. But am I certain? No."

"And Emma Chance? Did you suspect her?"

A slow smile curled the other man's lips. "I suspect everyone."

"Tell me about her."

"What's there to tell? She was a pretty little thing. Claimed she was here to sketch, although she was asking a lot of questions."

"About the Bonapartes?"

Pierce gave a low laugh. "I wouldn't know. She didn't ask me anything."

"Yet she drew your portrait."

"I didn't know that." Pierce drew up abruptly and turned to face him. "Why are you doing this? Why interfere? The villagers were content to believe she killed herself. So why stir them up?"

Sebastian felt a breeze kick up, swirling the damp mist against his cheeks. "Because she didn't kill herself."

"So? What the hell is she to you?"

"Nothing. And everything." Sebastian studied the other man's big-boned face, the hard light in his eyes. Sebastian knew the kind of men Jarvis employed. He had no doubt that Hannibal Pierce was more than capable of holding down a young woman for five minutes and watching her die a slow, agonizing death. "Did you kill her?"

Pierce stared back at him, his nostrils flaring with the violence of his breathing.

In the tense silence, the shifting of the branches of the ancient yews in the churchyard sounded unnaturally loud. Sebastian could hear a trickle of unseen moisture and the rustle of some night creature—

And the metallic *snick* of a flintlock's hammer being carefully thumbed back.

Chapter 14

"Get down!" shouted Sebastian, throwing himself flat as a roar of burning powder and whistling hot lead exploded from near the lych-gate.

The bullet hit Pierce high in the chest, spun him half around. He stumbled, then slowly crumpled.

"Bloody hell," swore Sebastian.

He could hear the shooter crashing through the churchyard, running away down the hill through the fog-shrouded tombs and crooked headstones. A shout sounded from one of the nearby cottages, then another. Sebastian pushed cautiously to his feet and went to crouch down beside the gasping man. As Sebastian lifted Pierce's head, a trickle of blood ran from the corner of his mouth.

Sebastian knew only too well what that meant.

"Who would want to kill you?" he asked, yanking off his cravat to press the wadded cloth against the man's ripped and bloody waistcoat.

Hannibal Pierce sucked in a shaky breath that blew bubbles in the wet sheen of his chest. His face was full of bewilderment, his thoughts and focus turning inward.

"Who shot you?" shouted Sebastian. He cradled the gravely wounded man in his arms, watched the warm blood seep through the cloth to run

down his fingers. And he found himself wondering what would have happened if he hadn't moved. Because given the angle of the shot and the way the two men had been standing, the bullet could easily have been intended for Sebastian himself.

"You didn't see anything?"

Archie Rawlins kept his voice hushed, although it was doubtful their words could wake the pallid, dying man in the bed beside them.

They were in Pierce's room at the Blue Boar. Dr. Higginbottom had arrived, bandaged the man's chest, pronounced there was no hope for him, and left. A single candle burned on the nightstand; the rest of the chamber lay in shadow.

"Nothing except the glow of burning powder in the fog," said Sebastian.

"It's bloody thick out there." The young Squire blew out a heavy breath and brought up one hand to rub the bridge of his nose with a thumb and forefinger. "I don't understand why this is happening. We've never had anything of this nature in Ayleswick. I mean, every once in a while some drunk will beat his poor wife to death, or somebody will get killed in a brawl. But never anything so . . ."

"Clandestine and premeditated?" suggested Sebastian.

"Yes, that's it." Rawlins nodded toward the dying man. "I never could figure out what he was doing here."

"He was keeping an eye on Lucien Bonaparte. For London."

Rawlins looked at Sebastian, his jaw slack. "Good God! How'd you know that?"

"Lady Devlin recognized him."

Archie Rawlins went to stand at the window, his gaze on the swirling fog. "I don't like where things are going," he said after a moment. "I find it difficult to believe this shooting isn't somehow connected to the murder of Emma Chance."

"Probably," said Sebastian. "Although it could conceivably be completely unrelated. Pierce told me Napoléon has someone here watching his brother."

Rawlins pivoted to stare at him. "Who?"

Sebastian shook his head. "He didn't know. He said he had some suspicions as to whom, but he couldn't be certain and he didn't name anyone."

"You're suggesting he was shot by a French agent? *Here?* In Ayleswick!"

"Perhaps." Sebastian watched the dying man labor to take a rattling breath. "It's also possible Pierce was hit by mistake. We were facing each other, and I moved when I heard the shooter pull back his hammer. A good marksman with a rifled, long-barreled pistol can reliably hit a target at fifty yards. But most men's accuracy goes all to hell beyond ten yards— and that's without the mist."

"How do you know the shooter was using a pistol?"

"I spent six years in the army."

"Ah." Rawlins frowned. "How far away would you say he was?"

"Twenty, maybe thirty feet."

"And you heard him cock his pistol? That's damned impressive."

"I have good hearing."

"I'll say." Archie swung away from the window, his features tightening as his gaze fell, again, on the man in the bed. "You think Higginbottom's right? That he's dying?"

"Yes."

He swallowed hard. "I was planning to ride into Ludlow in the morning. See if anyone at the Feathers can tell me more about Emma Chance."

"Let's hope you have some success."

"But . . . what about him? Whom do we notify if—when—he dies?"

The two men watched, together, waiting for Hannibal Pierce to draw another breath.

He didn't. And as the minutes passed and stretched out, it was as if they could see the life seeping out of him, his body shrinking until it became no more than an empty husk.

"I'll take care of it," said Sebastian, and reached out to draw the sheet over the dead man's face.

Later, Sebastian stripped off his clothes stained with the dead man's blood and sat on the side of the bed in the darkness beside his sleeping wife. The growing wind swirled the fog outside the window and rattled the branches of the ancient chestnut out on the green. He could smell the fecund odor of the fields surrounding the village, hear a lamb bleating in the night. He rested his hands on his thighs, opened and closed his fists. And still the tension hummed inside him, a stoked furnace of anger and alertness and rising urgency.

He felt the mattress shift as Hero rolled toward him to rest her hand flat against the small of his back. She had spoken to him earlier, while Higginbottom was tending his patient and grumbling that it was all a waste of his time since the man was certain to die anyway.

"Is Pierce dead?" she asked.

"Yes."

She was silent a moment. "You think that bullet was actually meant for you?"

"I wish I knew. If Pierce was indeed the target, it might help make sense of what's happening in this village. Otherwise . . . it could be damnably misleading."

"Or not."

"Or not."

She shifted to slip her arms around his waist and press her face against his side.

She was one of the most rational and levelheaded people he had ever known; calm and fiercely brave and utterly unflappable. Yet love makes us all vulnerable, and he felt the faint tremor that shivered through her as she let her breath ease out in a sigh.

"You will be more careful," she said.

"Yes, ma'am."

He saw her smile at him in the darkness, felt her hand slide across his back to his hip. He stretched out beside her, her body long and supple as she pressed against him. He buried his face in the dark, sleep-warmed tumble of her hair; breathed in the familiar scent of her, of lavender and musk and the lingering milky sweetness left by his infant son. And he felt the day's concerns begin to ease out of him.

He traced his lips along her cheek, captured her mouth, heard her breath catch as his hand closed over her breast. She wrapped her love and her body around him, and he lost himself in the wonder that was this woman and the all-consuming intensity of their union.

They had first come together just fifteen months before, in a desperate affirmation of life in the face of looming death. But death had not come. Instead, from those raw, tentative, unexpected beginnings had come Simon and a love so powerful and uplifting that it still filled him with a shaky wonder.

He kissed her forehead, her ear, her cheek; watched her face as he moved above her in the darkness. Once, he had faced danger with a recklessness born of a careless attitude toward living. But those days were in the past. And as he held her close, felt her heart pounding against his, heard the keening of her breath, he knew a deep and all-consuming thankfulness that he was here, now, alive and in this woman's arms.

Chapter 15

$\mathcal{T}$he next morning, Hero worked at coaxing Simon to eat some porridge while Sebastian sat at the table beside her and wrote a note to inform Lord Jarvis of Hannibal Pierce's death. He and Archie had combed through the dead man's effects, but they'd found nothing to shed any light on the two recent murders.

He was affixing a seal to the letter when Martin McBroom appeared at the parlor doorway. "Begging your ladyship's pardon for disturbing you so early," said the innkeeper with a jerky bow, "but I'm thinking your lordship will be wanting to see this." He held out a folded sheet of what looked like writing parchment, of the sort a lady might use for her correspondence.

"Where did this come from?" asked Sebastian, taking it.

"Mary Beth—the chambermaid—came across it while she was cleaning Mrs. Chance's room this morning. She said it'd fallen down behind the washstand."

Unfolding the sheet, Sebastian found himself staring at a list of numbered names written in what he recognized as Emma Chance's neat, flowing hand.

1. ~~Squire Rawlins~~

2. Lord Seaton

3. Major Weston

4. The man at the Ship

5. Reverend Benedict Underwood

6. Reuben Dickie

7. ~~Samuel Atwater~~

Two of the names—Squire Rawlins and Samuel Atwater—had a line through them, as if she had crossed them out.

Sebastian looked up to find Mr. McBroom watching him intently, his full, ruddy face glowing with curiosity. "Thank you," said Sebastian, refolding the paper.

McBroom's face fell with disappointment. "You'll be showing it to the young Squire?"

"I will, yes. Thank you."

"What is it?" asked Hero after the landlord had reluctantly taken himself off.

Sebastian handed her the paper.

She studied the list a moment, then looked up. "Men. They're all men."

"I hadn't thought about it, but you're right." He watched Simon thrust his fist into the porridge and give a toothless grin as it squished through his fingers. "Could this be a list of men whose portraits she drew?"

"No; it's not long enough. And the names aren't in the right order. Here." Setting the list aside, she carefully wiped Simon's face and hands and passed him to Sebastian.

"You've porridge behind your ear," Sebastian told his son while Hero went to retrieve Emma's sketchbook from the chest near the window.

"I made a list myself of the people in her portraits." Hero laid her own list on the table beside the paper found by the chambermaid.

Sebastian steadied his son on his lap and leaned forward to compare them.

1. Martin McBroom X
2. Archie Rawlins
3. Reverend Underwood
4. Reuben Dickie
5. Lucien Bonaparte X
6. Charles Bonaparte X
7. Samuel Atwater
8. Jude Lowe
9. Major Eugene Weston
10. Jenny Dalyrimple
11. Mary Beth the chambermaid X
12. Hannibal Pierce X

Sebastian said, "It looks as if she drew everyone on her list except Lord Seaton. Plus a few others who aren't on her list." He frowned. "I think I've heard of this Weston. But I can't place him at the moment."

Hero flipped open the sketchbook and held up a drawing of a middle-aged, mustachioed man posed before a modest brick house. He stood tall and erect, his posture hinting at a preening type of male vanity combined with a desperate attempt to draw attention away from his expanding waistline. "This is Major Weston. Recognize him?"

"No. But now I know where I heard the name. According to Reuben Dickie, Weston lives in what used to be the Dower House of Maplethorpe Hall." He caught Simon's hand as the baby reached for his quill. "Who is Jude Lowe?"

Hero flipped back a page. "Here. According to the chambermaid, he owns a tavern in a nearby hamlet."

Sebastian studied the lean, handsome man. He looked younger than Weston, probably closer to thirty-four or thirty-six, with dark hair, deeply set eyes, and a cleft chin. There was something about him— some faint similarity of features, or perhaps it came simply from the way he held his head—that reminded Sebastian of Jamie Knox. Emma had drawn him standing beside a tavern's swinging sign, its painting of a Spanish galleon flecked and worn but still clearly discernible.

"'The man at the Ship,'" said Sebastian. "And Atwater?"

Hero turned to the portrait of an unassuming-looking middle-aged gentleman. "Here."

Sebastian grasped both of Simon's hands, smiling as the boy pulled himself up to a stand, tiny fat legs wobbling as he balanced his feet on Sebastian's thighs. "So why are there 'Xs' behind five of the names on your list?"

"Those are the portraits that are unnamed: Martin McBroom, Lucien and Charles Bonaparte, the chambermaid, and Hannibal Pierce."

Sebastian looked over at her. "You're saying the only person Emma sketched and named who isn't on her list was Jenny Dalyrimple?"

"That's right. Jenny's also the only named woman Emma drew."

"How old is the current Lord Seaton?" asked Sebastian, his gaze still on the lurching, grinning child in his lap. "Any idea? Is he even of age yet?"

"Barely," said Hero. "The chambermaid says he's taken his sisters and the older Bonaparte girls to spend some time at an aunt's house in the Lake District. So he isn't here."

"Yet his name was on Emma Chance's list," said Sebastian. "I wonder why." He touched noses with the boy. "What do you think, young Master St. Cyr? Hmmm?" He caught Simon under the arms and lifted the baby high over his head as the boy squealed with delight. "Actually, why were any of those names on her list?"

He glanced over at Hero, but she simply shook her head.

It was one more question to which they had no answer.

Chapter 16

The innkeeper, Martin McBroom, seemed a logical source for information on the three relatively unknown men on Emma Chance's list—Samuel Atwater, Major Weston, and Jude Lowe.

Finding McBroom seated at a small, untidy desk in an alcove off the entry hall, Sebastian asked first about Samuel Atwater.

"Ah. Saw his name on the list, I did," said the innkeeper, shuffling papers around on his desktop.

"So who is he?"

"Could've told you before if you'd asked." McBroom kept his focus on his papers in a way that told Sebastian just how deeply he had offended the innkeeper earlier by not indulging the man's desire for a good gossip. "Happens he's steward out at Northcott Abbey. Some sort of cousin to her ladyship. From Yorkshire," he added in the faintly disparaging tone typically used by villagers when referring to "outsiders."

"How long has he been in Ayleswick?"

The landlord picked up his quill and inspected the tip. "Twenty, maybe twenty-five years, I suppose."

"And Jude Lowe?"

"Proprietor of the Ship, he is."

"And where might the Ship be?"

McBroom set about mending his quill with a knife. "At the cross-roads to the east of here. Just beyond the old gibbet." He raised his bushy eyebrows and threw Sebastian a sideways look over the tops of his spectacles. "Fitting, ain't it?"

"Oh? Why's that?"

Rather than answer, McBroom returned his gaze to his quill. "You gonna be talking to him?"

"Yes."

"Ah, well. Then you'll see, won't you?"

"And Major Weston?" asked Sebastian, fighting the urge to grit his teeth. "What can you tell me about him?"

According to the innkeeper, Eugene Weston, too, had arrived in the area some twenty to twenty-five years before, when his militia unit was billeted in the village. "Quite splendid to look at, he was in those days. Leastways, all the young women thought so—and more'n a few of the older ones who should've known better." McBroom sniffed. "Him and his scarlet regimentals and great flowing mustache. Course, he had eyes only for Liv Irving."

"Liv Irving?"

"Daughter of them took over Maplethorpe Hall."

"Oh?"

McBroom lowered his pen, his lips working silently over his teeth, the impulse to continue punishing the Viscount for his earlier snub warring with the urge to divulge the lurid past of one he obviously disliked.

The lure of the lurid won.

The main house had still been standing in those days, explained the innkeeper. It was a grand Palladian villa dating to the early eighteenth century, and the Irvings were unabashedly proud of their fine new estate. From the very beginning, they took to throwing large house parties to which they invited as many representatives of old or titled families as they could entice to come. The origins of the family's wealth were in trade, but they were determined to erase the stigma of having earned rather than inherited their fortune.

As a cousin of Lord Weston of Somersfield Park, the handsome young major was enthusiastically welcomed to the Irvings' endless round of dinners, rout parties, picnics, and balls. So eager were the Irvings to cultivate the well-bred and well-connected young officer that they failed to inquire too closely into his antecedents. By the time they discovered that the handsome young major's kinship to Lord Weston was distant and his father no more than an impoverished country vicar, the major had convinced sixteen-year-old Liv to elope. It was nearly a week before the couple returned, at which point the girl was hopelessly ruined.

There was nothing the Irvings could do at that point except put a brave face on it and hope for the best.

The Dower House lay at the end of a short drive that wound away from the main Ludlow road just beyond the crossroads. Built in 1789 for the late Mr. Irving's widowed mother, it was of moderate size, with symmetrically placed windows, a paneled central door, dentil-work cornices, and a dormered, hipped roof. The garden was small but exquisite, with both a formal section enclosed by a high yew hedge and a more natural area given over to wild roses and Leucojums and Camassias. When Sebastian reined in his chestnuts before the steps, he could see the blackened brick chimneys of Maplethorpe Hall itself just visible above the tops of the trees in a small spinney.

He dropped to the ground. "See if you can find a talkative groom," he told Tom. "I'd be interested to hear the servants' opinion of their master."

Tom grinned. "Aye, gov'nor!"

The front door opened, and Sebastian turned to find the major himself bounding down the shallow front steps toward him.

"Lord Devlin? It is Lord Devlin, yes?"

He was dressed quite nattily in a striped silk waistcoat, fine doeskin breeches, gleaming high-top boots, and a well-cut navy blue coat. He still sported a flowing, military-style mustache, although its once rich auburn was now beginning to fade to gray. In one hand he carried a crop, as if he had been on the verge of going out riding.

"Major?" said Sebastian with a bow.

"Yes, yes." The major bowed low and flashed a wide smile that displayed even white teeth. "I was just on my way into the village to see you. Heard you're helping young Rawlins. He's a promising lad, but there's no denying this sort of thing is beyond his capabilities. Far, far beyond."

The major was smaller than Sebastian had expected, the top of his head barely reaching Sebastian's chin, and of a narrow frame, with most of his weight tending to settle about his middle.

"Rawlins was clever enough to suspect that Emma Chance hadn't committed suicide," said Sebastian.

"Yes, well . . ." Weston brought up one hand to cover an unconvincing cough and glanced significantly toward the house. "What say we take a turn about the garden, eh? I'm afraid Mrs. Weston's a bit overset by all this."

"Of course."

They turned their steps down an allée of cordoned pear and apple trees, the green fruit just beginning to swell toward ripeness. "Why did you want to see me?" asked Sebastian.

Weston looked startled. "I beg your pardon?"

"You said you were on your way into the village to see me."

"Oh, yes, of course. Just seemed the thing to do, what? Let you know that if you need anything, you've only to ask. Only too happy to be of service."

"You met Mrs. Chance, I understand?"

"Oh, yes, several times."

"Why?"

"You mean, why did I meet her? She was interested in Maplethorpe Hall. Wanted to sketch what's left of it and very appropriately approached me to ask permission. Naturally I said yes."

"When was this?"

"That she spoke to me?" Weston frowned, his eyes narrowing against the brightness of the sun. "Let's see. . . . It must have been Sunday. Yes, it was—after church services. So definitely Sunday."

"And did she sketch the house?"

"She did. That very afternoon. I know because I saw her there."

"Sunday afternoon?"

"Yes."

"Did you speak with her then?"

"Yes, of course. Seemed only polite, eh?" Weston's tongue flicked out to wet his lips, his hazel green eyes crinkling with a smile that might once have been charming but now came off as faintly lecherous.

"What did you talk about?"

"Oh, this and that. She wanted to know more about the house—the way it used to be. She expressed interest in the Irvings' tradition of hosting extravagant entertainments, and I recall telling her about one grand hunting party we had in the autumn of 1791, at the beginning of partridge season. As it happens, I had particularly good luck that year. Bagged more than anyone nearly every time we went out."

"Did she ask about anything else?"

"Not so's I recall, no."

Weston stared out over the carefully tended borders, a faint smile of remembrance still warming his plump face. He was the kind of man who could remember with clarity everything he himself had said and done, but little else, for his focus was always firmly planted on himself.

"When did Maplethorpe Hall burn?"

Weston sucked on his back molars as if the answer required a moment's thought. "Must be ten—no, fifteen years ago now. Caught fire in the middle of the night. Mrs. Weston and I barely escaped the flames with our lives. Afraid m'wife's father was not so fortunate. He was bed-ridden, you see, and there was no getting to him in time."

Sebastian glanced back at the brick Dower House with its tall, white-painted windows and neat green shutters. The house was both charming and spacious, yet nothing, surely, to compare to the hall. So why hadn't Maplethorpe been rebuilt? Why had a man obviously as ambitious and as enamored of wealth and all its trappings as Weston retreated to life on such a reduced scale?

"We talked about rebuilding," said Weston, as if following the train of Sebastian's thoughts. "But somehow we never got around to it. In the end, we realized this place suits us fine. We were never blessed with children, you see." He smiled sadly when he said it, and Sebastian had the feeling it was an explanation he trotted out often: endearingly self-deprecating, faintly tragic, and patently false.

"I'm sorry."

Weston shrugged. "My wife keeps busy with the gardens, both here and at the ruins of the old house. It's her passion." He wafted one hand in an expansive arc that took in the exquisite borders backed by towering dark yew hedges. "This is all her work."

"It's lovely. She has a real talent."

Again, the self-deprecating smile—although this time it hid a venomous barb directed at his wife. "So I'm told. I'm afraid it's all just shrubs and flowers to me."

"When was the last time you saw Emma Chance?"

The abrupt change in topic appeared to disconcert him. "Why—that afternoon. Sunday."

"Did you know she drew your portrait?"

A faint, inexplicable hint of color tinged the major's cheeks. "No; did she indeed? Well, well, well."

"Did you happen to notice if she had one sketchbook with her, or two?"

"I only recall seeing one. But then, she had a canvas satchel with her, so I suppose she could've had another in there. Why?"

"We haven't been able to find the sketchbook she used for buildings and landscapes."

"No? That's odd."

They'd reached the spinney now, a thick stand of young oaks and field maple underplanted with hazel and dog roses and eglantine.

Sebastian said, "Who do you think killed her?"

It was a question he tended to ask essentially everyone he spoke with. But the major's reaction was definitely curious.

"Me?" Weston stared blankly at him, jaw slack. "Good God; how would I know? She was a pretty little thing. You're certain someone didn't try to have his way with her and simply carried things too far?"

It struck Sebastian as an unpleasantly euphemistic way to describe an act of attempted of rape leading to murder. "Why? Have there been instances of that sort around here in the past?"

Weston gave an odd, forced laugh. "Not to my knowledge, no."

"Mind if I take a look around the grounds of the old hall?"

Weston's smile faded away into something almost pained. "Whatever for?"

"It might help." Sebastian studied the other man's florid, sweat-slicked face. "Why? Is there a problem?"

Weston gave another of his oddly nervous laughs. "No, no, of course not. There's a gardener named Silas—Silas Madden. Lives in the old grooms' quarters over the stables and also functions as a sort of caretaker. He might try to run you off, but just tell him we spoke." He hesitated a moment, then smiled again as what looked like genuine amusement flooded his face. "They say it's haunted, you know. The old house, I mean."

"By your wife's father?"

"No, from before that. The daughter of the previous owners, the Baldwyns. Threw herself off the roof. She was their only child, and they died themselves not long afterward, of grief. Or at least, that's the way the story goes."

"Why? Why did she do it?"

"The usual: unrequited love." Weston rolled the last word off his tongue, lingering on the "l" and vowel sounds in a way that made a mockery of both the word and the emotion it stood for.

Sebastian felt his skin crawl. "What does the ghost do?"

The major's smile altered, became something faintly derisive. "Flits across the empty windows. Trails her icy fingers down your cheek. Alternately shrieks with laughter or sobs hysterically. Or so they say. I wouldn't know: I've neither seen nor heard her. There are those who say she started the fire—knocked over a candle left unattended."

"So how did the fire actually start?"

Weston stretched out his upper lip as he used a splayed thumb and forefinger to smooth his flowing mustache. "Oh, it was an untended candle, all right—knocked over by a windblown drape when the window was carelessly left open. But the ghost makes a much better story, don't you think?" And he smiled again, as untroubled by the thought of a grief-stricken girl plunging to her death as by the memory of his dying father-in-law's frantic shrieks on a wild, storm-tossed night.

Chapter 17

Major Weston was still standing in his drive, smiling faintly after them, when Sebastian drove away.

"So what did you learn?" Sebastian asked Tom.

Tom let out a scornful snort; in his own way, the tiger could be quite the snob. "It's a right shabby establishment, that one. Ain't but one groom, two 'acks, a showy 'unter that probably ain't got no bottom, and a mare t'pull the gig."

Sebastian turned the chestnuts onto the narrow, overgrown track that curled around the spinney toward the ruins of Maplethorpe Hall. "In other words, Major and Mrs. Weston are living in considerably reduced circumstances."

"Ain't they just. According to Andrew—'e's the groom there—the only reason they ain't in the poor'ouse is because Mrs. Weston got her da to change 'is will right afore he died. Seems 'e left everythin' tied up so's the major can't touch none of it. It's Mrs. Weston what controls things now."

"Interesting."

"Andrew says the major don't like it at all, though there ain't nothin' 'e can do about it. 'E don't cotton to all the ready she wastes on her gardens, neither. Andrew says they've 'ad some right royal rows 'bout it."

"Her gardens are lovely."

"Andrew says the Dower 'Ouse ain't nothing compared t'what she's done with the old hall."

At that moment, the gardens of the main house opened up on the far side of the spinney and Sebastian drew up for a moment as the glory of Liv Weston's creation spread out before them. It had become the fashion in recent decades to use ruins as decorative accents in gardens. Those without the good fortune to possess an authentic ruin on their estate simply built them—everything from imitation Greek temples to picturesque re-creations of romantic Crusader towers and crumbling medieval chapels. But Mrs. Weston possessed the real thing at the center of her gardens, and she had used it magnificently.

The hall might date back only to the early eighteenth century, but in its ruined state it looked much older, the ivy-hung walls looming over a Renaissance-inspired knot garden with arbors and turf seats and honeysuckle-draped pergolas. There was an Italian garden with a long canal flanked by tall, dark evergreens, and a medicinal herb garden, and a romantic, wild-looking nuttery and orchard underplanted with campanulas and daisies and poppies.

A stocky man pushing a wheelbarrow full of hedge clippings down a grass path paused to watch through narrowed eyes as Sebastian brought the curricle to a halt before the ruined house. The gardener wore a faded blue smock and wide-brimmed straw hat and held the stem of an unlit clay pipe clenched between his rear molars. He shifted the pipe thoughtfully with his tongue as he watched Sebastian hop down to the gravel.

"You must be Silas," said Sebastian, advancing on him. "Major Weston said you'd show me about the old hall."

The gardener's heavily featured face remained impassive. "He did, did he? And who might you be?"

"I'm Devlin."

Silas turned his head and spat. His skin was dark and coarse and deeply scored with lines from his years of work in the sun, although his sandy hair showed only the faintest touches of gray. He had a short but powerful build, with thickly muscled arms and legs, and was probably somewhere between forty and fifty. "I take it yer that grand London lord what's lookin' into the death of the lady?"

"That's right. I understand she was here Sunday afternoon, sketching the ruins. Did you see her?"

"Course I seen her. I'm here ev'ry day, all day, aren't I?"

"Did you speak with her?"

"'Spose I did."

Sebastian was remembering Hannibal Pierce's comment, that Emma Chance had been asking the villagers an unusual number of questions. "What about?"

"'Bout the garden and the house. What ye think?"

Sebastian stared out over the ripe summer borders of lavender and lilies, agapanthus and late-flowering clematis. "It's a lovely garden."

"Miss Liv done it all herself."

Miss Liv, Sebastian noticed; not Mrs. Weston.

"She's very talented," said Sebastian.

The muscles in the caretaker's face contracted in a grimace. "Better'n that prancing foreigner the previous Lord Seaton brought in to do the grounds of Northcott Abbey some years back. She's helpin' the young Squire with the gardens at the Grange now. Ye seen it?"

"Not yet."

"Course, she only started there this spring, so it'll be a while before everythin' grows up the way it's supposed t'. Gardens take time. Time, and a vision for how it'll all look someday."

Sebastian nodded to the nearby row of orange trees in tubs. "How long has she been working on the gardens here?"

"Since the fire. Changed it all around from when Mr. and Mrs. Irving was alive, she did."

"The fire must have been a terrible tragedy."

"A tragedy? Yeah, I guess ye could call it that."

"What would you call it?"

Silas shrugged and scratched a mosquito bite on his cheek with broken, dirt-encrusted nails.

Sebastian said, "Did Emma Chance ask about the fire?"

"Not so much. She wanted t'hear about the days when the Irvings was still alive. 'Bout the grand parties they used t'have."

"Oh?" Weston had also mentioned house parties—although his focus had been entirely on himself.

"She was partic'larly interested in the house party they had the year them Frogs nabbed their King and Queen and stuck 'em in prison."

Seventeen ninety-one again, thought Sebastian. He smiled encouragingly. "It must have been grand."

"Oh, aye; was it ever. They had more'n thirty guests that year, including titled lords and ladies from as far away as Worcestershire and Herefordshire. The gentlemen would go out shootin' ev'ry mornin', while the ladies strolled the gardens or did whatever it is ladies do with their days. And every night, there was such a big, fancy dinner they had t' hire near every woman and girl in the hamlet to help. And then at the end there was a masked ball, the likes of which ain't never been seen around here before or since."

"Were you also gardener here under the Baldwyns?"

"Aye. I was a young lad in those days, I was."

"Did Mrs. Chance ask about the Baldwyns?"

"Not so's I remember, no."

Sebastian gazed toward the brick stables and its attached coach house. "They were lucky the fire didn't reach the stables."

"Aye. Some sparks fell on the roof, but we was able to put 'em out."

"They're still maintained, I see."

Silas shifted his posture, as if drawing into himself, his arms coming up to fold across his chest. "I live there now. Use the old stalls 'n' carriage house for storage."

Sebastian studied the rutted track leading to the old carriage house. But all he said was, "I'm surprised the house was never rebuilt."

Silas hawked up a mouthful of phlegm and turned his head to spit downwind. "Old Mr. Irving, he was always right clever 'bout a heap of things. But he got sick near the end, and it made him foolish. Foolish as a child, he was, for a couple of years. Let the major do whatever he wanted." The gardener's jaw sagged, then tightened again as he clenched his teeth down hard on the stem of his unlit pipe.

Sebastian waited for the gardener to elaborate, but he simply stared out over the rows of quinces, plums, and apples in the orchard. It wasn't difficult to imagine what would happen to an estate under the stewardship of a man such as Eugene Weston, however temporary it might have been. The wonder was that anything was left at all.

Sebastian squinted up at the gaping, empty windows of the house's blackened facade, the broken tracery standing out stark against the blue sky. "I hear the place is haunted," he said with a smile.

He expected the gardener to scoff at the notion. Instead, Silas simply shrugged, although there was a noticeable increase in the intensity of his breathing.

"Do you ever see her?" asked Sebastian. "Marie Baldwyn, I mean. That was her name, was it not?"

"Ain't just her," said Silas, his voice quiet and gruff. "The dead don't rest when they been done wrong. And there's a heap of folks been done wrong hereabouts. A heap of folks." He turned back to his barrow. "Now you'll have t'excuse me. Miss Liv don't pay me t'stand about and natter."

Sebastian watched the gardener wrap his strong, sun-darkened fists around the handles of his barrow and lean into it, the wheel squealing faintly as he pushed it away.

A light breeze kicked up, shifting one of the long tendrils of ivy that hung from the walls of the ruined house. On the surface, the trag-edies suffered long ago by the ill-fated inhabitants of Maplethorpe Hall seemed to have nothing to do with Monday's death of Emma Chance beside the River Teme. Yet Emma had expressed an unusual interest in the history of this house. And Sebastian understood enough about human nature to suspect that there was probably more to those stories than he'd been told.

Chapter 18

*W*hen people said the Blue Boar was Ayleswick's only respectable inn, they didn't mean it was the area's only hostelry. For everyone who wasn't respectable, there was the Ship.

It stood at the crossroads to the east of the village, where the main road to Ludlow intersected the lane that led to Maplethorpe Hall's main gates before narrowing to a track that snaked south across the Teme. Once, this had been the site of a small hamlet. But only a few cottages were now left standing, the rest having long since collapsed into ivy- and thistle-covered mounds of rubble. It was a common enough sight in the English countryside these days, since the Enclosure Acts had squeezed an increasing number of small farmers and their even poorer neighbors off the land.

The Ship itself was a ramshackle, timber-framed affair with casement windows and a ratty thatched roof. Sebastian turned into its dusty yard to find a lean, dark-haired man currying a fine blood bay. He'd stripped down to his shirtsleeves, the muscles of his back and shoulders bunching and flexing with his work. As Sebastian reined in, the man looked up, his hand stilling at his task as he watched Sebastian hand the reins to Tom.

"You're Jude Lowe?" said Sebastian, hopping down from the high seat.

The man rested his bent wrists on his hips. "I am."

He had dark, almost black hair worn long over his collar, so that it gave him a faintly rakish look. His cheeks were cleanly shaven, his features rugged but handsome, his eyes a dark brown. Despite his task, he was dressed well, his linen clean and white, his boots worn but polished; the coat he'd taken off lay thrown over a nearby bench. And Sebastian found himself reminded again in some indefinable way of Jamie Knox.

"I'd like to ask you about Emma Chance," said Sebastian.

Lowe let out his breath in an incredulous grunt. "What makes you think I know anything about her?"

"She drew your portrait."

"Did she now? I didn't know that."

"When did you see her?"

Lowe tossed aside his currycomb and reached for a rag to wipe his hands. "Must've been Sunday, I guess. She was sittin' there"—he nodded toward the grassy bank on the far side of the road, beside the mound of some vanished cottage—"drawing a picture. She looked hot, so I walked over and offered her some lemonade."

"You knew who she was?"

Lowe's dark eyes gleamed with quiet amusement. "Ain't like we get a lot of strangers hereabouts, especially pretty young ladies drawing pictures. Of course I figured who she was. Everybody's been talkin' about her."

"Did you speak with her?"

"A bit. She wanted to know about the tavern. How long I been here—that sort of thing."

It struck Sebastian as a profoundly peculiar line of questioning for a young gentlewoman to have asked the owner of a wayside tavern. But then, Emma Chance had been asking a number of peculiar questions.

"So how long have you been here?"

Lowe shrugged. "Lived here my whole life. Took over from my father when he died back in 'ninety-seven."

Sebastian stared off across the treetops, to where the blackened chimneys of the ruined great house showed dark against a puffy white cloud. "So you were here the night Maplethorpe Hall burned?"

"Aye. Lit up the whole sky, it did. Ain't never seen nothin' like it."

Sebastian studied the tavern owner's strong cleft chin and straight brows. The resemblance to both Jamie Knox and Jenny Dalyrimple was definitely there. Although in an area this sparsely populated, Sebastian supposed most people were related to one another to some degree.

He shifted his gaze to the tumbled ruins of a nearby cottage. "How long has the hamlet been like this?"

Lowe's jaw hardened, a flinty look coming into his eyes. "Old George Irving pushed a Bill of Enclosure through Parliament in 'ninety-two. After that, those who could either left for London or immigrated to America. The rest died in the poorhouse. And then the old bastard howled when his poor rates went up." Lowe turned his head and spat. "May his blackened soul burn in hell forevermore."

"How long was he bedridden before the fire?"

"A year, maybe. I dunno. Why? What's any of this to do with the dead lady?"

"I'm told she was asking about the Irvings."

Lowe gave a soft laugh. "From what I hear, she was asking about anyone and everyone."

"Any idea why?"

"Said she wanted to know about the places she was sketching. Said it helped her to understand them. Sounds right peculiar, if you ask me. But then, I'm no artist, now, am I?"

"What do you think happened to her?"

Lowe stared at him a moment, his features tight, his eyes hooded and unreadable. "Why you askin' me?"

"You own a tavern. Men tend to talk in their cups."

"Not about murder. Not if they don't want to hang." Lowe reached for his nearby coat and slipped it on, his gaze still fixed on Sebastian's face as he carefully adjusted his cuffs. "Jenny tells me you knew Jamie."

"I did."

Sebastian waited for the tavern owner to remark on the resemblance between the two men. Instead, he said, "M'mother hasn't been well since he died. Took it right hard, she did."

My mother.

She buried three husbands, the Reverend had said of Heddie Kincaid. And Sebastian realized now that Heddie's first husband must have been Jamie Knox's grandfather; the second had fathered Jude Lowe, while the third was the unknown Mr. Kincaid.

"You're saying Heddie Kincaid is your mother?"

"Aye. Eleanor Knox was my sister—half sister, anyway, for all she was sixteen years older than me. I was only a babe myself when Nellie died, and m'mother raised her babies as her own. So Jamie and me, we grew up like brothers." Lowe tilted his head to one side. "I didn't believe Jenny when she said you looked enough like Jamie to be his twin. But 'tis true. Course, it's near twenty years since I seen him. Took the King's shilling when he was barely sixteen."

Sebastian was silent for a moment, his gaze drifting over the tavern's sagging roof and ancient walls. He'd been imagining Knox growing up in Heddie Kincaid's cottage beside the shady millstream. Now he realized the rifleman must have come of age here, in this tavern, in the midst of a dying hamlet strangled by the worst excesses of the enclosure movement.

It explained much.

Jude Lowe drew a deep breath that flared his nostrils. "I always meant to go up t'London and see him. Now it's too late."

"You know he left a son?"

"Aye. M'mother wants Pippa to bring the boy up here to her, but she won't hear of it."

"She may change her mind."

"She may."

Lowe watched in silence as Sebastian turned to leap up to his curricle's high seat. He waited until Sebastian was gathering the reins before saying, "Everybody in the village thinks that widow killed herself. What makes you so certain she didn't?"

"Because she was smothered."

Lowe shook his head in disbelief. "Don't know if I'd put much stock in anything old Higginbottom tells you. He told my granddad there was nothing wrong with him a good cupping wouldn't cure—and was still heating the damned cups when the old man keeled over dead. Charged us for the cupping too. Said it weren't his fault the man died before he finished."

"The bruises on Emma Chance's face are faint, but they're there," said Sebastian. "She was smothered."

Lowe reached for his bay's lead. "Never heard of such a thing. Who'd know how to kill without leaving no sign of it?"

Someone with experience at killing, thought Sebastian. But he kept that observation to himself.

Sebastian drove next to the dilapidated farm of Dr. Hiram Higginbottom.

He found the doctor in a pen near the barn, down on his knees beside a prostrate sick cow.

"She going to be all right?" asked Sebastian as Higginbottom lumbered to his feet with a grunt.

"Who knows? Maybe God—assuming God takes an interest in sick cows. I'll have to remember to ask the Reverend."

Sebastian watched the doctor bend to brush the dirt from the knees of his old-fashioned breeches. "Have you finished Emma Chance's post-mortem?"

Higginbottom straightened slowly. "I have."

"Anything interesting?"

The doctor stared at him a moment, and Sebastian suspected the man was tempted to tell him to wait for the coroner's inquest like everyone else. Then a gleam of nasty amusement came into his watery gray eyes, and he jerked his head toward the barn. "Come. I'll show you."

The dilapidated lean-to was even more hot, stuffy, and fly ridden than before, and thick with the stench of death. Emma Chance lay on the crude table where Sebastian had seen her before, her remains looking oddly shrunken now beneath a stained sheet that didn't quite cover her bare toes. Her clothes formed a jumbled pile on a nearby shelf beside several dirty, fly-covered tin bowls that held what he realized must be her internal organs.

He was aware of Higginbottom smiling at him openly now, eyes narrowed with malicious satisfaction. "Sure you're up to this?"

"Yes."

Higginbottom gave a disappointed grunt and shoved aside the sheet to pick up the cadaver's right arm. All traces of rigor had gone off by now, leaving the body limp. "There's a faint bruise here," he said, pointing to her forearm. "Course, she could've done it before, somehow. But it looks to me like the imprint of a man's thumb."

He let go of the arm, and it slid off the edge of the table to dangle down toward the dirt floor. "Other than that, the only thing of interest is this—" He rolled the body onto its side, revealing a long, slender bare back now purple with lividity. "Probably wouldn't have noticed if I hadn't had a couple of the lads move the table out into the sun while I did the postmortem. But I assume with your stellar eyesight you can see what I'm talking about?"

Sebastian studied the strange pattern of faint abrasions on Emma Chance's shoulder blades. "What are they from?"

"I haven't the slightest idea," said the doctor, letting the body flop back onto the table. He made no move to cover it again with the sheet.

"That's it?" said Sebastian.

"That's it."

"What about her lungs and heart?"

"They look normal enough."

"When do you think she was killed?"

"Sometime Monday, presumably. How'm I supposed to know?"

Sebastian reached to draw the sheet back over the dead woman's naked body. "I assume you looked at the contents of her stomach?"

Higginbottom glared at him from beneath bushy gray brows. "I did. She had a fair amount of half-digested food in there. But from which meal, I've no idea."

Sebastian paused with the sheet still in his hands, his gaze on Emma Chance's pale, waxy face. Her skin had taken on the color and texture of old vellum. And he found himself wishing that he could have met and spoken with her when she was still a laughing, breathing, vital, and talented young woman.

Before she was reduced to this husk of decaying flesh.

He drew the sheet over her face and turned toward the door.

"So who do you think did it?" asked Higginbottom, following Sebastian into the yard.

"I've no notion." Sebastian stood in the late-morning sunshine, his face lifted to the light as he sucked clean, fresh air into his lungs. "You're certain she wasn't sexually assaulted?"

Higginbottom fumbled in his pockets to come up with his pipe. "No sign of it."

Sebastian started to turn away.

"Did find one thing might be of interest, though," said Higginbottom.

Sebastian paused to glance back at him.

"She was still a virgin."

"You're certain? She was a widow, married seven years."

Higginbottom stared at him, one lip curling in contempt. "I may not know as much as your fancy London doctors, but this is one thing I do know. She was a maid, all right. When it comes right down to it, marriage is just a piece of paper; it's what happens afterward in the marriage bed—if not before—that makes a difference. Fact is, I ain't convinced she's twenty-eight, neither, like they're saying. Looks more like twenty or twenty-one, if you ask me. But then, what do I know? I'm just an old country doctor with more cows and sheep than patients."

Sebastian studied Higginbottom's dirty, unshaven face, the yellow teeth bared now in another of those malicious smiles. "The inquest is still scheduled for Friday?"

"It is." The smile widened. "You're lucky she's as fresh as she is, seeing as how you're staying at the Blue Boar." Inquests were typically held at inns and public houses, even in London, mainly because they were the only structures capable of holding such a crowd. "I remember last summer when they held the inquest over Nathan Black; cleared the place out, it did. He was in the Teme a week before they found him, and I sure as hell wasn't keeping him here. Half the jurors cast up their accounts before it was over. Although whether that was from the smell or the way he looked, I couldn't tell you."

"Have you given the postmortem results to Squire Rawlins?" asked Sebastian, refusing to rise to Higginbottom's bait.

"Ain't seen him. Said he was going to Ludlow to try and find out what he could about the dead woman's people. If he don't, the parish is gonna have to pay to bury her."

"I suspect when her goods are sold, there'll be sufficient funds to pay for her interment."

"That a fact? Well, lucky for her. Maybe she can pay for her own postmortem while she's at it."

Sebastian glanced back at that silent, still form, the stained sheet now thick with flies. *Who are you?* he wanted to ask her. *Who are you really?* It seemed everything from her name to her age to her true marital status had been called into question. About the only thing he knew for certain about the woman who'd called herself Emma Chance was that she was a gifted artist.

And that someone had wanted her dead.

Chapter 19

*S*hortly after Devlin left for the Dower House that morning, Hero sat down for an interview with the middle-aged chambermaid, Mary Beth Hodge, who in the process of tidying up had let slip the information that she'd been born and raised in the nearly abandoned hamlet that lay to the east of Ayleswick.

"You're certain this is all right with Mr. McBroom?" asked Mary Beth, nervously eying the notebook and pencil in Hero's hands.

"It is, yes; I've already spoken to him. I'm interested in knowing more about the effects of the Enclosure Acts on the area. Please sit down and relax, and tell me about your hamlet."

Mary Beth perched on the edge of one of the chairs near the cold hearth and clenched her hands together in her lap. "It was called Maplethorpe in those days, milady. That's why the Baldwyns named their big house Maplethorpe Hall—after the hamlet. Though there ain't many re-members that nowadays."

"Your father was a farmer?"

"He was, milady. Cut his hand real bad on a sickle and died from it, he did, when I was just fifteen. That's when I married my Nate."

"Your husband was a farmer as well?"

"Yes, milady."

"So you remember when George Irving's Bill of Enclosure passed through Parliament?"

A shadow touched the chambermaid's elf-like features, leaving her looking both older and sadder. "Don't I just, milady. We didn't know nothing about it till the commissioners come and posted the act on the church door. And by then, there weren't nothin' we could do about it, now, was there? The commissioners were the ones decided who got what, and of course they gave all the best land to Mr. Irving and divided up what was left amongst the rest of us. Only, we couldn't keep it unless we fenced it, and who could afford to do that? Plus, there was all sorts of fees we was supposed to pay. And why was that, when it weren't nothin' we'd ever asked for?"

She looked at Hero as if Hero might be able to supply some explanation. But she could only shake her head.

Mary Beth said, "It would've been bad enough, them dividing up the furlongs like that. But they took away all our rights to the commons and wasteland too. Nate and me used to keep a cow, we did. The milk from that one cow was worth half what a man could earn in a day. But once we'd lost the commons, we couldn't keep her no more and had to sell her. I had a little baby girl in those days; Julie was her name. I think maybe she'd have lived, if we'd still had the cow."

"It must have been a very difficult time for you," said Hero, although it was such a woeful understatement that it struck her as almost cruel.

Mary Beth nodded and rubbed the heel of her hand against one eye. "Everything was so different after that. We used to cut our firewood and peat from the wasteland, and gather berries there in the summer and nuts in the winter. It's where we'd get the rushes for our lights and the thatch for our roof, and even set our pigs t'foraging. But then we didn't have none of that no more. How was we supposed to live?"

"Were there any protests? Disturbances?"

A long silence followed the question. Then Mary Beth said, "He didn't tell you? Mr. McBroom, I mean."

Hero knew an uncomfortable prickling of premonition. "Tell me what?"

"About the troop of yeomen come up one night when a bunch of the lads had got together. Arrested more'n twenty, they did, my Nate and Lucas amongst them."

"Lucas?"

"Lucas was my boy. Sentenced him to serve in the army, they did, even though he was only twelve. Shipped him off to India." The chambermaid dropped her gaze to her lap, where her fingers worked plucking at the cloth of her apron. "Died of a fever when he weren't there more'n a month. Or so I heard."

"I'm sorry," said Hero, her voice now little more than a whisper.

"At least they didn't hang him, like they did my Nate. Nate, and my brother, John, both." Mary Beth drew a shaky breath. "That's when I came here, to work at the Blue Boar. Been here ever since. I was lucky, I was; most folks ended up in the workhouse. Or dead."

In the silence that followed her words, they could hear Martin McBroom in the distance, shouting at one of the stableboys.

"Don't seem right, somehow," said Mary Beth. "To take the land that once belonged to everybody and give it to those who already have so much. Just so's they can put a wall around it and arrest anybody dares set foot on it."

"It's not right," said Hero.

Mary Beth nodded, her lips pressed tightly together, the cords in her throat working as she swallowed hard. "There's a little ditty my Nate used t' sing to my Julie, before she died. You ever heard it?" And then she began to sing, her voice pure and sweet, but wavering now with the strain of her emotions:

"They hang the man and flog the woman,
That steals the goose from off the Common;
But let the greater villain loose,
Who steals the Commons from the goose.

The law demands that we atone
When we take things we do not own,
But leaves the Lords and Ladies fine
Who take things that are yours and mine.
And geese will still a Common lack,
Till they go and steal it back."

The aging chambermaid's voice faded away, leaving her staring at the cold hearth.

"I have heard it, yes," said Hero, quietly closing her notebook and setting it aside. Although the truth was, she'd heard the first four lines, but not the rest.

Mary Beth raised her gaze to Hero's face. "I can tell you this, milady: There weren't nobody around here was sorry, the night Maplethorpe Hall burned and took George Irving with it. Weren't nobody sorry at all."

Chapter 20

$\mathcal{A}$n hour or so later, just as the church bell was striking eleven, the Reverend Benedict Underwood's punctiliously correct wife, Agnes, paid a courtesy call on Viscountess Devlin. It was the done thing, for a vicar's wife to make a formal call on any ladies of stature visiting her husband's parish. Typically, the vicar's wife would leave a card and go away, never expecting to be honored with an actual visit. So Agnes Underwood was visibly stunned to be invited up to her ladyship's private parlor.

The Reverend's wife was a solidly built woman on the tall side, with a long, rectangular face and unmemorable features. She'd brought her husband a dowry of two hundred pounds a year, an additional income most welcome to a clergyman whose living could only be described as meager. And because she was inordinately proud of this fact, she made certain to impart the information to Hero within minutes of meeting her.

"I understand you had Emma Chance to tea," said Hero, handing the vicar's wife a cup of tea sweetened with three sugars.

"I did, yes. The Reverend invited her to the vicarage the first day she was here. Thought her a taking little thing and felt sorry for her." Something about the way she said it suggested that Agnes Underwood did not share her reverend husband's opinion—a suspicion that was confirmed when the woman leaned forward as if imparting a secret. "Although if you ask me, there was something undeniably *fast* about her. As I told the Reverend, I'm not surprised things ended the way they did."

Hero poured herself a cup of tea. "Oh? Why is that?"

"*Well,*" said the vicar's wife, her voice throbbing with meaning. "A young woman, gallivanting about the countryside with only an abigail? It's simply not the done thing, now, is it, Lady Devlin?"

"She was a widow."

"Yes. But . . . *still.*"

"Did she tell you anything about herself?"

The Reverend's wife thought about it a moment. "Not really. She mainly asked about the village."

"What about the village?"

"She was quite interested in the past. I gather her mother visited the area some years ago."

"Oh?" It was the first Hero had heard of any previous link between the dead woman and the village. "Did she happen to mention her mother's name?"

"Not that I recall, no."

Hero thoughtfully sipped her tea. "How long have you been at Ayleswick?"

"Twenty-one years as of last February."

"You were here when the Enclosure Act went through Parliament?"

"Oh, yes. Turbulent times, those were."

Parliament had passed thousands of Enclosure Acts over the previous three or four decades. Because each landlord pursued his own bill through Parliament on an individual basis, the slow erasure of England's ancient common rights had progressed piecemeal and thus provoked no unified, widespread resistance. But local instances of disorder were not uncommon.

"There were some rough elements in the village at one time," the vicar's wife was saying, her small mouth pursed. "I'm afraid they encouraged the others in their foolishness—firing ricks of hay, tearing down fences and leveling ditches, burning effigies. That sort of thing. But they're mostly all gone now, thankfully."

"Where did they go?"

"Botany Bay, the lucky ones. The rest are no doubt burning in Hades."

"You mean, they were hanged."

"Oh, yes—although not enough of them, if you ask me." Her eyes blazed; the vicar's wife was obviously not an advocate of Christian clemency.

Hero had seen a weathered gibbet standing near the crossroads to the east of the village. She wondered what it did to a small community like this one, when those with power and wealth took the lives of those without either. "When was this?"

"The hangings? A year or so after I arrived."

"And that ended it?"

"Oh, yes. That and the transportations."

"The village seems so peaceful now," said Hero, offering her guest a plate of small cakes. "One would never imagine it had such a violent past."

"Believe me," said the vicar's wife, nibbling on a cake. "It was quite terrifying at the time." Since vicars typically benefited from the enclosures at the expense of their poorer parishioners, it wasn't unheard of for rioters to set fire to churches and vicarages.

"Was anyone killed—apart from those hanged, obviously?"

"No. Although Lord Seaton's steward was threatened once by some ruffians with blackened faces."

"You mean Samuel Atwater?"

"Mmm."

Hero poured her visitor another cup of tea. "So, what do you think happened to Emma Chance?"

"Personally? I've no doubt that when all is said and done, the inquest will return a verdict of felo-de-se."

"Suicide? Really?"

"Yes."

"I suppose it's possible," said Hero.

"It's inevitable. We've never had a murder in the village. At least, not of the nature they're suggesting."

Hero studied Agnes Underwood's plain, complacent face. "Have there been other suicides?"

"Not for some years, no. Not since several girls did away with themselves after getting in the family way. Some silly fools whispered at the time that they'd been murdered. But in the end, the inquest found they'd died by their own hand, as expected."

Hero sat forward. "Oh? How did they kill themselves?"

"One drowned herself in the millpond. The other threw herself off the cliffs at Northcott Gorge."

"When was this?"

"Fifteen years ago."

"So about the time of the enclosure troubles?"

"A few years afterward, I believe. But . . . surely you don't mean to suggest that there is some connection—either between those suicides and the disturbances, or between what happened then and the death of this woman now?"

"No, of course not," said Hero, reaching for the plate of cakes. "Won't you have another?"

After the vicar's wife bowed herself out with a profusion of flowery compliments and effusive thanks, Hero changed into a walking dress of fine cambric, its hem embellished with a deep flounce edged in pale pink. She laced up a pair of sturdy half boots, tied on a wide-brimmed straw hat with a pink ribbon, pulled on a pair of fine kid gloves of the same delicate shade, and tucked her parasol under her arm. Then she went for a walk.

Following the village's narrow, winding high street, she turned east, skirting the edge of the green where Reuben Dickie sat on his step at the pump house, whittling another in a long line of small wooden animals. *He must have a veritable Noah's ark by now,* she decided, watching his fingers move with skilled ease. He glanced up and found her watching him, and though she smiled at him, he quickly ducked his head again in confusion.

She opened her parasol, tilted it against the strengthening sun, and walked on.

It was her intention to follow the coach road out to the gibbet that stood on the eastern fringe of the village. But as she neared the entrance to the sunken drive that led to the Squire's ancient manor house, three young lads came pelting down a lavender-edged cottage path toward her. They were shouting and laughing and pushing one another, and were so engrossed in their play that they nearly careened into her.

"Oye," shouted a man who appeared in the open cottage doorway behind them. "Mind where you're going there, lads! And apologize to her ladyship."

"Beggin' yer pardon, milady," chirped the three boys in unison before tearing off again up the road.

"If you'll allow me to apologize as well, my lady," said the man. He walked toward her, his head shaking as his gaze followed the three lads. He had one of those boyish Irish faces that are both ageless and charmingly engaging. But from the deep laugh lines beside his light gray eyes, she guessed he was probably somewhere in his late thirties or early forties. He was not, obviously, an ordinary cottager. His worn clothes were those of a gentleman, his speech and manner cultured, his accent only vaguely hinting at a Dublin lilt.

"Are they yours?" she asked with a smile.

"Oh, no, my lady. Those three young tearabouts belong to Jude

Lowe, keeper of the Ship. I'm nothing more than the humble village schoolmaster." He wasn't wearing a hat, so he couldn't sweep it off with a flourish. But he still managed to sketch an elegant bow. "Daray Flanagan, at your service."

She looked at him with renewed interest. "Ah, you're the one who was speaking to the miller's wife last Monday evening, right before she saw Emma Chance."

"I am indeed, my lady. And what a charming young gentlewoman she was. Such a pity, what happened to her."

"You spoke with her?"

"Not then, no. I came across her earlier, though, when she was painting a watercolor of the high street."

"When was this?"

"Must've been Friday or Saturday, I suppose. She had quite the talent, she did."

Hero studied his mobile, expressive face. "What do you think happened to her?"

"Me? I wouldn't be knowing, my lady. I've only been here a couple of years myself." The smile lines beside his eyes deepened, as if with pain. "I'd have said it was a peaceful, friendly place, this. Which just goes to show, now, doesn't it?"

"How do you come to be here?"

"Pure serendipity. I was passing through the village the day they were burying the old schoolmaster. Stopped at the Ship for a bite to eat and heard everyone talking about how they'd be needing to find someone to take the dead man's place. So I stayed."

It was an artless tale that glossed over much the teller chose not to dwell on, including where he'd been coming from, where he'd been going, and why he'd been content to take up such a lowly position. Some of his pupils might pay for lessons with shillings, but most doubtless paid in kind—and only when they could.

"Serendipity, indeed," said Hero.

Flanagan nodded. "My predecessor had been here forty years. The old Squire'd brought him in. Gave him—and me—this cottage rent free."

Hero had been thinking of Archie Rawlins's father as a drunken boor who foolishly set his horse at a wall he couldn't clear. Now she found she had to readjust that image. It wasn't unknown for landlords to take an interest in educating the children of their tenants and cottagers, but it was uncommon. Most saw the education of the masses either as unnecessary or as a misguided, dangerous folly.

Hero started to walk on, then paused to say, "You wouldn't happen to know anything about the gibbet out near the crossroads, would you?"

Flanagan's gaze flickered up the gently curving road, empty now in the morning sunlight. "I've heard it was set up for some poor fellow hanged for treason back in the early nineties. They say he was rotting up there for three months before somebody cut him down in the middle of the night and buried him who knows where. But I couldn't tell you the details. Folks around here don't like to talk about it much."

"It's been standing twenty years?"

"So I hear. Someone tried to burn it once. But the major, he had the fire put out. Even has old Silas Madden coat it with tar regularly, to help preserve it. Tends that gibbet with as much care as his wife tends her gardens, he does."

"I wonder why," said Hero.

But that was a question the Irishman was unable to answer.

Hero had just passed the last straggling cottage when she became aware of an elegant curricle coming toward her at a fast clip, its driver a down-the-road-looking man in a linen driving coat.

He drew up smartly beside her. "May I offer you a lift, my lady?"

Hero twirled her parasol. "You're not going in my direction."

"I can fix that," said Devlin.

The gibbet stood just before the sad remnants of the small hamlet at the crossroads. Towering some twenty or more feet high, its base set in a massive stone sunk in the ground, the thick post had strong bars of iron running up its sides as reinforcement.

"Someone obviously wanted it to last," said Hero, one hand holding her hat in place as she tipped back her head to stare up at the gibbet's projecting crosspiece. In the distant past, men were sometimes gibbeted alive—hung up in close-fitted, specially forged iron cages and left to die of thirst and exposure. But more often it was used to display the bodies of executed criminals, both as a way to extend their punishment after death and as a warning to others. Murderers were sometimes gibbeted. So were traitors and pirates.

"Care to tell me why you were so eager to walk out here and look at this?" asked Devlin, watching her.

She told him of her interview that morning and her conversation with the vicar's wife. "Mr. Flanagan says Major Weston rescued it from some anonymous arson attempt," she said, her gaze on the rusty hook sunk deep into the underside of the tar-blackened arm. "I wonder why."

"Who was gibbeted here?"

"Flanagan didn't know precisely; only that it was someone executed near the end of the last century. But . . . have you noticed how everyone keeps bringing up the past? Everything from extinct families and house fires to riots and suicides and hangings. I suppose villagers do tend to be more acutely aware of those who have lived out their lives in the same place before them. And yet . . ." Her voice trailed off as she struggled but failed to put her thoughts into words.

Devlin followed her gaze. "Emma Chance was asking an extraordinary number of questions about the past herself. And I'm not convinced she was motivated entirely by a desire to know the history of the buildings she was drawing."

Hero turned her head to look at him. "You think that could be why she was killed? Because she was asking questions someone didn't want answered?"

"I think it's certainly a possibility."

Together, they stared up at the old, fire-charred pole as a gust of wind fluttered the brim of Hero's hat and set the branches of a nearby elm to rubbing against each other. And though the air was warm, Hero found herself shivering, for it sounded exactly like the creak of rusty chains straining with the sway of a dead man's weight.

Chapter 21

That afternoon, Sebastian drove out to Northcott Abbey in search of the one person on Emma Chance's list of names he'd yet to meet: Samuel Atwater, the estate's longtime steward.

He found Atwater at a row of tenants' cottages on the far side of the estate. "Emma Chance?" said the steward in response to Sebastian's question. "I met her when Lady Seaton had her to tea last Saturday— but only briefly. Why do you ask?"

"That was the only time you encountered her?"

Atwater stood beside his horse, the reins held loosely in one hand as he considered his answer. He was dressed plainly in serviceable boots, buckskin breeches, and a coat, with a black cravat knotted at his throat. Before driving out to the abbey, Sebastian had quietly asked several villagers their opinion of the steward. All tended to agree he was a fair man, willing to work with tenants who fell behind on their rents for reasons of misfortune rather than incompetence or sloth. He had come to Ayleswick not long after his cousin's marriage, when Lord Seaton's aging steward retired to live with a daughter in Ludlow. He was both plainspoken and quiet, with the manner of a devout vicar—which was what his father had been.

"Well, I noticed her painting the high street one day," said Atwater. "But I didn't stop and talk to her."

"Did you know she'd drawn your portrait?"

"No. Did she now? Why would she do that?" he said in surprise. He was an ordinary-looking man in his middle years, with graying fair hair and typically Anglo-Saxon features, and it was obvious he couldn't imagine why anyone would want to draw his portrait.

Rather than answer, Sebastian said, "What did you think of her?"

"Can't say I thought much about her, to be honest. Pretty little thing. Tragic, her being a widow and all. But then, England's seen far too many widows and orphans these last twenty years and more."

"Did Lord Seaton secure his Enclosure Act from Parliament at the same time as George Irving?"

"Nah. The present Lord Seaton's grandfather did away with the old open-field system here at Northcott Abbey long before I came here. In the sixties or seventies, it must've been."

Enclosures had been taking place since the thirteenth century, when the price of wool began to exceed the price of grain. Although the practice had increased under the Tudors, it was never popular with them, as it tended to expand the number of poor beggars and vagrants. As a result, the monarchy eventually turned against the practice. But everything had changed in the last fifty years, when cheap cotton from America and India brought down the price of wool just as the cost of grain was skyrocketing. Now enclosures were seen as a way to increase crop yields. And this time, the King and his supporters had embraced the movement with gusto.

"The thing is," Atwater was saying, "the old Squire and his lordship's grandfather weren't greedy. Not like George Irving. The way Irving did it was naught but a giant swindle."

"I suspect my wife would be interested in interviewing you, if you're willing. She's writing an article on the effects of the enclosure movement."

"Is she, now? Well, there's a story to be told, that's for certain."

"I understand there were some significant disturbances around Ayleswick fifteen or twenty years ago."

Atwater's pleasant face hardened. "That there were, thanks to bloody old George Irving. Fixed it so that not only did the commissioners give him the best land, but they also exempted both him and the vicar from paying their share of either legal fees or fencing costs. It all fell to the smaller landowners. Those who couldn't pay—and that was most of them—were forced to sell. And Irving paid them next to nothing."

"It created unrest?"

"Of course it created unrest." The steward's nostrils flared with the intensity of his emotions. "Irving never understood country people. He came from merchant stock, you see; bought Maplethorpe when the last of the Baldwyns died out. He couldn't understand the centuries-old bonds that tie even the poorest Englishman to the land of his village. Take away people's rights to graze their cows and geese on the commons and cut fuel from the wasteland, and how are they supposed to live?" He shook his head in disgust. "Just because you use Parliament to make something legal doesn't mean it's right."

Sebastian looked at the steward with renewed interest. It was a fairly radical statement for anyone to make, let alone a man whose life had been dedicated to managing his wealthy employer's estate. "Tell me about the men who were hanged."

Atwater stared off across sunlit fields. "That was right ugly, it was."

"When was it, exactly?"

"'Ninety-three." He gave the date without hesitation or thought, as if it were painfully engraved in his memory.

"Why were they hanged? For pulling down fences and leveling ditches? Or did they fall afoul of the Black Act?" The Black Act had introduced the death penalty for more than fifty new offenses, most of which entailed countrymen trying to exercise the ancient communal rights of which they'd been deprived.

"Oh, they did all that and more. But they were actually charged with high treason—conspiring with the French, of all things. Crazy, it was."

Sebastian became aware of the plaintive cry of a curlew from some-where out of sight down the hill. "You don't believe they were guilty?"

"No. Never did. The man accused them of it was a spy planted by the government. Ask me, he made it all up out of whole cloth."

"How many were hanged?"

"Four, with another half dozen transported to Botany Bay and the youngest lads forced into the army. You can imagine what it did to the families around here—losing so many of their able-bodied men and boys all at once." He shook his head. "Wives, mothers, sisters, children, all left behind to fend for themselves, just when prices were rising and they'd lost all their old common rights. Was an ugly time, it was."

"How many were gibbeted?"

"Just one. The poor bugger identified as their leader."

"What was his name?"

"Dalyrimple. Alex Dalyrimple."

"Oh, my Lord," said Hero later, when Sebastian told her of his conver-sation with the steward. "Wasn't that Jenny Dalyrimple's husband?"

"Yes." He found it interesting that Jenny had identified herself as Alex Dalyrimple's wife, as if the man were still alive. She would have been just sixteen when the Crown made her a widow. Yet she'd never remarried, never forsaken her first love.

Sebastian said, "I've been thinking about the timing. Jamie Knox was thirty-six when he died, and he told me once he took the King's shilling when he was sixteen."

"In other words, in 1793." Hero tilted her head to slip the wire of a pearl drop through one earlobe. She had now changed into a scoop-necked evening gown of velvet-trimmed midnight blue silk in preparation for their dinner with Lady Seaton and her guests, the Lucien Bonapartes. "You think that's why Knox left Ayleswick and never came back?"

"I think it likely, yes."

She fit the second earring in place, then turned to face him. "I don't see how any of this—as tragic as it was—could possibly have anything to do with the murders of Emma Chance and Hannibal Pierce."

He touched the backs of his fingers to her cheeks. "I don't know that it does. But . . . there are an extraordinary number of secrets buried beneath the seemingly peaceful veneer of this village."

He was aware of her looking at him with quiet, thoughtful eyes. "Don't you think that's true of most villages?"

"Perhaps. But some secrets are more deadly than others."

Chapter 22

Sebastian had journeyed to Ayleswick-on-Teme that summer for two reasons. The first and most important was to deliver Jamie Knox's gift to his aged grandmother and, perhaps, learn from her some explanation for the uncanny resemblance between the two men. The second reason was more complicated and involved an ancient necklace with a mysterious past.

Cunningly wrought of silver and bluestone, the necklace had once belonged to Sebastian's mother—the beautiful Countess of Hendon, who had played her lord false before staging her own death and absconding to Venice with her latest lover. According to legend, the necklace had been a gift from the ill-fated Stuart king James II to his natural daughter, Guinevere. And Sebastian had recently learned that a portrait of a woman wearing the necklace was said to hang in Northcott Abbey's famous Long Gallery.

For the birthplace of Jamie Knox to be tied, somehow, to that hauntingly mysterious necklace seemed too coincidental not to be significant. Yet the problem was, what precisely did it signify?

Before they left for that evening's dinner with Lady Seaton, Sebastian watched Hero slip the old necklace into her embroidered velvet reticule.

"It could all be a mistake," he said. "The necklace in the painting could be similar but not the same."

She looked over at him. "Two necklaces with the same legend attached to them?"

He shrugged, although he doubted she was fooled by his assumption of insouciance. She knew him too well. Knew how vitally important this quest for the truth about his parentage was.

She said, "What will we do if Lady Seaton doesn't offer to show us the Long Gallery?"

He settled her cloak around her shoulders as a clatter of carriage wheels sounded outside the inn. "Then we'll just have to give her a little nudge."

Built of golden-hued sandstone late in the reign of Henry VIII, Northcott Abbey had something of the look of a medieval castle, with two square bays flanking the central entrance and a five-sided bay at each corner. But the rows of huge windows sparkling with myriad leaded panes showed that the massive pile had been built as a house, not a fortress; the mock parapet encircling its steeply pitched leaded roof was a sign of royal favor and purely for decoration.

"Impressive," said Hero, one hand coming up to grasp the carriage strap as she leaned forward to catch glimpses of the house through gaps in the gently undulating park's ornamental plantings of chestnut and lime, beech and oak. "I wonder what the man who built it did to receive such a choice allotment from his King's plundering of the church's wealth."

Sebastian studied the house's tall clusters of sixteenth-century twisting chimneys. "Well, amongst other services, he spent ten years as Good Ole King Henry's ambassador to Spain—surely a tricky position to hold when your king is in the process of divorcing a daughter of Spain. Henry thanked him by making him the First Baron Seaton."

She turned her head to stare at him. "However did you come to know that?"

"I looked it up before we left Brook Street." He smiled at her expression of astonishment. "What? You think you're the only one with research skills?"

"Huh. And the estate's been in the same family ever since? Impressive."

"Even more impressive when you consider that the Seatons have always been Catholic." Until the passage of the Relief Act in 1778, Catholics had been forbidden to buy or inherit land or even own a horse. But a surprising number had somehow survived.

"One wonders how they managed to hold on to the place all those years," said Hero.

"Extraordinary cleverness and lots of priests' holes, one assumes."

She stared up at the house's stately, undulating facade as the carriage drew to a halt before the grand entrance. "Why do you suppose Lady Seaton went out of her way to invite us to dinner?"

"Perhaps she doesn't want me to think she's keeping Napoléon's little brother hidden out here."

A liveried footman jumped to open the carriage door as Hero turned her head to look at Sebastian. "You mean, because she fears he may be involved in these murders?"

His gaze met hers. "Something like that, yes."

Northcott Abbey's state drawing room was a splendid eighteenth-century confection with an ornately plastered ceiling picked out in shades of pale pink, cream, and gilt. The walls were of pale blue and decorated with swirling cascades of carved shells and billowing ribbons of cream and pink; a matching pale blue silk covered the numerous scattered fauteuils, *bergers en gondola*, and settees, their curved, delicately carved arms and legs adorned with more gilt.

So vast was the space that it seemed to swallow the four people assembled there: the Dowager Lady Seaton, her houseguests Lucien and Alexandrine Bonaparte, and Northcott's steward, Samuel Atwater, who was looking decidedly uncomfortable at having been pressed into service to make an even six for dinner in such exalted company.

The resemblance between the Senator (as he liked to be called) and the Emperor Napoléon in his younger, slimmer days was as startling as Emma's sketch had suggested. His wife, Alexandrine, was a French-woman in her late thirties with a wide face, auburn hair, and a long nose. She was not unattractive, but neither was she a great beauty. This was a second marriage for both, a true love match that was said to have caused the final rift between the Bonaparte brothers when Lucien refused Napoléon's demands that he divorce his aging, common-born wife and accept a dynastic marriage.

Standing together now side by side, both vaguely smiling but obvi-ously ill at ease, they looked much like any ordinary, slightly dowdy couple more concerned with the happiness of their numerous offspring than with shifting strategic alliances and the movements of armies. But Sebastian had learned long ago that appearances could be deceptive.

"Lady Devlin," exclaimed Lady Seaton, coming forward to greet her new guests with both hands outstretched. "And my lord." Beside Hero's tall, Junoesque proportions, Grace Seaton appeared tiny, almost childlike. But she performed the necessary social niceties with admira-ble aplomb, as if it were an everyday thing, introducing the brother of her nation's greatest enemy to the daughter of the man who'd vowed to see the Bonaparte clan's numerous upstart regimes destroyed.

"This is delightful," said the Senator in heavily accented English, his smiling gaze fixed on Hero. "Your father is Lord Jarvis, yes? The Regent's cousin?"

"He is, yes," said Hero, settling on the tapestry-covered sofa indi-cated by their hostess. "Although his kinship to the King is not close."

"Yet you remind me so much of our dear brother's wife, Catharina of Würtemberg," said Alexandrine, with a friendly smile. "I believe she is your Regent's niece, yes?"

A moment's awkward silence followed her words, for it was a fact seldom mentioned in English drawing rooms that the granddaughter of an English princess had married the Beast's brother Jérôme. The match was a dynastic alliance, of course, with the young couple then being made King and Queen of Westphalia. But by all reports Catharina was utterly besotted with her husband. Unfortunately, Jérôme was blatantly and repeatedly unfaithful to his long-suffering wife.

"She is, yes," said Hero. "But my own kinship to the Queen of Westphalia is very distant indeed."

"Tell me," said the Senator, adjusting his tails as he took a chair near Hero, "what news do you hear of the war?"

"Only what we read in the papers, I'm afraid," she said.

"It seems every day brings news of more fighting somewhere," said Lady Seaton. "It must be an agony for those with sons, brothers, or fathers in either army."

Sebastian spared a glance for the estate's steward, who sat following the conversation yet contributing nothing to it himself. He had quietly arranged to be interviewed by Hero the following Monday. But beyond that, he seldom spoke. Atwater obviously believed it was not his place to put himself forward in any way. And Sebastian found himself wondering if Atwater's beautiful, wealthy cousin felt the same way. Or not?

"It's interesting Napoléon has pulled some of his men out of Spain," Hero was saying.

"Yes, and Vitoria was the result." Lucien Bonaparte flopped back in his chair. "Napoléon was a fool to entrust the defense of Spain to our brother Joseph. He knew Wellington was planning a major offensive. But what does Joseph do? Does he devote himself to drawing up a battle plan? No! He spends his days screwing women."

Alexandrine Bonaparte's eyes widened in alarm as her husband pressed on. "It's a family affliction, I'm afraid. Although none are quite as bad as my sister Pauline. She once spent five days in bed with a lover. Imagine, five days! I've heard she even—"

Sebastian choked on his wine, while Lady Seaton cleared her throat and said rather loudly, "I understand you have a new baby, Lady Devlin."

"Yes; Simon," said Hero, valiantly trying to turn her own choking laugh into a cough. "He's six months old."

"And you have him with you?"

"We do—along with his nurse, my abigail, Devlin's valet, the coachman, a footman, and Devlin's tiger. Needless to say, we do not travel lightly."

"Ah, yes," said Lady Seaton. "I remember those days." She turned her brilliant smile on her exalted guests. "Monsieur and Madame Bonaparte have a new wee one, as well. Born just this past January."

"Louis Lucien," said Bonaparte proudly. "Lady Seaton was gracious enough to allow us to baptize him in the private chapel she's built here at Northcott Abbey."

He then went on to tell a laughing tale about his youngest child's tendency to crawl backward. And it occurred to Sebastian as he watched the Emperor's brother glow with pride over his son's antics that here was a side of Lucien Bonaparte—the loving paterfamilias—that he hadn't expected to find. But then he reminded himself that this was a man who'd turned down a kingdom and risked his imperial brother's wrath in order to keep his family together.

"How many children do you have?" asked Sebastian.

It was Alexandrine who answered. "Eight, all together. Lucien's Charlotte and Lili are eighteen and fifteen; my Anna is fourteen, while our Charles is ten. The rest descend from there like organ pipes." She sketched a profile of steps with one hand.

"I've met Charles," said Hero. "He's a very clever lad."

Alexandrine smiled and shared a meaningful look with her husband. "We like to think so. Although I fear his sisters sometimes find him a bit tiresome."

"The Bonapartes' older girls have gone to the Lake District with my own daughters, Georgina and Louisa," said Lady Seaton.

"Yes, and you would not *believe* what we had to go through to get permission from the commissioner for them to travel so far," said Lucien. "Children!"

Sebastian took a slow sip of his wine as he studied the Corsican's swarthy, now disgruntled face. Lucien Bonaparte had been living in exile for nearly three years, his wife and children as much prisoners of war as he himself. Oh, their lives were comfortable enough—by all accounts Thorngrove was a grand estate. But their travel was still restricted, their correspondence read, their every move watched by spies from both Paris and London. As long as the war continued, their lives would remain in limbo. And then what would become of eighteen-year-old Charlotte Bonaparte, of age now to be wed? Or her younger sisters coming up behind her? What did such a future hold for little Charles, with his grand ambitions of scientific study and travel?

Only an unlikely peace or the decisive defeat of Napoléon would bring freedom for Lucien and his growing, ambitious family. Yet Napoléon's defeat would also mean the end of the closely knit Bonaparte clan's phenomenal wealth and power. So for which did Lucien and his no-nonsense wife secretly pray? Sebastian wondered. For Napoléon to keep fighting? Or for the Emperor to go down in a final defeat? If given the opportunity, would they actively seek to prop up Napoléon's fading fortunes?

Or would they work to bring their exile to an end, in any way possible?

It was over dinner that Hero, tired of waiting for Lady Seaton to spontaneously offer to show her guests the famous Long Gallery, gently brought the conversation around to the subject of art.

"I hear you have an impressive collection of paintings, Senator," she said, turning to Napoléon's brother.

Lucien's face shone with pride. According to reports, he had landed in England with a staggering number of servants and a baggage train that included not only scores of huge canvases but also life-sized Roman statues unearthed from his estate near Frascati. "I like to flatter myself that is so, yes. But you and Lord Devlin must come to Thorngrove yourself someday and give me your opinion." He nodded graciously toward their hostess. "Northcott Abbey also possesses an impressive picture gallery. Have you seen it?"

Lady Seaton fluttered one dainty hand through the air in a show of embarrassed disparagement. "Oh, believe me, it is nothing compared to Senator Bonaparte's collection."

"But I would love to see it," said Hero.

"If you like, of course. Although I should warn you that it consists mainly of family portraits, and very few by artists of any note."

"Perhaps we could explore it after dinner," suggested Alexandrine Bonaparte. "While the gentlemen linger over their port?"

For one intense instant, Hero's gaze met Sebastian's. It wasn't exactly what they'd had in mind, but it was better than nothing. "That would be lovely," she said with a wide smile.

Chapter 23

$\mathcal{B}$y the time they climbed the broad central staircase to Northcott Abbey's famous Long Gallery, the sinking sun was turning the hilltops a rich gold and casting long, cool shadows across the valley.

"I've always loved the way the light streams in the windows up here on a summer's evening," said Lady Seaton as they reached the brightly lit space.

"It's lovely," said Hero, and meant it.

Running the full length of the second floor, such galleries were a typical feature of late sixteenth- and early seventeenth-century estates. But Northcott's version was particularly stunning: a vast, high-vaulted space with a fancifully plastered ceiling and wide, soaring windows on three sides of the long, narrow room. One glance was enough to tell Hero that her ladyship had been unduly modest; the Seatons' collection of paintings was both large and impressive.

"This is the oldest portrait," said their hostess, leading the way to an oil-on-oak portrait of an aged, fifteenth-century gentleman painted as if bathed in intense light against a dramatically dark sea. "Sir Walter Seaton, Baronet. My husband liked to call him a privateer. But if you ask me, he was a pirate."

"He does rather look like a pirate," agreed Alexandrine Bonaparte.

Hero studied the long-dead baronet's sun-darkened, white-bearded face and rich velvet robes. "But a very successful one."

"Oh, he was very good at what he did," said Lady Seaton.

She kept up a running commentary as they moved slowly past the rows of dead Seatons, ladies in crespines and high-waisted velvets with detached sleeves gradually giving way to their descendants in snoods and narrow gowns with V-shaped waists. Hero was careful to affect an expression of intense interest and murmur appropriate compliments. But the truth was, she wanted nothing more than to rush through these earlier portraits. The woman she was looking for would have been painted much later, in the late seventeenth or maybe even the early eighteenth century. It was only with effort that she kept her gaze from straying down the gallery.

"It's hard to believe women actually used to shave their foreheads and eyebrows, isn't it?" said Lady Seaton, pausing before a trio of eyebrowless sixteenth-century ladies with complexions so white they could have come only from makeup disastrously mixed with lead. "How did they ever think it looked attractive?"

"And those towering headdresses," said Alexandrine Bonaparte, studying one portly matron's elaborate, sail-like confection. "It makes my neck ache just looking at them."

"Yes, but I must admit I do like a man in doublet and hose," said Hero, shifting to an early seventeenth-century portrait of a dashing Lord Seaton in a plumed hat.

The other women both laughed and continued on.

After what seemed like forever, hose began to give way to breeches, and ruffs disappeared in favor of broad linen and lace collars. And Hero felt herself tensing as she searched each heavy, gilded frame for the unknown woman with a silver and bluestone necklace.

And then she saw her.

Long necked and regal, she'd been painted at a time when it was

fashionable to have one's portrait done in a style known as "romantic neg-
ligence" or "undress." Thus, instead of the stiff court dress typical of the
age, she wore a loosely draped, white satin gown over a deep blue under-
dress with voluminous pleated sleeves and a wide neckline scooped low
to reveal the upper swells of her pale breasts. Traditionally, such portraits
showed their subjects with short strands of pearls nestled at the base of
their throats. But this woman wore a thick chain of curiously wrought
silver from which hung a gleaming triskelion superimposed on a smoothly
polished bluestone disk.

Hero had no need to compare the painted necklace to the one she'd
tucked into her reticule. They were identical.

"Who is this?" asked Hero, pausing before the painting when their
hostess would have moved on.

"That's my late husband's great-great-grandmother, Guinevere Stuart. She was said to be a natural daughter of James II."

"And she married a Seaton?" said Hero.

"Actually, it was her granddaughter Isabella who married a Seaton."
Lady Seaton indicated the portrait that hung beside Guinevere Stuart's,
of an auburn-haired girl captured in the first blush of youth and beauty.

Hero kept her gaze on the portrait of Guinevere Stuart. "That's an
interesting necklace she's wearing."

"Isn't it? They say it was a wedding gift from her father. According
to the legend, it was once worn by an ancient Druid priestess and possessed special powers."

"Special powers?" said Alexandrine Bonaparte. "Sounds fascinating.
What sort of powers?"

"Supposedly, it brought long life to anyone who possessed it. Not
only that, but it was said to choose its next owner by growing warm in
the hand of the woman destined to possess it."

Hero stared up at the woman in the painting. She looked to be
somewhere in her early thirties, her thick dark hair cascading in loose
curls around her shoulders. She had inherited her royal father's oval

face, full lips, and strong chin. There was wisdom in the gentle composure of her features, and strength. But her eyes were clouded as if with sadness and an unflinching awareness of painful disasters to come.

"And did she have a long life?" Hero asked.

"She did, yes; they say she lived to be over a hundred years old. Although I'm afraid her life wasn't exactly happy." Lady Seaton paused. "I suppose the necklace didn't promise that."

"Why?" asked Hero. "What happened to her?"

"Her father married her to a Scottish laird named Malcolm Gordon. She had eight children by him, seven sons and a daughter. But once King James was deposed in the Glorious Revolution, she went from being an asset as a wife to a potential liability. Not only that, but all of her sons rallied to the Jacobite cause after the death of Queen Anne and were either killed in the Risings or exiled. In order to save himself—and acquire new sons—Gordon divorced her."

"She took refuge here, with her granddaughter?"

"Briefly. But I'm afraid the Lord Seaton of the day wasn't particularly happy to be seen giving refuge to a Stuart."

Not surprising, thought Hero, *given that he was a Catholic desperately trying to remain invisible.* She looked up into the long-dead woman's lovely, sad face. "So what happened to her?"

"I believe in the end she went to her daughter in Wales."

"And the necklace?" asked Alexandrine Bonaparte, obviously intrigued by its story. "Do you still have it? Does it glow warm in your hand?"

Lady Seaton gave a light laugh. "I wish I had it. But I've always assumed it must be in Wales—if it even still exists. It's such a plain, old-fashioned thing, I can see some new bride who didn't know its history simply tossing it out." She moved on to a large portrait farther down the row. "And this is probably one of the best paintings in the collection. It's a Van Dyck."

Hero followed their hostess on down the gallery, her features schooled into an interested expression even as her thoughts remained on the sad-eyed, ill-fated woman in the portrait behind them.

She couldn't have said precisely what she'd hoped this visit to the Long Gallery would accomplish. Yes, she had confirmed the existence of the portrait and the link between Lady Hendon's necklace and the Seatons of Northcott Abbey. But it provided no real clue to the identity of the unknown man who'd presumably fathered both Devlin and Jamie Knox.

For the eyes of Guinevere Stuart were a pale blue, as were her granddaughter's. And though Hero carefully scrutinized each of the many portraits hanging in the gallery, not one of that long line of Seaton ancestors hanging memorialized in oil had yellow eyes.

Later that night, in the hours before dawn, Hero awoke to the sound of a cow lowing in the distance and the whisper of the wind through the limbs of the ancient chestnut out on the village green. Somehow she knew even without moving that she was alone in her bed.

She opened her eyes to see Devlin silhouetted against the window's pale glow, his body limned by the wind-tossed light of the moon.

"Did I wake you?" he said. "I'm sorry."

"How did you know I was awake?"

She heard the amusement in his voice. "I saw your eyes open."

"Dear God, you are unnerving sometimes."

She rose to go to him and loop her arms around his shoulders. He tilted his head back against hers, and she saw he held the necklace in his hand, the silver triskelion gleaming in the soft glow from the window.

He said, "Thirty years ago, an old woman in the wilds of northern Wales gave this to my mother. She always told my sister and brothers and me that she didn't want to take it, but the woman insisted. And truth be told, I think the legend fascinated my mother. She swore the stone grew warm as soon as the old woman placed the pendant in her hand."

"Who was the woman?"

"I'm not certain my mother ever knew. She said the woman was very old, and I've always pictured her as some haggard, ancient crone. But was she really?" He shrugged and shook his head.

Hero reached to lift the necklace from his hand and felt the warmth of the stone against her palm. She had never told him of her own reaction to the stone, for it seemed too fanciful to credit. And yet . . .

"I suppose the old woman could have been a descendant of Guinevere Stuart," she said. "Lady Seaton did tell us she took refuge in Wales."

Devlin smiled. "Where's a *Debrett's Peerage* when you need one?"

She laughed softly, then sobered as a shadowy movement out on the village green caught her eye. "What was that?"

But of course Devlin could see quite clearly what—or, rather, who— it was. "Just Reuben Dickie," he said.

The door of the corner cottage on the far side of the green opened, spilling golden light into the lane. A man walked from the cottage to the pump house; a large man with a bullet-like head and thickly muscled arms and thighs. They watched him converse with Reuben for a moment. Then the two turned and entered the cottage together.

"Reuben's brother, Jeb, must be home," said Devlin. "Last I heard he was hauling a load of timber to Wales."

The cottage door closed against the night. Hero said, "It looks as if he takes good care of his brother."

"Or at least he tries."

Hero glanced at Devlin. "What does that mean?"

But Devlin simply shook his head.

She studied the tightly held features of his handsome, moonlit face. "I thought you didn't suspect Reuben."

"I don't. He's not smart enough to try to make a murder look like suicide, and however clever brother Jeb may be, I doubt he's much of a Shakespearean scholar."

"But you still don't like him."

He smiled. "Let's just say I don't think he's as harmless as he'd like to appear."

Hero stared up the hill to where the squat, bulky tower of the church showed dark against a starry sky. "It seems so peaceful here. Idyllic. But it's not, is it?"

"It has a dark history. But then, what place does not?" He nodded to the now-deserted green below. "I was sitting here thinking about all the generations of men and women who've walked these same lanes, who plowed the same fields century after century and listened to the same church bells toll the hours of their lives, and then buried their dead in the same churchyard."

"Is it significant, do you think, that neither Emma Chance nor Hannibal Pierce was from the village?"

"It could be." He turned to face her. "I think I'd like to take a look at the ruins of the old priory tomorrow."

"Because Emma Chance was there the day she died?"

"Partially. But also because it's such an integral part of the history of this village. And I can't shake the idea that knowing the past is the key to understanding what is happening here, now."

Chapter 24

Thursday, 5 August

What was left of the ancient Benedictine priory of St. Hilary lay beside a sparkling, swift-flowing stream at the base of a gentle slope. Once home to dozens of choir monks and lay brothers and surrounded by closely cultivated fields and well-tended orchards, the ruined sandstone walls now rose from a swath of green meadow kept cropped close by a sizeable flock of sheep.

"It's beautiful," said Hero, pausing beside Sebastian at the edge of the meadow to gaze at the shattered cluster of monastic buildings. They had approached the site by way of the footpath that led from the coach road along the stream, coming upon it suddenly when they rounded a bend and broke through a thin copse of oak and ash. A melancholy silence hung over the site, broken only by the purling of the water and the bleating of a lamb and the sigh of a warm breeze through row after row of empty window openings. "What I wouldn't give to have seen it before Good Ole King Henry got his greedy hands on it."

"You mean, back when it was still crawling with smelly monks who delighted in burning witches and heretics and thought women the spawn of Satan?"

She laughed. "Yes. Then."

Watched by half a dozen or so interested ewes, they crossed the meadow toward the ruins, the morning sun drenching the timeworn walls with a rich golden light. Most of the scattered outbuildings—the gatehouse and infirmary, guesthouses and mill—had long ago been reduced to unrecognizable piles of weed-choked rubble. But nearly the entire west end of the church with its three processional doorways and huge rose window was still intact, along with large stretches of the main mass of monastic buildings.

While Hero poked around the outside the complex, Sebastian went to stand in the church's ruined central portal. The roof was long gone, leaving the once elegant interior open to the blue, cloudless sky. A row of weathered columns marched along the south side of the nave, separating it from the aisle, and tall pointed arches still marked the crossing. He drew in a long, slow breath and felt the haunting, melancholy beauty of the place call to something deep within him.

"I'd like to have seen Emma Chance's drawings of this place," he said when Hero came to stand beside him. "I'd think an artist could easily spend days here."

"Is this the last thing she drew, do you think?" Hero asked, her gaze on the weathered carvings of saints and sinners that decorated the deep portal.

"I suppose she could have done some sketches down by the river after she left here. We still don't know exactly when or even where she was killed."

They picked their way across the ruined interior of the church, to an opening that led to what would once have been the cloisters. Substantial sections of the chapter house, refectory, and dorter that had once clustered around the cloisters remained, along with sections of the cloister's exquisite fan vaulting.

The monastery might have been founded in the eleventh century, but it appeared to have undergone a massive rebuilding during the late twelfth and thirteenth centuries, with little of the earlier Norman work remaining. The steady stream of pilgrims attracted by the miraculous powers of St. Hilary's Virgin had brought great wealth to the once humble priory. For the greater glory of their God and as an inspiration to his followers, the monks had rebuilt their church to soaring new heights and adorned it with magnificent carvings and frescoes and glorious stained-glass windows. They'd filled their library with illuminated texts and adorned their altars with precious plate of silver and gold. And for the old and sick, they had built a two-story infirmary and a lepers' hospital.

Sebastian's own belief in the religious instruction of his youth hadn't survived the ugly realities of war. But that didn't alter his respect for the centuries of tonsured men who'd once devoted themselves to a spiritual life of contemplation and prayer and service. And he found himself wondering what it must have been like for those nameless, humble men to stand and watch, helpless, while those who claimed to worship the same God destroyed everything they'd worked so hard to build up in his name.

Much of what was valuable—starting with the lead from the roofs— would have been stripped and sold. But far more would have been left to the destruction of the elements. The beautifully carved wooden rood screens and misericords had probably been broken up for firewood by the poor, while the library's ancient, beautifully illuminated manuscripts were hauled off by the cartload to soapmakers or torn up to line workmen's boots and furnish a bountiful supply of rare, soft rags for the village jakes.

That's what haunts this place, he thought. It's the despair and anguish of the monks who poured their energy and joy, their very lives, into this monastery, only to see it destroyed. And he wondered, when they watched the windblown rain ruin the frescoes and carvings left open to the sky, when they heard the screams of their brethren burned alive for choosing devotion to God over duty to king, did they still believe in their god? Somehow, he suspected they did.

But he couldn't help but wonder about the greedy, powerful men who'd torn the lead off the monastery's roofs and sold it. How could they still claim to be good Christian men even as they pocketed their ill-gotten silver? And he found his gaze straying up the hill, to where the massive Tudor chimneys of Northcott Abbey rose high above the leafy treetops of its vast park.

Hero said quietly, "I thought I'd feel her here. But I don't."

"No. The past is too strong here," he said, conscious of a welling of frustration tinged with what he recognized as anger directed toward himself. Nearly three days had now passed since Emma Chance's death, and he was no closer to understanding what had happened to her than he had been standing in the water meadows on that first misty morning.

What he needed, he realized, was to talk to someone who knew the village well yet remained apart from it. Someone who combined an insider's knowledge and understanding with an outsider's perspective.

Someone like Ayleswick's new schoolmaster.

Daray Flanagan was sitting on his front stoop when Sebastian walked up and introduced himself.

The Irish schoolmaster's feet were bare except for his darned socks, and he had an apron tied over his clothes as he worked at blacking a pair of worn boots.

"You've caught me at a most ungentlemanly occupation," said Flanagan, grimacing down at his dirty hands.

"Boots are important," said Sebastian.

"That they are." Flanagan reached for a rag and began polishing his left boot. "You're here about the murders, I take it? Don't know how much I can help you. Only spoke to the unfortunate young gentlewoman briefly when I saw her painting one time. And I can't say I recall encountering the fellow from London at all."

Sebastian propped one shoulder against the cottage's dark, half-timbered framing. "Why do you think they were killed?"

Flanagan shook his head as he blew out a long, sorrowful breath. "I'd have said I understood this place and the people in it fairly well by now. But . . . it's obvious I was mistaken."

"Any chance it could have something to do with the presence here of Lucien Bonaparte?"

Flanagan slanted a sideways look at him. "Never tell me you're thinking Bonaparte killed them."

"Not personally, no."

"So one of his servants? Is that what you're suggesting?" The schoolmaster rubbed the toe of his boot in thoughtful silence. "Why would he?"

"I suppose that would depend on why Emma Chance was here."

Flanagan was no fool; he understood immediately what Sebastian was suggesting. "You're saying she could have been sent to spy on him?"

"It's possible."

Flanagan shifted his attention to the boot's heel, his jaw set hard. "Me, I wish the French bastard had never come within a hundred miles of Shropshire. I've had more than enough of the French and their killing to last me a lifetime—and then some."

Technically, Bonaparte was Corsican, not French. But Sebastian simply said, "How well do you know Lady Seaton?"

Flanagan's face creased with amusement. "How well you think I know her, then? Her being a grand lady, and me a poor Irish schoolmaster? Or were you thinking she invites me out to Sunday mass at her little private chapel there at Northcott Abbey?"

"You're Catholic?"

"I was. My father used up all his savings to send me to the seminary to be trained as a priest."

"What happened?"

"The Revolution happened."

At the time of the French Revolution, Catholic seminaries were illegal in Great Britain and Ireland; as a result, anyone wanting to become a priest was forced to study on the Continent. Sebastian said, "I take it your seminary was in France?"

Flanagan reached for his second boot and said simply, "Nantes."

Sebastian studied the Irishman's inscrutable profile. He now understood Flanagan's earlier passing comment about the French and their killing.

A beautiful, ancient city at the mouth of the Loire River, Nantes had been the site of one of the most horrific episodes of the Revolution. The revolutionaries had slaughtered so many of the city's inhabitants that Madame Guillotine quickly proved inadequate. In the end, thousands of men, women, and children—most guilty of nothing more than being in the wrong place at the wrong time—were stripped naked and thrown into the river to drown.

"You managed to escape before the worst of the Terror?" said Sebastian.

"No, I wasn't that wise. But I was one of the lucky ones: the troop of soldiers they sent to our seminary gave us a choice: renounce our religious vows and join the army, or be drowned in the river." Flanagan's eyes narrowed with something that looked like amusement but was not. "Guess which I chose?"

"I doubt anyone could blame you for that."

"You don't think so? M'father never forgave me. Died cursing me, or so I've been told. Having a son who was a priest—or at least a martyr—was supposed to be his ticket into heaven, and I let him down. I've always wondered what he'd done that was so bloody awful he figured he needed my help staying out of hell."

"How long were you with the French army?"

"Two endless years. I suppose I could have tried to make a break for it sooner, but I figured all I'd succeed in doing would be to get myself shot as a deserter. So I waited until we were down by the Swiss border, then just walked across it one dark night. Almost starved to death before I found an English family in Geneva willing to take me on as a tutor for their son."

"Did you ever go back to Ireland?"

"Never did, no."

"Because your father was dead?"

Flanagan gave a short laugh. "No. Because my mother is still very much alive. Would break her heart, it would, to know I've lost my faith. And I couldn't hide it from her. I suppose there are some as can witness such things and retain their belief in a benevolent, all-wise God. But I fear I'm not one of them."

Flanagan had given up on his boots. For a long moment the two men simply shared a silence, their thoughts lost in a painful past.

Flanagan said, "Course, the French are all good Catholics again, now that Napoléon's been cozying up to the Pope." He eased his right foot into its boot. "Amazing what a difference twenty years and a shift in official policy can make."

Sebastian watched Flanagan reach for his second boot and asked again, "Who do you think killed Emma Chance?"

The schoolmaster hesitated, that pinched look back around his eyes. "I knew one of the men in charge of the drownings in Nantes: a lawyer by the name of Renard. If anyone had asked before the Revolution what manner of man I thought he was, I'd have said he was gentle, devout, kind. Yet he personally supervised the murder of thousands of men, women, and children. *Thousands*—some no more than babes in arms. He herded them naked and begging for mercy onto barges, and then he towed them out into the middle of the river and drowned them. I'm told it's a hideous way to die, drowning."

"Like suffocating," said Sebastian.

Flanagan turned his head to look at him, his face held tight and flat. "Twenty years ago, in Nantes, I couldn't begin to understand how

Jacques Renard could do the things he did. And I can't understand here, today in Ayleswick, how someone I know could have murdered that beautiful and talented young woman. Yet someone did."

"There aren't many men could do such a thing," said Sebastian. "Hold a woman down for three to five minutes and watch her slowly die."

Flanagan grunted. "You think so? If there's one thing the French Revolution and the noyades of Nantes taught me, it's that most people's capacity for evil is infinitely greater than we'd like to believe.

"Infinitely," he said again, then slipped his left foot into its boot and stomped down hard.

Chapter 25

Archie arrived home from his expedition to Ludlow early that evening. He was hot, dusty, tired, and cranky.

"Two blasted days!" said the Squire, hunching forward on his bench to prop his elbows on the boards before him when he and Sebastian compared notes over a couple of tankards of ale in the Blue Boar's taproom. "I spent the better part of two days interviewing everyone from the Feathers' innkeeper to the ostlers and scullery maids. And I didn't learn a blessed thing."

"I take it Emma Chance left no permanent address with them either?"

"No. Which is strange, don't you think?"

"Yes."

"She was there five days. The chambermaids say she must have done a fair amount of shopping, for she had any number of boxes and parcels delivered from dressmakers and milliners and such. But beyond that, no one could tell me anything."

"How did she arrive there? By the mail?"

"If only! That would at least have given us some indication of where she'd traveled from. But she came in a gig, and no one was familiar with the lad who drove her. He simply let her off and went away again."

"And she traveled without her own abigail?"

"She did. Told some tale about the girl breaking her leg, which is why she needed to hire a new one."

Sebastian swiped a thumb across the condensation on his tankard. "I'd say you learned something."

Archie stared at him. "I did? What?"

"You learned that she went out of her way to disguise who she was and where she'd come from."

"I suppose I did. But . . . why? Why would she do such a thing?"

Sebastian took a folded sheet of paper from his pocket and slid it across the table to the young magistrate. "The chambermaid found this list of names when she was cleaning Emma Chance's room."

Archie frowned as he ran through the list. "Good God; I'm on here." He looked up at Sebastian. "Why is my name here? And why has it been crossed out? Mine and Samuel Atwater's. *Samuel Atwater?* What does it mean?"

"I've no idea. But it's an interesting collection of individuals. The only one I've yet to speak with is young Lord Seaton, who isn't here."

Archie nodded. "He's gone to Windermere." He read through the names again, his frown deepening.

Sebastian said, "Tell me about him."

"Crispin?" Archie looked up. "We were great friends as young lads. But the Seatons are Catholic, you know. So while my father was able to send me to Eton, Crispin had to go to Stonyhurst." Catholics were forbidden to attend schools such as Eton and Winchester or Oxford and Cambridge. It was only in the last two decades that they'd been allowed to establish their own educational institutions; before that, they'd had to send their sons and daughters to the Continent. Archie shrugged. "We sort of went our separate ways after that."

"What's he like?"

"Well . . ." Archie shrugged again with all the discomfort of one little given to analyzing his fellow men. "My father always said he was an idealistic dreamer with more passion than sense. But then, my father could be a bit harsh in his judgments." He set the list aside. "Crispin's been gone for at least a fortnight. So why is his name on this list?"

Sebastian took a slow sip of his ale. "Have you spoken to Higginbottom?"

"About the postmortem, you mean?" Archie turned a bit pale. "I stopped by there on my way back from Ludlow. He's a sadistic bastard, isn't he? Showed me her heart and lungs and wanted me to see the rest of her, but those bits were enough for me, I'm afraid."

Sebastian said, "I'd be interested to take a look at the clothes she was wearing when she was killed."

"I can ask Nash to pick them up in the morning when he collects the body for the inquest." Emma Chance's inquest was scheduled to begin at ten the following morning. Because the coroner and a fair number of the jurors would be coming from Ludlow, the county was saving money by scheduling Hannibal Pierce's inquest directly after hers.

As a witness to the death of Pierce, Sebastian had received an official summons from the coroner requiring him to give testimony. But without any suspects, neither inquest was likely to be more than a necessary formality to be gone through before the bodies could be released for burial.

Archie hesitated a moment, then said, "Why do you want to see her clothes?"

"They might tell us something. I doubt Higginbottom paid much attention to them."

Archie chewed thoughtfully on the inside of one cheek. "Did Higginbottom tell you she was still a maiden?"

"He did."

"It happens sometimes, I suppose. Doesn't it? With a marriage of convenience or . . . or some sort of physical irregularity, perhaps?"

"Perhaps," said Sebastian.

The young magistrate blinked. "But you don't think so?"

"Very little about Emma Chance seems to add up." Sebastian drained his tankard and set it aside. "I suspect if we could figure out why, we'd be a fair ways toward discovering who killed her—and Pierce."

Archie scrubbed his hands down over his face. "I still can't believe there've been two murders in the village in less than a week. What the devil is going on around here?" His gaze met Sebastian's, and Sebastian read in his troubled gray eyes another question, one the young Squire couldn't quite bring himself to voice:

Is it going to happen again?

That night, long after they made love, Hero was aware of Devlin still lying awake beside her.

After more than a year of sharing this man's life, she knew how personally he took each murder, knew the way he came to live and breathe each investigation. But she'd never known him to be as troubled as he was by this one. She suspected it had something to do with his own reasons for coming to this village. But it also had something to do with the village itself.

"You need to sleep," she said, resting her hand on his shoulder.

He slipped an arm beneath her and drew her closer to his warm, hard body. "I will."

"When will you sleep? After you've caught this killer?"

"I'm flattered you think I'm going to catch him."

"You will," she said, and saw him smile in the darkness. "Will they bury Emma Chance tomorrow, do you think?" she asked. "After the inquest?"

"Probably. And Pierce as well." Once Pierce's family received notification of his death, they might choose to move the body later, come winter. But he needed to be buried now.

Hero raised herself on her elbow so she could see him better. "I've been thinking about what Archie Rawlins told you—that the chambermaids at the Feathers said Emma Chance had received a number of deliveries from dressmakers and milliners while she was there."

Devlin speared his fingers through the fall of her hair, drawing it back from her face as he cradled her head. "And?"

"You said the gray gown she was wearing when she was killed looked new, and her gray traveling dress certainly was. So if she did all that shopping, it means she probably bought them both in Ludlow right before she came here. She had only one gown—a muslin she'd dyed black—that wasn't new."

"Yes," said Devlin, still obviously not quite certain where she was going with this.

"I suppose it's possible she decided to change from full to half mourning right before she came here. But I've also been thinking about what Higginbottom said—that she was still a maid, and seemed younger than she claimed to be. So what if she did all that shopping in Ludlow because she wasn't actually a widow in mourning? What if she was in fact a maiden in her early twenties? What if she claimed to be a widow nearing thirty because it made what she was doing—embarking on a sketching trip around Shropshire with only her abigail—seem slightly less scandalous?"

Hero watched his eyes widen. "Lady Devlin, you are brilliant."

She smiled. "No. I'm simply all too familiar with the constraints under which gentlewomen in our society must labor. And the ways we sometimes devise to get around them."

She saw the flare of some nameless emotion in his eyes. Then he drew her back down into his arms and held her tight against him.

After a moment, he said, "If you're right—and I think you very well may be—then the question becomes, Did she concoct the hoax because she wanted to go on a sketching expedition through Shropshire? Or was the sketching story only another part of the deception?"

Hero snuggled her head against his shoulder. "You're thinking she was here because of Lucien Bonaparte, aren't you?"

"Yes. The problem is, who sent her—and why?"

Chapter 26

Friday, 6 August

*T*he coroner from Ludlow arrived shortly before ten the following morning, riding in a ponderous, antiquated traveling carriage with peeling gilt paint, drawn by a pair of badly mismatched bays.

"His name is Magnus Fowler," said Archie, peering out one of the Blue Boar's front windows as a wizened, bandy-legged figure in an old-fashioned frock coat and powdered wig descended the coach's steps and batted away the hand of the footman who offered to assist him. "They say he was mayor of Ludlow back in the eighties. But he's been the coroner as long as I can remember. M'father used to say it doesn't matter whether he's presiding over the inquest of a dead child or a horribly mutilated corpse; Fowler is always as bored as he is unmoved."

The coroner paused for a moment beside his carriage while a short, plump clerk, dressed in a worn, shiny black coat and clutching a satchel to his chest, scuttled down the steps behind him. Fowler let his gaze rove over the village green and the half-timbered houses ringing it, his nose twitching with obvious derision. Then he turned to enter the Blue Boar.

By English law, any sudden, violent, or unnatural death required an inquest. Sworn in by the county coroner, a jury of between twelve and twenty-four "good and honest men" was impaneled to view the body of the deceased, hear testimony from relevant witnesses, and present its findings. More legal than medical in form and function, the inquest was a legacy from the days of the Norman Conquest, when the Crown's main interest had been in taxing any Saxon populations that could be found responsible for the murder of a Norman.

Inquests were always something of a public spectacle, and the Blue Boar's taproom was crowded that morning with curious villagers as well as the summoned jurors, many of whom had ridden in from as far as Bromfield and Ludlow. Sebastian recognized Jude Lowe and the large, heavily muscled carter they'd seen two nights before with Reuben Dickie. Samuel Atwater was there, escorting both Lady Seaton, who had encountered Emma shortly before her death, and young Charles Bonaparte, who had discovered the body; both would be required to give testimony. Even Major Eugene Weston was in attendance, his hat dangling from one finger against his thigh as he stared down at Emma Chance's beautiful, pale young face.

Because one of the most important duties of the jury was to view the corpse, Emma's body lay on a board table in the middle of the room, her flesh waxen and just beginning to show signs of turning a mottled purple and black. Sebastian was both surprised and relieved to see that Higginbottom had had the decency to drape her with a cloth covering so that only her head, shoulders, and arms were exposed. It was not uncommon for victims at inquests to be displayed naked for all the curious to gawk at.

Magnus Fowler entered the taproom with a flourish, his sharp, bony features bland with disinterest as he glanced at the draped corpse laid out in the center of the room. "I assume this is the deceased?" he snapped to no one in particular.

"One of them," said Archie, stepping forward. "We thought it best to leave the other body in the parlor for now."

Fowler raised one bushy gray eyebrow. "We? And who, pray tell, are 'we'?"

A hint of color showed high on Archie's cheekbones. "I'm the justice of the peace, Archibald R—"

"I know who you are," said Fowler with a dismissive wave of one
hand. "Heard your father was dead. Pity." He sniffed in a way that indicated his expression of sympathy was not directed at Archie. "I've a
game of whist scheduled for two this afternoon and I've no intention of
being late for it. Let's get this business under way." He turned to Webster Nash. "You still constable?"

Nash drew himself up as stiff and proudly officious as a sergeant at
a trooping of the colors. "I am, yer honor. Constable Nash, yer honor."

"Thank goodness someone around here knows what he's doing,"
muttered Fowler. "How many jurors?"

"Fifteen, yer honor. There were—"

"Fifteen will do," said Fowler, going to fling himself into the somewhat battered armchair positioned behind a small table set up especially
for him. "Well, let's get started, man. What are you waiting for? And
you—" He skewed around in his chair to glare at Martin McBroom.
"Bring me some ale and be quick about it."

The air filled with men's coughing and the scraping of benches as
the fifteen jurors and the assembled witnesses took their seats, while
the onlookers pushed and shoved to gain the best viewing positions
behind them.

Constable Nash cleared his throat and announced in a booming
voice, "Oyez, oyez, oyez! Ye good men of this county are summoned to
appear this day in the presence of Emma Chance lying dead here before
ye to inquire for our Sovereign Lord the King, when, how, and by what
means she came to her death." He paused to audibly suck in air. "Answer
to yer names as ye shall be called."

The names of the jurors were duly called, with the first named
being appointed foreman. All solemnly swore their oaths with a hand
on the Bible, while Magnus Fowler took out a pocketknife and began
paring his nails.

"What'd you say the dead woman's name was?" he asked without looking up.

"Emma Chance, yer honor. Relic of one Captain Stephen Chance."

"Do we know how and when she died?"

"She was found dead Tuesday morning. But Dr. Higginbottom did a postmortem, yer honor."

"Then swear him in, man. We haven't all day."

Higginbottom shuffled forward to take his seat with such painful slowness that Sebastian suspected the irascible doctor of doing it deliberately to spite the impatient coroner.

"Well?" snapped Fowler. "How did she die?"

"Death was caused by the exclusion of air from the lungs," said Higginbottom. He paused. "In other words, she was smothered."

A faint murmuring spread through the assembled crowd. A good portion of the villagers were obviously still expecting the verdict to be felo-de-se, or suicide.

Higginbottom waited for the muttering to die down, then said, "Both heart and lungs appeared normal on examination. The only marks of any significance on the body are a slight bruise under the chin, an even smaller discoloration on the left cheek, and a faint mark on the right arm."

The coroner stared at him from beneath his brows. "Are you trying to tell me that a woman can be smothered without it leaving more than the faintest traces?"

"If the assailant knows what he's doing, yes."

"Huh." Fowler glanced over at his clerk, who was scribbling furiously at the other end of the table. "And when did you say she died?"

"Sometime Monday afternoon or evening."

"Anything else?"

A faintly amused light crept into the old doctor's eyes, but he simply shook his head and said, "No."

"Go away, then," snapped the coroner. He waved one hand at the jury. "You will now inspect the body—but be quick about it."

With more coughing and scraping of benches, the fifteen members of the jury rose to file past the displayed corpse. Some stared at it long and hard, trying to find the bruises reported by the doctor; others gave the dead woman barely a glance before returning to their seats.

The abigail, Peg Fletcher, was called next to testify that Mrs. Chance had gone off sketching sometime after midday and never returned. Lady Seaton testified with great dignity to having encountered the victim at the priory at approximately two o'clock. Then the miller's wife was sworn in.

A merry-faced, husky woman in her late forties with a massive bosom and soft brown hair wrapped around her head in plaits, she reported seeing the lady walking toward the river shortly after five that afternoon.

Magnum Fowler—who to all appearances had by this point fallen asleep—opened one eye and said, "Do you possess a watch?"

Alice Gibbs laughed. "Oh, no, sir. Where would the likes of me get a watch? And what would I do with it if I had one?"

"Then how did you know it was five o'clock?"

It was an acute question. But Alice simply laughed again and said, "Why, I'd just been talkin' to the village schoolmaster and we heard the church bells strikin' the hour. He said he hadn't realized it was so late. That's how I come to remember the time."

"Huh. That will be all, then." Fowler turned to the constable. "Where did you say the deceased was found?"

"In the water meadows to the west of the village, yer honor."

"By whom?"

"Young Master Charles Bonaparte, yer honor."

"He's here?"

"He is."

"Call him as witness."

There was a stir as Charles was ushered forward. The jurors from Ludlow and Bromfield—most of whom had never been privileged to set eyes on a real, live Bonaparte—gawked openly at this diminutive relative of the Great Beast.

Alexandrine Bonaparte had obviously gone out of her way to make her rambunctious offspring presentable, for he was dressed in neat nankeens and a spotless frilled shirt, and clutched to his chest a brimmed round hat of straw with a wide ribbon band. He looked vaguely intimidated by the formality of the proceedings but also, boy-like, secretly proud of the role he'd been called on to play in this exciting drama. He swore his oath in a firm voice that carried not a hint of his parents' Corsican or French accents.

"I frequently go down to the water meadows at dawn," he said when asked what he was doing by the river that morning. "It's a fine place to watch for birds. I'm very interested in birds, you see."

Sebastian found himself sitting forward on his bench, his gaze on the boy's smooth, sun-browned face. They'd been wondering why Emma Chance's killer had staged her suicide at that particular spot. Now Sebastian found himself wondering whether it was possible the murderer had known young Bonaparte planned to visit the river that morning. Had he hoped the boy would be the one to stumble upon the body?

The idea seemed both preposterous and yet, somehow, possible. But who would do such a thing? And why?

"At first, I thought she was simply having a rest," Charles was saying, "It seemed a bit strange, given the hour, but, well, people sometimes do strange things. I said good morning to her, but she didn't answer. And then I saw an ant crawl across her face, and that's when I realized she might be dead. So I ventured to take a closer look, and when I touched her hand, she was cold. So I ran to the Grange and told Squire Rawlins."

Nash glanced over at Fowler, but the coroner had no more questions. The boy was released.

Archie took the witness stand last, to describe in detail the position of the dead woman's body at the time of discovery.

"Any indication the corpse had been moved after death?" asked Fowler.

"There was, yes, sir. The paths to that part of the river were still muddy from a recent rain, you see, even though the roads had all dried. Yet there was no mud on her half boots. So she must have been killed someplace else and brought there."

"But you've no idea where precisely she was killed?"

"No, sir."

Fowler sank his chin into his cravat and scowled at the young magistrate. "And that's it? You've no more witnesses? No suspect to be held in gaol to answer for the offense?"

A muscle bunched along the side of Archie's jaw. "No, sir."

The coroner gave a loud, derisive snort and nodded his dismissal.

"Well," said the coroner, adopting a loud, formal tone and pressing himself back in his seat with his hands wrapped around the chair's threadbare arms. "It is obvious we're dealing with a homicide. But the question is, homicide in which degree? In light of the medical testimony given, a verdict of felo-de-se must be ruled out. Yet that still leaves murder, manslaughter, justifiable homicide, and homicide by misadventure. Without more evidence"—here he paused to cast a withering glance at Archie Rawlins—"we've no way of knowing if the homicide was committed with malice and forethought, or accidently by one simply endeavoring to keep the victim quiet, or in some other way entirely which eludes us. Of course," he added, his gaze now fixed on the jury, "I am giving you my own personal judgment and not directing you, for the finding and verdict of this inquest are yours; my duty is simply to take and record it. But under the circumstances, I see no reason to order a recess. Mr. Foreman, how do you find Emma Chance came to her death and by what means?"

The foreman's eyes widened. After an instant's startled silence, the jurors took to murmuring amongst themselves. Then the foreman pushed awkwardly to his feet and said, "We find the lady came to her death by being smothered, yer honor—like the good doctor says. But by whom or with what intent, we've no notion."

Fowler nodded. "The clerk will draw up your verdict in legal form for you to sign." He flicked his bent hands before him in a kind of sweeping motion. "Now, Constable; get this body out of here and bring in the next one. And you'll need to reswear the jury too, so be quick about it."

The inquest into the death of Hannibal Pierce preceded much as had Emma Chance's, except that, due to the nature of his fatal wound, the major's body was displayed in all its naked, well-muscled, bloody glory. Because his cause of death was obvious and known to all, Archie had spared the purses of the county's ratepayers by declining to order a post-mortem. Sebastian gave his testimony as witness to the shooting. The information about Pierce's ties to Charles, Lord Jarvis, he kept to himself.

He was followed by those who had rushed to the scene after Pierce was shot. Then, when the constable tried to call Higginbottom again, the coroner glared at the doctor and hissed, "Sit down. We don't need your testimony. Any fool can see how he died."

Magnus Fowler loudly cleared his throat. "Now. Once again we see laid here before us a victim of homicide. Again, felo-de-se must be ruled out, and, one supposes, justifiable homicide. Nevertheless, that still leaves manslaughter and homicide by misadventure, as well as murder, so one cannot say with certainty that this act was committed by one lacking the fear of God before his eyes or being moved and seduced by the instigation of the devil." He glared at the foreman and snapped, "Verdict?"

The jury quickly returned a verdict of homicide by shooting, by party or parties unknown. Magnus Fowler flipped open his pocket watch and frowned down at it. "I will, of course, sign warrants to the effect that inquisitions have been held this day in view of the bodies now lying dead in your parish, so that they may be lawfully buried." He snapped his watch closed and looked up. "But the open nature of these findings is disturbing. And for a village of this size to experience not one but two inexplicable homicides in as many days is as outrageous as it is intolerable." He rose to his feet and nodded toward the still frantically writing clerk. "The jurors and all witnesses must sign before they are allowed to leave.

And you, innkeeper"—he glanced at Martin McBroom—"I'll have dinner served in your best private parlor. Immediately."

Then he swept through the door without another glance at the pallid man who lay dead in the center of the room.

"Insufferable bastard," grumbled Archie later, after the coroner had disappeared into the Blue Boar's parlor. He roughened his voice and rolled his "r's" in a credible imitation of Magnus Fowler's Shropshire accent. *"'For a village of this size to experrrrience not one but two inexplicable homicides in as many days is as outrrrrageous as it is intolerrrrrable.'* What the blazes does he think I should be doing that I'm not?"

"He hasn't the slightest idea," said Sebastian, although the reassurance did nothing to ease the young man's scowl.

They were standing in the lane outside the inn. The sky above was a clear blue, the noonday sun drenching the village in a white heat. A fair number of the villagers and even some jurors were still milling about, talking and laughing loudly, so that it was a moment before they became aware of the sounds of an altercation coming from the direction of the churchyard, the Reverend's soothing tones alternating with a younger man's voice, obviously cultured but ragged now with emotion.

"For God's sake, Reverend. You must let me see her! Please tell me it isn't her. *Oh, God; Emma, Emma . . .*"

"Who is that?" asked Sebastian.

"Good heavens," said Archie, his features going slack as he turned to stare up the hill. "It's Crispin Seaton."

Chapter 27

The Reverend Benedict Underwood had stopped Lord Seaton at the church porch by planting himself in the archway, his arms out-stretched and his jaw set with determination.

"You can't go in there, my lord," the Reverend was saying as Sebastian and Archie came up. "Mrs. Underwood is supervising Margaret in the preparation of the body for burial. Wouldn't be proper for you to see the lady in such a state."

Lord Seaton raised both hands to clutch the sides of his head, elbows splayed. "But don't you understand? I must know if it's her!" A handsome young man in his early twenties, he had a tumble of golden curls and large, deep blue eyes in an open, earnest face. A splendid chestnut grazed nearby, reins trailing across the grass, as if the young lord had ridden into the churchyard and dismounted only at the church steps.

"My lord," said Underwood. *"Please."*

"Who do you think she might be?" asked Sebastian.

At the sound of a stranger's voice, Crispin whirled around, his cheeks flaming with color, his eyes wild. "Who're you?"

"Devlin." Sebastian studied the younger man's haggard face. "You knew Emma Chance?"

Crispin shook his head. "I don't think her name is actually Chance."

"Who do you think she is?"

The young lord swallowed hard, the belligerence and angry fire seeming to drain out of him. "Miss Emma Chandler."

"How old is this Miss Chandler?" Archie asked his childhood friend.

"Twenty-one."

"Can she draw?" asked Sebastian.

Crispin sucked in a shuddering breath. "Like a Renaissance master."

Sebastian turned to the Reverend, who had dropped his arms to his sides and was now standing in the porch, looking from one man to the next. "Ask your good wife to have Margaret cover Emma Chance's body with a sheet. I think Lord Seaton needs to see her."

She lay in a small room at the base of the ancient west tower. A branch of candles flickered near her head, for the tower's walls were thick, its lancet windows small and high.

Crispin Seaton drew up just inside the low arched door to the room. Sebastian heard him draw a quick, rasping breath, saw his head shake from side to side in instinctive, hopeless denial. "No!" he screamed, his voice raw with anguish. "*Oh, God, no.*"

Sebastian caught him as he crumpled.

"Her name was Emma Chandler," said the young Lord Seaton in a hushed, strangled voice. "Not Chance. Chandler."

They were in the parlor at the vicarage; Crispin perched at the edge of a chair beside the empty hearth, a glass with a hefty measure of the Reverend's Scotch in one hand.

"Who was she?" asked Archie, leaning against the sill of a window overlooking the churchyard.

"She was—until a few months ago—a parlor boarder at Miss Rowena LaMont's Academy for Young Ladies in Tenbury."

Archie and Sebastian exchanged glances. Parlor boarders were a special classification of boarding school students. Living at a school the year around, they typically enjoyed their own bed and were granted the privilege of sharing the headmistress's parlor in the evening. Such students were frequently wealthy orphans or motherless children of men posted overseas.

But sometimes they were the illegitimate, hidden offspring of a wealthy family.

"What happened a few months ago?" asked Sebastian.

"She turned twenty-one and came into her inheritance."

"How did you happen to meet her?"

Crispin looked up from the brooding contemplation of his Scotch. "My two sisters attend Miss LaMont's academy. Last winter, I inherited a small manor house nearby from a great-aunt. It was in a shocking state of disrepair, and I spent some time there setting it to rights. Emma— Miss Chandler—was my sister Georgina's particular friend, and often came with her to see me."

"Were you in love with her?"

Crispin pressed his lips together into a tight line and nodded as if he didn't trust his voice.

"Who were her family?" asked Archie. "They should be notified."

Crispin stared at him. "But I don't know who they are. She didn't know who they were."

"Why was she here?" asked Sebastian.

"I don't know."

"But you did know she was here."

"No!" The vehemence of the denial took Sebastian by surprise. "I was on my way back from leaving my sisters and the Bonaparte girls with my aunt in Windermere when I heard that a young woman named

Emma Chance had been killed in Ayleswick. She sounded so much like my Emma that I . . . I . . ." He paused to take a long gulp of his drink. "She used that name sometimes, you see—Emma Chance. Like it was a joke, although I never thought it very funny."

Chance child. It was a polite euphemism for a bastard.

Sebastian studied the young man's bowed head and rigid frame. His grief was real. But Sebastian couldn't shake the suspicion that the young lord was being less than honest about something.

"Who do you think killed her?" Sebastian asked.

Crispin glanced up, his face blank. "I've no notion. Why would anyone want to kill her?"

"Who knew of your interest in Miss Chandler?"

"No one." Crispin thought about it a moment, then added, "Well, my sister Georgina, I suppose. And Louisa. But they would never tell anyone."

"Your mother didn't know?"

Crispin surged to his feet, his face white, his fists clenched. "What the bloody hell do you mean by that?"

"You didn't tell her?"

"Not yet, no, damn you! And if you're suggesting that my mother would—that she would hire someone—"

Sebastian hadn't actually suggested it. But he found it more than interesting that Seaton's mind had instantly leapt to that possibility.

"Take a damper, Crispin," said Archie Rawlins.

Crispin turned his head to glare at his childhood friend.

Archie said, "*Someone* killed her, Crispin. She told everyone in the village that she was a twenty-eight-year-old widow on a sketching expedition. Now we find out she's someone else entirely. That changes everything; don't you see?"

"You can't be suggesting she was killed because of me!"

"No," said Sebastian. "Although I suspect she was here because of you."

Crispin stared at him, his jaw slack. "But why would she come here and pretend to be someone else? It makes no sense."

"Where has she been living since she left the school?"

"In Little Stretton. It's a village to the north of here, near the Long Mynd. There's a teacher who used to be at the school—Miss Owens is her name; Jane Owens. She has a cottage there. Emma was very fond of her." He paused, his lips quivering. "She had this scheme of the two of them opening a school together." It was obvious from the way he said it that Seaton had not been in favor of the idea.

"Can you tell us anything—anything at all—that might shed some light on what happened to Miss Chandler?"

"No. You think if I knew anything, I wouldn't tell you?" Seaton drained his Scotch and set the glass aside with a hand that was far from steady.

Sebastian exchanged glances with Archie.

An already puzzling investigation had just become considerably more complicated.

"So the Reverend decided to bury only Hannibal Pierce?" said Hero.

Sebastian was standing in their private parlor, their small son in his arms. A portmanteau packed by his valet, Calhoun, stood near the door, and a message had been sent to Tom to bring round the curricle. He planned to leave for Little Stretton on the hour. "Seems wise," he said. "Why bury her amongst strangers if someone can tell us who she is?"

"Crispin Seaton says Emma Chance—or rather, Chandler—didn't know anything about her family."

"No. But her school must."

"So why not go to Miss Rowena LaMont's Academy in Tenbury?"

"I intend to. But first I want to know what Emma was doing here, in Ayleswick, and I'm hoping this Miss Jane Owens can tell me." He smiled as Simon reached out one splayed hand to explore his father's nose. "Hopefully I won't be gone more than a couple of days."

Hero said, "I'm thinking I might spend some time looking into those two earlier suicides the vicar's wife was telling me about."

"What about your interviews for the article on the effects of the enclosure movement?" He worried sometimes that marriage to him was distracting Hero from the life she'd once intended to have.

She met his gaze, her face solemn. "Finding this killer is important to me too, Devlin—particularly if Emma Chandler isn't the first young woman he's murdered." She paused, her nostrils flaring on a deeply indrawn breath. "Were they buried at the crossroads, do you think? Those other young women who were thought to have committed suicide, I mean."

It was the practice in England to bury those convicted of the crime of felo-de-se at the crossroads, with a stake driven through their hearts— the idea being that both the stake and the constant traffic above would keep their restless souls from wandering. He shook his head. "I don't know, but probably. Superstitions die hard in areas like this."

He saw her jaw harden, saw the glitter of outrage in her eyes. To steal a young woman's life was bad enough. But to convince others that a murder victim was responsible for her own death, thus condemning her to an ignoble burial, added another vile outrage to an already despicable act.

His gaze fell to the pile of women's clothing delivered that morning by Constable Nash. All were now neatly folded. He said, "You looked at her clothes?" Hero had declined to attend that morning's inquests.

"I did."

"Anything interesting?"

She went to where the clothes rested on a straight-backed chair. "It's a lovely walking dress, probably made by a modiste in Ludlow and quite new. I did notice this—" She picked up the dress and turned its back toward him. "It looks as if dirt has been ground into the shoulders."

He carried Simon over to study the delicate cloth. "Makes sense, given how she was killed." He shifted the baby's weight so he could finger the slightly abraded cloth. "It probably also explains the faint scrapes on her back. Her killer was pinning her down, and she was struggling."

"How perfectly ghastly."

"It is, yes."

Hero set the dress aside. "I don't think she was wearing her spencer when she was killed. It's not dirty at all."

"The day was quite warm. The spencer was found folded beside her."

"The back of her hat is smashed, though; I'd say she was wearing it when she was killed." Hero reached for a soft kid glove. "And there's this," she said, holding it out to him.

"What about it?"

"There's only one."

Sebastian remembered noticing a glove lying with Emma's hat and spencer in the meadow. Had its mate been there too? He couldn't recall. He said, "Knowing Constable Nash, he probably dropped the other one somewhere. But you might ask Archie to look into it if you should happen to see him while I'm gone."

From the lane in front of the inn came the jingle of harness and the sharp cockney accents of Tom cajoling the chestnuts.

Sebastian brushed his lips against his son's cheek and breathed in the sweet baby scent. "For days now—ever since Hannibal Pierce was shot—I've been thinking this is all somehow connected to the presence in the neighborhood of Napoléon Bonaparte's brother. God help me, I was even willing to entertain the idea that Emma might be an agent sent from Paris. Now I'm wondering if I made a mistake assuming the two murders are connected. They may not be at all. Or Pierce could have been killed simply because he saw something that endangered whoever murdered Emma."

Hero reached to take the child from his arms. "But why kill an innocent young artist?"

He expelled a long breath. "Hopefully this Miss Jane Owens can help answer that question." He cradled her cheek in one hand and kissed her hard on the mouth. "Promise me you'll be careful?"

"That's my line," she said, and he laughed.

Chapter 28

*S*ebastian reached the village of Little Stretton late in the afternoon of a long, golden August day.

Lying some fourteen miles to the north of Ludlow on the main coach road that led to Shrewsbury, the village nestled at the base of a stretch of highlands known as the Long Mynd. Its cottages were a charming mix of half-timbered, red brick, and weathered gray stone, its gardens of holly-hocks and tumbling roses well tended, the breezes sweeping down from the hills above sweetly scented by the slopes' tangle of gorse, bracken, and heather.

Miss Jane Owens lived in a somewhat dilapidated whitewashed cot-tage situated on the banks of the River Ashes Hollow. She answered the door herself, a small, slim woman in her forties with a no-nonsense starched white cap covering short, curly brown hair barely touched by gray. Her forehead was high, her mouth small, her gray eyes wide with surprise at finding a fashionably dressed lord standing on her porch and an elegant curricle with a well-bred pair of spirited chestnuts at her gate.

"Miss Owens?" he asked with a bow.

"Yes?" she answered pleasantly. But she was obviously good at read-ing people, because whatever she saw in his face caused her smile to falter. "There's something wrong, isn't there? What is it? Dear God, what has happened?"

"I think you'd best sit down before I tell you," said Sebastian. He had come equipped with a letter of introduction penned by Lord Seaton. But it didn't look as if he would need it.

She gripped the edge of the door, her lips pressed tight. "No, tell me now."

"It's Emma Chandler," he said.

The horror and dread that leapt into her eyes told him just how much the younger woman meant to her. "Please say she's all right."

"I'm sorry," he said, and saw her brace herself for what was to follow. "I'm afraid she's dead."

"I've been an educator for more than twenty-five years," said Jane Owens later, as they walked along the banks of the swiftly rushing river. "Every child is unique and distinctive, each in his or her own way. But I never had a student quite like Emma."

"She was an extraordinarily talented artist," said Sebastian.

"She was beyond extraordinary. I firmly believe she had the talent to be as famous as Lawrence or Reynolds, if that was what she wanted."

"But it wasn't?"

A faint smile touched the older woman's lips. "No. She wanted to open a school—a school for girls like her."

"You mean, chance children?"

Jane Owen cast him a thoughtful glance. "Have you known many such children?"

Sebastian stared across the narrow, rocky river, toward the barren slopes of the Long Mynd rising gently above them. Amongst those of his class, such children were most often handed over to foster families and forgotten—if they weren't simply abandoned on the parish. Some were hidden away in schools, as Emma had been. But only a rare few were raised within the family, usually disguised as a "distant cousin," their true identity carefully hidden even from the children themselves.

"Not really," he said.

She nodded. "I've taught several over the years. They . . . they have problems it's difficult for the rest of us to understand. Those of us who grow up within a family—" She gave a quick, dry laugh. "Even if it's not one we particularly like—that family still helps us define who and what we are. It's so much a part of us that we tend to take that aspect of our identity for granted."

Sebastian remained silent, his gaze on the swirling waters beside them. He'd grown up thinking he knew his family, only to realize that it had been a lie, that half of his heritage was a question mark, a dark, mysterious unknown that alternately intrigued, tormented, and repelled him. It was as if a yawning hole had opened up inside him that he was both desperate and terrified to fill.

"But these children," Jane Owens was saying, "the ones who are given away or secluded and kept a secret—they have no sense of who they are, of who and what they come from. They can only imagine . . . dream . . . wonder. It tends to make for troubled youngsters, full of sadness and anger. They can be quite difficult to deal with."

"But not Emma?"

"Oh, no; if anything, Emma was the most secretive, rage-filled child I've ever met. She was fifteen when I first arrived at the academy. That's an age at which all children are trying to establish who and what they are. Except, children such as Emma have nothing to work with beyond what they invent themselves. They're adrift, essentially alone in the world. They feel terribly abandoned . . . confused . . . afraid. And angry. Very, very angry."

"Yet you were able to get through to her."

Jane Owens gazed down at the sun-sparkled waters beside them, her thoughts obviously troubled and far, far away. "I understood her. I think that's what was important. Rowena LaMont believes such children should be humble and endlessly grateful. She could never understand that by trying to force Emma to deny and hide her true feelings, she was only making matters worse."

Sebastian studied the older woman's intent profile. And he found himself wondering why she had left the academy, and how she had come to be here, in her rose-covered cottage on the banks of the River Ashes Hollow.

"Do you know why Emma went to Ayleswick?" he asked.

"Not for certain, no. But I can guess. She was trying to discover who her parents were. When she was younger—when I first met her—Emma always insisted she didn't want to know. She said that if they were ashamed of her—if they didn't want to have anything to do with her—then she didn't want to know who they were or have anything to do with them." Again, that sad smile touched her lips. "She used tell the most marvelous stories to the younger children at the school, all about stolen heiresses and lost princesses and children who were switched at birth. I often thought that was the real reason she didn't want to know the truth—that she preferred her own world of fantasy, where anything was possible. She realized that once she learned the truth, she'd need to give up imagining and accept what might be a very unpalatable reality."

"So what changed her mind?"

"Maturity, I suppose. Plus, there were so many questions she wanted answered. She wanted to know simple things—like why she had gray eyes, or where her artistic talents came from. But I think there was more to it than that. I think she was desperate to know if her mother ever loved her—if she regretted giving her up. She wanted to know where she belonged, even if the family that should have welcomed her didn't want her."

"And she thought she belonged in Ayleswick?"

The older woman looked stricken. "I don't know. She wouldn't tell me anything."

"You never knew her family's name?"

"No. But Rowena LaMont might. She always dealt with a firm of solicitors in Ludlow, but I wouldn't be surprised if she learned the truth years ago."

"The Ludlow solicitors also handled Emma's inheritance?"

A frown line appeared between her brows. "How did you know about that?"

"Lord Seaton told me."

"Ah."

"You knew he was in love with her?"

"Oh, yes."

"Was Emma Chandler in love with him?"

Jane Owens paused beside an old stone bridge that spanned the river. "I believe she was, yes. But . . ."

"But?" prompted Sebastian.

"She was . . . strange with him. I think she was afraid of being hurt."

"Understandable, given his youth and the marked disparity in their ranks."

"Yes. But I do believe he was sincere in his feelings for her."

"Did he ask her to marry him?"

"He did ask her, yes."

Sebastian thought about the anguished young man he'd first encountered on the church porch. So Seaton had asked Emma Chandler to marry him, yet somehow never managed to work up the courage to tell his mother he'd fallen in love. "And?"

"She told him he needed to give her time to think. I suspect it's a part of what made her finally decide she wanted to know the truth about who she was. It was as if she couldn't accept his offer until she knew."

"She knew the name of the Ludlow solicitors?"

"She did, yes—from when she'd dealt with them over the inheritance. So she went there first."

"When was this?"

"A month or so ago."

Sebastian frowned. "Not a fortnight ago?"

"Oh, no, it's been at least a month or more. I warned her they'd never tell her what she wanted to know, but somehow she managed to get it out of them. I fear she may have bribed one of the clerks."

"Enterprising."

"Oh, yes. Emma was an extraordinarily enterprising young woman. Once she determined she wanted to do something, she wasn't one to let either her fears or societal expectations hold her back."

"But she didn't tell you what she'd discovered?"

Miss Owens pressed her templed hands against the lower part of her face. "No. Whatever it was obviously disturbed her. She was gone several days, and when she came back, she was very quiet and thoughtful. And then she left again."

"When was this?"

"That she left again? A fortnight ago."

"Did she tell you where she was going that time?"

"No. Although I gather it must have been Ayleswick?"

"Yes," said Sebastian. Although she had stopped at Ludlow again on the way. She'd registered at the Feathers Inn as Mrs. Emma Chance and then set about assembling a wardrobe appropriate for a woman claiming to have been widowed some six months.

Miss Owens rested her outstretched palms on the top of one of the low stone walls edging the bridge and leaned into her arms. The air smelled of clean running water and blooming heather and sun-warmed earth, and she was silent for a moment, her gaze on the rippling waters flowing beneath them.

Then she looked over at him. "I don't understand. Why would someone kill her? How could anyone do that? She was so full of life, so passionate, so brilliant and strong. She had her entire life ahead of her—so many dreams and plans, so much to give. And someone took it all away."

Sebastian found it hard to meet the woman's pain-filled gaze. "Is there nothing you can tell me—nothing at all—that might help make some sense of what happened to her?"

"No. I can't think of anything."

"Would you mind if I looked at her room?"

The request seemed to take her aback. Then she blew a harsh breath out through her nostrils and nodded. "No. I can see it must be done."

"I would like your assistance."

She nodded again and pushed away from the bridge.

Chapter 29

Emma Chandler's chamber was one of two that lay at the top of the cottage's steep oaken staircase. With whitewashed walls and dormer windows set into a sloping ceiling, it was a pleasant room, the view from the windows looking out across the tumbling river toward the Long Mynd. The furniture was sturdy and plain. But Emma had covered the walls with her own exquisite art. In addition to simple sketches, there were also watercolors and oils, with brooding views of the Long Mynd hanging beside thought-provoking, character-filled faces of the very old.

"She purchased a few items after she came into her inheritance," said Miss Owens as Sebastian let his gaze drift around the room. "A silver brush and comb set, some new clothes, a trunk—and lots of art supplies, of course. But she was mainly focused on finding a house, something large enough that we could turn into a school. She wanted to stay in the area. It's a good location for a school, halfway between Ludlow and Shrewsbury."

"How much did she inherit? Do you know?"

"Ten thousand pounds."

Sebastian turned to look at her in surprise. He'd been imagining a legacy of several hundred pounds, perhaps, at most. Ten thousand pounds was a substantial sum. "Who does she leave it to?"

Miss Owens gave him a blank look. "I've no idea. Why? Surely you don't think her inheritance could be the reason she was killed?"

"It seems unlikely. But I don't think we can discount it entirely." He went to scan the titles of a row of books on a shelf mounted on the wall near the window. The volumes were simply bound but well-worn, and he noted works by Blake and Donne, Coleridge and Shakespeare. There was a copy of *Hamlet*, but when he took it down and turned to the last page, he found the last line intact.

"What are we looking for?" asked Jane Owens, watching him.

Sebastian slipped the book back in place. "Anything that might explain what happened to her."

She nodded and went to open the top drawer of the small chest beside the bed.

They worked their way quietly around the room. It didn't take long, for Emma Chandler's possessions had been few, her habits neat and tidy. It wasn't until he noticed a pencil sketch of Crispin Seaton tacked up near the window that something occurred to him.

"Did Lord Seaton ever write to Emma?" he asked.

Jane Owens glanced up from her search. "He did, yes. She received a letter from Windermere not long before she left."

"Have you come across it?"

She shook her head. "No, I haven't. You think that's significant?"

"I don't know."

Jane Owens was searching a small cupboard built into the wall beside the fireplace when Sebastian noticed a strange charcoal drawing affixed to the inside of the cupboard door. A young girl of perhaps twelve or thirteen stood before a building engulfed by a raging fire, her dark hair loose and flying across her face as the fierce air currents driven by the flames whipped the hem of her dress around her. In her arms she held another child she'd obviously rescued from the fire. A child whose face, he suddenly realized, was identical to her own.

"Emma did that years ago," said Miss Owens, following his gaze as she straightened. "I think she told me once that she was twelve."

"It's amazingly good."

Jane Owens nodded. "You wouldn't recognize it, but the burning house is Miss LaMont's Academy."

They stood in silence for a moment, studying the troubling and yet powerfully uplifting image.

"She's rescuing herself," Sebastian said after a moment.

"Yes. That was Emma."

Jane Owens closed the cupboard door and leaned back against it. They had discovered nothing.

He said, "Do you know the name of the firm of solicitors in Ludlow?"

"No; I'm sorry. Rowena LaMont could tell you." She hesitated, then pulled a face and added, "Although if you desire her cooperation, it might be best not to mention our meeting."

"She didn't approve of Emma's decision to join you once she came of age?"

"Miss Lamont and I did not part under the most amiable of circumstances."

Sebastian studied the schoolteacher's pinched, tightly held face. "It was over Emma, was it?"

She hesitated, and he thought she meant to deny it. But then she nodded. "Fortunately, a cousin who'd died six months before had left me this cottage and some land I rent to a local farmer. So I had someplace to go. The worst part was leaving Emma."

"When was this?"

"Two years ago. She asked if she could come to me when she turned twenty-one, and of course I said yes."

"Did she know then about the inheritance?"

"She knew she would come into something, but she had no idea of the amount."

"And Miss LaMont never said anything that might suggest who her family are?"

She frowned with thought. "I know Miss LaMont was extraordinarily impressed by them, whoever they are. Unfortunately, it somehow never translated into kindness to Emma. In fact, it was as if Rowena LaMont was determined to punish the child for the parents' transgression. But she was always extraordinarily tight-lipped about their identity."

Jane Owens was silent a moment. Then her eyes widened as if with a sudden thought. "Dear God. If that's why Emma was in Ayleswick, could *they* have killed her? Her own family?"

Her gaze met Sebastian's. He knew from the hopeful look in her eyes that she wanted him to tell her she was wrong.

Only, he couldn't.

Chapter 30

*L*ater that afternoon as the sunlight deepened to a rich golden hue and rooks swooped in to nest in the dense branches of the churchyard's ancient elms and yews, Hero walked up the hill to Ayleswick's sprawling vicarage and asked to see the Reverend's wife.

"My dear Lady Devlin," exclaimed Agnes Underwood some minutes later, hurrying into the parlor where Hero had been left waiting by the awestruck young housemaid. "My most sincere apologies for not coming sooner. But Bella—silly girl that she is—didn't have the sense to interrupt when I was speaking to the butcher just now."

"I do hope you didn't break off your discussion with him on my account," said Hero, gently disengaging her hands from Mrs. Underwood's tenacious grip.

"Oh, it's nothing, nothing, believe me. Please have a seat, Lady Devlin. I've already sent Bella for tea and cakes, so it shan't be but a moment." Her hostess settled on an uncomfortable-looking settee and clasped her hands in her lap. "Is there something I can do for you?"

"Actually, I was hoping you could tell me more about the two young women who died in the village some ten or fifteen years ago."

The smile slid off Agnes Underwood's face. "The young women . . ."

She pursed her lips and pulled her chin back against her neck like a turtle drawing into its shell. "Whatever for?"

"You said that at the time of their deaths it was believed the women committed suicide."

The vicar's wife clicked her tongue against the roof of her mouth with disdain. "There is no greater sin against God than to take one's own life."

It was a sentiment that Hero had never been able to understand. How was it worse to take one's own life than to steal the life of another? At least someone committing suicide had the permission of his or her victim. But she kept that thought to herself, saying simply, "Tell me about them."

"Well . . . the first was Sybil Moss. Her father is a cottager on Lord Seaton's estate. *Quite* the flighty little thing, she was. Beautiful, of course." Agnes Underwood sniffed contemptuously. She was the kind of woman who considered beauty an outward sign of frivolity and actually saw her own plain features as a mark of her innate superiority. "Gave her notions far above her station, I'm afraid."

"How old was she?"

"Fifteen or sixteen, I believe."

"Was she seeing anyone in particular?"

"In particular?" Agnes huffed a scornful laugh. "As to that, I couldn't say. But she certainly had half the men in the parish trotting after her like dogs after a bitch in heat. And not only the young ones, either, if you know what I mean."

"Oh?" said Hero encouragingly.

The vicar's wife leaned forward and dropped her voice. "It was *quite* the disgusting spectacle. Why, even Lord Seaton was falling all over himself, sniffing around the Moss cottage and—"

She broke off as the young housemaid, Bella, staggered in under a heavy silver tray loaded with teapot, cups and saucers, and plates of small cakes and biscuits.

Hero waited until the tea was poured and Mrs. Underwood passed her a cup before saying casually, "So why did Sybil kill herself?"

The vicar's wife looked up from stirring her own tea, one arched eyebrow cocked. "Why do you think? Got herself in the family way, of course."

"And she killed herself over it?" said Hero incredulously. An unmarried gentlewoman who found herself with child faced endless shame and social ruin, while for a housemaid it could mean instant dismissal followed either by a descent into prostitution or slow starvation and a wretched death. But the consequences were typically not so dire for a simple cottager's daughter. "Did her father turn her out the house?"

Agnes Underwood shrugged. "Who knows? One assumes so. I mean, why else would she throw herself off the cliffs of Northcott Gorge?"

"There was never any suggestion at the time that someone might have pushed her?"

"Good heavens, no. What makes you ask such a thing?"

"It is possible, isn't it?"

"No. I mean, who would want to push her?"

"The man who got her with child, perhaps?"

Agnes Underwood fingered her teacup, her features pinched and twitching with the turbulence of her thoughts. But she remained silent.

Hero said, "Nothing came out at the inquest?"

"Of course not. The verdict was felo-de-se, although the Reverend was able to argue successfully that the girl wasn't in her right mind when she committed the act. He's very compassionate, you know—some might say *too* much so. If you ask me, she should have been buried at the crossroads, naked and with a stake driven through her heart. Wicked, wicked thing."

It was with effort that Hero kept the distaste provoked by her hostess's remarks off her face. "And the other girl?"

"That was the blacksmith's daughter, Hannah. Hannah Grant. Drowned herself in the millpond, she did."

"Was she likewise with child?"

"I assume so."

"Surely there was an autopsy?"

"No. There was no need. It was quite obvious that the silly girl had drowned, so why waste parish funds? The old Squire was very careful about such things. Parish rates are quite high enough already."

"So it is possible she could have been murdered as well."

Agnes Underwood gave another of those humorless laughs. *"Dear Lady Devlin, what a thing to suggest."*

"If she wasn't known to be with child, then why was she thought to have killed herself?"

"Love sickness, the silly chit."

"She was in love? With whom?"

"Who knows? Kept it a secret. Probably some married man, I'm afraid. She was as pretty and flighty as Sybil, so it was no surprise when she came to a similarly bad end."

Hero took a slow sip of her tea. She suspected that any attractive young woman who laughed and enjoyed the attentions of men would be condemned as "flighty" by the vicar's wife. "Precisely when did these deaths occur?"

Mrs. Underwood screwed up her face with thought. "Well . . . let's see. It was before Maplethorpe burned, so it must have been 'ninety-six or 'ninety-seven."

"Had any other young women died under similar circumstances before that?"

"Well, there was Marie Baldwyn. Threw herself off the roof of Maplethorpe Hall, she did. But that was before my time. And I believe the family succeeded in convincing the coroner's jury that she had simply slipped and fallen to her death."

"What about in the years since then?"

"Good heavens, no. Two were quite enough, thank you. Three, if you count Marie Baldwyn."

"Four if you count Emma Chandler," said Hero. "Whoever killed her also tried to pass that death off as a suicide."

The vicar's wife looked vaguely affronted. "Surely you don't mean to suggest that there's any sort of connection? It's been years!"

"So it has." Hero took another sip of her tea and smiled. "I had a second purpose in visiting you this evening. I was wondering: Do you have a copy of *Debrett's Peerage?*"

Agnes Underwood settled back on her seat, obviously too relieved by the shift in topic to be puzzled by it. "Why, yes."

"May I borrow it? As well as any histories of seventeenth- and eighteenth-century Scotland and Wales the vicar might have?"

"Of course." She waited expectantly to have the request explained to her.

But Hero simply smiled, said, "Thank you," and left it at that.

Later that evening, Hero sent Jules Calhoun up to the Grange with a message for Archie Rawlins.

Then she settled down beside her sleeping son and opened the vicar's books in search of Guinevere Stuart Gordon.

Chapter 31

Saturday, 7 August

*S*ebastian left for Tenbury early the next morning, after having stopped the night at an old, half-timbered inn on the edge of Little Stretton. The day had dawned cool and misty, with heavy white clouds that hugged the tops of the trees and obscured the upper heights of the Long Mynd. He made the drive in easy stages, resting his horses along the way.

A middling-sized, ancient market town surrounded by orchards of apples, damson plums, and pears, Tenbury lay on the southern banks of the River Teme where the counties of Worcestershire, Herefordshire, and Shropshire all came together. In the spring, when the fruit trees bloomed, the town could be lovely, with clouds of colorful, piercingly sweet petals that billowed through the narrow old streets. But on this wet, dismal morning, Tenbury seemed brooding, somber.

Miss Rowena LaMont's Academy for Young Ladies lay on a quiet street of stern, gray stone houses with steeply pitched slate roofs, its garden hidden by a high wall topped with spikes.

"Ain't the most cheery-lookin' place, is it?" said Tom.

Sebastian stared up at that bleak, silent facade and found himself remembering twelve-year-old Emma's drawing of the school engulfed in hellish flames. "Perhaps it looks better in the sunshine," he said, and handed the boy the reins.

Miss Rowena LaMont proved to be as prim and forbidding-looking as her house. A tall, thin woman somewhere in her late fifties, she had unusually pronounced cheekbones and a small, tight mouth. Her dark blue gown was both fashionable and finely made, but cut high at the neck, its severity relieved only by a thin band of good lace at the collar.

She received him in a comfortable parlor as elegant as her gown. Around them, the house was quiet, with most of the students presumably home for the summer holidays.

"Lord Devlin," she said, sinking into a curtsy. "How do you do? Please sit down and tell me how I may help you."

He knew by the avaricious gleam in her eyes that she thought him the parent of a prospective student. He took the comfortable seat she indicated and said bluntly, "I'm here because I'm hoping you can answer some questions about Miss Emma Chandler."

Avarice receded behind a frozen facade of bristly caution. "Emma? I'm sorry to disappoint you, my lord, but Miss Chandler is no longer a student at the academy."

"I know. You have heard, I assume, that she was murdered earlier this week in Shropshire?"

The headmistress's expression never altered. "I read about it in this morning's papers, yes. I gather there was some initial confusion as to her proper identity."

"It must have come as a sad shock to you."

Miss Rowena LaMont obviously had any shock she may have experienced well under control, and Sebastian found himself doubting she'd felt even the slightest twinge of sadness. She regarded him steadily. "Surely you aren't suggesting her death is in any way connected to her time at the academy?"

He gave her a reassuring smile. "Of course not. But the local magistrate has asked for my assistance in the investigation, and we were hoping you might be able to tell us more about her. At the moment, the circumstances surrounding her death remain a complete mystery."

Miss LaMont pursed her lips and plucked at her high collar with a nervous thumb and forefinger. "I'm sorry, but surely you can appreciate my position? The privacy of our students—both present and past—must always be respected."

"I understand," said Sebastian with a smile, rising to his feet. "I had assumed you would prefer to speak with me. But I see now I should have had Bow Street send one of their Runners to interview you. My apologies for—"

"Wait!" Miss Rowena's eyes widened in alarm. The last thing the mistress of a school for young ladies wanted was for it to be known that her premises had been visited by Bow Street Runners. "Please, my lord, do sit down." She folded her hands in her lap. "Now, what would you like to know?"

Sebastian settled back into his seat. "How long was Miss Chandler a student here?"

"Fourteen years. She came to us at the age of seven."

The thought of Emma spending two-thirds of her short life in these bleak, cold surroundings struck him as profoundly sad and troubling. But all he said was, "Tell me about her."

Miss LaMont gave a tight little smile. "What is it the Jesuits say? 'Give me a child to the age of seven, and I will give you the man'—or, in this case, the woman? I'm afraid Emma's character was essentially formed by the time she came to us."

"Where had she lived, before?"

"Some farm family. Foster parents, of course. But she should have been removed from them much, much sooner. She was a wild thing when she arrived, with the manners and speech of a country bumpkin. Needless to say, we took care of *that* in short order, although I'm afraid she never quite fit in with the other students."

"Why not?"

"Why? Because of who she was, of course."

Which she was never allowed to forget, he thought. Aloud, he said, "So who was she?"

Miss LaMont lowered her voice, as if what she was about to say was too shocking to be expressed aloud. "A natural child."

"Of whom?"

"As to that, I fear I cannot say."

"Yet she obviously came from a wealthy family."

"Oh, yes. Her bloodline must always demand respect, even if the stain of illegitimacy remains indelible."

Sebastian studied the schoolmistress's self-satisfied, supercilious expression. If Rowena LaMont considered Emma Chandler's bloodline worthy of respect, then the girl must have been of gentle birth. The by-blow of a mere merchant or tradesman, no matter how wealthy, would never be considered possessed of superior blood.

"Had she any close friends amongst the other students?"

"Oh, no. I always took care to discourage the formation of any schoolgirl attachments in that direction. My students' parents would hardly thank me for allowing their daughters to form such a connection, now, would they?"

"But she was friendly with Georgina Seaton."

Miss Lamont stiffened. "She was, yes. But then, girls of Georgina's age do sometimes have a tendency toward willfulness. If Emma hadn't been leaving the academy, I would have taken more forceful steps to end the friendship. But as it was . . ." She shrugged.

Sebastian found he liked the absent Georgina Seaton, although he had never met the girl. It couldn't have been easy for her to befriend someone so obviously marked as an outcast by the school's headmistress.

He said, "Did you know that Miss Seaton's brother, Crispin, had formed an attachment to Miss Chandler?"

Rowena LaMont's small pale eyes grew narrow and flinty. "I was aware of his interest, yes."

"Did you by chance inform Lady Seaton of that interest?"

"If I had thought it serious, I would not have hesitated to notify her ladyship. But the boy is only—what? Twenty-one? Twenty-two? Young gentlemen of that age tumble in and out of love with startling rapidity and frequency. I saw no need to trouble her ladyship with something that would inevitably blow over."

"Had you had any communication with Emma since she left the school?"

"No. Why would I?"

Emma Chandler had shared this woman's table and parlor for four-teen years, yet she found his question strange?

Something of his thoughts must have shown on his face, for she said, "To coddle the fruits of sin is to condone the act that created them, and I believe we must never be lured into such errors by the tempta-tions of misplaced kindness." She smoothed one hand down over her fine skirt. "Emma Chandler could with justice have been consigned to a short, brutal existence in a parish workhouse. Instead, she was given a life of rare comfort and privilege. Yet far from being grateful or suitably humble, she was angry, resentful, and willful."

Sebastian found his hands tightening on the arms of his chair, so that he had to deliberately relax them. "Can you think of anyone who might have wanted to cause her harm?"

Miss LaMont gave a forced, mirthless laugh. "Good heavens, no."

"Do you have any idea what might have taken her to Ayleswick?"

"No idea whatsoever." She glanced pointedly at the small gold watch she wore pinned to her bodice. "And now you really must excuse me, my lord; I have duties to which I must attend."

"Of course." He rose to his feet. "If you could furnish me with the name and direction of her family?"

She rose with him. "Sorry, but that's quite out of the question."

He gave her a smile that showed his teeth. "Well, if you'd rather deal with Bow Street . . ."

She pursed her lips, her nostrils flaring with indignation. He thought for a moment that she still meant to refuse him. Then she said, "Wait here," and swept from the room.

She reappeared a moment later to slam a folded piece of paper down on the rosewood table beside the door. "You didn't receive this from me. And if you try to claim otherwise, I shall give you the lie to your face. Good day, my lord. One of the maids will show you out."

After she had gone, Sebastian went to unfold the slip of paper and stare down at what she had written. *Lord Heyworth. Pleasant Park, Herefordshire.*

He folded the paper again and put it in his pocket.

He was tempted to start for Herefordshire that afternoon. But one look at his tired horses told him the chestnuts had gone as far as they should in one day.

"Did ye find out who she was?" asked Tom as Sebastian leapt up to take the reins.

"Not exactly. But I now have a very good idea of where to look."

Chapter 32

Shortly after breakfast, Hero hired a pretty little gray mare from Martin McBroom's stables and, accompanied at a respectful distance by a groom, rode out to the Moss family's cottage on the far edge of Lord Seaton's estate.

It was one of half a dozen such cottages in a row, all neatly white-washed and newly thatched, each with its own croft and toft. The young Baron—or at any rate his sober, middle-aged steward—obviously took good care of the estate's tenants.

She reined in before the open front door of one of the middle cottages, where a towheaded child of four or five who'd been playing in the dirt beside the step looked up at her in openmouthed awe. "Good morning," said Hero with a smile, dismounting without her groom's assistance. "Is your mother or father around?"

The child gaped at Hero a moment, then pushed to her feet and darted inside, screaming, "Mumma, Mumma! Come quick!"

A slim, pleasant-looking woman appeared in the doorway, her flaxen hair in striking contrast to her still smooth, sunlit skin, the child now balanced on one hip and sucking her thumb.

"Mrs. Moss?" asked Hero. If this was Sybil's mother, she must be in at least her mid-forties by now, and she was still startlingly beautiful.

"Aye, milady," said the woman, sinking into a deep curtsy.

Hero found herself hesitating as she looked into the woman's faintly smiling but puzzled face. *How do you tell a mother you want to reopen the wounds of the past?* she thought. How do you gracefully bring up the death of one of her children? How do you ask her to confront, in daylight and before a stranger's eyes, a pain normally kept tucked out of sight and revisited only in solitude during the darkest hours of the night?

"I need to talk to you about the death of your daughter Sybil," Hero said bluntly, and watched the smile fade from the older woman's soft blue eyes, leaving them stark and hurting.

"She was my firstborn," said the woman who introduced herself as Anne Moss. They were seated beside the cottage's cold hearth, a nearby casement window thrown open to the cool summer breeze. She held the little fair-haired girl in her lap and kept touching the child's cheek, her arm, her leg, as if to reassure herself of this living child's presence. "She was so pretty, my Sybil. As pretty as any angel in one of those Popish holy pictures."

Hero wondered where the cottager's wife had seen such an image but kept the thought to herself.

"Barely sixteen, she was. She'd always been such a good child. But you know what girls of that age are like—willful and feeling their oats."

Hero found she could picture Sybil Moss quite clearly: a younger version of her mother, beautiful and nubile and joyously aware of her ability to turn heads and attract men. Lots of men. She would know she was desirable, know that her youth and beauty gave her a special kind of power—fleeting, perhaps, but rare and valuable.

"Is it true she was with child?" Hero asked, because she suspected the mother would not voluntarily betray her daughter's condition.

A faint line of color appeared high along her cheekbones. "She was. But she didn't kill herself over it. I don't care what that high-and-mighty coroner from Ludlow said. She didn't throw herself off the cliffs of the gorge because she was with child. She was happy about the baby."

"Do you know who the father was?"

Anne Moss shook her head. "She wouldn't say. It was something she hugged to herself, a secret. But it was a secret she was proud of; I'm sure of that. She weren't ashamed of it."

"How did your husband feel about it?"

Anne Moss hesitated, then lifted the little girl off her lap and said, "There now, Lizzy; run along and play."

She watched the child dart out the door, and sighed. "To be frank, I don't think John was surprised. She was so very pretty, our Sybil. He was hoping she'd take up with one of the more prosperous farmers here-abouts, someone who could give her a good life. But . . ."

"But?" prompted Hero when the woman lapsed into silence.

"I worried. She was so pretty—prettier than I ever was, and she knew it. Gave her grand ideas, I'm afraid."

"Who do you think was the babe's father?"

Anne Moss brought up one hand to rub her forehead. "I don't know. But she let slip a thing or two, enough to make me think he was a gen-tleman. Someone she should've known better than to go lying with."

"You mean, someone like Lord Seaton? Or perhaps the old Squire?"

Sybil Moss's mother nodded, her lips pressed into a pained line. "I even wondered about Major Weston or maybe—God forgive me—the vicar himself. Man of God he might be, but it never stopped him from having an eye for the pretty ones."

Was it a coincidence, Hero wondered, that Sybil Moss's mother had named four of the seven men on Emma Chandler's mysterious list? Somehow, she doubted it. "What about Samuel Atwater?"

The older woman's face lightened with unexpected amusement.

"Oh, no chance of that. Samuel Atwater's never had eyes for anyone but Lady Seaton. He'd marry her tomorrow, if she'd agree to it."

Hero remembered the steward's quiet, intense focus on the pretty, petite dowager, and wondered why she hadn't figured that out for herself. "Tell me what happened the day Sybil died."

Anne Moss stared down at the cold ashes on the hearth beside them, her face drawn and suddenly much older looking, her fingers plucking at the cloth of her apron. "It was Midsummer's Eve," she said, as if that explained much, as indeed it did.

The pagan origins of the rites of the summer solstice might be lost in the darkness of millennia past, but the date was still an important one in country villages. It was a time of drinking and dancing, when bonfires were lit along the fields so that their herb-scented smoke might drift across the crops to ward off evil sprits and ensure a successful harvest. Young girls decked themselves in garlands of golden calendula and marigolds and Saint-John's-wort, symbols of the sun and the light and life it gave.

Yet there was a marked undercurrent of darkness to this homage to the power of the sun. For on Midsummer's Eve, the boundaries between this world and the next were said to be thin and weak, and fairies roamed the land. Even as one celebrated the warmth and light of the sun, there was an acknowledgment that on this day, the sun reached its zenith. In the days to come, the hours of light would shorten as the year cycled inexorably toward autumn and the cold, dark death of winter.

"When did you last see her?" Hero asked quietly.

Anne Moss lifted her gaze to the window. "She must have slipped away sometime after the bonfires were lit. I didn't even realize she'd gone until the fires had all died and she still hadn't come home. And even then, I only thought she was . . ." Sybil's mother brought up a hand to press her fingertips to her lips, the sinews in her throat corded with an old, festering guilt that was never going to go away. "God help me, I was so angry with her. I went to bed and lay there thinking about how I was going to give her what for when she got home."

"But she never came home?"

Anne Moss shook her head. "I knew the next morning something was wrong—knew she wouldn't worry me like that. My John and some of the other cottagers went looking for her. One of his lordship's shepherds said he'd seen her over by the gorge, so they . . ." Anne had to pause and swallow before she could go on. "They found her lying on the rocks beside the river. Her neck was broke."

"Where in the gorge, exactly? Do you know?"

Hero was afraid the woman might find the question strange, but she answered readily enough. "She was lying at the base of a rocky outcropping called Monk's Head. They say that years ago, one of the young monks from the priory fell in love with a village girl. He tried to get out of his vows, but they wouldn't let him. So the two of them—the monk and the girl—jumped to their deaths there. Don't know if it's true, but it's a popular trysting spot for the young."

"Could she simply have fallen?"

"I suppose it's possible. But I doubt it. What was she doin' there all by her lonesome, anyway?" Sybil's mother turned her head to stare defiantly at Hero. "I think she was pushed. I think she went there to meet whoever planted that babe in her belly, and he pushed her."

"Did you tell that to the coroner?"

"I tried. He didn't want to hear it. Of course he didn't want to hear it." She fell silent, her thoughts lost in the past.

In the sudden hush, Hero became aware of the sounds of a child's laughter and the barking of a dog. Then Sybil's mother drew a deep, shaky breath and said, "The vicar was kind. He convinced the jury she was so overset by findin' herself in the family way that she wasn't in her right mind when she killed herself. Gave her a good Christian burial, he did, although we had to do it after dark, and she's lyin' on the very edge of the churchyard. Don't get me wrong; I appreciate what he done for us—truly, I do. But it weren't true, what he said. She wasn't out of her mind, and she didn't jump off the cliffs of the gorge. I'll believe that till the day I die myself."

Hero found she had no difficulty imagining a scenario in which a pretty, naive young girl, oh so proud of the gentleman's babe in her belly, might suddenly find her joy turned to despair when her wellborn seducer abruptly rejected her. But Hero wasn't about to suggest that possibility to the grief-stricken mother before her.

She said instead, "Of all the men you named, who do you think killed your daughter?"

Anne Moss stared at her long and hard. "You truly want to know?"

"Yes."

"I think it was Lord Seaton—his present lordship's father."

Hero was seated by the window and leafing thoughtfully through the portraits in Emma Chandler's sketchbook when Archibald Rawlins knocked tentatively at the door of the private parlor.

"I got your message," he said, standing awkwardly in the center of the room with his hat in his hands. "I asked both Nash and Dr. Higginbottom about the gloves. But neither could remember noticing if there was one or two."

"So it was probably dropped somewhere along the way," said Hero.

"I wouldn't be surprised. I'm afraid Nash isn't as careful as he should be." He hesitated a moment, then said, "You haven't heard from his lordship?"

"Not yet, no."

Archie nodded. "I was thinking about driving over to Ludlow on Monday. Crispin says Miss Chandler dealt with a firm of solicitors there. He couldn't remember their names, but if I can find them, they might be able to tell us more about her."

"That's an excellent idea," said Hero, giving him an encouraging smile. "Tell me, how well do you remember Lord Seaton's father, Leopold?"

"I don't really. I was maybe six or seven when he died."

Hero knew a quickening of interest. "He died around 'ninety-seven or 'ninety-eight?"

"Something like that, yes. Why?"

"Sybil Moss died in July of 1797."

"Did she? I couldn't have told you exactly. I barely remember it."

"When did Hannah Grant die?"

"Around then sometime."

"Her father is the village blacksmith?"

"He is, yes. I could talk to him—ask him about it, if you like."

"Is Hannah's mother still alive?"

"She is, yes."

"Then I'll talk to her instead."

A vague shadow passed over the young Squire's features. "If you'd prefer. Only, you might want to do it when the smith isn't around. He has a tendency to get a bit agitated whenever anyone mentions his daughter."

"Don't worry," said Hero. "I'll be careful."

Chapter 33

*L*ater that afternoon, as a thick white band of clouds settled low over the village, Hero walked up the high street to the blacksmith's shop and the slate-roofed, sandstone cottage that stood beside it. Remembering Archie Rawlins's warning, she carried with her a large, unusually heavy reticule.

She could see Miles Grant still at his forge, the fire glowing red-hot as he worked the massive bellows, his sweat-gleamed face bent to his task. In the yard of the nearby cottage, his wife was taking down clothes from a line strung between a lean-to shed and a mulberry tree, her arms moving methodically as she unpinned and rolled her wash to stow it in the basket at her feet.

If Mary Grant had ever been as pretty as her long-dead daughter, Hannah, all traces of those days were gone. The passage of hard years had etched deep lines in her face, sagged her cheeks, and tugged down the corners of her mouth and eyes, so that she looked as if she were melting—as if life were dissolving her a little more every day.

"Good evening," said Hero with a friendly smile.

The woman looked around and froze, and Hero saw the nasty bruise riding high on her left cheek, so purple it was almost black.

"God above," whispered the blacksmith's wife as she cast a wary glance toward her husband's forge. "I know why you're here, milady, but please—oh, please—just go away."

Hero watched the nerves in the older woman's face twitch with her distress. "I'm sorry, but I need to know about Hannah."

Mary Grant's pinched eyes widened with alarm at the sound of her daughter's name. "Miles, he don't like me talkin' about her," said the dead girl's mother. "Won't even let me mention her name in his hearing, he won't. Says she shamed us."

Hero was careful to keep her voice as bland as her expression. "You think she killed herself?"

Mary Grant jerked one of her husband's shirts off the line, sending its pins flying. "It's what they said at the inquest, ain't it?"

"When exactly did she die?"

A painful spasm crumpled the mother's face. "The twenty-fourth of January, 1798."

"Do you know if she was seeing anyone in particular at the time?"

The smith's wife paused, the shirt clutched forgotten in her arms, a faint, faraway light kindling in her eyes. "She was so pretty, all the lads in the village were in love with her—and more'n a few who weren't lads, if you take my meaning? Even his lordship's father fancied her, he did. I know because I saw him smiling at her once or twice. He always had an eye for a pretty face, he did. I told her not to make too much of it, that his lordship never meant well by any girl he smiled at. I think she listened to me. She weren't one for being foolish."

Hero studied the older woman's tightly held, intense face and suspected she spoke as much to convince herself as to persuade Hero.

"So who was she in love with?" asked Hero.

"I didn't ever know. I mean—" She broke off, her head jerking toward the blacksmith's shop as Hero became aware of a beefy man in a leather apron descending on them, his powerful arms crossed at his chest, his broad, heavily jowled face dripping sweat, the cords in his neck rigid with his fury.

"I'm sorry," said the smith's wife in a rush, bundling up the shirt in her hands and thrusting it into her basket. "I can't talk no more. Truly I can't." She seized the basket and disappeared into the cottage, leaving half the clothes still hanging on the line.

"What ye doin', comin' round here?" shouted Miles Grant, his voice booming out as his long stride closed the distance between then. "Comin' round here, makin' trouble? I'll teach ye to go pokin' yer fancy nose where it don't belong." He uncurled his arms, his knotted fists coming up as he descended upon her. "I'll show you."

Hero calmly withdrew the small, brass-mounted flintlock pistol from her reticule and thumbed back the hammer. "Come any closer and I will kill you. Without hesitation or compunction."

He drew up abruptly, eyes widening with surprise as much as anything else. She knew from the twitching of his heavy straight brows that the definition of the word "compunction" eluded him. But he understood the meaning of a loaded flintlock leveled unflinchingly at his chest.

"Ye wouldn't shoot me," he said, although his voice lacked conviction.

"Believe me, I would more than welcome an excuse to put an abrupt end to your miserable, brutish existence."

He obviously believed her because he took a wary step back, his hands dangling loosely at his sides, his face dark and swollen with the impotence of his fury.

She wiggled the muzzle of her pistol. "Now turn around and go back to whatever you were doing."

"Ye can't order about a man in his own house!"

Rather than keep the pistol leveled on his chest, Hero readjusted her aim so that the muzzle now pointed at his crotch. "Let me assure you that I am an excellent shot. Now, turn around and go away. You are boring me."

He didn't turn around. But he did back away from her, one step at a time, his dark, angry gaze fixed on her face. She waited until he'd backed all the way to his forge before she calmly walked away, the pistol still in her hand.

She doubted he would actually have been so foolish as to harm her, although she had no intention of taking any chances. More likely he had intended to use his size and his aggressive maleness to intimidate and frighten her. But she also had no doubt that he was dangerous, and this day's events had both humiliated and enraged him. She had challenged his comfortable belief that as a man he was superior to any female, no matter how wellborn.

And if he came at her again, it wouldn't be directly or out in the open where anyone could see.

Chapter 34

*P*leasant Park, the ancestral home of the powerful Turnstall family, lay to the southwest of Tenbury, in the rolling, verdant country of Herefordshire.

Nursing his chestnuts in easy stages, Sebastian arrived there in the afternoon. The sky was still overcast, with thickening gray clouds that robbed the day of light and warmth and cheer. Stately and pretentious, the house rose at the end of a sweeping, oak-lined carriageway. Its walls were built of massive, carefully hewn sandstone blocks, the roofline bristling with tall chimneys that thrust up pale against the dark foliage of the wooded hillside behind it. The gardens were as stiff and formal as the house, with close-cropped lawns, trim yew hedges, and old-fashioned box-edged parterres.

"Gor," breathed Tom as Sebastian reined in before the house's grand, Palladian-influenced portico. "'Er family owns *this?*"

"This, and another half dozen estates, besides," said Sebastian, hopping down to the gravel sweep.

To arrive unexpected at such a grand country estate was considered bad form, so Sebastian wasn't surprised when he was shown to a small waiting room by a stately butler and left to cool his heels for a number of minutes. He'd about decided the current Earl must not be receiving when the butler returned with a bow to say, "This way, if you please, my lord?"

He led Sebastian to a cavernous salon with figured pink silk–covered walls, richly colored marble pilasters, ormolu-mounted marquetry bureaus, and clusters of stately, throne-like chairs and settees gathered around each of the room's three marble-decked fireplaces.

Albert Felton Turnstall, Third Earl of Heyworth, stood beside the room's central hearth, one arm laid along the mantelpiece in what was meant to be a relaxed pose but instead came off as studied. He was of average height but slight of frame, with reddish blond hair and swooping curly side-whiskers. Sebastian knew him slightly, for the Turnstalls spent some months of every year in London. He was somewhere in his early to mid-thirties, which meant that Emma Chandler was most likely the natural daughter of this man's father, the Second Earl.

The Earl's mother, the Dowager Countess of Heyworth, sat nearby on a tapestry-covered chair, her stout body rigid with anger, her color high, and her head thrown back. Sebastian had the distinct impression that mother and son had argued over whether to receive him and that both knew the reason for his visit.

"Lord Devlin," said Heyworth with a smile that did not reach his eyes. "What an unexpected pleasure." The emphasis on the word "unexpected" was subtle, but there.

The formalities were punctiliously observed, polite utterances mouthed, and Sebastian invited to sit. Yet all the while, the room vibrated with an undeniable tension.

Sebastian smiled at his host and said bluntly, "I gather you know why I'm here."

Heyworth expelled his breath in a startled, nervous laugh. "Why, no. Are you by chance in the neighborhood?"

"Not far. At Ayleswick, in Shropshire. I assume you've heard of the recent murders there?"

Heyworth and the Dowager Countess exchanged guarded glances. Sebastian thought for a moment the Earl meant to deny all knowledge of the subject. But then he obviously realized the folly of trying to claim ignorance of something that had set the entire West Midlands to talking.

"Yes. Shocking, to be sure. I understand you've involved yourself in the investigations?"

"I have, yes. And I'm afraid we've recently discovered that the dead woman's name was not Chance as previously believed, but Chandler." He hesitated. "Emma Chandler."

The Dowager Countess remained rigidly silent. But Heyworth, who had resumed his stance beside the fireplace, lifted one eyebrow in a show of polite interest. "Oh?"

"The name means nothing to you?"

"No. Should it?"

Sebastian glanced, again, at the Dowager Countess. She was perhaps sixty years of age, deep of bosom and round of face, with dark blond hair fading rapidly to gray. Once, she might have been pretty. But sixty years of haughtiness, conceit, contempt, and petulant self-indulgence had etched themselves into her face in ways that were not attractive. Sebastian had the impression that if it had been up to the Dowager, she would have denied him, that it was Heyworth who had insisted they brazen out the interview.

Sebastian said, "I should think it would, given that your family paid her fees at a Tenbury academy for something like fourteen years."

Heyworth gave another of his breathy, unconvincing laughs. "I'm sorry, but whoever told you such a thing was mistaken."

"Indeed?" Sebastian looked from the Third Earl to his silent, angry mother. "Well then, my apologies for disturbing you."

"Not at all," said Heyworth. "Shall I ring for a footman to show you out? I do hope you have more success elsewhere."

"Perhaps I shall." Sebastian rose to his feet. "Emma will be buried in the churchyard at Ayleswick, should you wish at any point in the future to pay your respects to your sister."

"*She was not my sister,*" hissed Heyworth.

Sebastian smiled and started to turn toward the door. Then he paused, his attention arrested by the large painting that hung on the far wall.

A massive canvas, it was a life-sized portrait of an eighteenth-century family grouping set against a leafy background. Dressed in the splendid silks, velvets, lace, and opulent jewelry of a gentleman of the late 1780s or early 1790s, the Second Earl of Heyworth stood with one hand propped on his waist, his gaze off to one side as if he were surveying his estate with pride. He had his son's sharp features but a much stronger chin, his long wig powdered and crimped in the style of the day, his half smile one of calm self-satisfaction and pride.

His Countess reposed beside him on a stone bench. The Dowager had indeed been quite lovely when young, her figure slender and well formed, her eyes a deep, almost violet blue, her hair fashionably powdered. Two children relaxed in the grass at her feet. The future Third Earl, Albert Felton Turnstall, looked to be perhaps twelve or thirteen years of age, his bored conceit captured by the artist with startling clarity. But it was the young girl beside him who drew and held Sebastian's attention.

Some fifteen or sixteen years at the time she was painted, she was laughing down at a small kitten that clambered over her lap. Her smile was both vibrant and warm, and yet there was something about her posture that made her seem vaguely detached from both the artist painting her and the other members of her family. Her natural, unpowdered hair was the same rich, reddish blond as her brother's, although she lacked his sharp nose and rather weak chin. In fact, she looked very much like a younger version of the woman sitting behind her.

The resemblance of both mother and daughter to the pallid young woman Sebastian had last seen being prepared for burial was unmistakable.

Sebastian felt a heavy weight of sadness as the implications of what he was seeing sank into him. He had assumed Emma Chandler must be the natural daughter of the Second Earl of Heyworth, carelessly begotten on some mistress or village girl. But he realized now that the actual truth was probably far more tragic, that Emma was in all likelihood the child of this laughing young girl whose exact name—and fate—were unknown to him.

He swung around to stare back at the stony-faced Dowager who still sat with her hands clenching the gilded arms of her chair. He'd thought her anger and cold indifference to Emma's fate the product of a proud woman's resentment of her husband's bastard. But if his suppositions were correct, then Emma Chandler was this woman's granddaughter.

He might have apologized for so callously breaking the news to her of her granddaughter's death. Except that he had no doubt she'd already known.

And didn't care.

Sebastian was waiting for Tom to bring the curricle round when Lord Heyworth's butler came to stand beside him.

An aged, dignified man with thick white hair, a deeply lined, impassive face, and a fiercely upright carriage, the butler gazed out at the carriage sweep before the house and said, "You'll be wishing to stop somewhere for the night, my lord?"

Sebastian studied the man's stoic, unreadable profile. "Can you recommend something?"

The butler kept his gaze fixed straight ahead. "The Black Lion in Kirby is quite comfortable, my lord. The innkeeper's wife once served as governess to Lord Heyworth and his sister, Lady Emily. A Miss Rice, she was then. Did you know Lady Emily, my lord? She died twenty-one years ago now, at the tender age of seventeen. Tragic, it was."

Sebastian watched Tom bring the chestnuts to a stand before them with a cocky flourish. "Yes, it must have been. Thank you for the recommendation. My horses have already gone far enough for one day."

The butler gave a stately bow and withdrew.

Chapter 35

The Black Lion proved to be a neat, eighteenth-century brick inn with white casement windows and a steep slate roof. It stood in the center of the village of Kirby, a small cluster of houses centered around a soaring fifteenth-century jewel of a church.

The innkeeper was a large, jolly-looking man named Will Hanson. In his late fifties with an ample girth, three chins, and ruddy cheeks, he bustled forward to greet Sebastian with a wide smile, his voice booming, "Welcome! Welcome!" But when he heard Sebastian's name, the smile faded into something pained. "Ah," he said with a heavy sigh. "You're here about the poor lass was killed up Ayleswick way."

Sebastian paused in the act of swinging off his driving coat in the inn's flagged hall and looked over at his host in surprise. "How did you know?"

"Stayed with us some three or four weeks back, she did." The innkeeper motioned over a lanky, half-grown lad. "Here, Richard, take his lordship's portmanteau up to the best bedchamber while I have Bridget fetch some hot water." To Sebastian, he said, "And then I reckon your lordship will be wishing to speak with my wife?"

"Yes, please."

"I arrived at Pleasant Park when Lady Emily was eight and her brother, Albert, had just been breeched," said Sarah Hanson. She was a plump woman a few years younger than her husband, with silvery gray hair framing a plain, kind face. "I was very young at the time myself. My father was a vicar in Worcestershire, but he died when I was nineteen, and I had no brothers. Fortunately, my father had seen that I was given a good education, and his successor was kind enough to assist me in locating a position."

They were walking along a narrow, shady lane that wound around the village's ancient churchyard, toward the fields beyond. The evening was as overcast and somber as the day, the air cool and damp and filled with birdsong from the rooks, jackdaws, and thrushes coming in to roost in the soaring tops of the chestnuts and beech overhead.

"I used to wonder what would have happened to Emily if I hadn't come along," said the former governess. "She was so very different from the other members of her family. She told me once that she felt like a changeling—although of course she was not. From what I've heard, I suspect she took after her grandfather, the First Earl, who was by all accounts a remarkable man. But he was dead by the time Lady Emily came along. She was a very unhappy child."

"How long were you with the family?" Sebastian asked.

"Nearly ten years."

"So until Lady Emily died?"

Sarah Hanson's face pinched with an old but still raw grief. "She died in my arms."

"In childbirth?"

"No. They killed her—her family, I mean. Oh, they could never be charged, of course. But they killed her, just as surely as if they'd run her through with a sword."

"Can you tell me what happened?"

She looked up at him, her gaze steady and solemn. "I can tell you what I know."

It began innocently enough, late in the summer of 1791, when Lady Emily was just sixteen, young and beautiful and filled with a joyful zest for life.

A message arrived one afternoon at Pleasant Park from the Irvings of Maplethorpe Hall, inviting Lady Heyworth and her daughter to a country house party to be held the first week of September. Predictably, Lady Heyworth turned up her nose at the invite, saying with a sniff, "How impudent of them. Do they seriously think I would even consider accepting? The family positively reeks of the shop. Why, when I encountered Mrs. Irving at the assembly in Ludlow last spring, she told me her great-grandfather was a butcher!" Her ladyship gave a scornful titter. "Can you imagine?"

But Lady Emily was eager to attend her first real, grown-up house party. And so she assembled a carefully rehearsed list of arguments and approached her mother in her sitting room several mornings later.

"About the house party at Maplethorpe Hall . . . ," she began.

Lady Heyworth was busy embroidering a fire screen and barely glanced at her daughter. "What about it?"

"I agree that Mrs. Irving isn't quite the thing," said Emily, clenching her hands behind her back. "But I do like her daughter, Liv. And you said yourself that I need more practice going into company before my Come Out in London next spring."

Lady Heyworth kept her attention focused on her needlework. "Your Come Out is precisely why you must take care to avoid such entertainments. It would do you no credit for it to become known that you had lent your presence to a gathering of vulgar, pushing mushrooms."

"But that's just it, you see; the guest list is quite select—Liv wrote me all about it. Lady Dalton is taking Julia, and . . ." Here Emily paused to draw a deep breath in preparation for what she hoped would be her most persuasive argument. "Lord Stone will be there."

Lady Heyworth's hands stilled at their task as she looked over at her daughter. "Stone? You're quite certain?"

Edward, Lord Stone, might be only a baron, but his estates were worth forty thousand pounds a year. Set against so grand a fortune, the fact that he was thirty-five years old, stout, and addicted to opera dancers and highflyers was inconsequential; Lady Heyworth had decided he would make a marvelous catch for her daughter and was already scheming of ways to bring Emily to his lordship's notice. Emily had no intention of satisfying her mother's ambitions in that direction, but she wasn't above using the lure of Lord Stone's presence to achieve her own ends.

"Well, why didn't you say so before, you silly chit?" exclaimed her ladyship. "Of course you must go." She pulled a face. "Although I won't deny that the thought of having to endure that Irving woman for a good week is enough to bring on my spasms." Then a happy thought occurred to her. "You say Lady Dalton will be there with Julia? I wonder if I could prevail upon her to take you into her charge."

A letter of inquiry was duly dispatched to Lady Dalton, and a favorable response received. The fact that Lady Heyworth would be sending her sixteen-year-old daughter off to a country house party under the lax chaperonage of a woman known to be as lazy as she was fond of card games and discreet love affairs was not seen as an impediment.

"I had serious forebodings," the former governess told Sebastian now as they paused beside an ancient, moss-covered stone wall to gaze out over the churchyard. "But between Lady Emily's determination and her mother's ambitions, no one would listen to me."

"She went?"

"She did, yes. She had a marvelous time at first. How could she not? She was away from her mama's censorious eye, and she was so pretty, and she was in the company of a good dozen men with whom to strike up a flirtation."

"Who was there besides Stone?"

"Let's see. . . . Lady Dalton brought her twenty-two-year-old son, George, as well as Julia. And Stone had several boon companions in his train—men of a similar ilk, I'm afraid. There were others as well, although I can't recall them now. She wrote me a letter while she was there, talking about some of the people she'd met. I saved it. In fact, I showed it to Emma Chandler."

"May I see it?"

Sarah Hanson pushed away from the churchyard wall and turned back toward the inn. "If you think it would be helpful, yes."

Chapter 36

The letter was yellowed with age and worn, as if its recipient had pored over it again and again in search of an elusive clue that might bring understanding—or at least some sort of comfort.

Sarah Hanson slipped the folded pages from between the leaves of a Bible that rested on the table beside a comfortably worn chair in the Hansons' private parlor. She fingered it a moment, as if reluctant to have Sebastian read it, lest he harshly judge one who'd been so dear to her. "Remember: She was very young when she wrote it," she said, finally holding it out to him. "Just sixteen."

Lady Emily's handwriting had been graceful and delicate, her enthusiasm for her first grown-up house party readily obvious in the letter's numerous underlinings and exclamation points.

My dear, dear Miss Rice,

Oh, I am so <u>glad</u> Mama was convinced by the lure of Lord Stone's presence to allow me to come to Maplethorpe, for I am having the most marvelous time!

Thankfully, Lord Stone has shown not the slightest interest in me. I hear he prefers his women "mature and experienced"—no innocents need apply!—which suits me just fine. (Do you think if I tell Mama, she will abandon her matchmaking schemes? Or will she simply blame me for not putting myself forward enough?) His lordship and his companions are out most of the day shooting, and when they do return to the house, their attention is consumed by the billiards table, the contents of Mr. Irving's extensive cellars, and some foul-smelling things I'm told are called cheroots. Fortunately, the same cannot be said of most of the other gentlemen present, so it is only during the day that we ladies are forced to amuse ourselves with our needlework and reading and letter writing, or rambling walks through the countryside and to the village.

I already wrote Mother and Father about my fellow houseguests, so shall I tell you instead of the village? There are several of what Mama calls the "better sort" of families in the neighborhood. The gentlemen have been invited to join the houseguests in their shooting and they also come in the evening with their wives to dinner. From the Grange comes Squire Rawlins and his quiet little mouse of a wife. The Squire is like a character out of Chaucer—large, gruff, loud, opinionated, and so addicted to snuff he is always liberally dusted with the stuff. He is even older than Lord Stone and interested in nothing beyond his horses and his hounds and his port—oh, and his land and herds, of course. He told me to my face he has no patience for struggling to make conversation with some chit barely out of the schoolroom! How I feel for his wife, for she is not much older than I.

Far more congenial is Lord Seaton of Northcott Abbey, a fine estate that lies to the west of Ayleswick. His lordship also has a wife, although they say she is increasing and ill as a result, so she seldom goes into company these days. Liv tells me there are <u>whispers</u> about his lordship, if you know what I mean. And I must say his behavior does seem to bear them out, for he has been quite marked in his attentions to me, and he is so handsome and charming that my head would surely be turned were it not for Liv's warnings.

There is also a Major Weston, who is a frequent guest at Maplethorpe. He is quite gallant and likeable, although Lady Dalton bestirred herself from her flirtation with one of Lord Stone's cronies long enough to warn me he is utterly without fortune and must make his own way in the world. He is related to Lord Weston of Somersfield Park, but while that must obviously make him attractive to Mrs. Irving (Liv tells me her mama is <u>most</u> anxious for her to make some noble connection), I know my own mama would take to her bed for a week were she to learn that her daughter had so much as <u>smiled</u> at a mere major. And if she were to hear about the brooding and romantically dashing young man down at the Ship! Well, I do believe she would suffer an apoplexy. But not to worry, my dear Rice, for I am mindful always of what is owed my house, and am content merely to attempt to capture <u>that</u> young man's likeness in my sketchbook. If only my humble talents were equal to the challenge!

On Sunday, those of us who were astir trooped down to the village for church services. I wish you had been there so that I might have heard your opinion of the local vicar, one Reverend Benedict Underwood. He is only recently ordained—I believe the living was a gift from some uncle.

His sermon on Galatians 5:19–21 was both thought provoking and scholarly (although I fear it sailed over the heads of the vast majority of his parishioners!). But I found his delivery most peculiar, for he reminded me of a thespian on a stage—quite self-consciously dramatic and so very proud. He is an attractive man for a vicar (if you like that look; I do not), although not, surely, quite as handsome as he believes himself to be. I told him in all sincerity how much I enjoyed his sermon and was tempted to add that I would love to hear him expound on 1 Samuel 16:17. But I was a good girl and held my tongue!

It was while we were still on the porch that a strange lout of a boy from the village—Reuben Dickie is his name—tried to chase a billy goat right into the church! They claim he is harmless—"half-soaked and yampy," as they say here in Shropshire. His brother soon put a stop to the lad's antics, with the assistance of Samuel Atwater, Northcott's strangely solemn steward. But as they led Reuben away, he threw me such a look over his shoulder that I've quite made up my mind to avoid the village from now on.

But never fear, my dear Miss Rice, for I am having a marvelous time. I can't wait until next February, when we go to London! And now I must dash off, for Mrs. Irving has got up an expedition to Northcott Gorge, which is said to be quite lovely and haunted by the ghosts of two star-crossed medieval lovers. I will write more later.

Your devoted pupil,
Emily

Sebastian was silent for a moment, caught by the pathos of the long-dead girl's joyous enthusiasms. He folded the letter and handed it back to the former governess.

"She never wrote again?"

Sarah Hanson tucked the letter back into the book. "No. She came home three days later. I knew the instant I saw her that something dreadful must have occurred, but she refused to speak of it. I didn't learn the truth for another two months."

"When she realized she was with child?"

She nodded. "She was forced. Although I'm afraid Lady Turnstall refused to believe her. Insisted that if Emily hadn't given herself willingly, then she must have done something to make the man think she would welcome his advances."

"She never named the father?"

"No. All she would say was that he was one of the men she had written me about, and that marriage to him was impossible. Once—after the child was born—I heard her whisper to the baby that she had her father's hair. But that was the only hint she ever gave."

"So the father was dark."

"Yes."

Sebastian thought of the men named in the letter. He understood, now, the origins of the list they'd found in Emma Chandler's room. Of all the men mentioned in her mother's letter, only Lord Stone had been missing from Emma's list. But then Stone—nearly sixty now and riddled with syphilis—was famous for his full head of bright ginger hair.

"What happened when Lady Turnstall discovered her daughter was with child?" Sebastian asked.

"She sent her away. I had a cousin living in reduced circumstances in a large house in Barmouth, overlooking the estuary, and she was happy enough to have us come stay with her. Lady Emily was introduced to the neighborhood as the tragic young widow of a major recently killed in the American colonies."

"A useful fiction," said Sebastian. And borrowed by Lady Emily's daughter herself decades later, although for a slightly different reason.

"The child came dreadfully early," said the former governess, going to stand at the window overlooking the village high street. "She was so small and weak, I thought sure she would die. But she didn't. Most women in her situation would have hated the product of such a conception, but Emily was besotted with the infant from the moment she first held her. She was desperate to keep her."

"The Turnstalls refused?"

"How could they do otherwise? I tried to reason with her, but Emily remained hopeful she could bring them around. Then, one morning in late August, we went for a walk along the estuary. It came on to rain not long after we left, so we turned back toward the house. A carriage was just pulling away from the gate as we came up. The instant she saw it, Emily started to run. Somehow she knew what was happening, even before we saw the face of her father's solicitor in the window. She screamed and begged for them to stop, but the coachman only whipped up his horses faster. She ran after the carriage until she could run no farther. Then she simply collapsed in the middle of the road, sobbing."

Sebastian watched the former governess swallow hard, her hands clenching around the edge of the windowsill before her. He remained silent, waiting until she was able to continue.

"She lay there for what seemed like forever, curled in a ball, hugging herself, while the rain poured down around us. I kept saying, 'Lady Emily, you must get up. You'll catch your death.' Finally she looked at me and said, 'You think I care?'"

"She took sick?"

"It didn't seem so at first. I finally persuaded her to let me help her inside. Then she went wild—demanded we return at once to Pleasant Place so that she could confront her father. We left for home that very day. I never knew precisely what passed between them, but I believe she threatened to shame the family and destroy her own reputation by taking out an advertisement in all the London papers proclaiming the child's birth—and abduction—to the world."

"Would she have done it?"

"For the sake of the child? Oh, yes. And her father knew it. In the end, they reached a kind of compromise. She agreed to give up the child and keep its birth a secret, and he gave his word that the child would be educated and eventually inherit half of Lady Emily's dowry— or all of it, should she never marry."

"So what happened to her?"

"That very night, after her interminable meeting with her father, she collapsed with a raging fever and putrid sore throat. She was dead in a week."

"Yet he kept his word?"

"He did, yes. There was much not to like about the Second Earl. But he was a man of his word. He genuinely loved his daughter—and mourned her death. He set things up so that even in the event of his own death, his solicitors would see that the child was sent to school at the age of seven, and that her inheritance would be safe from his son, Albert."

"When did he die?"

"Four years later."

"The new Lord Heyworth knew of the arrangements?"

"I assume he was told as soon as he came of age, although I can't say for certain. The truth is, I've had little contact with his lordship since Emily's death. Will asked me to marry him right after the funeral." Sarah Hanson gave a short, sharp laugh. "Lady Heyworth was beyond horrified when I accepted. She actually tried to forbid me to do any such thing. After all, what would people think when they learned that her children had been taught by the local innkeeper's wife?"

Sebastian smiled, "What, indeed?" He studied the former governess's plump, good-natured face. Sarah Hanson might be both better educated and considerably better bred than her innkeeper husband, but the truth was, she'd been extraordinarily lucky to marry him. Most impoverished, aging gentlewomen lived out their lonely lives in fear and want.

Sebastian said, "Did Emma Chandler know who you were when she came here?"

"No. In fact, she registered under the name Emma Chance. But I knew who she was the instant I set eyes on her. She was so very much like her mother—only darker haired, of course."

"Did you tell her you recognized her as Lady Emily's daughter?"

"Not at first, no. I was tempted. But it didn't seem right, putting myself forward like that. She hired Richard to drive her out to Pleasant Park the next morning. She told me later that she knew nothing about Lady Emily; all she knew was that the Turnstalls had been paying her fees at Miss LaMont's Academy."

"Did she give her name as Emma Chance when she went out to Pleasant Park?"

"She did, yes. I think she was afraid they'd refuse to see her if she identified herself to the staff as Emma Chandler. And she was right. It was the Dowager who met with her. As soon as Emma told her ladyship her real name, Lady Heyworth flew into a shaking rage. Called the poor girl a brazen, lying hussy and set up such a fuss that the Earl himself came on the run. It was Heyworth who told Emma he'd call the constables if she ever dared show herself near the estate again."

"Charming."

Sarah Hanson's nostrils flared on a deeply indrawn breath. But all she said was, "Alfred Turnstall is very much his mother's son."

"Why was Emma given the name Chandler? Do you know?"

"Chandler was the name of the farm family that fostered her for the first seven years. She told me they were very kind to her. She had no idea Molly Chandler wasn't her mother until one day when a solicitor from Ludlow arrived to carry her off to Miss LaMont's Academy." Her voice hardened. "It was such a cruel, heartless thing to do."

"Yes," said Sebastian.

It explained how the Turnstalls had known the reason for Sebastian's arrival. Even if they hadn't been closely following events in the papers, they would know that "Emma Chance" was really Emma Chandler. And with all the talk generated in the region by the Ayleswick murders, they would also know that Sebastian was investigating her death.

"When Emma came back from the park," Sarah Hanson was saying, "she was devastated—both because of the way they'd treated her and because they'd refused to tell her what she was so desperate to know."

"You mean, the names of her mother and father?"

"Yes. She broke down crying on the stairs up to her room."

"And that's when you told her what you knew and showed her the letter?"

"Yes." Sarah Hanson turned to look at him, her face stricken. "I wish to God I hadn't. It's why she went to Ayleswick, isn't it? She was trying to figure out who her father was. She went there, and now she's dead."

"How did she react when you showed her Lady Emily's letter?"

"At first, she was excited to read it. But by the time she finished, she was pale and shaking. If anything, she seemed more devastated than when she'd returned from Pleasant Park—although I could never understand why."

"She didn't tell you she was in love with a young man from Ayleswick?"

He read the dawning comprehension and horror in her eyes. "Dear God, no. What was his name?"

"Crispin, Lord Seaton—the son of one of the men who may have raped her mother."

Chapter 37

*E*arly the next morning, before he left the village of Kirby, Sebastian visited the small fifteenth-century church with its flying buttresses and fan vaulting and soaring stained-glass windows.

Even in death, the grand inhabitants of Pleasant Park refused to mingle with the common folk of the village. Rather than be buried in the churchyard, generations of Turnstalls lay in a private crypt beneath their own chapel in the north transept. An ornate jewel of Italian marble, delicate tracery, and masterfully carved, life-sized effigies, the chapel was crowded with memorials to past generations of Turnstalls, some extraordinarily ornate and pretentious, others less so.

Emma's mother had warranted only a small brass plaque inscribed, LADY EMILY TURNSTALL, MAY 1775–AUGUST 1792.

Pausing before it, Sebastian ran his fingertips along the engraved letters and felt the tragedy of the young woman's death hollow him out inside. *How many women?* he wondered. As one century followed the next, on down through the ages, how many women had seen their lives shattered by an unintended pregnancy that ran afoul of their society's cruel, unforgiving conventions?

He wondered if Emma Chandler had come here to the church before she left the village. From Sarah Hanson she would have heard the answer to two of the questions that had haunted her since childhood: She would have learned the name of the woman who had given her life and she would know that her mother had both loved her and wanted desperately to keep her.

Yet the discovery would have been bittersweet, for the mother she had sought was long dead, never to be seen or touched. Standing here, reading her mother's stark memorial, she would have felt the awful finality of it, the inescapable sadness of realizing she would never know her mother's smile, never breathe in the scent of her skin or hear the sound of her laughter. Never hear her say, *I love you.*

And he wondered, had anyone ever said those words to Emma before Crispin Seaton? Probably not since she'd been dragged away from the happy farm of the couple who had given her their last name. What would it have done to her to read her mother's letter and realize that she might lose Crispin too? There were seven men mentioned in Emily's letter. The odds were slim that her mother's rapist would turn out to be the father of the man Emma loved. Yet the chance was there.

She could have decided to ignore what she'd learned, turned her back on the past, and embraced the future she surely wanted. Instead, she'd been driven to learn the truth. Disregarding her society's conventions, she'd disguised herself as a widow on a sketching expedition and gone to Ayleswick.

Had Emma somehow discovered the information she sought? Sebastian wondered. Was that why she had died? Had her reappearance in her father's life threatened the guilty man so much that he had killed her? Killed his own daughter?

It was possible. Horrifying, but definitely possible.

Chapter 38

Shortly after breakfast, Hero left Simon with Claire and took the shady path that rambled through stands of old-growth oak and beech, to the water meadows.

It had rained during the night. But now the air was clear and fresh with the new day, the sunlight filtering down through the leafy branches overhead golden and warm. Wrapping her arms around her bent knees, Hero sat on the moss-covered log where Emma's body had been found and stared out at the slow-moving river. Devlin was right; there was nothing particularly picturesque or unusual about this stretch of the Teme. So why had Emma Chandler's killer chosen this spot to stage her suicide?

Why?

A hawk circled overhead, riding an updraft, and Hero tipped back her head, watching it. The silence and isolation of the place settled heavily upon her. She could hear nothing but the sigh of a faint breeze through the treetops and the whine of unseen insects. Then a boy called to his dog somewhere on the opposite bank, and the moment was broken.

"What happened to you?" she whispered, as if the dead woman's spirit still lingered there, haunting this place. "What, and why?"

Why would someone kill an unknown young woman? Lust was the

obvious answer, except the girl hadn't been violated and there were no signs that she had been killed trying to resist a sexual assault. Which suggested that either the killer knew exactly who she was and why she had come to this small, out-of-the-way village, or . . .

Or her identity was meaningless and she'd died simply because she'd somehow seen or learned something her killer didn't want known.

Hero was contemplating this last possibility when she became aware of a strange sensation creeping over her, tense and unsettling.

She was being watched.

Holding herself very still, she glanced around the water meadow, her gaze raking the reeds down by the river and the tangled undergrowth of the stand of alders and willows that pressed in close. She was not a fanciful woman, but she profoundly regretted not bringing her pistol with her. She was searching about for a stout stick when a vague rustling drew her attention to a nearby patch of blackberries.

"Hullo," she said, recognizing the short, squat man barely visible through the brambles. "It's Reuben, isn't it? Reuben Dickie?"

"Aye, ma'am." He stepped reluctantly from behind the blackberries, obviously discomfited to have been seen. And she wondered how often he did this—watched people quietly, without their knowing.

"Why were you watching me?" she asked with a smile. She hoped the smile didn't come off looking as tight and forced as it felt.

He touched his forelock and bobbed his head. "Didn't mean nothin' by it, ma'am."

"Do you come here often?"

"Sometimes." He sniffed and wiped his nose with the back of his hand. She realized that his other hand gripped a small book, elegantly bound in blue leather. But he was holding it awkwardly against his leg, as if anxious to hide it from her view.

"You have a book, I see," she said, still smiling.

"What? Oh, aye, ma'am." His small eyes slid away.

"Where did you get it?"

"Found it, I did."

"Oh? Where?"

"I dunno. Just found it."

"When?"

"When? Few days ago, I reckon."

"It looks like a lovely book. May I see it?" She held out her hand, and though he hesitated, she kept her hand out and gave him a stern look.

He stumbled forward and surrendered the book.

Somehow she knew, even before she saw it, what she would find engraved in gold lettering on the spine.

Hamlet. William Shakespeare.

She opened the book to the last page with hands that were not quite steady. Where the final words of the play should have been was now only a gaping hole. The last sentence had been neatly sliced away by a knife.

"Where did you say you found it?" Hero asked again, flipping to the inside front cover.

"I dunno. Always finding things, I am. Things other folks throw away."

"You think someone threw this away? It's a lovely book."

"Well, they must've, else how would I have found it?"

"Only you don't remember where?"

"No, ma'am."

"Was it around here?"

"Oh, no, ma'am."

"How can you be certain, if you don't—"

Hero broke off, her attention arrested by the owner's name written in a small, cramped script on the flyleaf.

The Reverend Benedict Ainsley Underwood.

"I had no idea it was missing," said the Reverend, staring down at the small, leather-bound volume in his hands. "You say Reuben claims to have found it?"

"You think he might not be telling the truth?" asked Hero.

They were seated in the Reverend's book-lined study overlooking the churchyard. An ornate ormolu clock on the mantel ticked loudly in the sudden silence. The Reverend cleared his throat. "Let's just say that Reuben sometimes invents his own truths."

"He also claims not to remember precisely where he found it."

"Yes, well, that doesn't surprise me. There's nothing wrong with Reuben's memory. But if he thinks he might be in trouble, he is not above playing up his mental deficiencies for sympathy."

"Why would he think he might be in trouble?"

The vicar exhaled a long, pained breath. "Some years ago, when he was younger, Reuben . . . Let's just say he had a habit of roaming at night and peeking into people's windows, especially cottages with pretty young girls. The old Squire, he told Reuben he was going to put him in the stocks if he was caught doing anything like that again—forbade him ever to be out after dark, in fact. But I'm afraid he does still go out at night, probably far more than anyone realizes. I wouldn't be surprised if he found the book on one of his illicit midnight sojourns and that's why he won't admit to remembering anything."

Hero thought about the night she and Devlin had seen Reuben on the village green, and the way his brother, Jeb, had come out to coax him back inside.

The vicar ran his fingertips along the small book's spine. "It's disconcerting—frightening, even—to think that poor young woman's killer could actually have been *here*, in my house . . . stealing my books. . . ."

"When do you think the book was taken?"

"I've no idea. It's been several years since I last read *Hamlet*. It could have been gone for some time without my knowing it." He rose to inspect a shelf that Hero saw contained a row of several dozen small, similarly bound volumes. They must have been tightly packed in before, because the space left by the missing play was not obvious.

"Have any others been taken?" she asked.

He stooped to inspect the titles. "Doesn't look like it, no." He straightened and cast a bewildered look at the towering, crowded cases around them. "Although I can't with any honesty say nothing has been taken from any of the other shelves."

"You have an impressive collection," said Hero.

The Reverend smiled with obvious pride. "Thank you."

"Do you remember who might have been in here last Sunday or Monday?"

"You mean around the time that unfortunate woman was killed?" He shook his head. "No, I'm sorry. One day does tend to blend into the next."

"Could you perhaps recall the names of those who might have been here in the last several weeks?"

He looked vaguely uncomfortable. "Perhaps. But . . . I really don't think I ought to be providing such information to anyone. We may not be Papists, but we are still bound by the sanctity of the confessional."

She shifted her gaze to the window and the expanse of worn, leaning headstones that stretched beyond it. "I'm told Sybil Moss is buried in your churchyard."

"Sybil?" Underwood's face went slack with puzzlement. "She is, yes. Why do you ask?"

"I'd like to see her grave."

Chapter 39

Hero stood beside the low, lichen-covered wall separating the churchyard from the rocky hillside above. The weathered gray stone at her feet was small and unmarked, with a freshly picked bunch of lavender resting against it.

She pressed the fingers of one hand against her lips as she felt an oppressive sadness wash over her. She could think of no greater sorrow for a mother than to bury her child. The very air here seemed heavy with despair, as if Anne Moss's grief clung to this place, keeping her dead child company even when she was elsewhere.

The angry caw of a blackbird cut through the silence. Hero looked up to see a tall, lean gentleman in doeskin breeches and an exquisitely tailored coat working his way toward her through the scattered tombs. There was dust on his fashionable beaver hat and traces of mud on his black top boots, and she waited until he came right up to her before saying, "How many miles have you driven in the last several days?"

"Too many," said Devlin, and swept her into his arms.

It was a raw kiss, full of want and need, and probably totally inappropriate for a churchyard. And she knew then that whatever he'd discovered had left him troubled and unsettled.

He let his hands slide down her arms, his forehead resting against hers for a moment before he released her.

He nodded to the small, plain marker beside her. "Whose grave is this?"

"Sybil Moss's."

"So she wasn't buried at the crossroads after all."

"No. The vicar managed to convince the jury she wasn't in her right mind." Hero paused. "The other girl, Hannah, wasn't as lucky."

She was aware of him studying her face and wondered what he saw there. "You still think the deaths of those two young women are linked to what happened to Emma?"

"Yes. Although I can't understand how."

He reached out to take her hand in his. "I think I may have an idea."

They sat beneath a gnarled old yew on a bench looking out over the churchyard's undulating turf and ancient, timeworn gravestones. He told her what he had learned about the woman called Emma Chandler and the tragic young earl's daughter who had given her birth.

"That poor girl," said Hero when he had finished.

"Which one? Lady Emily or her daughter?"

"Both, actually. I never cared for Lady Heyworth. But I hadn't realized quite how despicable she actually is."

" 'To coddle the fruits of sin is to condone the act that created them,' " quoted Devlin.

"She said that?"

"No; that was Miss Rowena LaMont."

"Lovely."

She understood now why what he'd discovered about Emma Chandler had affected him so profoundly. Like Devlin, Emma had been desperate to learn the truth about her birth and had come to this seemingly quiet, picturesque village on a quest to discover the identity of the unknown man who had fathered her.

"Is that why Emma crossed Squire Rawlins's name off her list?" said Hero. "Because she was actually looking for Archie's father and she realized the man was dead?"

"Except she didn't cross off Lord Seaton's name even though she knew before she came here that he's dead too. She crossed off Atwater, although he's still very much alive. And she drew Archie's portrait, remember?"

Hero thought about the way she herself had scrutinized the paintings in the Long Gallery at Northcott Abbey, searching for some elusive trace of resemblance between Sebastian and those centuries of long-dead Seatons. "Emma was an artist, accustomed to analyzing her subjects' facial features. Perhaps that's why she drew Archie—because she was looking for a likeness between him and herself, and she eliminated him when she didn't find it."

"It's possible. Or perhaps she crossed him off her list when she discovered the old Squire was as fair as his son."

"Was he?"

"I don't know. But Atwater is sandy haired."

Hero lifted her gaze to the ruins of the old medieval watchtower on the hilltop above them. "Sybil's mother doesn't believe her daughter killed herself—she says the girl was proud of the baby she was carrying. Although of course that could have changed very quickly if the baby's father rejected her, which is quite likely if he was a gentleman."

"Was he?"

"Her mother thought so."

"What about the other girl?"

"Hannah Grant? If she was with child, her mother didn't know about it. But they never did a postmortem, so she might have been." Hero stared out over the scattered gravestones, more sparse on this, the north side of the church. The north was traditionally considered unlucky, so people didn't like to be buried there. "You think the same man could have killed all three young women? Sybil and Hannah because they were carrying his child, and Emma because she was his child?"

Devlin squinted against the westering sun. "If he did, then our list of possible suspects has just been reduced to two: the Reverend Underwood and Major Weston."

She looked at him in surprise. "What makes you say that?"

"Atwater is fair-haired; Seaton and Rawlins are dead; and I can't see anyone else in the village caring how many chance children he begets—or being educated enough to come up with an appropriate Shakespearean quote. Thanks to the old schoolmaster Archie's father brought in, a fair number of the villagers are literate. But I doubt any of them are devotees of Elizabethan plays."

Hero said, "Not only is Atwater fair, but according to Anne Moss, he's been desperately in love with Lady Seaton ever since he came here as steward. And when I think about the way he looked at her at dinner, I believe it."

"Which brings us back to Weston and Underwood."

She told him then about the discovery of the vicar's copy of *Hamlet*. "Underwood claims someone must have taken the book from his library."

"You believe him?"

"I don't know. Sybil's mother told me the vicar has always had an eye for pretty girls. Which is interesting because the vicar himself used the exact same phrase—pretty girls—when we were talking about Reuben Dickie. Seems Reuben has a nasty habit of peeking though the windows of cottages with attractive young women. He's not supposed to go out after dark, but as we know, he does."

"Interesting. Have you told Archie?"

She shook her head. "He's gone off to Ludlow in search of Emma Chandler's solicitors."

The bell in the church tower began to peal, slowly counting out the hour as Devlin rose to his feet. "I think I need to have a little chat with Reuben Dickie. He knows damned well where he found that book."

Hero rose with him. "What I don't understand is, why would he lie?"

"I suspect the answer to that depends on where he actually found it."

Chapter 40

*T*he village pump house was empty, the green deserted except for a couple of fat, waddling ducks that quacked at Sebastian as he stood for a moment beside the weathered old building. Then he went to knock at the last of that line of half-timbered, thatched cottages overlooking the broad expanse of turf.

The door was opened by a slight, aging woman with a deeply lined face and white hair so thin it showed the pink scalp beneath. At the sight of Sebastian, she sucked in a startled breath and bobbed an awkward curtsy. The room behind her was small and low ceilinged, with dark, heavy beams and a vast, old-fashioned stone hearth from which rose the pleasant aroma of stewing mutton and onions.

"Mrs. Dickie?" said Sebastian with a smile as he politely doffed his hat. "Sorry for disturbing you, but I'm looking for your son Reuben."

"Reuben?" She clutched the edge of the door with gnarled, arthritic hands. "What's he done?"

"Nothing. I simply had some questions I wished to ask him."

"He's usually at the—" She broke off, her eyes narrowing as she gazed beyond him, to the pump house. "Oh."

"You wouldn't happen to know where he might have gone?"

Her gaze met his, then slid away. "He likes to wander, ye know. Always goin' off, he is. But he should be back by dinnertime. He does like his dinner, our Reuben. Ye want I should tell him yer lookin' for him, my lord?"

"That would be helpful. Thank you."

She bobbed another curtsy. But her face was tight, her eyes pinched with a fear that was both furtive and telling.

Hiring a hack from Martin McBroom's stables, Sebastian rode out to the former Dower House of Maplethorpe Hall.

He could see Liv Weston deadheading spent blooms in the long border when he reined in before the house's simple portico. She had an unfashionable straw hat tied over her fair hair and an apron protecting her serviceable, faded gown of dark blue muslin; a deep, weathered basket hung by its handle on one crooked arm.

"My husband isn't here," she said when Sebastian left his horse in the groom's care and walked up to her.

"Actually, I'd like to speak with you, if you don't mind."

She tilted her head to one side. "Why would I mind?"

Her face was faintly lined and browned from her days spent in the garden, her nose small and upturned, her cheeks rosy. She didn't strike Sebastian as the type of woman who would succumb to a fit of the vapors if she chanced to overhear her husband discussing an unknown woman's murder. So why had Weston been so anxious that first day to keep Sebastian away from his wife?

He said, "We've recently discovered that Emma Chance—or rather, Chandler—was the natural daughter of Lady Emily Turnstall. I understand you knew her."

Liv Weston's face went slack with surprise. "Emily? I knew her, yes. We were in school together for a year, in Hereford. I had no idea she—"

She broke off, her breath hitching. "Dear God, is that how Emily died? In childbirth?"

Sebastian shook his head. "No. Although it wasn't long afterward. When was the last time you saw her?"

"It must have been . . ." She paused, thoughtful. "Yes—it was at a house party my parents gave the autumn before she died."

"Did she ever contact you after that?"

"She wrote to thank us, of course. But when I sent her a letter several weeks later, she never answered." Liv Weston was silent a moment, obviously doing sums in her head. "When was her child born?"

"Late May. I'm told it came some weeks early."

Sebastian watched as a strange hardness crept over her features. "Who fathered her child? Do you know?"

"No. It's why Emma Chandler was here, in Ayleswick; she was trying to find out. Did you not recognize her? She resembled her mother quite strongly."

Liv Weston shook her head. "No. To be honest, I have only the vaguest recollections of what Emily looked like. It's been so long. But . . . good heavens. Are you suggesting that's why the young woman was killed?"

He met her gaze squarely. "I think it a strong possibility, yes. How well do you remember that September? Do you have any idea who might have fathered Lady Emily's child?"

"Honestly? No. I was seventeen and very much wrapped up in my own affairs, while Emily . . . She was quite pretty, you know. Pretty and fabulously wellborn as well as wealthy. I remember being rather envious of all the admiration and attention she attracted from everyone without even trying." She paused. "It's not something I'm proud of."

"Yet you invited her."

"I did, yes. We were friends at school. I liked her. But that didn't stop me from being jealous once I saw how all the gentlemen reacted to her. When I heard that next summer that she had died, I felt . . . very small."

It was a startlingly frank admission. Liv Weston was obviously one of those rare people who had no difficulty acknowledging her faults. In that, she was most unlike her husband.

Sebastian said, "Whoever fathered Lady Emily's child forced her."

"Please tell me it wasn't someone at our house party."

"Not a houseguest, no. She told her governess it was someone who lived in the area."

Liv Weston was silent again, and he knew she was running through the possibilities in her mind. Had she noticed Major Weston's long-ago flirtation with the pretty young earl's daughter? Sebastian wondered.

Surely she had.

He said, "Do you remember anything—anything at all—from those days that might help make sense out of what is happening now?"

"Not really. You know what house parties are like. Lots of harmless flirting and some not-so-harmless affairs." She let the basket slide down her arm to her hand and set it on the grass path at her feet, the secateurs resting atop the cuttings. She straightened slowly, the fingers of her hands knit together before her. "There is one thing. . . . Emily had what I thought at the time a rather strange fascination with a boy down at the Ship."

"You mean, Jude Lowe?"

She shook her head. "No, not Lowe; his brother. He was slightly younger than she was, but so very attractive. It was as if she were obsessed with him. I remember he had the strangest yellow eyes; I'd never seen anything like them. I mean . . ." She stared at Sebastian, a faint touch of color riding high on her cheeks, then looked pointedly away.

He said, "You mean Jamie Knox?" Knox wasn't actually Lowe's brother. But the two had been raised together like brothers, and Sebastian could see Liv Weston making the mistake.

"Yes, that was his name. He went away a few years later, after the trouble we had. Frankly, I was glad to see the back of him. He may have been young, but he was dangerous. If anyone forced Emily, I'd say it was him. Jamie Knox."

Sebastian was seated at a table near the front leaded window of the Ship's public room, a tankard of ale before him, when Lowe came to pull out the opposite chair, turn it around, and straddle it.

"I hear you've been away for a few days," said the publican, resting his forearms along the chair's back.

Sebastian took a long swallow of his ale. "I have."

"And did you discover what you were looking for?"

"Partially." Sebastian set the tankard aside. "What can you tell me about the deaths of Sybil Moss and Hannah Grant?"

Lowe regarded him fixedly for a moment before answering. "Why are you asking about things that happened fifteen years ago?"

"Because I'm not convinced their deaths were suicides."

Lowe blew out a long, harsh breath. "You and a fair number of other people."

"Oh? How well did you know them?"

"Well enough. I was more than a bit sweet on Hannah when I was a lad, and Sybil was my niece."

"Anne Moss is your sister?"

"My half sister, yes."

Sebastian was reminded, again, of just how interwoven the relationships between the inhabitants of a small, isolated village like this could be. "Do you know who the girls were seeing?"

"Everybody knew. It wasn't as if he ever tried to hide it."

"He?"

"Seaton—the present lord's father. Acted like he had some sort of medieval droit du seigneur over the prettiest girls in the village. Most of them lay with him willingly enough. But he wasn't above forcing those who resisted."

Sebastian studied the publican's lean, dark face. "You think he could have killed them?"

Lowe shrugged. "Somebody did. I always figured he was as likely as anyone else."

"What manner of man was he?"

"Leopold Seaton? Arrogant. Selfish. Thought the world owed him anything and everything he ever wanted. He was a rich lord—came into his inheritance when he was quite young. What do you suppose he was like?"

Sebastian sipped his ale. "You wouldn't happen to recall a young gentlewoman named Lady Emily Turnstall? She was a guest at one of the Irvings' house parties back in the early nineties."

The publican's mouth twisted in wry amusement. "Me and the Irvings, we were never exactly on visiting terms, you know."

"I'm told she was rather taken with Jamie Knox."

Lowe held himself very still. "Ah. I think maybe I do remember the lass, though I couldn't have told you her name or even what she looked like. She wanted Jamie to let her draw his picture."

"And did he?"

"He did, yes."

"Was she a good artist?"

"Not bad. Nothing near as impressive as the young widow was killed last week, mind you. But not bad."

Emma's artistic ability obviously hadn't come from her mother. So where had it come from? Sebastian wondered. Or had it been a gift, a talent that was uniquely her own?

"What's she got to do with anything?" asked Lowe.

"Perhaps nothing."

Lowe grunted. "Right. That's why you're asking about her, is it?"

Sebastian ran one finger up and down the side of his tankard. "Why did Knox leave Ayleswick?"

"M'mother told him to go. She was afraid he was gonna end up like Alex."

"You mean Alex Dalyrimple?"

"Aye."

"Who cut Dalyrimple down?"

Lowe's hard gaze met Sebastian's and held it. "He was Jenny's husband. You think we were going to leave him up there to rot?" He looked around as two carters came into the public room, covered with dust from the road and calling loudly for ale.

Sebastian kept his gaze on the tavern keeper. "Is it true what they say? That he was conspiring with the French?"

"True?" Lowe gave a mirthless laugh. "Since when did the Crown ever care about the truth of their charges? Oh, Alex was a member of the local Corresponding Society; he never denied that. Thought every man should have the right to vote and even run for Parliament, if he wanted. That's a far cry from 'conspiring' with the French. But a lot more dangerous when it comes right down to it, don't you think?"

Sebastian studied the publican's lean, handsome face. Jude Lowe would have been just sixteen or so himself in those days. What part had he played in the incidents that ended with four men hanged, six transported, and Alex Dalyrimple's body rotting in chains on a gibbet?

"When did Leopold Seaton die?" asked Sebastian.

"Few years after they killed Alex. Why?"

"Did Seaton play a part in that? Alex's execution, I mean."

"Not so much."

"How did he die?"

"Seaton? Fell off his horse drunk one night, riding home from the Blue Boar. Hit his head on the side of the bridge not too far from his gatehouse." Lowe wrapped his hands around the back of his chair, his dark eyes narrowed, thoughtful. "It all happened long ago. Why are you bringing it up now?"

Rather than answer, Sebastian said, "Knox's sister, Jenny, never remarried?"

"No. She had a boy, Nicholas, born just a few months after they hanged Alex. I think he's what kept her going at first. But the lad died when he was still a wee tyke. And when he did, it was like any joy she had left in life just drained away. Those were hard years hereabouts. Right hard."

"Hard and dangerous," said Sebastian.

But Lowe simply shrugged one shoulder, as if for the villagers of Ayleswick the two were one and the same.

Chapter 41

After Devlin left, Hero hired the little mare again from Martin McBroom's stables and rode out to Northcott's home farm for her appointment with Samuel Atwater. She found the steward supervising the storing of a load of newly harvested grain in the ricks.

"Devlin tells me you're a critic of the enclosure movement," she said after her groom had taken the horse off and they turned to walk up the lane.

"That surprises you?" said Atwater.

She found herself smiling. "Actually, it does. I would think that as a steward, you'd be the first to criticize the ancient open-field system."

The laugh lines beside his eyes deepened as he squinted into the distance. "Perhaps I'm simply getting old. I liked England the way it was when I was a lad. But we'll never see those days again, will we? And it isn't only the look of the land that's changed, I'm afraid; the people have changed too. Time was, Englishmen were part of a community; they had a stake in the land they worked. But not anymore. The enclosures have changed our entire sense of who and what we are."

"You must admit the old ways were wasteful," said Hero.

"You mean, the three-course rotation system? Oh, aye; but that wasn't the fault of the open-field system. Four-course rotation can work in an open field as easily as on a rich man's enclosed estate."

"Yet surely it's easier to get one man to change his ways than to get fifty to agree to it?"

"Not if those fifty are educated. But then, that's the last thing those pushing for enclosure want, now, isn't it? Education makes men dangerous."

It was a remarkably radical thing to say, and Hero found herself wondering if Samuel Atwater, like Alex Dalyrimple, had been a member of one of the Corresponding Societies that sprang up across England in the first days of the French Revolution.

"Those are the arguments used to justify enclosures," he was saying. "But they make about as much sense as the argument that access to commons makes men too lazy to work for wages." He gave a rough laugh. "I wonder how willing the likes of Malthus and Burke would be to spend sixteen hours working in a factory for a shilling a day."

"Or down in a mine," said Hero.

He threw her a quick, penetrating glance. "You've read Adam Smith?"

"I have, yes."

"Smith claimed the best way to help the poor is by making the rich richer. And we've seen how well that's worked, now, haven't we? I suppose that's why the population of America is swelling with all the families we've pushed off the land here. Those who lived long enough to make it there, at any rate."

Hero watched the sun slip behind the oak trees lining the lane, leaving them in shadow. She said, "I've seen what's left of the hamlet of Maplethorpe. It's very sad."

"You should have seen it back in 'ninety-five, when wages were falling as fast as prices were rising, and folk took to wearing shirts made of sackcloth and eating acorns. A lot of the little ones died—the little ones, and the old." He took a breath that lifted his chest. "The thing is, you drive the cottagers and small farmers off the land, and most everyone else suffers too, don't they? How're the millers and thatchers, the carpenters and shoemakers, to feed their families if there's no work for them? Only ones don't suffer are the rich men in their big houses."

"Yet George Irving is dead, and his big house a ruin."

"Aye, that's true enough."

"I'm told you had a run-in some years ago with a group of men in blackface."

"I did, yes. But they did me no harm. You'll find no mantraps or spring guns on Northcott—not while I'm steward here, at any rate. It's a sorry state of affairs when a rich man's deer, hare, and pheasant are allowed to eat a poor man's crops, and there's nothing he can do about it without hanging."

"Was Irving behind the hangings and transportations that took place in the parish twenty years ago?"

"Of course he was. He couldn't catch the protestors at what they were doing, so he hired someone to make things up. And it worked, didn't it?"

"Do you believe the fire that killed him was an accident?"

Atwater glanced up at the dark shapes of swifts darting across the sky above. "You've heard about the Earl over in Oxfordshire who evicted all his cottagers and leveled their village so he could expand his park, only to go hunting one day and fall down the abandoned well of one of the cottages he'd leveled? His greed killed him, didn't it? It doesn't happen often, but every once in a while people do get what they deserve in this life."

He drew up then and turned to face her. "Never tell me you're thinking there's some connection between the events of fifteen and twenty years ago and what's happening now?"

"Devlin thinks it a possibility, yes."

He frowned. "You've read Goldsmith's poem? 'The Deserted Village'?"

"Yes."

Atwater nodded. "It's good you're writing this article. Someone needs to explain what the enclosures are doing—someone besides the poets. A hundred years from now, their words will be dismissed as romantic sentimentalism—if they're read at all."

Hero studied the steward's plain, earnest face and knew a whisper of disquiet. "We still read Shakespeare."

"We do. So we do," he said quickly, clearing his throat in a way that made her wonder if his thoughts had paralleled hers. "And now you must excuse me. I see another wagon coming in from the fields. Shall I send a man for your groom?"

Later, when the sun was high in the sky, Hero walked up the lane to the ruined medieval tower that overlooked Ayleswick and its surrounding countryside. She was sitting with her back to one of the crumbling walls, her gaze on the ghostly traces of the lost furrows and ridges of the past, when she noticed Sebastian climbing the hill toward her.

"It's an impressive view," he said, coming to sit beside her.

She shifted to lean gently against him. "I keep thinking that if I stare at it long and hard enough, everything will make sense."

"Is it helping?"

"No," she said with a laugh. "I had an interesting interview with Samuel Atwater this morning. He's . . . very radical."

"He is, indeed."

"You think that might be significant?"

"I think it could be." He told her then of his conversations with Liv Weston and Jude Lowe. When he had finished, she said, "Is it possible Leopold Seaton was Emma's father?"

"I'm beginning to think he was. But we may never know for certain."

She was silent a moment, her gaze on the rain clouds bunching over the Welsh mountains to the west. "While you were gone, I borrowed the Reverend Underwood's copy of *Debrett's Peerage*, along with a weighty history of Scotland and another of Wales."

He turned his head to look at her. "And?"

"Guinevere Stuart did marry a Scottish laird, Malcolm Gordon. In addition to her seven ill-fated sons, she had a daughter she named Addienna after her mother."

"So that part of the tale is true."

"It is. Addienna married a Welsh nobleman, the Earl of Penlynn, and had two daughters and four sons."

"And it was one of those daughters who married a Lord Seaton?"

Hero nodded. "Isabella. It was with Isabella Seaton that Guinevere first took refuge after her husband divorced her. But the Lord Seaton of the time wasn't comfortable with her presence, so Guinevere lived the last years of her life in Wales with her daughter Addienna."

Hero hesitated, and after a moment Devlin said, "There's something else; what is it?"

She met his strange yellow gaze and held it. "It's about Guinevere's daughter, Addienna—the one who married the Earl of Penlynn."

"Yes?"

"Three of her four sons joined the Jacobite cause along with her seven brothers and were all killed. But the eldest son, Edwyn, publicly repudiated his brothers and became, in time, the next Earl of Penlynn. By all accounts, he was a rather unpleasant fellow and eventually died without a son of his own. But he did have one daughter, Katherine, born late in his life. Katherine married unwisely, probably out of desperation to get away from her father."

Devlin kept his gaze on her face, and she wondered what he saw there. "Hero, what are you trying to tell me?"

She sucked in a deep breath that did nothing to ease the strange pressure in her chest. "Katherine married the Earl of Atherstone and died giving birth to a daughter, also named Guinevere."

Devlin stood up abruptly and went to stare out over the valley below. "I take it this daughter is the same Guinevere who married the Marquis of Anglessey several years ago?"

"Yes." It was through Guinevere Anglessey that Devlin had recovered his mother's necklace when it was found clasped around the beautiful young woman's dead body.

It was a long moment before he spoke, his voice scratchy with the intensity of his emotions. "Someone told me once that Katherine Atherstone's great-grandmother was burned as a witch. But that can't be true if her great-grandmother was Guinevere Stuart."

Hero went to stand beside him. "No; Guinevere Stuart lived to be a hundred and two. But such tales are often corrupted and twisted as they're passed down through the generations. It could have been some earlier ancestor."

"Perhaps. Yet none of this explains why my mother was given the necklace."

"No."

They watched as a tall, slender young woman with a basket over one arm left the cottage near the millstream and turned toward the village. After a moment, Sebastian said, "I sometimes wonder if the problem is that I keep trying to find connections where none actually exist—between my mother and the necklace and the women who once possessed it, and between the dark past of this village and these recent murders."

"There's a connection," said Hero, slipping her hand into his. "In both cases. We simply haven't discovered it yet."

Chapter 42

Some twenty minutes later, Sebastian was waiting outside the village shop while Jenny Dalyrimple exchanged the two pounds of butter she'd made for a length of candlewicking and other supplies. She packed her purchases in her basket, then cast him a decidedly hostile look as she left the shop and turned toward home.

"What you want with me?" she asked as he fell into step beside her.

"I want to know how Alex Dalyrimple came to be accused of working with the French."

She kept walking, her gaze on the road ahead. "What difference does it make to you?"

"It does. Isn't that enough?"

For a long moment, he didn't think she meant to answer him. Then she said, "You ever hear of Colonel Edward Despard?"

Sebastian suspected there were few in England who hadn't heard of Colonel Despard. An army officer who had served with distinction from Jamaica and the American colonies to Honduras, Despard was accused by a government informant of plotting to seize control of the Bank of England and kill King George III. It was true that Despard had become a vocal member of one of the many Corresponding Societies that sprang up across Britain in the years after 1789. But the Corresponding Societies were legal in those days, and the evidence for the outlandish charges against him was laughably weak. That didn't stop the attorney general, Spencer Perceval, from putting him on trial, along with six coconspirators. Admiral Nelson himself testified in Despard's behalf, but all seven were nevertheless convicted of high treason and sentenced to be hanged, cut down while still alive, disemboweled, beheaded, and quartered.

At the last minute, fear of a public revolt caused the government to abandon the medieval ritual of torture and dismemberment they'd planned, and Despard was simply hanged and beheaded. But Sebastian had never believed the colonel guilty of anything more than admiration for the principles espoused by Thomas Paine and the American and French Revolutions.

That, and marrying a beautiful young black woman descended from slaves.

He said, "I'm told your husband was a member of the local Corresponding Society."

"He was. But so was lots of others, back then." She stared off down the winding road, the features of her face held tight. "Alex dreamt of a day when every Englishman rich or poor would have the right to vote and run for Parliament. When every child could learn to read and write, and a man couldn't be thrown in prison for the crime of speaking his mind. But that doesn't mean he didn't love his country. It was because he loved England so much that he wanted it made better for everyone— not just for the likes of George Irving or Lord Seaton."

"Who accused him?"

"A nasty little weasel named Wat Jones. We learned later he was paid to do exactly what he did—worm his way into the local Corresponding Society so he could then denounce all his friends to the authorities with a pack of lies."

"Who paid him? George Irving?"

"I always thought so. But it could even have been the high-and-mighty

Earl of Powis himself, for all I know. Alex stirred up the whole county with his ideas. That's why they knew they had to find a way to kill him."

"How old was he?"

"Twenty-two."

They'd reached the cottage, and she drew up to turn and face him. "Alex's been dead twenty years, and nothing he dreamt of seeing has ever come to pass. The hamlet of Maplethorpe is little more than a memory, and now Jamie's dead too."

"It will come to pass someday," said Sebastian. "The things he fought for. They will."

She gave a sharp, disbelieving laugh. But there was a fragility, a bleakness about her that touched his heart. "So saith his lordship, son and heir to the great Earl of Hendon."

Rather than answer her, Sebastian said, "Jamie told me once that his father was either an English lord, a Welsh cavalryman, or a simple stable hand. Could the English lord he suspected have been Lord Seaton?"

"Not his lordship, no. But he was some sort of relative of the Seatons. They both were—the English lord and the captain both."

"And the stable hand? Who was he?"

"Just some good-looking lad m'mother fancied."

"From Northcott Abbey?"

She tipped her head to one side, her gaze on his face. And he knew she both sensed and understood the quiet desperation that drove his questions. "No, from Maplethorpe Hall."

He thought for a moment she meant to say something more—that she knew more.

Then she turned and entered the cottage, closing the door behind her.

Chapter 43

Sebastian was headed back toward the Blue Boar when he noticed Reuben Dickie sitting on the pump house step, his head bowed over his carving.

"I've been looking for you," said Sebastian, walking over to him.

Reuben froze, his eyes darting this way and that, as if he were thinking of bolting. "Mumma said you was. It's 'cause of the book, ain't it? But I already told the lady, I don't remember where I found it."

"Do you remember when you found it?"

Reuben shook his head slowly back and forth. "It's been a while."

"Was it by the river? Or somewhere else?"

"I dunno."

"Did you find anything with it?"

Reuben's nostrils flared on a suddenly indrawn breath. "What would I find with it?"

"A satchel. Or a sketchbook, perhaps."

"No. Oh, no."

The man was an appallingly bad liar.

Sebastian said, "You won't get into trouble for it, you know. In fact, you'd be a hero, for finding something we've all been looking for."

Reuben dug the toe of one clog into the dirt. "You're trying to trick me, aren't you? You think I'm stupid. Well, I'm not stupid."

Sebastian tried a different tack. "I hear you like to go out at night."

"I ain't supposed to go out at night."

"But you do sometimes, don't you?"

Reuben shook his head again, harder and faster this time. "Things happen at night. Things people don't want you to see."

"Oh? Such as?"

Reuben quit shaking his head as a sly smile crept over his features. "You don't know, do you? You think I'm so stupid, but there's lots of things I knows that you don't."

Sebastian leaned against one of the pump house's worn columns and crossed his arms at his chest. "If I wanted to find out about those things, where would you suggest I look?"

Reuben's tongue crept out to lick his lips. "Depends what things you want to know about."

Sebastian simply stared at Reuben expectantly, and after a moment his silence goaded the other man into saying, "Ain't nothin' there now, but if you'd looked in Maplethorpe Hall's old carriage house a few days ago, ye might've seen somethin'."

"How many days ago?"

"Oh, maybe around the time that pretty young widow was kilt," Reuben said airily, and went back to his whittling.

Sebastian watched the man's short, incredibly deft fingers peel away curls of wood to reveal what he now realized was a badger.

"Saw her, too, you know," said Reuben abruptly.

"You mean, the night before she was killed?"

Reuben sucked his lower lip between his small, oddly spaced teeth as he focused on his carving. "I ain't allowed out at night, remember? But she was up real early that mornin'."

"You saw Emma Chandler on Monday morning?"

Reuben kept his attention focused on his carving. "Mm-hmm."

"Did she have her sketchbook with her?"

"What's a sketchbook?"

"The notebook she drew pictures in." Was it significant, Sebastian wondered, that Reuben hadn't asked, *What's a sketchbook?* when Sebastian first inquired after it?

"Reckon she did," said Reuben.

"Where did you see her, Reuben? And don't pretend you don't remember, because I won't believe you."

Sebastian said it with just enough menace in his voice that Reuben's hands went slack, the knife tumbling from his grasp as his mouth formed a startled "O."

"The old pack bridge, down past Maplethorpe," he said in a rush, scrambling after his knife. "She was paintin' a picture of it in that notebook of hers. What'd you call it?"

"A sketchbook. Did you speak with her?"

"Jist to say she was up awful early."

"And what did she say?"

"She said she hadn't been able to sleep, so she figured she may as well come paint the sunrise."

"At the pack bridge?"

Reuben nodded vigorously. "Said it was real pretty, she did."

A single arch of dark, old red brick, the pack bridge was a relic of an earlier age, when England's roads were so abysmal that most goods were hauled across country not in wagons or by canals, but on pack animals. Its track was narrow and seldom used now, but not entirely abandoned.

Sebastian stood on the grassy bank of the River Teme, the tip of his riding crop tapping against his high-topped boots. The sun was beginning to sink in the sky, the air heavy with the scent of the mint that grew in the dark, damp shadows of the bridge.

It was an out-of-the-way, deserted place for a young woman to visit alone, even in broad daylight. What the hell had possessed Emma to come here early on the morning of the day she was fated to die?

He climbed back up the bank to where he had left his rented hack, his gaze narrowing as he turned again to study the track that crossed the bridge and disappeared into the wasteland on the opposite bank. A marshy, uncultivated stretch of bracken and scrub, it extended as far as he could see. But somewhere to the south, he knew, lay the estuary of the River Severn and Bristol Channel and, beyond that, the North Atlantic Ocean.

And France.

Maplethorpe's caretaker-gardener, Silas Madden, was weeding a bed at the far end of the water garden when Sebastian turned into the old hall's once grand, formal drive.

Sebastian continued on around the ruined, blackened walls of the burned house to where the stable block and carriage house still stood. He dismounted, his gaze on the wagon ruts he'd noticed that first day, dry and crumbling now in the heat of the afternoon. From the distance came a man's shout.

Sebastian ignored him.

A long, narrow structure built of the same red brick as the burned hall, the carriage house was quite large, with a row of six arched double doors. Each door sported a well-oiled and surprisingly heavy hasp and padlock, although most of the locks hung open.

Ain't nothin' there now, Reuben had said.

Sebastian thrust open the first set of doors, the afternoon sun throwing his shadow before him across the beaten-earth floor. It was a cavernous space, once home to traveling carriages, tilburies, whiskies, and dogcarts, but empty now except for a pile of discarded sacking, some cracked old harness hanging on a wall, and several bales of hay that looked very new indeed. A number of incongruous but undeniable scents lingered in the dusty air—pungent aromas left by recent stores of tobacco, wine, and brandy.

A noise from the near door brought Sebastian's head around. His gaze met Silas's.

"Tell Weston I want to see him," said Sebastian. "Here. Now."

Chapter 44

Major Eugene Weston arrived in less than ten minutes.

By then Sebastian was seated on a stone bench in the lea of one of the garden's high yew hedges. The major came striding up the track through the spinney, arms swinging, face red from a combination of physical exertion and righteous indignation. He drew up abruptly at the sight of Sebastian.

"I say," blustered Weston, hands clenched into fists at his sides. "It's not exactly the done thing, now, is it? Poking about without anybody's leave? Sending a man messages by his servants? How would you like it if—"

"In my experience," said Sebastian, crossing his arms at his chest and leaning back in his seat, "smuggling gangs have a nasty habit of turning lethal when they find themselves in danger of being exposed. Is that what happened? Did Emma Chandler accidently stumble into your little operation here? Is that why you killed her?"

"Kill her? Me? What a preposterous notion. And as for smuggling . . ." Weston gave a tinny laugh. "This isn't exactly Cornwall or Kent."

"True. Which makes it so much easier to maneuver, doesn't it? Far more comfortable to land your goods near Newport or Chepstow without all those annoying revenue officers sticking their noses into everything. Part of each cargo is probably sent directly to Hereford and Worcestershire, while from here you can supply all of Shropshire and a good section of the hills of eastern Wales, as well."

Weston gave Sebastian a wooden stare. "I don't know what you're talking about."

Sebastian heaved a pained sigh, his gaze on the major's flushed, sweaty face. "You basically have two options: You can tell me what I need to know, or you can answer some decidedly awkward questions posed by His Majesty's revenue men."

Weston spread his arms wide and smiled. "There is nothing here for anyone to find."

"Not now. But that can be fixed."

The smile slid off the major's face. "What does that mean?"

"Use your imagination. And if you take one more step, Silas," Sebastian added calmly as he shifted his weight to draw a small, double-barreled flintlock pistol from his pocket, "I'll blow your bloody head off. First yours, and then the major's."

Silas, who had been sidling toward him along the hedge with a pitchfork gripped purposefully in his hands, froze as Sebastian pulled back both hammers with an audible *click*.

Weston turned a sickly shade. "That will be all, Silas," he said, his voice wheezing. "Thank you."

For a moment, Silas looked as if he might balk. Then he shouldered his pitchfork and turned toward the stables.

Sebastian shifted the muzzle of his pistol to the major. "Make up your mind. I don't have all afternoon."

Weston waited until the caretaker was out of earshot, then cleared his throat, a tic spasming the flesh beside his right eye. "I have your word as a gentleman that if I answer your questions, you won't inform the revenue men?"

"Not unless I discover Emma Chandler was killed because of your little adventure."

Weston licked his dry lips. "What do you want to know?"

"What night did your latest cargo arrive?"

"A week ago yesterday."

"Sunday night?"

"Yes."

"And you sent it on again when?"

"The next night."

"So, Monday?"

Weston nodded, his jaw thrust forward in a way that pursed his lips.

The shipment would have been brought in from the estuary by pack-horses, then reloaded here into wagons and sent on its way buried beneath grain or some other legitimate product. And Sebastian found himself thinking about Reuben Dickie's brother, Jeb, and the shipment of timber he'd recently hauled to Wales.

"That's the night Emma Chance was killed," said Sebastian.

"Yes. But the one has nothing to do with the other. Absolutely nothing."

"Emma Chance didn't come back here again that evening and see something you didn't want her to see?"

"Of course not. How careless do you imagine we are?"

"And you're certain the shipment wasn't already in the carriage house the day she came to sketch the hall?"

"No! I tell you, it arrived that night, long after she'd finished and gone away. Besides, Silas was watching her the entire time she was here, just in case she got too curious."

"Pitchfork at the ready, one assumes."

"Don't be ridiculous."

"And the next night? What time did the wagons leave?"

"Just before dawn—so Tuesday morning, actually. Any earlier and there's always a danger of arousing suspicions."

"Were you here Sunday night?"

"Good God, no. You don't seriously think I deal with any of this myself?"

"No," said Sebastian.

Weston's role was undoubtedly minimal and would extend little beyond supplying the critically necessary funds. Smuggling was a lucrative but capital-intensive business. Because customers paid for their smuggled goods only on delivery, the money to finance each run up front had to come from the likes of merchants and landowners—wealthy men who risked their investment but not their lives.

The real dangers were run by others: by the crews of the black-hulled cutters that plied the channel; by the fishermen who ferried the cargo ashore in their small boats; by the impoverished, starving countryfolk who served as tubmen and batsmen, or who guided ponies loaded with ankers of brandy and wine or oilskin-wrapped packets of tobacco, silk, and lace. Moving under cover of darkness from one isolated safe house to the next, they were the ones who ferried the goods inland, the hooves of their pack animals muffled with rags. They were the ones who faced death or transportation if caught.

But while their risks were high, they were paid pennies. The handsome profits generated by their labors were pocketed by men like Weston, who were seldom caught. Yes, he allowed the old hall's carriage house to function as a way station. But if it were ever discovered, he could simply claim it was used without his permission or knowledge. The actual management of the operation would be handled by someone else—someone with the kind of skills needed to negotiate with ships' captains and coordinate the laborers who actually moved the goods. Someone who probably didn't even live in Ayleswick.

"What about Monday night?" said Sebastian. "Were you here then?"

"Of course not. What do you think? That I plow my own fields and shear my own sheep as well?"

"So how do you know what actually happened on either night?"

"Because I would have been told, had anything untoward occurred."

"Silas handles everything here, does he?"

"He's very reliable."

"I've no doubt that he is," said Sebastian. "How long have you been dabbling in the free trade?"

Weston's jaw jutted out mulishly. "What the devil business is it of yours?"

Sebastian pushed to his feet. "If you'd rather answer the questions of His Majesty's revenue men—"

"Fifteen years," snapped Weston. "What else was I to do, after Liv wheedled her father into leaving his will the way he did? He was in his dotage by then, you know. The will never should have been allowed to stand, but it was. So what would you have me live on? Pin money doled out by my own wife, just so she can waste the ready on her damned gardens? I had no choice!"

"It's her fault, is it?"

"Of course it is!" Weston stared at him, eyes wide, nostrils flaring with his hard, quick breaths.

Sebastian studied the man's flushed, overfed countenance. "Do you remember a young woman named Lady Emily Turnstall?"

Weston looked confused. "Who?"

"Lady Emily Turnstall. She attended a house party given by the Irvings in September of 1791. She was just sixteen, and very pretty."

Weston huffed a disbelieving laugh. "Do you seriously think I remember every green girl I ever met?"

"She was the daughter of the Earl of Heyworth. Quite richly dowered."

Weston shook his head. "Sorry. If I ever met her, I don't recall it. What has she to do with anything?"

"How about Alex Dalyrimple?" said Sebastian, ignoring the question. "The man who was gibbeted in 1793. You do recall him, don't you?"

"Of course I do. Radical bastard. If you ask me, he should have been drawn and quartered as well as gibbeted."

"Why?"

"What do you mean, *why?* The brute terrorized the entire parish for months. If he'd had his way, they'd have set up a guillotine on the village green! No man or woman of birth or breeding would have been spared."

"Took it personally, did you?"

"Who wouldn't take it personally?"

His tone was one of moral outrage. But there was an element of bluster there too, that told Sebastian the man was being less than honest.

About any number of things.

Chapter 45

The discovery that Ayleswick was part of an established smuggling conduit opened up a disturbing new possibility.

Free traders had long been used by both London and Paris to secretly slip men and messages back and forth across the Channel. And Sebastian had no doubt that Paris had moved quickly to exploit a smuggling operation that was already in existence when Lucien Bonaparte arrived in Shropshire as a paroled prisoner of war. From his days as an exploring officer, Sebastian knew enough about the way these things worked to have a pretty good understanding of how messages would move along the route, first to Ayleswick, and then to whatever trusted courier finally delivered the sealed packets to Bonaparte himself.

It was possible Eugene Weston knew his smuggling operation was being exploited by Paris, although Sebastian found that unlikely; the man's role was that of financier and nothing more. Yet given the distance of some thirty or more miles between Ayleswick and the Bonapartes' estate in Worcestershire, forwarding such messages would have been both time-consuming and delicate. Was that the real reason Lucien had brought his family to spend the summer at Northcott Abbey? To be in closer contact with Paris now that the situation on the Continent was

sliding toward disaster? Were the repairs to his estate simply a convenient excuse? And if so, what was Lady Seaton's role in all this? Did she
know of her guests' contact with Paris? Or was she simply being used?

Pondering the possibilities, Sebastian rode through the village,
then spurred his horse on to Northcott Abbey. As he rounded a bend
thickly planted with rhododendrons, a vista opened up before him and
he found himself looking down on the ornamental lake, its normally
placid, reflective surface now ruffled by a stiffening breeze. A familiar
figure clothed in breeches, high-top boots, and a well-tailored coat
paced back and forth before the picturesquely sited Roman temple.

Sebastian checked for a moment, then wheeled his horse down the
slope toward the lake.

The drum of hoofbeats brought Lucien Bonaparte around, his brow
furrowed with the agonies of poetic composition. But at the sight of
Sebastian, his face cleared. "Good afternoon, my lord! This is a pleasant
surprise."

Sebastian swung from the saddle and dropped easily to the ground.
"Good evening, Senator. How is the epic coming?"

Lucien Bonaparte heaved a weary sigh. "There is a reason the
ancients personified the Muses as female. I fear Calliope is a fickle creature, capricious and at times damnably difficult to woo."

"You come here every day to write?" asked Sebastian, his attention
shifting to the folly beside them. Although built as a ruin, the temple's
roof was more than solid enough to provide a poetically minded guest
with shelter from sun and rain. Through the single row of thick Doric
columns, Sebastian could see that Lady Seaton had even softened the
temple's stone benches with mounds of plump cushions in delicate
shades of teal and peach.

"Every day except Sunday, from ten to one," said the Senator with
obvious pride. "And sometimes, as today, I return again to work in the
late afternoon."

"Art requires dedication."

"It does, it does." Lucien's good-humored smile remained in place, but his eyes were shrewd and watchful. The man was no fool; he knew Sebastian wasn't here to discuss his epic poem on Charlemagne. "So tell me, my lord; how is your investigation into these dreadful murders progressing?"

"It's interesting, actually. I've just discovered that a shipment of French spirits passed through Ayleswick the very day Emma Chandler was killed."

Lucien Bonaparte kept his face admirably blank. "Oh?"

"Mmm. And it occurs to me that a message may have come with it—say, from Napoléon to you?"

In the sudden, tense silence, Sebastian could hear a thrush singing in a nearby stand of beech and the gentle slap of the wind-ruffled water lapping against the reeds edging the lake. The Corsican cleared his throat. "My brother and I are estranged. That is why I fled the Continent."

"Oh, I've no doubt you quarreled. Napoléon has quarreled—sometimes violently—with every one of his brothers and sisters multiple times over the years. But yours is still an extraordinarily close family. You always seem to make up your differences and come to each other's aid when threatened. And Napoléon has never been more threatened than he is now."

Lucien Bonaparte brought up a hand to tug at his earlobe, his dark eyes hooded, his gaze on the lake.

"What worries me," said Sebastian, "is the thought that Emma Chandler might somehow have stumbled upon a meeting between you and your brother's messenger, and that's why she was killed."

"But there is no communication between my brother and me."

"What about between you and your mother?"

Bonaparte fiddled with the chain of his pocket watch. "I am allowed to send letters to my mother through the commissioner."

"And if you wish to say something you don't want the commissioner—and everyone at Whitehall—to read?"

"Unfortunately, that is one of the inescapable trials of being a prisoner."

"Not so inescapable, surely?"

Bonaparte drew himself up to his full height. "Monsieur! One of the conditions of a gentleman's parole is that he not communicate with anyone except through the commissioners. I have given my word. You insult me."

"Do I?" Sebastian met the Senator's outraged gaze. He'd learned long ago that the rulers of this world operate on a different moral plane than other mere mortals. Their decisions—whether careless or calculated—often wreaked suffering and death on a scale unimaginable to anyone else. Taken all together, Sebastian figured the Bonaparte brothers were collectively responsible for the deaths of anywhere between three and six million people. When set against that level of carnage, what difference would the murder of one insignificant young woman make to someone like Lucien Bonaparte? And as he studied the Corsican's swarthy, Mediterranean features, so similar to those of his more famous, older brother in his prime, Sebastian knew a rush of raw anger and revulsion that he controlled with difficulty.

"If your presence in Ayleswick has anything to do with these murders," said Sebastian, "*anything*, then the deaths of both Emma Chandler and Hannibal Pierce are on your head and on your soul. Think about that while you wrestle with your recalcitrant muse," said Sebastian.

And he walked off and left Bonaparte there, beside the wind-ruffled lake and its pillow-filled folly.

Chapter 46

That evening, Sebastian and Archie met to compare notes over brandy in the Grange's ancient, oak-paneled hall. A relic of a bygone era, the hall was a cavernous space with a soaring, trussed-oak roof, thick walls, and flagstone paving. Even on an August night, it was chilly enough to warrant a small fire on the vast, old-fashioned hearth.

Archie listened, his face grim, while Sebastian told what he'd learned of Emma Chandler's determination to identify the man who had raped her mother. "My God," said the young Squire when Sebastian had finished. "Could my own father have done something like that? His name was on her list."

Sebastian took a slow sip of his brandy. "What color was your father's hair?"

"Lighter than mine. Why?"

"Because whoever raped Lady Emily was dark. It's probably why Emma crossed off his name—she somehow discovered your father was fair."

Archie stared at him. "She did! She actually asked me. And she did it so adroitly it didn't even occur to me to wonder at it."

He thrust up from his saggy armchair and went to throw another log on the fire. Then he stood with a palm braced against the aged chimneypiece as he stared down at the flames. "This changes every-thing, doesn't it?" he said after a moment. "How horrifying to think she could have tracked down her father only to have him kill her for it."

"If he did, it narrows our list of suspects considerably."

Archie looked over at him questioningly.

Sebastian said, "Like your father, Samuel Atwater is fair; Leopold Seaton and Jamie Knox are dead; and we both know Reuben Dickie is incapable of concocting such an elaborate ruse."

"Which leaves Underwood and Weston. Have you spoken with them?"

"Not Underwood. But Weston denies even remembering Lady Emily."

"Well, he would, wouldn't he?"

Sebastian swirled the golden brown liquid in his glass and said nothing. He had decided not to tell Archie about his discovery that afternoon at Maplethorpe Hall, or of his subsequent conversation with Lucien Bonaparte. Partially it was because he had given Weston his word as a gentleman that he wouldn't report his activities to the cus-toms officials, and he suspected that wouldn't sit well with the earnest young justice of the peace. But it was also because he was beginning to realize that Archie had a tendency to go off half-cocked after each bit of new information, and Sebastian wasn't yet convinced that what he'd learned had anything to do with Emma Chandler's murder.

"I'll admit I've never liked the man," Archie was saying. "And my father abominated him. But . . . do you actually think Weston is capable of murdering a young woman he thought was his own daughter?"

"We know he once seduced an innocent young girl simply to get his hands on her wealth. So I'd say, yes, someone that selfish could con-ceivably kill if he felt his interests or security were threatened. He'd simply convince himself the murder was the victim's own fault for ask-ing questions about something that happened twenty-two years ago." Sebastian paused. "Or for being so thoughtless as to fall pregnant."

Archie's features had taken on a pinched, troubled look. "In other words, Sybil Moss and Hannah Grant?"

Sebastian nodded. "I can't get past the idea that their deaths are linked to what's happening today. In my experience, once a man kills, it becomes much easier for him to kill again."

"Because he thinks that if he got away with it once, he can get away with it again?"

"That's part of it. But there's also a certain kind of man who discovers he enjoys killing. He likes the feeling of power it gives him."

"I must say, that does rather sound like Weston."

"It does, yes." Sebastian drained his brandy. "Tell me about the Ludlow solicitors."

It had taken Archie most of the day to track down the right solicitors, an old firm called Bieber and Smythe with offices on a narrow, winding street near the castle. Then the principal partner, Daniel Bieber, had insisted on accompanying him back to Ayleswick to view Emma Chandler's body and personally verify that she was, indeed, dead.

"Was he satisfied it's her?" asked Sebastian.

"Said he was—after he finished casting up his accounts behind one of the tombs in the churchyard. Thank God the Reverend will be able to bury her in the morning. I don't think anyone will be able to recognize her soon."

"Did Bieber tell you who she named in her will?" asked Sebastian.

"He balked at it, initially. But he finally had to agree it might be important. Seems she left everything to that former teacher of hers up in Little Stretton."

"Jane Owens?"

"Yes."

Sebastian watched the flames lick up around the new log on the hearth, his thoughts drifting to the sad-eyed woman in the simple thatched cottage beside the River Ashes Hollow. He knew even without being told how Jane Owens would use Emma's money: to open the school for chance children that had been the young woman's dream.

"There's something else," said Sebastian as Archie moved to refresh their drinks. "Something Lady Devlin discovered."

"Oh?"

While Archie poured another hearty measure of brandy in each glass, Sebastian told the young Squire about the Reverend's edition of *Hamlet*.

"You're saying the killer stole Underwood's copy of the play?" Archie set aside the decanter. "But why would he do that?"

Sebastian took the glass he held out. "Because he's too clever by half. He tucked the line from *Hamlet* into Emma's hand to reinforce the impression that she'd killed herself. But at the same time, the book could also be used to throw suspicion on the vicar if we ever realized her death was actually murder."

Archie came to sprawl in his chair again. "But unless the killer knew why Emma was here, what possible motive could he imagine the vicar might have?"

"None that I can see. Which brings us to the second possibility."

"Which is?"

"That Reverend Benedict Underwood is himself the killer, and he never intended his book to turn up."

Archie's eyes widened. "Good God."

Sebastian drained his glass in one long pull. "We need to know where Reuben Dickie found that damned book."

"I'll get it out of him first thing in the morning," said Archie. "Even if I have to beat it out of him."

But it was just after dawn the next morning when a cottager collecting firewood in the wasteland along the river found Reuben dead.

Chapter 47

Tuesday, 10 August

*R*euben Dickie lay sprawled facedown at a gravelly bend in the Teme, his arms flung wide, the side of his head a pulpy, bloody mess. More blood soaked the back of his smock where a jagged slice in the worn cloth showed a gaping, purple wound in the pale flesh beneath. He was close enough to the water's edge that one hand bobbed with the movements of the river as pond skaters flitted around his stiffening, puffy white fingers.

"Looks like he was stabbed in the back and had his head bashed in," said Archie, his face grim and slicked with sweat as he batted at the flies buzzing around them.

Sebastian crouched down beside the body. "Someone obviously wanted to make quite certain he was dead." Reuben's one visible eye stared back at him, wide and filmed with the beginnings of decay. From the distance came the slow, mournful echo of the funeral toll. The vicar had decided to go ahead with Emma Chandler's funeral despite the discovery of yet another murder, which meant that Constable Nash wouldn't be along until he'd finished his duties as bell ringer and sexton.

"How long do you think he's been dead?" asked Archie, making no move to come any closer.

Sebastian yanked off a glove to touch the dead man's cheek. "A while. He's cold."

"What I don't understand is, why would a killer go through the trouble of carefully staging Emma Chandler's death—and the others before her—to look like suicides or accidents, only to now start shooting people or bashing in their skulls?"

"Because once we'd figured out Emma's death wasn't a suicide, there really was no point anymore, was there?"

"I suppose not." Archie cast an uncomfortable glance around. "Was he killed here, do you think?"

"It looks like it. But then, I'm no expert. The gravel strikes me as rather convenient."

Archie shook his head. "I don't understand."

"No footprints."

"Ah. Yes." Archie stared across the river at a flock of geese that had been turned out into a recently harvested field. Later, cows would be set to graze on the stover, and later still, sheep. In the spring, the dung and the roots would all be plowed under in preparation for the planting of a new season's crop.

After a moment, Archie said, "Who would want to kill Reuben? I mean, yes, he could be damnably annoying. But he was essentially harmless."

"Whoever killed him obviously didn't think so."

An oilskin satchel lay half-hidden beneath the dead man's body, and Sebastian carefully eased it free. "Ever see Reuben with anything like this?"

"No."

"Then I think we know where he got it."

The satchel opened to reveal a lady's plain black reticule, a selection of drawing pencils, two erasers, and a large sketchbook.

"Good God," said Archie, his hands falling to his sides. "It's Emma

Chandler's." His gaze met Sebastian's. "Could Reuben have killed her after all?"

"If he did, then who killed Reuben?"

Archie huffed a startled laugh. "Ah. I hadn't thought of that."

Sebastian opened the sketchbook to find himself staring at a peaceful, idyllic watercolor of the village green. "I think it more likely that Reuben came upon Emma Chandler's body sometime late Monday night or early Tuesday morning, before young Charles Bonaparte found her."

"And simply took her satchel? What a ghoulish thing to do! Was the book with it, do you think?"

"Perhaps. Perhaps not. But if it was—and he did take the satchel from her body—it certainly explains why he didn't want to say where or when he'd found the vicar's book." Sebastian flipped several pages in the sketchbook and stopped at a somber charcoal drawing of the churchyard.

"What it doesn't explain is why he was killed."

"And here I was thinking the second sketchbook had disappeared because its contents would somehow implicate Emma's killer," said Hero. They were in their private parlor at the Blue Boar; Sebastian had laid Emma's sketchbook open on the small round table beneath the window.

"I thought the same," said Sebastian, beginning to turn the pages.

The first sketches were general scenes of the village, most done in pencil or charcoal, with a few more detailed studies in watercolors. There was the green with its timeworn pump house and a couple of fat ducks waddling across the grass. Then came pictures of the gently curving high street and the row of picturesque, half-timbered cottages that lined the green. And it occurred to Sebastian that it was possible to follow the passage of Emma's days at Ayleswick, simply by noting the order of her pictures.

On Saturday morning, at the same time she'd drawn Archie's

portrait, she'd also sketched some half dozen views of the Grange's ancient, ivy-draped tower and quiet moat. Invited to Northcott Abbey that afternoon by Lady Seaton, Emma had drawn the graceful old house from several angles, as well as the Greek temple overlooking the park's ornamental lake and the famous Long Gallery.

"Ah," said Hero, staring at Emma's exquisite rendering of the long, narrow room's soaring windows and elaborately plastered ceiling. "She must have asked Lady Seaton to show her the family portraits. Clever."

Simon started fussing from his rug near the cold hearth, and Sebastian went to pick up the boy, swinging him high. "Is there a portrait of Leopold Seaton in the Long Gallery?"

"There is, yes. Lady Seaton pointed it out to me. He was a startlingly handsome man."

"As is Crispin."

"Yes. But I didn't see much of a resemblance between father and son. The father was dark haired."

"Which explains why Emma didn't cross his name off her list," said Sebastian, coming to stand beside Hero again as she turned the next page.

They found themselves staring at the ruins of Maplethorpe Hall. Emma had drawn the house at eerie angles, so that the blackened walls seemed to loom over the viewer in a way that made it appear oppressive, almost threatening.

"Must have been strange for her, visiting the burned-out husk of the house that had played such a pivotal role in her mother's life," said Hero. "I wonder if she knew before she came here that the hall had burned."

"She may have heard about it from Crispin or his sisters. They must surely have spoken to her of their village long before she realized her own connection to Ayleswick."

Hero looked over at him. "I hadn't thought of that. Most of the names in her mother's letter were probably already familiar to her."

Emma had drawn some half dozen sketches of the burned old hall before moving on to the crossroads, where she captured the melancholy of the nearly abandoned hamlet and the bedraggled thatch and leaning chimneys of the Ship. Then came a haunting image of the gibbet, its blackened arm stark against a glaring sky.

"Do you think she did all these drawings to support her story of being on a sketching expedition?" said Hero. "Or was she simply intent on recording her father's village?"

"Could have been both."

Hero flipped the page to reveal an unexpectedly pastoral scene with cows grazing on the side of a long, grassy mound set against a background of old oaks.

"What the devil is that?" asked Sebastian as Simon began to fuss again.

Hero reached out to take the baby. "Mr. McBroom was telling me there's an ancient barrow several miles to the east of here, on the way to Ludlow. This must be it."

Sebastian studied the low, earthen mound, noting now the weathered stones thrusting up from the grass at one rounded end. "So when did Emma go there? And why?" He turned the page to find himself staring at a beautifully detailed watercolor of the pack bridge, its single brick arch silhouetted against a rising sun. "Huh. This was obviously painted on Monday morning. So she must have walked out to the barrow on Sunday evening. Why would she do that?"

He looked up, his gaze meeting Hero's. But she simply shook her head.

After the watercolor of the bridge came several drawings of Ayleswick's squat Norman church, then a sketch of a majestic rose window rising empty and solemn against a cloudless sky.

"The priory," said Hero.

There were two more drawings of the ruins. In one, a scruffy mongrel Sebastian recognized as the Seatons' dog, Barney, trotted nose-down along the remnants of the cloister. The other was a striking view of the ruins of the chapter house.

The next page was blank.

"Well, hell," said Sebastian.

Hero shifted Simon's weight to her hip. "Let me see the sketch of the barrow again."

Sebastian flipped back to the earlier drawing. It had rained later that evening, and Emma had drawn the storm clouds already pressing down dark and threatening over the landscape. But now, as he studied the ancient tumulus and the stand of trees that encroached upon it, he realized the scene was not entirely deserted. A half-grown, dark-haired boy in nankeens and a torn short coat stood near the trees, his head thrown back as he watched a peregrine circling overhead.

"Good heavens," said Hero. "That looks like Charles Bonaparte."

"Sunday?" said the Emperor Napoléon's precocious young nephew. He sat on the top rail of the paddock fence where Hero and Sebastian had found him watching a groom put a colt through his paces. "Yes. I was out by the barrow. Why?"

"Do you recall seeing Emma Chandler there?" asked Hero.

Charles looked confused. "Chandler?"

"We've discovered that was Emma Chance's actual name," explained Sebastian.

"Was it really?" The boy's eyes brightened with interest. "You mean, she was here under an alias? What was she? A spy? An assassin? A—"

"Did you see her at the barrow?" Sebastian asked again.

"Yes, sir." He gripped the top rail and swung his legs back and forth in a way that reminded them that he was still very much a child. "She asked what I knew about the place. I told her that long barrows like that date back to the Stone Age and were probably used for burial chambers. She was very interested." His eagerness faded away. "She was a nice lady. I'm sorry she's dead."

"Did you see the picture she drew out there?"

"I did, yes. She showed it to me. I wish I could draw like that. Wouldn't it be grand?"

"Which of you left first?" asked Hero.

The boy looked from Hero to Sebastian, and back again. "She did. Why?"

Sebastian said, "Did she walk toward the village?"

"I don't think I noticed which way she turned when she left. But I did see her again later, when I was on my way home."

"Oh?"

"She was near the top of that small rise—you know the one? Just before you reach the crossroads."

"What was she doing?"

"She was just standing by the hedgerow, talking to Crispin." The boy hesitated, then added, "I think she was crying. And Crispin, he looked as angry as all get-out."

Sebastian stared at him. "You mean, Crispin Seaton?"

"Yes, sir."

"Are you certain?" asked Hero.

"Oh, yes, ma'am," said young Master Bonaparte. "I don't think he saw me because he was focused so intently on her. But I remember it because I was surprised to see him. I mean, I thought he was still in the Lake District."

"Did you tell anyone you'd seen him?" asked Sebastian.

"I said something to Mama the next day. But he never showed up at Northcott, and my mother told me I must have been mistaken."

"Do you think were?"

Charles Bonaparte met his gaze, and there was something about his expression that made the boy seem older than his years. "I know I wasn't."

Chapter 48

Crispin Seaton sat beside the raw earth of Emma Chandler's grave, his head bowed, his forearms resting on spread knees. He didn't look up when Sebastian walked across the sunlit grass toward him. The sky was still brutally cloudless, and Crispin's small bunch of meadow daisies and poppies was already beginning to wilt in the heat.

Sebastian said, "I'm sorry."

The younger man nodded, his throat working hard as he swallowed. "I've been sitting here thinking about the first time I kissed her. The fields were dusted with a late snow and it was so cold, her nose was red, like a child's. But then I kissed her, and her lips were so warm. I remember looking into her eyes, and they were so soft, so beautiful, I knew then that I could look at her forever and never tire of it. And now . . . now she's down there in the ground. She can't see or feel anything, and I'll never be able to touch or look at her again. Ever."

Sebastian raised his gaze to stare up the hill, toward the ruined medieval watchtower that stood guard over the village. "You told me you heard about Emma Chance's death on your way back from the Lake District and suspected she might be Emma Chandler. Except, now I discover that you were actually here in Ayleswick that Sunday, the evening before she was killed. You saw her and you spoke with her. So why the lie?"

Crispin held himself very still, his hands dangling limply. Then his head fell back, displaying a face ravaged by grief. "How did you know?"

"You were seen."

The younger man's features pinched with puzzlement. "But . . . I didn't ride all the way into Ayleswick. I hadn't even reached the cross-roads when I saw her walking along the road." He drew in a shaky breath. "I couldn't believe it was her."

"You stopped?"

"Of course I stopped."

"Did she tell you why she was here?"

Crispin nodded, his throat working visibly as he swallowed.

"Why was she crying?"

Crispin stared at him. "How did you know she was crying?"

"I told you; you were seen." It said something about the intensity of the exchange between the two young lovers, that Seaton hadn't even noticed Charles Bonaparte trotting down the road behind them. "Why was she crying?"

Crispin swiped a shaky hand over his face. "We were . . . arguing."

"About what?"

"Does it matter?"

"I rather think it does."

The young Baron nodded and shifted to clasp his hands around his bent knees. "She told me she'd discovered her father was someone from Ayleswick, so she'd decided to come here posing as an officer's widow on a sketching expedition so she could find out who he was. I wanted to know how the blazes she thought we could ever marry when everyone in the village now thought she was someone she wasn't."

"What did she say?"

He stared at the new grave before him. "She said, How could she marry me when there was a chance that *my* father was also *her* father?"

Sebastian held himself very still. He was finding it oddly difficult to draw his next breath, much less ask the questions he needed to ask in a calm, even voice. "Had she made any progress in discovering her father's identity?"

Crispin shook his head. "She said she'd eliminated the old Squire because Archie told her his father was fair-haired, and Samuel Atwater for the same reason. But that was about it."

"I'm not quite certain I understand how she thought she could possibly discover the truth."

"I don't know either. What was she going to do? Come right out and ask Major Weston if by chance he'd raped some earl's sixteen-year-old daughter two decades ago? Ask the *vicar*, for Christ's sake? I had the impression she thought she'd somehow recognize her father when she saw him."

"Except that Emma looked like her mother," said Sebastian. "Why didn't you tell me this before?"

A faint hint of color crept into the younger man's cheeks as his gaze drifted away. "I was afraid that if you knew I'd been here and then left—that we'd quarreled—then you might think I'd killed her."

"Where did you go, after you came upon her on the road?"

"What do you think? My God! I'd just discovered that the woman I loved and wanted to marry thought there was a very good chance she was my sister! You can have no idea what that's like. No idea at all."

Sebastian stared out over the sun-soaked tombstones around them, conscious of a familiar pounding in his temples. Because the truth was that he understood only too well what Crispin Seaton was going through. He'd been through it himself.

"I turned my horse around and rode back to Ludlow," Crispin was saying. "I took a room at the Angel and set about getting mind-numbingly drunk. I stayed that way for days. It's . . . it's all just a blur. I finally woke up on Friday determined to ride back here and have it out with her. Except, by then everyone was talking about the inquests being held down in Ayleswick. I heard the name Emma Chance and—" His shoulders shook and he dropped his face into his hands, muffling his voice. "I kept telling myself it had to be some kind of mistake. She couldn't be dead. She just couldn't."

Sebastian understood now why Emma had told Reuben early Monday morning that she hadn't been able to sleep. Upset by the previous evening's confrontation with the man she loved, she'd finally given up even trying and left her bed before dawn to go down to the river to paint a pack bridge used by smugglers. She must have been exhausted all that day.

And by dawn the next morning she was dead.

He studied the younger man's bowed head, the wind-ruffled fair hair gleaming golden in the sunlight. He believed Crispin Seaton's grief was genuine. But he knew, too, that Crispin wouldn't be the first murderer to weep at his victim's graveside.

Chapter 49

*L*ater that afternoon, as the sun sank toward the Welsh hills, Sebastian sat at the large central table in their private parlor with Emma Chandler's two sketchbooks spread open before him. He was comparing the sequence of her landscape sketches with that of her portraits.

He stared at them a long time, trying to make sense of what he knew of this woman's death and the others that had both flowed from it and preceded it. Finally he said, "I know why Emma named the subjects of some of these portraits but not others."

Hero looked over at him from where she was mending one of Simon's dresses in a chair beside the window. "Why?"

"Her main purpose was obviously to draw and name each of the men mentioned in her mother's letter. But three were already dead, so she drew Archie in the hopes that he bore some resemblance to his dead father, and Jenny Dalyrimple because she must somehow have realized 'the man at the Ship' referred to in her mother's letter was actually Jamie Knox, and Jenny is Knox's twin."

"So why did she draw Martin McBroom and Hannibal Pierce?"

"Because she was an artist, and both men have interesting faces. As does the chambermaid, Mary Beth. But she didn't name them because their identities weren't important."

"She didn't draw Crispin," said Hero.

"No. But she knew exactly what he looked like, didn't she?"

They had found Crispin's last letter to Emma tucked into her reticule, and its presence there told them all they needed to know about her feelings toward him. Now Hero set aside her sewing and came to stand behind Sebastian, looking over his shoulder as he flipped slowly through the dead woman's drawings. She said, "Do you think Crispin could have killed Emma?"

"I'd think it more likely if she'd died that night—if he'd killed her in a rage. But I find it difficult to believe he rode off, only to come back twenty-four hours later to put his hand over her face and quietly smother her to death."

"But he could have done it. He did lie."

"He did. Although I'm beginning to think he may have lied to protect his mother."

"Lady Seaton?" Hero sank into the chair beside him. "You can't be serious."

"I wish I weren't."

She shook her head. "I'm not following you."

"Let's suppose, for argument's sake, that the man who raped Lady Emily Turnstall twenty-two years ago was the same gentleman who impregnated Sybil Moss and Hannah Grant."

"We don't know for certain that Hannah was with child."

"No. But bear with me a moment. We've been assuming that Sybil and Hannah were killed by whatever gentleman seduced them—namely Lord Seaton, the Reverend, or Major Weston—with Seaton being eliminated because he's now dead. But what if those women were actually killed by the guilty man's angry, jealous wife?"

"What a ghastly thought," said Hero. "Although if you're right, it means Agnes Underwood and Liv Weston should also be considered suspects."

"True. Except Reverend Underwood and Major Weston are both still very much alive, whereas Leopold Seaton is long dead. Supposedly he fell off his horse one dark night riding home drunk from the Blue Boar and cracked his head open on a conveniently situated stone bridge."

"You're suggesting his loving wife actually bashed in his head, instead? And then killed Emma when she found out the young woman was her husband's child?" Hero was silent for a moment. "But Lady Seaton didn't know why Emma was here."

"We think she didn't know, but that doesn't mean she didn't. Apart from which, she could actually have an entirely different motive if Emma was killed because she accidently stumbled upon a meeting between Lucien Bonaparte and someone delivering a message from Paris."

"If there was a message from Paris that day. And if Lady Seaton knows of Lucien's contact with Paris. That's three ifs," said Hero.

Sebastian found himself smiling. "You're right; it is."

Hero began slowly turning the pages of Emma's second sketchbook. "When one meets her, Lady Seaton seems so feminine and eventempered. Could she really be that different? That . . . evil?"

Sebastian stared down at Emma's sketch of Northcott Abbey, its leaded windows sparkling in the summer sunshine. Virtually every aspect of a gentlewoman's existence, from her tastes and talents to her behavior and basic personality, was expected to conform to their society's narrow definition of womanhood. Some women were lucky: They were born fitting into that tight, predetermined mold. But most struggled their entire lives to cope with the discrepancy between the reality of who they were and the illusion of what their society expected them to be.

Some, like Hero—and, he realized, Emma Chandler—were independent minded enough to go their own way regardless of the consequences. But few were that brave. Most learned early to affect a false persona, to hide their intelligence and determination and tuck away their true selves behind a gentle, smiling, unnatural facade. And he had no doubt into which category Grace Seaton fell.

"I think Lady Seaton is very good at playing whatever role other people expect her to play. What she's actually like is anyone's guess."

"But how could she have managed it? Physically, I mean. She's so tiny. And then there's what happened to Hannibal Pierce. Even if she's a marvelous shot, I can't imagine her ladyship creeping through a misty churchyard with a rifled pistol to shoot Hannibal Pierce. Or hiding in the bushes beside the river to leap out and bash Reuben Dickie over the head."

"No. But she has a very devoted cousin."

"Samuel Atwater?" Hero considered this possibility in silence for a moment. "Ironically, I can believe her capable of murder easier than I can him. I find him rather likeable."

"So do I." Sebastian went to stare out the window at the lane leading up the hill to the ancient church, where a yellow-wheeled whiskey stood beside the lych-gate, the reins of its glossy bay held by one of the village lads. "Of course, it's always possible that Leopold Seaton really did fall off his horse and crack open his own head, and I should be looking into Liv Weston and her pitchfork-wielding gardener instead."

Hero came to stand beside him, her gaze, like his, on the elegant woman now weaving her way through the churchyard's scattered tombstones. "If you are right, how can you possibly prove it?"

"I don't know." He turned away from the window and reached for his hat and gloves. "Whoever is doing this has in all likelihood killed at least six people. And I have absolutely nothing but supposition to go on."

Sebastian found Lady Seaton in the same place he'd come upon her son that morning: at Emma Chandler's graveside.

She wore a demure light blue carriage dress with a round straw hat, her golden curls clustered poignantly about the pale, delicate features of her face. She held her hands nestled one inside the other and pressed against the gown's high waistband, and she had her head bowed. But her eyes were open and she appeared more lost in thought than engaged in prayer.

At the sound of Sebastian's footfalls, she raised her head to look at him. She did not smile. A sheaf of purple heather and spiny yellow gorse rested against the new grave's bare dirt; it was a strange offering, but he did not need to ask to know that she had brought it. She stared at him for a long moment, and he knew again the sense that this was a woman who kept all genuine thoughts and emotions carefully hidden from public scrutiny.

She said, "Crispin told me of his conversation with you this morning."

Sebastian stood on the far side of the grave, his hat dangling in one hand. "Did he tell you he was in love with Emma Chandler?"

She nodded. "He confessed that to me days ago."

Confessed. The word choice struck him as significant.

She said, "Georgina had spoken to me several times of her friend at school, so I recognized her name, once it became known."

"She'd told you of Crispin's interest in Emma?"

"No." She smiled faintly as she said it, drawing out the long vowel sound. "That she kept to herself. But then, Georgina and her brother have always been close. He asked her to keep it quiet, and she did."

Lady Seaton fell silent again, her gaze dropping to the raw earth between them. "I wish she had told me why she was here. I might have been able to help her."

Sebastian found his imagination boggling at the thought of Emma confiding to this elegant, cool gentlewoman her suspicions that Lady Seaton's dead husband might have been guilty of rape. He said, "You met Lady Emily Turnstall?"

"I did, yes. But only briefly."

"How much do you remember of that long-ago September?"

"Little, I'm afraid. I was increasing at the time and most dreadfully unwell. But . . ." Her voice trailed off, her nostrils flaring on a suddenly indrawn breath. "Surely you're not suggesting that's why she was killed?"

"I think it very likely, yes."

She ran her hands up and down her arms as if she were cold, although the evening was still golden warm. "And the others—Reuben Dickie and that man from London? What have they to do with a house party twenty-two years in the past?"

"Probably nothing. But they may have seen something the night Emma was killed, something that could betray her killer's identity." He hesitated, then said, "It's possible the same person was also responsible for the deaths of Sybil Moss and Hannah Grant."

Her gaze flew to his, her pretty mouth going slack with surprise. He caught an unexpected flicker of what looked very much like fear lurking in her startlingly blue eyes. Then she lowered her thick lashes and looked away again. "But Sybil and Hannah committed suicide."

"I think not."

She gave a little shake of her head. "Those women died years ago. How can you possibly think there's any connection between their deaths and what happened to Emma Chandler?"

"Because someone in Ayleswick obviously likes to solve his problems with murder." *Or her problems*, thought Sebastian. "Did you never consider it?"

"That the two girls hadn't killed themselves?" She hesitated. "There was talk at the time. But I never credited it for an instant. What a troublesome thought."

He said, "I understand you invited Emma to Northcott on Saturday."

"I did, yes." She looked both puzzled and vaguely suspicious. "Why?"

"I was wondering how you met her."

"We were introduced by Agnes Underwood when I stopped by the vicarage Friday afternoon. She mentioned Emma was interested in sketching the historic buildings in the area, and I suggested she visit Northcott Abbey."

"Did she ask about your late husband?"

A faint frown puckered her pretty forehead. "She may have. I don't recall now exactly what we spoke of." She gathered her skirts. "And now you must excuse me, my lord. I don't like to leave Devon—my horse—waiting too long."

He watched her walk away, her head held high, her features comfortably settled into a look of gentle goodwill she'd been practicing since childhood.

Before he left the churchyard himself, Sebastian turned to enter the old parish church.

The passage of the most recent Catholic Relief Act had enabled the Seatons to build a small, unobtrusive Catholic chapel on the grounds of Northcott Abbey. But for generations before that the family had had to hide their faith, attending services at the village church on Sunday and burying their dead in its crypt.

Built without aisles, the church of St. Thomas was the same age as the earliest construction of the priory that now lay in ruins to the west. Its sandstone walls were thick, its windows small and rounded, the air permeated with the odor of cold, dank stone and lost centuries of incense and blessed candles.

Memorials to those interred in the crypt below lined the worn sandstone walls and floor of the nave. The oldest were those dedicated to the first generations of Rawlinses; but the most elaborate were those of the Seaton family. It didn't take Sebastian long to find the engraved marble slab of Lady Seaton's lord. Leopold Seaton had died on the sixth of February 1798, less than two weeks after Hannah Grant was found floating in the millpond. A coincidence? Possibly. But Sebastian doubted it.

He was turning away when another memorial caught his eye, this one small and heartbreaking in its brevity:

SHELBY WILLIAM
BELOVED SON OF LEOPOLD AND GRACE SEATON
2 NOVEMBER 1797 TO 16 APRIL 1798

Sebastian stared at that pitiful memorial, conscious of an upwelling of empathy for the beautiful, self-contained woman who had buried her infant son within months of losing her husband.

He searched the surrounding memorials, wondering if she had lost other children, but found no evidence of any. In her seven years of marriage, Grace Seaton had given birth not to three, but to four children: Crispin, the son and heir, followed by two girls, Georgina and Louisa, and then, finally, a second son.

And three months later, Leopold Seaton was dead.

Sebastian tilted back his head, his gaze on the mellow blues, greens, and reds of the stained-glass window above the altar. The land and wealth of noble families were traditionally entailed, thus enabling the family's fortune to pass virtually intact from eldest son to eldest son on down through the ages. Failing a son, both land and titles would pass instead to the nearest male in the paternal line, be he a brother, nephew, uncle, or distant cousin. Any noblewoman left widowed without a son was generally to be pitied, for her home and her husband's wealth would all pass to some distant relative.

As a result, most wives were anxious to bear not just one healthy son, but two. "An heir and a spare," they called it. And shortly after the birth of his "spare," Lord Seaton had died.

A coincidence? Possibly. But a murderous woman unwilling to tolerate her lord's philandering any longer might well wait until after the birth of a second son before putting an end to her husband's straying once and for all.

It was past time, Sebastian realized, that he learn more about the death of Leopold, Lord Seaton.

Chapter 50

Wednesday, 11 August

The next morning dawned cool and blustery, with thick clouds that hung low enough to obscure the mountains to the west. With Archie at his side, Sebastian rode out to the old stone bridge where Leopold, Lord Seaton had died.

"I was still a small boy when it happened," said Archie, reining in at the edge of the weathered fieldstone bridge that spanned a small rivulet some hundred yards from Northcott Abbey's gatehouse. "But I still remember listening to my father talk about how Lord Seaton's brains were splattered all over the bridge. It made quite an impression on me."

"I would imagine it did," said Sebastian, his mount moving restlessly beneath him as he studied an ancient stand of oak thickly undergrown with witch hazel that encroached close to the road here.

Archie's eyes crinkled with a faint smile of remembrance. "For years, I couldn't pass the bridge without looking to see if I could spot some trace of all those splattered brains. Somehow I always managed to convince myself that I did." Archie's smile faded as he squinted up at the roiling clouds overhead. "You really think Seaton's death could some-how be connected to what's happening now?"

"The timing is interesting," said Sebastian. "Sybil Moss died on Midsummer's Eve in 1797. Less than seven months later, Hannah Grant was found floating in the millpond. And just two weeks after that, Lord Seaton falls off his horse at one of the few places between the Blue Boar and home where he's guaranteed to do himself some serious damage. You don't find that suspicious?"

"When you put it that way, yes. It's damnably suspicious."

Sebastian said, "Do you know if there was an autopsy?"

"I doubt it. M'father was always ranting and raving about the parish rates. He wouldn't have paid to hold an inquest if it hadn't been required."

"I gather the inquest's verdict was death by misadventure?"

Archie nodded. "Seaton's horse—a sweet-tempered white mare named Cleo—was declared a deodand. Liv Irving bought her. Rode her for years."

Under English common law, chattel found to have been involved in a death was known as a deodand and had to be forfeited, whether it was a horse, a cart, a boat, or tree. All deodands passed to the Crown and were usually sold, although owners could pay a fine equal to their value to keep their property. It was less common now than it had once been. But Sebastian wouldn't be surprised if Archie had had to pay to keep his father's hunter, Black Jack. For some reason, Lady Seaton had evidently not chosen to do so.

Archie's face had taken on a flat, empty look, as if his thoughts were suddenly far, far away.

"What is it?" asked Sebastian, watching him.

Archie swallowed. "If you're right—and I'm afraid you may very well be—then that's three murders my father missed: Sybil, Hannah, and Lord Seaton. Three!"

Sebastian was tempted to say, *There may have been more.* But he kept that possibility to himself.

"My God," said Archie, his voice rough. "Poor Hannah Grant was buried at the crossroads with a stake through her heart!"

"Whoever is doing this is clever—clever, and devious enough to make most of his murders look like suicides or accidents. Under the circumstances, your father's mistake was easy to make."

Archie shook his head, his eyes narrowed and hard. "I want to find him. Whoever's doing this, I want to find him, and hang him."

Sebastian remained silent. He'd told Archie his suspicion that Leopold Seaton's death might be linked to the other murders. But he'd yet to divulge the rest of his thinking. It was all still speculation, too unproven.

He shifted his gaze to the crenelated sandstone gatehouse that guarded the entrance to Northcott Abbey's long, stately drive. The big house itself was out of sight, hidden by the heavy late-summer canopy of the plantings that dotted the estate's rolling, expansive park. And he found himself thinking about the family that had lived here, carefully hiding their religious faith generation after generation, on down through the centuries. What did that sort of pervasive, inescapable fear do to people? he wondered. What would it be like, living endlessly with that level of distrust and suspicion and duplicity? All while gazing down on the crumbling ruins of the priory from which your wealth had been seized?

He said, "Was Lady Seaton a Catholic before she married?"

Archie looked puzzled but answered readily enough. "She was, yes. I understand she's related to the Nevilles and Howards." Both were famous Catholic families who had managed to maintain their wealth and power despite their religion. "Why?"

Sebastian shook his head. "Just wondering."

Archie gathered his reins, then hesitated. "Have you ever not caught a killer?"

"Not one I wanted to catch."

"But . . . what if we never figure out who's doing this?"

"Then I suspect he'll eventually kill again," said Sebastian, and saw the color drain from the young Squire's face.

Chapter 51

*H*ero was writing up some of her interview notes at the table in the private parlor when a timid knock sounded at the door.

"Come in," she called, expecting Mary Beth, the chambermaid.

The door opened to reveal a slight, white-haired old woman, her heavily lined face swollen and twisted with grief. "Beggin' yer ladyship's pardon fer disturbing ye," said the woman, wringing her hands nervously before her. "McBroom, he told me to take meself off, so I nipped up the back stairs when he weren't lookin'."

Hero paused with her quill still in her hand. "May I help you?"

The woman bobbed an awkward curtsy. "I'm Becka—Becka Dickie. Reuben's mother."

Hero rose to go to her. "I am so sorry for what happened to your son. Please, come in and sit down."

The Widow Dickie's eyes widened. "Thank you kindly, milady, but it wouldn't be proper for me to sit, it wouldn't."

"Nonsense. I insist."

It took some work, but the old woman finally allowed herself to be coaxed to a seat beside the empty hearth while Hero gave the bell a sharp tug and ordered a tray with tea and toast.

"Did you have something you wished to tell Lord Devlin?" she asked, settling opposite the woman. "I'm afraid he's not here at the moment."

The Widow Dickie shook her head. "It was ye I was wantin' to see." She hesitated, then pushed on. "It's about me Reuben. He wasn't supposed to go out after dark, you see. The old Squire, he said he'd clap Reuben in the stocks every day for a week if the poor boy ever so much as stuck his nose out at night again. But Reuben, he never was real good at doin' what he was told."

Hero waited, and after a moment, the old woman started up again, her voice hushed, ragged.

"He was out the night that pretty lady was kilt. Come back real spooked, he did. Wouldn't tell me what'd happened. But whatever it was, it scared him bad."

Hero leaned forward in her chair. "You think he might have witnessed her murder?"

Reuben's mother plucked at the worn, stained cloth of her dress. "I dunno. To be honest, milady, I have wondered, ever since they found her dead. You see, Reuben was scared, but he was also excited—the way he'd get when he had a secret. He did like his secrets."

If Reuben had seen Emma Chandler's murder, it would have been a dangerous secret to keep, thought Hero. It might very well have ended up getting the simpleminded man killed.

"He'd gone out the night before too," Reuben's mother was saying.

"Oh?"

Silent tears began to slide unchecked down the old woman's cheeks. "Was out most the night, he was. Didn't come back till the sun was up, which was right foolish of him—and so I told him, ye can be sure of that."

"Do you know where he would go at night?"

She shook her head. "He'd just wander. Sometimes he'd tell me things he'd seen, but not always."

"Did he tell you what he saw Sunday night?"

"I know he was by the pack bridge at dawn, because he told me he come upon that lady down there. Paintin' a picture, she was."

"Yes," said Hero. "Reuben told Lord Devlin he'd seen her there."

The Widow Dickie nodded. "The thing is, milady, I don't think Reuben told his lordship that was the *second* time he'd seen her that mornin'."

Hero found her attention well and truly caught. "It was?"

The old woman shifted uncomfortably in her chair, not quite willing to meet Hero's gaze. "I don't like to be carryin' tales, 'specially not about a man of God, but . . ."

"Yes?"

The Widow Dickie gripped the arms of her chair with gnarled, workworn hands. "The Reverend's got this cousin, ye see. Rachel Timms is her name. She's a widow, she is. Her husband, he was kilt in the war some years back. The vicar, he's got this little cottage tucked into the side of the hill, just above the churchyard; Hill Cottage, it's called. The old sexton used to live there, but Nash, he's got his own cottage, so he don't need it. So when Mrs. Timms's husband was kilt and she had no place to go, the Reverend, he let her come and live at Hill Cottage."

"That was very kind of him," said Hero, not quite certain where any of this was going.

"He did the same for another cousin of his. Maybe eight years ago, it was. Rose Blount was her name." Reuben's mother chewed on her lower lip. "Only, she died after a few years."

Hero studied the older woman's age-lined, troubled face. "Mrs. Dickie, what are you trying to tell me?"

The old woman met her gaze squarely. "Rose Blount died in childbirth, milady—her and the babe both. She never told nobody who her baby's father was. But, thing is, from the first week the vicar brought her here, my Reuben, he was telling me how he'd see the vicar sneakin' over there to her cottage in the middle of the night when there weren't nobody else around. And then, after she died, why, the vicar, he didn't let more'n a few months go past afore he's got his cousin Rachel livin' in that cottage, and Reuben tells me the vicar is visitin' her at night too."

Hero felt her stomach tilt with revulsion. "Are these women actually his cousins, do you think?"

"Oh, yes, milady. I truly believe they are. Everybody thinks he's such a fine, generous man, lettin' 'em live in Hill Cottage fer free. But there ain't nothin' kind or generous about it, and he ain't lettin' 'em live there for free, if you get me drift?"

"Do you think his wife knows what he does?"

The Widow Dickie snorted. "How could she help but know? You ask me, she don't mind the way things are one bit, so long as it keeps him outa her bed."

"How many people in town know about this?"

"As to that, I can't say. There may be some as suspects it. But ain't nobody gonna talk about it—him bein' the vicar 'n' all. I've argued with meself for days, thinkin' maybe I should tell somebody what me Reuben seen. And now me boy's dead, and I can't help but wonder if . . ." She swallowed. "Maybe if I'd spoke up sooner, Reuben would still be alive."

"I don't exactly understand what this has to do with the death of Emma Chandler," said Hero.

"But that's just it, milady. The churchyard is the first place Reuben told me he seen the pretty lady early that morning, even before the sun come up. She'd walked up the hill from the Blue Boar and was standin' by the lych-gate when the Reverend left Rachel Timms's cottage."

"Did Reverend Underwood see her?"

"How could he help but? I mean, it ain't like she was tryin' to hide. He walked right by her. Reuben said the Reverend mumbled somethin' about a sick parishioner. So he seen her, all right."

"Did he see Reuben?"

"I don't rightly know."

Hero watched Becka Dickie pluck at her skirts again. The woman hadn't come right out and said she suspected Benedict Underwood of having killed both her son and Emma Chandler. But the implications were obvious.

"I've always felt right sorry for Mrs. Timms," Reuben's mother was saying. "Just like I did for Rose Blount. A woman shouldn't have to turn herself into a whore for her own cousin, jist to have a roof o'er her head."

"How do you know she's not willing?"

Becka Dickie stared at Hero with unblinking, wise eyes. "Ye talk to Rachel Timms. Ye'll see."

Hill Cottage lay just to the north of the churchyard wall, tucked into a slight dip in the slope. Built of whitewashed fieldstone with a roof of lichen-encrusted slate, it was small and doubtless dark inside, with its front shutters closed even at midday, as if against prying eyes. Once, the cottage might have boasted a garden. Now there were only a few scraggly, half-dead rosebushes and some forlorn-looking poppies struggling to survive in a patch of dirt scratched nearly bare by a flock of dispirited-looking chickens.

Hero rapped with one gloved fist on the worn door, then stood listening as the sound faded away into windblown silence. She waited, then knocked again. She could feel the other woman standing—breathless, wondering, afraid—on the other side of the door's weathered panels.

"Mrs. Timms?" said Hero softly. "Are you there? I need to speak with you. It's about the young woman who was killed in the village last week. Mrs. Timms?"

Silence.

"Blast," whispered Hero under her breath. She was turning away when the door was suddenly yanked open about a foot and then stopped.

A painfully thin woman appeared in the gap. She looked to be perhaps ten years older than Hero, with a long, oval face and the sallow complexion of someone who'd once lived in a fiercely sunny climate but now rarely ventured out of doors. Her pale blond hair was already lightly touched by gray and unfashionably secured in a tight roll at the nape of her neck. Her dove gray gown was plain and threadbare, the hand gripping the edge of the door reddened and chapped by work. There was nothing about either her appearance or her manner to suggest the kind of woman who regularly received furtive midnight visits from a forbidden lover.

"Good morning," said Hero. "I'm sorry for disturbing you. I'm Lady Devlin."

"I know who you are," said Rachel Timms, her voice well-bred and cultured, but timid, breathy. "What makes you think I know anything about the woman who was killed?"

"May I come in, please?"

Rachel Timms's nostrils flared on a quickly drawn breath, her chest jerking as she struggled to choose between two equally frightening prospects: to risk being seen with Hero on her doorstep or to invite her inside. And Hero found herself wondering if anyone besides Benedict Underwood had entered Hill Cottage since Rachel Timms's arrival here five or six years before.

"It's important," said Hero.

She thought for a moment that Rachel Timms meant to close the door in her face. Then she stepped back and opened the door wider.

"Come in—quickly, please."

Chapter 52

*T*he Reverend Benedict Underwood was inspecting that year's crop of small, unripe apples in the ancient walled orchard beside the vicarage when Sebastian walked up the lane toward the church. Sebastian had just spent the last half hour listening to Hero's account of her meeting with Rachel Timms, an experience that left him hard put to maintain his equanimity.

"Looks as if you should have a good harvest this year," he said, his head tipping back as he surveyed the trees' gnarled, heavily laden branches.

The vicar's face settled into his habitual, benevolent half smile. "Yes— God willing."

"I'm sorry I was unable to attend yesterday's funeral," said Sebastian, looking out over the low wall that separated the orchard from the churchyard. Because this was the favored south side, the weathered, lichen-covered gravestones were thick here.

The vicar winced. "I heard about what happened to Reuben Dickie. Poor wretched soul. He was always carving little wooden animals for the village children, everything from sheep and horses to foxes and deer. He was amazingly talented at it."

"I'd wondered what he did with them," said Sebastian as the two men turned to walk between the rows of old fruit trees.

Underwood glanced sideways at him. "Any idea who could possibly have done such a thing?"

"We have a few theories."

"Oh?"

"It seems Reuben had a habit of wandering at night."

The vicar nodded sadly. "I know. He wasn't supposed to, but . . ." He shrugged.

"It's very likely that he was killed because of something he saw."

Underwood blinked and said again, "Oh?"

"Mmm. Perhaps the night Emma Chance was killed, although his death could also be linked to something he saw late the previous night— or, more accurately, something he saw early that morning."

"You mean, Monday morning?"

"Yes." Sebastian kept his gaze on the vicar's bland face. "As it happens, he and Miss Chandler both saw you leaving Hill Cottage shortly before sunrise."

Underwood bent to pick up an unripe apple that had fallen amongst the roots of the tree beside them. He tossed it up and down for a moment, as if considering his response. When he looked over at Sebastian, he had his faint, concerned smile firmly back in place. "I'm afraid I don't know what you're talking about."

"Indeed? Do you imagine your visits to Rachel Timms a secret? They're not. Oh, no doubt some of your parishioners think you a good, generous man for lending a hand to your indigent female relatives. It would probably never occur to them that their own vicar fathered the child whose birth killed Rose Blount. I wonder: Did your cousins know what they were letting themselves in for when they took up your seemingly generous offer to come live in your cottage? Somehow I doubt it. But once they were here, you had them at your mercy, didn't you?"

The vicar's smile was still eerily in place, but his eyes were hard and glittering with righteous anger. "Are you somehow imagining Rachel unwilling? Believe me, you flatter her. She's a widow, not some silly shrinking virgin. Rose was the same. Eager enough to spread her legs in exchange for a roof over her head."

Sebastian thought about the desperate woman Hero had described to him—frightened, isolated, shattered, and ashamed, betrayed by one she'd trusted. His hands curled into fists, and he had to force himself to unclench them.

"It still feels like rape," Rachel had told Hero, shoulders shaking with her quiet sobs. "He's been doing it to me three nights a week for over five years now, and every time, it still feels like rape. But it's not, you know. I've never fought him; never told him no. How can I? I've nowhere else to go. He's turned me into his whore, but I let him do it. There isn't a day goes by I don't think of killing myself. But my father was a vicar too; I understand that God has sent this trial to me, and the penance for my weakness and sin is that I must endure it."

To which Hero had replied, "Have you thought about killing him?"

Rachel's gaze flew to meet Hero's; then she looked away and gave a quick, jerky nod. "God help me, I have, yes. But even if I did somehow escape hanging for it, Ayleswick would then have a new vicar. So I would lose Hill Cottage anyway—and burn in hell for all eternity for what I'd done."

Now a small rabbit showed its head amongst the tall grass at the edge of the orchard, and Underwood chucked the green apple at it. The rabbit disappeared.

Sebastian said, "In a little over a week, three people have been murdered in Ayleswick. And you had a motive to kill at least two of them."

Underwood swung to face him, his mouth sagging open. "You can't be serious."

"Oh, but I am. You see, we now know why Emma Chandler was here in Ayleswick. It had nothing to do with a sketching expedition and everything to do with discovering who out of a list of seven men raped her mother twenty-two years ago. Your name was on her list—"

"Are you mad?"

"—and we now know you're the kind of man who has no qualms about forcing himself on unwilling women. All of which leads to the obvious conclusion that Emma somehow discovered you were her father, and you killed her to shut her up. You killed her, and then you staged her death to look like a suicide—complete with a poetic verse cut from your own bloody copy of *Hamlet* tucked into her dead hand."

"Don't be preposterous. Why would I then leave my book lying around where it could be found?"

"I don't know that you did. It's possible you thought you'd hidden the book or disposed of it in some way. Only, Reuben Dickie found it—probably because he saw you hide it. That's why you killed him: because you were afraid of what else he might have seen."

The vicar stared at him, chest jerking with the agitation of his breathing, his jaw set hard. "But this is ridiculous! Utterly ridiculous."

Sebastian said, "I also wouldn't be surprised if you killed Sybil Moss all those years ago, as well—either because you were worried your parishioners might find out you'd fathered the child she was carrying, or because she refused your unwelcome advances and you were afraid she might tell someone about how you'd tried to force yourself on her. Her and Hannah Grant both."

"Good God. What sort of monster do you take me for?"

Rather than answer, Sebastian found his gaze drifting down to the picturesque, deceptively peaceful-looking village curled around the base of the hill. The wind was scuttling the clouds overhead in a way that sent shifting patterns of shadow and light chasing each other across the broad green and the ancient, half-timbered buildings that edged it. Fifteen years before, the Reverend had successfully convinced a coroner's jury that Sybil Moss hadn't been in her right mind when she supposedly killed herself. Had it been a gesture of disinterested kindness or of guilt?

He'd been unable to do the same for Hannah Grant.

"You're wrong," said Underwood. "You hear me? You're wrong."

Sebastian brought his gaze back to the pale, sweat-slicked face of the man beside him. "If you killed Emma Chandler and the others, I will see you hang for it; make no mistake about that."

Underwood was shaking now, an odor of sour sweat rising from his cassock. "But I didn't. I swear to God I didn't kill her. I didn't kill any of them!"

"Then I suggest you pray to him for salvation—if you have any reason to believe he'll listen to you," said Sebastian, and turned to walk off and leave him there, standing rigid and unmoving in the tall, drying grass of the old orchard.

Chapter 53

For any man, let alone a man of God, to take advantage of his impoverished female relatives' vulnerability to satisfy his lust was as despicable as it was repellent. There was no doubt that Benedict Underwood was a vile human being who conceivably had a motive to kill everyone from Sybil Moss to Reuben Dickie.

But that didn't necessarily make him guilty.

What it did was explain why a killer would use Underwood's edition of *Hamlet*, and why he wouldn't destroy the book after cutting it up. Given Underwood's rape of Rachel Timms and Rose Blount, there was little doubt that those four simple words sliced from the vicar's book, *The rest is silence*, would be enough to see the Reverend hanged should he ever go on trial for Emma's murder.

But for some reason he couldn't have explained, Sebastian still wasn't convinced. And the nagging certainty that he was still missing something drove him back to the private parlor at the Blue Boar. Opening Emma Chandler's two sketchbooks on the room's large, central table, he stood staring down at them, his fingers curling around the table's edge. He kept coming back to the idea that the key to what had happened to Emma

Chandler lay in the pattern of her movements on that last, fatal day. And as he turned the pages of her sketchbook for what must have been the hundredth time, he realized it wasn't just one thing he'd been missing, but two.

Half an hour later, he was still staring at Emma's last sketch when Hero came in from taking Simon for a walk. She brought with her the scent of fresh country breezes and sun-warmed ripe grain, and paused in the doorway to watch him in silence for a moment.

"You've figured something out," she said.

"I have indeed." He spun the sketchbook with the drawings of the priory around to face her. "I don't know why I didn't grasp the significance of it before, but think about this: Unless Emma's killer took off her gloves for some inexplicable reason, then she must not have been wearing them when she was killed. So what does that tell us?"

When visiting, a gentlewoman generally removed her gloves only to eat. But according to Hiram Higginbottom, Emma had been killed several hours after her last meal.

Hero looked puzzled for a moment. Then enlightenment dawned. "She would have to take off her gloves to sketch! That means she was killed while she was drawing something. But . . . what?"

"Whatever it was," said Sebastian, "she obviously never had a chance to actually begin sketching it. Nothing has been torn out, and the last drawing in her book is of the priory, and it looks finished to me."

"You think she really did go back to draw Maplethorpe Hall again for some reason? And the smugglers killed her?"

"That's what I was thinking, at first. Except—" He broke off to flip back through the sketchbook. "Look at this: she drew six pictures of the Grange, five of Northcott Abbey, but only three of St. Hilary's Priory. Why?"

Hero came to stand at his side. "Perhaps she was more interested in the Grange and Northcott Abbey because either of them might have been her father's home, whereas the priory was simply an attractive ruin."

"Perhaps. Except I remember thinking when we were at the ruin what a beautiful, inspiring site someone with her talents must have found it. She'd already drawn one of these three pictures by the time Lady Seaton claims to have seen her at two o'clock. Yet according to the miller's wife, Emma didn't leave the priory and climb back over the stile until five. In other words, it took her three hours to do the last two sketches."

Hero began turning the pages of the book.

He said, "How long do you think one of these sketches would take?"

"If they were detailed renderings, she could have spent days on one. But they're not. They're just quick, loose impressions. And if she did six similar sketches of the Grange—plus a portrait of Squire Rawlins—in one morning, then surely she didn't spend an hour and a half on each of these last two drawings." Hero raised her gaze to his. "What are you suggesting, Devlin?"

"One of three things: Either she went someplace else after she left the priory but before she climbed over that stile at five o'clock—"

"Someplace like Northcott Abbey, you mean? A second visit no one has told us about?"

He nodded. "Either that, or the miller's wife was wrong about when she saw Emma climb over the stile."

"I was under the impression Alice Gibbs was quite certain about the time."

"She was. And we all simply accepted her testimony without question. But she could have been wrong. It's even conceivable that for some reason I can't begin to imagine, she's lying."

Hero untied the ribbon of her hat and pulled it off. "You said there's a third possibility."

His gaze met hers. "The third possibility is that the miller's wife didn't see Emma that afternoon at all, because Emma never left the priory alive. In other words, she died there."

❧

Alice Gibbs was hoeing a row of beets when Sebastian turned his curricle into the short lane that led to the neat stone cottage beside the mill. She straightened slowly, one hand self-consciously smoothing her skirts as she watched him hop down from the carriage's high seat.

"Milord," she said, bobbing a curtsy. "If it's Miller Gibbs you're looking for, I'm afraid he's gone off to see the smith about getting a shaft fixed."

"Actually," said Sebastian, "you're the one I came to see, Mrs. Gibbs. I wanted to ask about the evening you saw Emma Chandler—or Chance, as she called herself. I understand you were out in your garden?"

"Yes, milord. Pickin' some radishes, I was, when Mr. Flanagan stopped by to talk about our Henry." The miller's wife beamed with maternal pride. "Doin' ever so well with his studies, is our Henry."

"That must make you very pleased."

Her smile widened. "It does, yes, ever so much, milord. Never learnt to read or write meself, you see. So I can't tell you what it means to me, seeing my boy catchin' on so quick."

Sebastian turned to glance up the narrow, leafy lane toward the coach road, a distance of some two to three hundred feet away. He himself could have identified someone at many times that distance. But then, his vision was uncommonly acute.

"You must have very good eyesight," he said.

Alice Gibbs laughed, her face rosy and full cheeked. "Me? Och, no, milord. Anybody in town can tell you I wouldn't recognize me own husband if I was on one side of the church and he was on the other. I wouldn't have known it was Mrs. Chance at all if Mr. Flanagan hadn't told me."

"Oh?" said Sebastian, still smiling pleasantly. "What did he say?"

She thought about it a moment. "I reckon he said somethin' like, 'There goes that widow what's been drawing all the old buildings hereabouts. She must've been sketching the priory.' And I said, 'She picked a lovely day for it,' and we talked a bit about the nice spell of weather we'd been having."

"And then what?"

If she found the question odd, she didn't show it. "Well, he'd just been tellin' me how he had a meetin' at half past five, so then he said he'd best be hurrying along."

It was a detail Sebastian had heard before, but he hadn't paid any attention to it. Now it struck him as blindingly significant, as if Flanagan had gone out of his way to make certain the miller's wife remembered the time.

She was still smiling broadly, eager to be of assistance and proud of her ability to tell him what he wanted to know. He said, "The village is lucky to have Mr. Flanagan."

"Och, aren't we just. He's ever such a kind, scholarly man."

"Exactly how long has he been here?"

"Well, let's see. . . . Must be more'n two years now. He come right after poor old Mr. Coombs passed away."

"Mr. Coombs was the previous schoolmaster?"

"He was, yes, milord."

"And he died two summers ago?"

"More like that February or March, it was."

In other words, thought Sebastian, just months after Lucien Bonaparte was sent to Shropshire. Aloud, he said, "How did he die?"

"Something hit his stomach, it did."

Sebastian found himself wondering if what hit the unfortunate Mr. Coombs's stomach had been poison. Someone had obviously been making Ayleswick-on-Teme an extraordinarily unhealthy place to live for quite some time now.

He bowed his head and touched his hand to his hat. "Thank you for your assistance, Mrs. Gibbs. You've been most helpful."

"Anytime, milord. Anytime."

He'd almost reached the curricle when a thought occurred to him, and he paused to turn back and ask, "Could you see Miss Chandler well enough to tell what she was wearing?"

Alice Gibbs laughed as she reached down to pick up the hoe she'd dropped. "I could see that, milord. Had on a light gray cloak, she did."

There'd been a gray cloak hanging on one of the hooks in Emma's room at the Blue Boar. But she hadn't had it with her when she was found. She hadn't even been wearing her spencer, which was folded up beside her. "Bit warm for a cloak, wouldn't you say?"

"It was, indeed. I remember thinkin' she must've put it on that morning, worryin' meybe it was gonna come on to rain again."

"That must be it," said Sebastian.

She smiled at him again, totally oblivious to the fact that she hadn't actually seen anything she claimed to have personally witnessed.

Chapter 54

Sebastian found the front door and windows of the schoolmaster's cottage standing open to catch whatever breeze might chance to stir the close air of the sultry afternoon.

"Mr. Flanagan?"

He paused on the flagged stoop, his gaze drifting over the vaguely untidy, low-ceilinged front room, the massive bookcase stuffed with an assortment of tattered volumes, the battered, ink-stained table that looked ancient enough to have once graced the stately halls of the old priory.

"Mr. Flanagan?" he called again.

Through a doorway in the room's rear wall he could see a section of the smoke-blackened kitchen hearth; a steep staircase to one side presumably led to a dormered sleeping chamber above. But the silence in the cottage was absolute.

"Flanagan?"

Sebastian hesitated, then walked around the outside of the cottage to the cobblestoned yard at the rear. In addition to the woodshed and other typical outbuildings, he was surprised to find a small but relatively new barn and fenced paddock. A neat black mare with powerful

hindquarters and a deep chest thrust her head over the fence and whin-
nied at him expectantly.

"Aren't you a fine girl?" said Sebastian, going to stroke the mare's muzzle.

There weren't many schoolmasters who could afford to keep such an
elegant mount. True, Flanagan had neither wife nor children to feed, and
he'd reportedly been riding through Ayleswick on his way to Wales
when he learned of the recently vacated position of village schoolmaster.
But a different explanation for the mare's presence was forming in Sebastian's mind.

A man carrying messages, first to Ludlow, then to Worcestershire,
would need a good, reliable horse.

The mare butted her head against his chest. He said, "Where's your
master? Hmmm?"

With growing disquiet, Sebastian gave the mare a final pat and
turned toward the open door of the hay barn. Stepping into the darkened interior, he listened to the telltale drone of flies, smelled the cop-
pery stench of spilled blood.

And then, when his eyes adjusted to the gloom, he found what was
left of Daray Flanagan.

"Maybe we're making a mistake, trying to make sense of all this," said
Archie, his voice oddly hollow sounding as he stared down at the schoolmaster's sprawled, bloody body. The flies were buzzing thick around
them, but the Squire was making no attempt to bat them away from his
face. "Whoever this killer is, he must simply be mad."

Like Reuben Dickie, Flanagan lay facedown, the back of his head a
pulpy mess. A bloodied length of firewood lay discarded nearby. Sebastian studied the marks on the barn's dirt floor. From the looks of things,
the Irishman had been struck elsewhere—probably in the cobbled
yard—and dragged into the barn.

"I don't think so," said Sebastian, going to stand in the barn's open doorway. "I think whoever's doing this has a very deliberate, rational purpose for everything he's done."

Archie stayed where he was. "How did you happen to come here, anyway?"

"I had an interesting conversation this afternoon with Alice Gibbs. She tells me she's myopic. Famously so, in fact."

"She is, yes." Archie gave a hoarse laugh. "I remember one time she thought a billy goat menacing a couple of m'father's dogs was her own daughter Elizabeth."

Sebastian narrowed his eyes against the light as he searched the yard for traces of blood. "So how do you suppose she was able to recognize Emma Chandler from a distance of two or three hundred feet?"

Archie opened his mouth, took a deep breath, and closed it. "I don't know. I didn't think about that."

"She tells me it was actually Flanagan who identified the figure climbing over the stile that afternoon as Emma. Alice simply saw what she'd been led to believe she was seeing."

"But what difference does it make if it was Flanagan or Alice Gibbs who saw Emma?"

"Because I don't think the person they watched was actually Emma. According to Alice Gibbs, the figure she saw climbing over the stile was wearing a gray cloak. Now, it's possible that at some point before Emma was killed, she went back to the Blue Boar and left the cloak in her room. But I doubt it. I think she was killed before five o'clock, and it was all just an elaborate ruse to disguise the actual time and place of her death."

"But why? Why was it so important to cover up when and where she died?"

"It would be of vital importance if she was killed because she'd accidently stumbled upon a meeting between Lucien Bonaparte and someone delivering a message from France."

Archie stared at him. "You can't be serious."

"I wish I weren't."

A dark smear on the cobbles near the woodshed caught Sebastian's attention, and he went to have a closer look.

"Is that blood?" asked Archie, watching him.

"It is. From the looks of things, I'd say Flanagan was killed here, then dragged into the barn out of sight—probably either late last night or early this morning." The blood had long since dried. "Hopefully Higginbottom will be able to give us a better idea—that is, if he ever gets around to it." The last they'd heard, the old doctor had yet to begin the postmortem on Reuben Dickie, despite the inquest scheduled for that Thursday. He said his cow was still sick.

Archie watched Sebastian push to his feet. "But how do you know Flanagan didn't simply *think* he saw Emma and got it wrong. I mean, how do you know he was deliberately misleading Alice Gibbs?"

"Because he's dead."

"Oh." Archie went to sit on the mounting block in the corner of the yard, his head in his hands. He sat there for a long time; then he dropped his hands and lifted his head to stare at Sebastian. "So who was in the gray cloak?"

"The killer," said Sebastian. "And he's just eliminated his accomplice."

Sebastian had no doubt that whoever killed Flanagan was clever enough to have removed anything from the dead schoolmaster's cottage that might implicate him. But they searched the cottage anyway. Even clever people make mistakes.

Slowly and methodically, they went through every drawer and cupboard, checked each room for loose floorboards or chimney bricks, inspected the undersides and backs of each piece of furniture. As they searched, Sebastian told Archie of the previous day's encounter at Maplethorpe's carriage house. "I gave Weston my word as a gentleman I wouldn't report him to the authorities unless I had reason to believe his smuggling operation had something to do with Emma Chandler's death. But now I do."

Archie looked up from searching the contents of a pantry shelf. "You think *Weston* is the killer?"

"He could be, although I doubt it. In all likelihood he's just a greedy bastard taking advantage of the war to run contraband. He probably has no idea the French have been using his smuggling line to pass messages back and forth between Napoléon and his brother."

"Through Flanagan?"

"He arrived shortly after Bonaparte was sent to Shropshire, didn't he? March of 1811?"

"He did, yes. But . . . why would Paris send someone to Ayleswick, then? I mean, yes, Lucien is here this summer, but two years ago he was in Ludlow. And after that he moved to his estate in Worcestershire."

Sebastian shifted his search to the front room. "How often would Flanagan go out of town?"

"Fairly often," admitted Archie, hunkering down to peer beneath the desk. "He has a cousin keeps a tavern near Warwick he used to—" He broke off when he realized what he was saying and muttered, "Bloody hell."

After that, he worked in silence for some minutes, obviously turning the information over in his head. Then he said, "What I don't understand is, if Flanagan was the one delivering the messages, then who's the killer?"

Sebastian pushed a chest back into place. "I don't know."

"Lucien Bonaparte must know," said Archie, standing in the center of the front room, his hands dangling loosely at his sides. "Damn that bloody French bastard all to hell. He not only knows who's doing this; he was probably there when Emma was killed."

"Perhaps. But I doubt it." Sebastian went to scan the titles in the sagging old bookcase. "In all likelihood, Bonaparte only dealt with Flanagan. It's probably another reason Flanagan was brought in—to help protect the identity of whatever agent was already in place. I wouldn't be surprised if Napoléon is more than a bit suspicious of his brother's loyalties."

"You're saying the French have someone else here in Ayleswick? My God. Who?"

Rather than answer, Sebastian reached for a volume of eighteenth-century Scottish sermons and opened the flyleaf to a scrawled, nearly illegible signature. *Alistair Coombs.* He looked up. "These books belonged to the village's previous schoolmaster?"

Archie nodded. "Most everything you see here was his. He had no heirs that we knew of, so we just left it all for Flanagan. He was happy enough to have it."

Sebastian closed the book and slipped it back into place before pulling out another, then another.

"What are you looking for?" asked Archie, watching him.

Sebastian opened a volume of John Donne's poetry and turned the flyleaf to face the young Squire.

"Well, I'll be," whispered Archie as he stared down at the familiar signature written in a tight, cramped hand.

The Reverend Benedict Ainsley Underwood.

Chapter 55

*I*n the end, they found nearly half a dozen books from the vicar's library tucked in amongst those left by Alistair Coombs.

"What the devil!" swore Archie as Sebastian opened yet another of the vicar's volumes. "I want Underwood clapped in irons! The sanctimonious, traitorous, murdering bastard."

Sebastian calmly set the volume aside. "A moment ago you were convinced the killer was Major Weston."

Archie stared at him, breath coming hard and fast enough to visibly jerk his chest. "You're saying you *don't* think Underwood is the killer? But his books are here!"

Sebastian studied the titles of the small stack of volumes. Old Alistair Coombs's reading tastes had run mainly to histories and sermons. But the books borrowed from the vicar's library were all poetry. "Think about this: Why would Underwood go through the trouble of killing Flanagan, yet not bother to remove his books from Flanagan's shelves?"

"Maybe he forgot they were here. Or—or maybe he was interrupted before he had the chance to gather them up."

"Perhaps. By all means, I think you should ask the good Reverend for an explanation."

Archie went to stand in the open doorway, his hands on his hips as he watched Constable Nash and one of the cottagers load Daray Flanagan's body into a cart. "When is this killing going to end?" he said after a moment, his voice less angry now, more shaken.

"When anyone who could possibly identify the killer is dead."

Archie turned to meet Sebastian's gaze, resignation mingling with a wild look of lost innocence in the young Squire's eyes.

While Archie stormed off to confront the vicar, Sebastian quietly called for his curricle and drove out to the Dower House. Except he didn't expect to find Major Eugene Weston there.

There were times when one simple piece of evidence, read wrong, could throw a murder investigation entirely off course. In this case, that bit of evidence was a short line of poetry from an Elizabethan play.

The rest is silence. Those four words, tucked into Emma Chandler's dead hand, had suggested a killer who was not simply literate, but erudite. A killer who, in casting about in his mind for one more clue that might point to suicide, was educated and well read enough to come up with a Shakespearean quote. That, combined with the revelation of Emma's search for the gentleman who'd raped her mother, had inevitably led Sebastian to focus on a narrow segment of the parish's residents.

He wondered why it hadn't occurred to him before, that there might be more than one killer at work here. Was it simply too difficult to believe that this small, seemingly peaceful village harbored not one but two murderers, even though he already knew its bucolic atmosphere to be deceptive? Was it really that simple? Two killers: one a new arrival to Ayleswick, educated, and so fond of poetry that he occasionally helped himself to volumes from the vicar's library. And the other . . .

Who?

Virtually any one of the district's "better sort" could conceivably be involved with Major Weston in his smuggling venture, and each could likewise have had a reason to kill Sybil Moss and Hannah Grant all those years ago. But the death of Daray Flanagan opened up an entirely new possibility, one Sebastian pondered as he drove through fields ripe with golden grain. Because if it was Flanagan who had tucked that Shakespearean quote into Emma Chandler's hand, then the field of other suspects had just been thrown wide-open. There was no need for the second killer to be literary. He need not even be literate.

It was a realization that produced a significant shift in how Sebastian viewed everything he'd learned that past week. It forced him to reevaluate every assumption he'd made and each conclusion he'd reached. And when he stepped back from all he'd thought he understood and looked at the village and its troubled history again with fresh eyes, a different pattern emerged.

A pattern that was as compelling as it was profoundly, personally troubling.

Liv Weston was pruning an overgrown hedge of roses at the base of her garden when Sebastian turned his chestnuts into the Dower House's narrow, weed-choked drive. Looking up, she paused with one heavily gloved hand clutching her secateurs, her eyes narrowing as she watched him rein in before the house's modest portico. A large, battered basket rested on the turf at her feet. As Sebastian dropped from the high seat to the gravel sweep, she deliberately turned her back on him and resumed shaping her hedge.

Without bothering to mount the steps and knock on the front door, he turned and walked toward her.

"Good afternoon, Mrs. Weston," he called. "Is the major around?"

She kept her gaze on her work. "I'm afraid not, my lord."

"Any idea where I might find him?"

"Sorry, no. As it happens, I haven't seen him since yesterday."

Sebastian drew up beside the lanky hedge. It should by rights have been cut back weeks ago, shortly after it had finished blooming. "Did he say when he would be home?"

Snip, snip, went Liv Weston's secateurs. "Actually, we expected him for dinner last night. Mrs. Carmichael made braised pork. Always one of his favorites."

Sebastian studied her half-averted face and saw there the faintest hint of a smile, a bubble of what might have been called suppressed hope if it hadn't had such a nasty edge to it. "You're not concerned?"

"Not really."

He became aware of the almost unnatural silence around them, broken only by a single thrush chattering in the branches of a nearby maple. Despite the cloud cover, the heat of the day had become oppressively close and still.

He said, "Has something happened to your husband, Mrs. Weston?"

"I've no idea. But a woman can dream, can't she?" She paused to glance over at him. "Does that shock you? You think I should feign concern? Truly? After you've spent the last week poking into all our lives, uncovering all our secrets?"

"Not quite all of them, I'm afraid."

"I think you underestimate yourself, my lord."

Sebastian watched her cut off a long cane with a quick snip. Until that moment, he'd had sympathy for this woman, or at least for the young and vulnerable girl he imagined she'd once been. Now he began to wonder if some of that sympathy hadn't been misplaced.

He said, "How long has your husband been dabbling in smuggling?"

Her attention was all for her roses. "I am a woman. What would I know of such things?"

"You know."

When she remained silent, he said, "Tell me this, Mrs. Weston: Why does your husband take such care to preserve the old gibbet that stands near the crossroads?"

Her hand momentarily faltered at its task. "Why do you ask?"

"Just curious."

She shrugged. "He would tell you that gallows and gibbets, like whipping posts and stocks, play an invaluable role in reminding the lower orders of the folly of forgetting their proper place in the scheme of things. But the truth is, my husband is a nasty, vindictive man. He hated Alex Dalyrimple with the kind of passion not even death can satisfy, and he maintains that gibbet as a testament to what he sees as his victory over an enemy. If my husband had had his way, Dalyrimple's body would still be moldering up there."

"Why? Because Dalyrimple dared try to oppose your father's Bill of Enclosure?"

"In part. But mainly because Dalyrimple was nothing more than a base-born, self-taught wheelwright, yet he was ten times the man Eugene Weston could ever hope to be—and Eugene knows it."

Sebastian watched her step back to evaluate her work. He wondered when she had realized the folly of her marriage. Before her father's death, obviously, given that she had successfully persuaded the enfeebled old man to tie up her inheritance in a way that kept what was left of it from Weston's grasp. Was that truly when Weston had turned to smuggling? he wondered. Or had it started before? Perhaps even before the erection of that tar-blackened gibbet at the crossroads.

Sebastian touched his hat with a slight bow. "When your husband returns, if you would be so kind as to tell him I'd like to speak with him?"

"Of course," said the major's wife, that eerie little smile still curling her lips. "If he returns."

"You think the major done run off after killin' all them people?" asked Tom when Sebastian returned to the curricle.

Sebastian craned around to stare at his tiger. "How did you know Weston is missing?"

"Heard the cook talkin' about it with the groom. They can't think why else 'e ain't come home."

Sebastian could think of another very good reason for Major Weston to have disappeared. But he kept that possibility to himself as he drove back to the village.

"See the chestnuts taken care of," he told Tom as they drew up before the Blue Boar. "Then I want you to find Squire Rawlins and suggest that it might be a good idea to send his constable out to nose around Maplethorpe's carriage house."

The boy scrambled to take the reins, his sun-reddened face sharpening with sudden understanding. "'Oly 'ell! Ye think the major might be *dead?*"

"His wife certainly thinks it."

"'Oly 'ell," said Tom again. "What'll I tell the Squire if 'e asks where you've gone?"

"Tell him . . . Tell him I've gone for a walk."

Chapter 56

$\mathcal{S}$ebastian had just passed the outskirts of the village when Lucien Bonaparte came thundering toward him mounted on a magnificent dapple-gray Arabian.

"My lord," said Napoléon's brother, the gray sidling and tossing its head as he reined in hard beside Sebastian. "I was coming to see you."

"Oh?" Sebastian kept walking. He was in no mood to deal with the Emperor's spoiled, self-indulgent brother.

"Is it true what they're saying? That Daray Flanagan is dead?"

Sebastian glanced up at the Corsican's pale, slack face. "Why? Are you admitting you knew him?"

"So it is true? He is dead? *Mon Dieu.* This is dreadful."

"It's certainly dreadful for Flanagan."

The Corsican kicked his feet from the stirrups and dropped awkwardly to the ground. "There is something I must tell you," he said, tugging at his rucked-up waistcoat as he fell into step beside Sebastian.

"Yes?"

"I fear I was not quite truthful when I said I am not in contact with Paris. Not with Napoléon, you understand, but with my mother."

"I'd already figured that."

Bonaparte's jaw sagged. "You had?"

"I take it Flanagan was sent here as a courier?"

"He was, yes. But . . . how did you know?"

"Call it a good guess. You met with him on Monday? At the priory?"

The Corsican nodded miserably. "At three o'clock."

Sebastian drew up abruptly and swung to face him. "Who was with him?"

Whatever Bonaparte saw in Sebastian's face caused him to take a quick step back. "No one."

"You're certain?"

"Yes."

"Who arrived at the priory first? You or Flanagan?"

"Flanagan."

"So he was waiting there for you?"

"He was, yes." Bonaparte looked puzzled. "That's important. Why?"

Sebastian said, "And you saw no sign there of Emma Chandler?"

"No, nothing. And now Flanagan is dead, and I've just learned that young woman was at the priory that afternoon as well, and—"

"You didn't know that?"

"That she was there? No! Not until just now, when I heard Lady Seaton discussing it with her steward."

Emma's presence at the priory that afternoon was known by everyone who had attended Emma's inquest. But then, Lucien Bonaparte hadn't been present at the inquest; he'd sent his son in the company of Lady Seaton and Samuel Atwater.

Bonaparte sucked in a quick, nervous breath. "Is it someone sent by Whitehall who's doing this? I know that man, Hannibal Pierce, was their creature—"

"How do you know that?"

"Flanagan warned me. I wondered why he always insisted on passing me the packets from Paris in broad daylight rather than under cover of darkness. But he said anyone I met at night would immediately be suspect, whereas we might briefly encounter each other during the day without attracting undo attention."

"Did you order Pierce killed?"

"No! I haven't ordered anyone killed! I don't kill people. I have never killed anyone. Never."

"The message from Paris; what was it?"

"I can't tell you that!"

Sebastian suppressed the urge to grasp the Corsican by the lapels of his coat and shake him. "Bloody hell. At least four people are dead because of that message—if not six."

"You don't know that!"

"You know it too. It's why you're here."

Napoléon's brother brought up two shaky hands to swipe them down over his face. "My mother wrote to say that if the armies of this new alliance continue to march against us, France will surely fall. Even the world's most brilliant general needs an army, and there simply aren't enough men between the ages of fourteen and sixty left to defend our borders. She wants to know if London would be agreeable to Napoléon abdicating in favor of his infant son, the King of Rome."

"I could answer that question for her."

Lucien nodded sadly. "I fear the time for such an action has passed. But I have sent out feelers to Castlereagh."

Sebastian understood why Lucien had been reluctant to divulge the contents of his mother's message. It was one thing for malcontents on the streets of Paris to whisper about Napoléon abdicating in favor of his son. But it was something else entirely for the Emperor to actually be considering it.

"The other French agent here in Ayleswick," said Sebastian, "who is it?" It was a question he was afraid he already knew the answer to, but he found he was still hoping to be proven wrong.

Lucien Bonaparte chewed the inside of one cheek and gave Sebastian a glassy stare.

"God damn it; who is it?"

"I don't know. Flanagan always called him 'our friend.' But I never learned his identity. It's the way these things are structured; you must know that. The messages are sent in a sealed packet from Paris to the ship. Then, once the ship arrives off your shore, the packet is handed to whoever is in charge of the horses that collect the cargo from the beach. They carry it here to Ayleswick."

"And give it to whom? Weston?"

"*Pphff.*" Bonaparte pushed a derisive breath out between his front teeth. "The man is an idiot content to pocket a few dollars here and there. Who would trust him?"

"So who? Who took delivery of the packets and passed them to Flanagan to carry to you? He's the man who's actually been running Weston's little smuggling operation from the very beginning, isn't he? From long before you were sent to Shropshire."

"I don't know who he is! You must believe me."

"Why the bloody hell should I?"

"Because it's the truth." Bonaparte's horse began to sidle, and he tightened his grip on its reins. "I don't understand the reason for all this killing. Why is it happening?"

"Because Emma Chandler was at the priory sketching when Daray Flanagan and the man you call your 'friend' arrived. She must have accidently seen or heard something that betrayed their links to Paris, and they killed her for it."

"But Flanagan's friend wasn't there!"

"Just because you didn't see him doesn't mean he wasn't there. You say Flanagan knew about Hannibal Pierce. If that's true, his 'friend' probably came along that day for the sake of security."

"And you're saying this man has now killed Flanagan? But why?"

"Because he's afraid of being exposed. Flanagan was expendable, but his 'friend' isn't; another courier can always be brought in."

"But all this killing! It's too much. Too much."

"You're certain you don't know who he is?"

"No!"

"Then you'd best hope he believes that."

Lucien Bonaparte gave him a strange look. "Why?"

"Because I wouldn't put it past him to kill you too."

"Me?"

"Why not?"

The Corsican opened his mouth to answer, then closed it again.

Sebastian said, "Still certain you don't know who he is?"

Lucien Bonaparte gave a short, jerky shake of his head, his forehead beaded with sweat, his lips twitching with fear.

And in spite of himself, Sebastian believed the man.

Chapter 57

The hollow *twunk* of an axe slicing into wood echoed in the sultry stillness of the afternoon as Sebastian approached the small stream that led to the old priory.

He followed the sound around the side of Heddie Kincaid's cottage, to a dirt yard where Jenny Dalyrimple was chopping lengths of wood into kindling. Her face was flushed and sheened with sweat, and she threw him a quick glance over one shoulder before reaching for another section of wood to rest on the block before her.

He came to a halt some distance from her. "Tell me about your cousin, Sybil Moss."

Jenny swung her axe, and the wood on the block shattered. "What about her?"

"Do you know the name of the gentleman she was seeing at the time she died? The one who put a babe in her belly?"

"Course I know it."

"Tell me about him."

She reached for another length of wood but simply held it, her gaze on his face. "You really want to hear it?" The words were like a challenge thrown at him.

"Yes."

She set the section of wood on the block and swung again, splitting it neatly, the lean muscles in her shoulders and arms working beneath the thin cloth of her dress. Then she turned to face him, her breath coming hard and quick from her exertion. "All right; I'll tell you, then. It was Leopold Seaton—the present Lord Seaton's father."

Sebastian searched her tightly held, sweat-sheened features, looking for some sign of calculation or deception. But he found only contempt and an old, old anger.

He said, "Is it possible Lord Seaton killed her?"

For a long moment, Sebastian didn't think she meant to answer him. Then she set her jaw and shook her head. "No. Not in the way you mean."

"What about Lady Seaton? Could she have done it?"

Jenny tilted her head to one side. "Why you care how Sybil died?"

"Because I don't believe she threw herself off the cliffs of Northcott Gorge, just as I don't believe Hannah Grant drowned herself in the millpond or Leopold Seaton simply fell off his horse coming home drunk one night from the Blue Boar. I think they were murdered. And I think whoever killed them is now responsible for the death of Emma Chandler and all the other killings that have followed on from it."

Jenny swung her axe to sink the blade deep into the chopping block beside her. "You're wrong. Sybil did throw herself off the cliffs of Northcott Gorge."

"How can you be so certain?"

She swiped her sweaty face with the sleeve of one crooked elbow. "Because I was there."

"At the gorge?"

Jenny lowered her arm, her hands dangling loose at her sides as she silently stared back at him.

He said, "Tell me what happened."

She continued to stare at him, and there was something about her face in that moment that reminded him so much of the last time he'd seen Jamie Knox that it tore at his gut.

"Why?" she said at last.

And he thought, *Because I don't want to believe that the man who was like a brother to Jamie is a killer, although I am very, very afraid that he is.*

But all he said was, "It's important."

She twitched one shoulder. "Sybil never made any secret of the fact she was lying with his lordship—had been for months. She was so pretty, no one was surprised when she caught his eye. He went after all the pretty girls."

Sebastian studied the flaring line of Jenny's cheekbones, the gentle curve of her lips. She was still an extraordinarily attractive woman. And he found himself wondering if she herself had once attracted Leopold Seaton's attentions. If so, Seaton must have quickly realized that this woman was far too dangerous to trifle with.

She drew a painful breath. "But Sybil . . . Somehow she convinced herself things were different with her. She was so excited when she realized she was carrying his child. She thought once he knew, he'd set her up in a fine house in Ludlow with servants and a carriage and fancy clothes and jewels. I tried to warn her, but she wouldn't listen to me. Said I was jealous and didn't want her to be happy."

"So what happened?"

"She told him about the baby on Midsummer's Eve, during the bonfires. At first he just laughed at her for thinking he'd acknowledge one of his bastards. But she didn't take it well, so then he flew into a rage. Told her if she tried to claim he'd fathered her brat, he'd have her taken up for being a whore and whipped through the village at the cart's tail." Jenny swiped at her forehead again. "He was like that. He could be smiling and oh so handsome one minute, and then, just like that"—she snapped her fingers—"he'd turn mean and ugly. In the end, he pushed her away from him hard enough to send her sprawling. Then he just walked off and left her there on the ground."

She fell silent. Sebastian held himself very still, waiting for her to continue.

She said, "I went to help her up; put my arms around her and told her everything was gonna be all right. But she wouldn't stop crying. She was talking wild, about what a fool she'd been and how she just wanted to die—that she ought to go throw herself off Monk's Head. Then she pulled away from me and ran off into the night."

He could picture the scene all too well. The hellish glow from the bonfires lighting up the darkness and reflecting on the young girl's tears. The warm night air heavy with herb-scented smoke. The laughter and excitement of villagers drunk on cider and a primitive tradition older than anyone knew.

"What did you do?" he asked quietly.

"What you think I did? I found Jude, and we went after her."

"To Northcott Gorge?"

Jenny nodded. "Jude, he didn't think she'd really do it, even though she was standing at the edge of the cliff when we got there. The wind was whipping at her skirts and blowing her hair across her face. I begged her to get back from the edge, and Jude, he told her not to be such a damned fool. She looked over at us—didn't say anything, just looked at us in a quiet, steady way that scared the hell out of me. There was a full moon that night, and I could see the determination in her eyes. Then she just . . . stepped over the edge into nothing."

Jenny fell silent again, her gaze fixed unblinkingly on the distance, and Sebastian knew she was seeing again the young woman's skirts billowing in the moonlight, hearing the bone-breaking thump and tumble of her body hitting the rocks as she plummeted into the gorge.

"You didn't tell anyone?"

Her features hardened. "Why would we? So they could bury her at the crossroads with a stake through her heart? That's the last thing we wanted. We told anyone and everyone who'd listen to us that she was laughing the last time we'd seen her, that she was *happy*. That there was no way she'd deliberately kill herself. But the coroner's jury didn't believe us."

"When Lord Seaton died a few months later, did you never think someone might have killed him?"

"I figured maybe Miles Grant—the blacksmith—got him."

"Was Hannah also carrying Seaton's child?"

"I don't know. But she was lying with him. That I do know."

"How do you know that?"

"Because she told—" Jenny broke off, her nostrils flaring on a sudden intake of breath.

"She told—whom? You? Or someone else?"

"I don't remember," she said, staring boldly back at him, not caring that he knew she was lying.

"Was Hannah Grant your cousin as well?"

"No. Her people moved down here from Ludlow." She lifted her chin. "So you see, there's no connection between Sybil's death and what's happening in the village now."

Sebastian wondered if she actually believed that, or if she was simply trying to convince him, the way she'd tried to convince the village that her cousin had fallen to her death. He said, "Did you know Daray Flanagan is dead?"

Her lips parted, the sinews of her throat tightening. "When?"

"Sometime last night or early this morning."

He expected her to say, *Why would anyone kill Daray Flanagan?* He waited for her to say it, because it was the logical, inevitable response to such an announcement.

But she didn't say it. Then he saw the stark bleakness in her eyes and knew with a sinking certainty that she didn't ask because her mind was quick. She already knew why someone would kill Daray Flanagan, just as she had a pretty good idea as to who had done it.

It wasn't obvious or easily discernible, the twisted, thin cord of anger and revenge that connected one untimely death to the next. But it was there, the passion and outrage of youth leading to a mature and ruthless instinct for self-preservation.

And Sebastian wondered, had it begun on that long-ago Midsummer's Eve, when Jude Lowe watched the young niece he'd known and loved all his life step off a cliff into oblivion? Or had the origins of that murderous fury begun earlier, with the tarred, blackened body of a childhood friend hung up to rot in the cold embrace of a gibbet's iron cage?

He wondered, too, if Hannah Grant really had drowned herself in that millpond, or if the last thing she'd known was the angry, brutal grasp of a jealous young man. A man who'd once loved her, only to be rejected when she turned from him to a wealthy lord he knew to be both selfish and cruel.

"I was more'n a bit sweet on Hannah myself when I was a lad," Jude had told him. *"More'n a bit . . ."*

The wind gusted up, shivering the leaves of the elms edging the stream and bringing with it the scent of coming rain. It was all conjecture, of course. Sebastian knew only too well that just because an explanation fits neatly doesn't mean it's true. Never in his years of solving murders had he so desperately wished to be wrong. But he felt the rightness of it like a sick certitude deep in his gut.

He was aware of Jamie Knox's twin staring at him, her fine, intelligent eyes flat and still, as if she could will from their depths any betraying glimmer of the truth. And he wanted to say to her, *You know, don't you? You might not have known it before, but you've figured it all out now. You know the secret, violent soul of the man who's always been more like a second brother to you than an uncle. You know he swore to kill Leopold Seaton all those years ago. You know where he gets the fine brandy that he hides in his cellars and the inexplicable wealth he must be careful not to show to anyone he doesn't trust. You know he was the one who supposedly urged Daray Flanagan to stay when the Irishman so conveniently came riding through town on the day of Alistair Coombs's funeral, and you've always suspected why, even if you never admitted it to yourself. Just as you've always suspected that the flames that consumed Maplethorpe Hall had nothing to do with a candle and a windblown curtain and everything to do with that tar-soaked gibbet and a government informant brought in specifically to end the subversive protests against George Irving's ruthless Bill of Enclosure.*

"Whatever happened to him?" Sebastian asked, and she shook her head, not understanding his question. "Wat Jones, I mean. The squatter you told me lied at Alex Dalyrimple's trial."

"He went away."

Which he undoubtedly did. Although Sebastian suspected he didn't get far.

He stared across the stream at the stile Emma Chandler had climbed the afternoon of her death—but only once, not twice. And the irony of her fate struck him suddenly as both cruel and heartrendingly senseless. She had come to Ayleswick to uncover the truth about her parents in the hopes of better understanding who and what she was. And all she had found was her own death.

He said, "Is there another way to get to the priory ruins besides following the stream here?"

"You can come at it from Northcott. And there's a footpath starts across from the village church and cuts through the wood."

"Thank you," he said, touching his hand to his hat.

"Did it never occur to you," she said as he turned away, "that if you hadn't interfered—if you'd let that young woman's death be ruled a suicide—then Hannibal Pierce, Reuben Dickie, and Daray Flanagan would all still be alive today?"

He paused to look back at her. "Are you suggesting their deaths are my fault?"

"Death follows you," she said, her hands coming up to grip her upper arms and hug them to her. "You brought it here."

He forced himself to meet her gaze. "Ayleswick was no stranger to violent death long before I arrived, and you know it."

He thought she might deny it.

But she didn't.

Chapter 58

He found Hero and Simon watching the ducks on the village green.

She turned, the child in her arms, her brilliant smile of welcome fading when she saw his face. "Devlin. What is it?"

He stood beside her and watched as their son prattled gibberish at the quacking, waddling ducks. He wanted to say, *I came to Shropshire because I can't seem to let go of this need to know. To know the true identity of my father, to know if I lost a brother the day Jamie Knox died, to know why my eyes are yellow rather than a deep St. Cyr blue. Except, all I've found are more questions. More questions, and a murdered young woman on a painful quest so similar to my own. And now, in the process of solving her murder, I'm afraid I'm about to destroy what's left of a family that has already suffered too much because of me.*

But he didn't say any of those things. Instead, he squinted up at the dark clouds building over the distant hills and said, "Think we can make it out to the priory before the storm hits?"

They left Simon with his nurse, then took the path that led from the ancient parish church of St. Thomas, through a dense wood of beech and elm.

As they walked, he told her of his conversations with Lucien Bonaparte and Jenny Dalyrimple, and of the long-ago, tragic death of Sybil Moss and everything he believed had followed it.

She said, "You think Lucien Bonaparte was lying when he claimed only Flanagan was at the priory that day?"

"I think he believed he told the truth. But that doesn't mean Jude Lowe wasn't there; only that Bonaparte didn't know it."

The wind was kicking up, thrashing the limbs of the trees overhead, and he saw her tilt back her head, her lips parting as she gazed up at the sky. "Could Jude Lowe really be that evil?"

"I doubt he sees himself as evil. I'm sure he thinks he had a good reason for everything he's done."

"He's evil," said Hero.

Sebastian shrugged. "As far as he's concerned, he's fighting a war—a war against centuries of oppression and exploitation by the likes of everyone from George Irving and Leopold Seaton to the English Crown. He looked at what the revolutionaries were trying to accomplish across the Channel in France, and he wanted those kinds of reforms here. I don't know how long he's been cooperating with the French, but I doubt it was before the hangings of 1793. In fact, I wouldn't be surprised if it was that spate of judicial murders that initially pushed him toward the French."

They'd reached the stream at the edge of the wood, and she paused for a moment, her gaze on the ruins of the old priory thrusting up pale and somber against the roiling clouds in the west. "I can understand his killing Seaton and Irving," she said, "even if I don't condone it. But there is no possible justification for the murder of Emma Chandler. She was completely innocent of anything."

"Yes. But that's what happens when a man appoints himself as judge and executioner of his fellow beings. What begins as a moral, righteous impulse can all too quickly degenerate into what's convenient for him."

They crossed a rugged bridge to the meadow, the flock of sheep scattering before them as thunder rumbled in the distance. Following a passage through the monastery's confused tumble of fallen stones and ruined walls, they came out in the central cloister. Hero had brought the satchel with Emma's sketchbook, and she opened it now to the final drawing.

"Emma must have been standing about here when she drew this," she said, positioning herself in the cloister by comparing the ruins of the chapter house to Emma's sketch. Then she lowered the sketchbook, her face pinched as if with pain.

"What?" he asked.

"I don't understand why Flanagan and Lowe felt they needed to kill her. I mean, if they found her here sketching, why not simply go away and arrange for Flanagan to pass the message from Paris to Bonaparte another time?"

"I suspect they didn't realize she was here until she'd already seen or overheard something that betrayed what they were about. That's why they killed her."

"But surely they would have looked around when they first arrived, to make certain they were alone?"

"I've no doubt they did. Which tells us that by the time they arrived, Emma was no longer here in the cloisters."

Hero turned in a slow circle, her gaze scanning the broken walls and weed-choked walks around them. "So where was she?"

He found himself staring at what was left of the refectory, the lacey sandstone tracery of its outer row of soaring, pointed-arch windows showing pale against the increasingly storm-darkened sky. Running nearly the entire length of the cloister's south walk, the monk's stately dining hall had been built above an undercroft, both to provide storage for foodstuffs and as a deliberate echo of the *cenaculum*, the upper room in Jerusalem where the Last Supper was said to have taken place. The grand portal that once marked the entrance to the refectory's main stairs had long ago collapsed. But a second, narrower set of steps, its barrel vault still intact, led down to the chamber below.

Hero looked from Sebastian to the undercroft's entrance and whispered, "Oh, my Lord."

A growing wind buffeted their faces and flattened the lank grass as they crossed the cloister. The ancient stone steps were crumbling with age and littered with debris, and she was about to descend when he put out a hand, stopping her.

"Look," he said.

Two distinct sets of men's footprints showed in the dust of the centuries: one smaller, the other noticeably longer. The men had passed up and down the steps several times, nearly obliterating a third set of prints left by a woman's half boots.

Dainty footprints that went down but did not come back up.

"She died down there, didn't she?" said Hero, her voice hushed.

"I'm afraid so."

They picked their way down the ancient stairs in silence, his stomach hollowing out with the implications of what they had found. He imagined Emma finishing her sketch of the chapter house and then turning, sketchbook still in hand, to notice the steps to the undercroft. Intrigued, she must have ventured down the steep steps, surely as awed as they were when the beauty of the ancient, vast chamber opened up before her, its sturdy stone vaulting and central row of stout Norman piers perfectly preserved, its outside range of round-headed windows echoing the Perpendicular windows of the refectory above.

Had she been planning to make a sketch of the undercroft? he wondered. Was that why she lingered? Or did she hear Flanagan's and Lowe's voices and decide to remain out of sight, lest she discomfit them by her unexpected appearance?

If so, it was a decision she surely came to regret.

"I wonder how they knew she was here," said Hero.

"She may have accidently made some sound. Or Lowe could have decided to search down here and came upon her by chance."

"And so he killed her," said Hero, her words echoing eerily in the cavernous space. "He pinned her down against the rough flagstone floor and quietly smothered her."

"Yes."

A single lady's glove lay beside one of the undercroft's central octagonal piers, and Sebastian bent to pick it up.

He had no way of knowing for certain, but he suspected Flanagan had been horrified when he discovered what Lowe had done. They would have had to leave Emma's body here, in the undercroft, until nightfall, using the remaining hours of daylight to trick Alice Gibbs into helping them obscure the time and place of Emma's death. Then, under cover of darkness, they would have returned to shift the body to the water meadows, carefully staging the scene to look like a suicide.

But in the darkness, they had overlooked one dropped glove, and the telltale footprints on the stairs. Nor had they seen Reuben Dickie watching them from the undergrowth at the edge of the river.

"It all seems so pointless," said Hero. Thrusting Emma's sketchbook back into the satchel, she crossed the chamber to stand at one of the empty windows that looked out on the trickling stream and the wind-tossed wood beyond. After a moment, she said, "Do you ever think about the simple, seemingly inconsequential decisions people make in the course of going about their lives? Decisions that can inadvertently get them killed? If Emma had picked a different day to walk out here and sketch the ruins—or if she simply hadn't noticed the stairs to this undercroft—she'd still be alive today."

"As would the rest of them." Thunder rumbled around them in a crashing crescendo of fury that rolled on and on, and he said, "We need to get back."

A few scattered drops of rain pattered on the stones in the cloisters above, filling the air with the scent of wet dust as they turned toward the stairs. "What will you do next?" said Hero as he followed her up the steps.

"That depends on whether Major Weston is alive or dead."

"And if he's d—"

She broke off, and he saw her stiffen as she emerged from the barrel-vaulted stairwell into the growing fury of the storm.

"What is it?" he asked—or started to ask. Except by then he'd reached the top of the steps himself. In the gathering gloom he could plainly see the tall, lean figure of Jude Lowe.

And the long-barreled, flintlock pistol Jude held with the muzzle pressed against the side of Hero's head.

Chapter 59

"Don't move," said Jude.

Sebastian froze, his gaze locking with Hero's. He could feel his pulse racing in his neck, feel the wind buffeting his suddenly sweat-slicked face. "Let her go," he said, even though he knew it was useless. "Your quarrel is with me. Not my wife."

Jude tightened his grip on Hero's upper arm, keeping her between them as he dragged her back one stumbling step. "Put your hands where I can see them and back away—slowly. *Do it,*" he snarled when Sebastian hesitated.

Overhead, the sky was a turmoil of roiling dark clouds rent by quick, bright flashes of lightning. Sebastian splayed his hands out at his sides and placed one foot behind the other, moving cautiously over the uneven, rubble-strewn ground. He knew that if he tried to rush Jude, Hero would be dead in an instant. But he knew, too, that while Jude might intend to kill Sebastian first, the innkeeper would never allow Hero to leave the priory alive.

"That's far enough," said Jude, thumbing back the hammer on his flintlock. "I didn't want to have to kill you."

"Why? Because I look like Jamie?"

"That must be it." Jude's nostrils flared on a suddenly indrawn breath. They could smell rain in the wind, hear the roar of the storm descending on them. "You should have left well enough alone."

"Perhaps you shouldn't have killed an innocent young woman."

Jude shook his head. "She gave me no choice. Like you."

Sebastian watched Jude's hand. His only hope was to throw himself sideways at the last instant when the innkeeper fired, and he felt his body tensing as he waited for Jude's finger to tighten on the pistol's trigger.

Then, out of the corner of his eye, he saw Hero shift her grip on Emma's satchel. When Lowe shifted the muzzle of his pistol toward Sebastian, Hero swung the satchel up to send it smashing into Jude's right hand. The pistol exploded into the air in a flash of flaming powder and went clattering across the fallen stones.

"You bloody bastard," swore Sebastian and threw himself forward.

Jude shoved Hero aside as Sebastian rammed into him, hands fisting in the cloth of Jude's coat, his momentum driving both men backward across the cloisters. Jude's heel hit a loose stone and he lost his balance, grabbing Sebastian's forearms to pull Sebastian over with him as he fell.

Sebastian came down hard on his knees, the two men breaking apart as Jude pivoted to take the impact on one shoulder and hip and kept rolling. Sebastian started to lurch up, but he'd made it only half-way when Jude jackknifed forward to wrap his arms around Sebastian's legs and pull him down again.

Drawing back his arm, Sebastian slammed the heel of his hand into Jude's face as they fell. The innkeeper's nose smashed in a wet, hot smear of blood, the impact rocking Jude back, breaking his hold on Sebastian and sending the innkeeper sprawling on his back in the rubble-strewn grass. Then Jude's fist closed over a chunk of stone and he pushed up to swing it at Sebastian's head.

It was raining harder now, big wet drops that splattered the dust around them. Sebastian jerked out of the way, the rock grazing his shoulder as he kicked out. He landed a glancing blow on Jude's thigh but lost his balance and went down again just as Jude pulled a knife from an unseen sheath at the small of his back. Sebastian fumbled for the double-barreled flintlock he'd tucked into his pocket and felt the hammer catch on the edge of his pocket.

Bloody hell. He jerked the pistol free just as Jude reared up, kicking the gun out of Sebastian's hand and slashing at him with the knife.

Sebastian lunged sideways but felt Jude's blade rip through the cloth of his coat to slice a line of fire through the flesh beneath. He turned the lunge into a roll, reaching down to yank his own knife from his boot as he came up again in a crouch.

Then he leapt back just in time as Jude slashed again, this time toward his face.

The rain came down in a torrent, drumming on the old weathered stones of the priory around them and flattening the grass in the clois-ters. Sebastian was dimly aware of Hero circling around them. She'd retrieved his double-barreled flintlock from where it had fallen and now held it in a strong, two-handed grip. But the two men were too close together for her to risk a shot.

Then Jude plunged his knife toward Sebastian's chest.

"No!" she shouted.

For one critical moment, she caught Jude's attention and his focus wavered. Sebastian slammed his left fist into Jude's wrist, knocking the blade aside as he stepped in to drive his own knife hard, like a sword, deep into the innkeeper's heart.

Their rain-washed faces now just inches apart, Sebastian's gaze met that of the man he'd just killed. He saw the shock in Jude's dark brown eyes, saw his knowledge of imminent death fade to bewilderment and something else. Something that looked very much like confusion and hurt.

"Jamie?" Jude whispered, his eyes rolling back in his head as he col-lapsed.

Sebastian caught his weight as he fell, eased the innkeeper's body down into the rubble-strewn grass. Then he straightened, his breath coming hard and fast enough to jerk his chest.

Hero came to stand beside him, his flintlock pistol still held loosely in one hand. "Is he dead?" she asked, her gaze on the blood-smeared face of the man at their feet.

"Yes."

"Good."

Sebastian didn't say anything because there really was nothing to say. And she wrapped her arms around his neck and held him close while the rain poured around them and his breathing eased.

Chapter 60

Thursday, 12 August

*T*he inquest into the death of Jude Lowe was held less than twenty-four hours later, immediately after those that had already been scheduled. The verdict was justifiable homicide.

Afterward, Sebastian and Archie Rawlins walked out to the crossroads, where the blacksmith and two of his sons were working with pickaxes and shovels to dig up what was left of Hannah Grant. No one had given them official permission, but Sebastian suspected no one was going to stop them either, just as he had no doubt the vicar would allow Hannah to be reburied in the churchyard. There was much that was disgusting about Benedict Underwood, but there was some good there too.

Sebastian watched in silence as Miles Grant, his face wet with silent tears, tenderly placed his daughter's skull in a wide-topped basket. Then Sebastian's gaze shifted to the Ship, deserted now in the late-afternoon sunlight. He'd learned only that morning that Lowe was a widower, that his wife had died of fever less than a year ago. And he found himself thinking of Lowe's three boys, and what would happen to them now.

Archie said, "I'm still having a hard time getting used to the idea that Jude Lowe has been killing people around here for fifteen years and more."

"From the sound of things, he stopped for quite a few years in there."

"I wonder why."

"Perhaps there was no one he wanted dead."

Archie pushed out a strangled huff of air. "I suppose that's something to be grateful for." He was silent for a moment, then said, "There've been so many deaths these last ten days. It's not going to be easy for the people of the village to absorb it all. They've lost too many, over the years."

"At least it's finally over."

Archie nodded. "I don't know how to thank you for what you've done. I never would have figured this out if you hadn't been here."

"You don't know that."

"Yes, I do. If it'd been up to me, I'd have hanged the vicar. The vicar!"

"Jude Lowe was a very clever man."

"He certainly fooled me. I hope to God I never have to face anything like this again."

"You'll do all right. Just keep an open mind and remember that simply because an explanation seems to fit doesn't mean it's true."

They turned back toward the village, the towering old gibbet casting its long shadow across a section of the coach road left muddy by the previous day's rains. After a moment, Archie said, "So how do you know when you finally have it right?"

"I'm not sure. You just do," said Sebastian, and Archie threw back his head and laughed.

Later that evening, as the sun slipped toward the purple hills of Wales, Sebastian climbed the lane to the churchyard. He stood beside Emma

Chandler's graveside for a long time, while the rooks flew in to roost in the nearby yew, fluttering and cawing as they settled in for the night.

He felt an intense, painful bond with this woman he had come to know only after her death. They had both come to Ayleswick-on-Teme in the hopes of discovering the identity of the man who had sired them. Both had failed. But only Emma had lost her life in the quest.

So adrift was he in his own thoughts that it was a moment before Sebastian heard a woman's faint footfalls and the swish of fine cloth, and realized he was no longer alone.

"Am I interrupting you?" asked Lady Seaton, walking up to him. She wore a simple muslin dress with a light blue spencer and a wide-brimmed straw hat that framed her golden curls in a way that made her look deceptively young and vulnerable.

"No, not at all," he said.

She tipped back her head to look up at him, the warm evening breeze fluttering the blue satin ribbon of her hat across her cheek. "I wanted to ask you something."

"Of course."

"I believe I told you I once met Lady Emily."

"Yes."

She drew a deep breath and nodded, as if confirming the truth of her earlier statement or perhaps simply encouraging herself to go on. "What I didn't tell you was that we met on the last night of the Irvings' house party. They held a grand ball—a masquerade—and although I wasn't well, Seaton insisted I attend. He felt the need to trot out his wife on occasion, you see, to reassure the local gentry that despite the irregular nature of his activities he still retained my love and devotion."

Sebastian said nothing, and after a moment, she went on. "Leopold was an extraordinarily attractive man with a most deceptively charming manner. He had a way of paying attention to a woman, of smiling at her, that could make her feel the most beautiful, most fascinating and desirable woman in the world."

"And he turned his charms on Lady Emily?"

"He did, yes. I watched them. You might think it was because I was jealous, but it wasn't. Not by then. I knew what he was like, and I worried about her."

Sebastian remembered the words the sixteen-year-old girl had written to her governess. *He is so handsome that my head would surely be turned were it not for Liv's warnings. . . .*

"I could tell she was flattered—how could she help but be? She was so young and innocent. But she was wise enough not to forget that he was a married man. And while she seemed happy enough to have the opportunity to practice the arts of flirtation with a master, I could see that she was becoming increasingly uncomfortable with the tenor of his attentions. In the end, she excused herself and went outside for some air. She was trying to get away from him, of course. But I'm afraid he took it the wrong way."

"He followed her?"

She nodded. "I should have gone after them immediately. Instead, I waited, hoping she'd come back. And then Lady Irving buttonholed me as I was headed toward the terrace. She was so persistent, I'd only just managed to extricate myself when I saw Leopold slipping back in through the glass doors. He was vaguely disheveled, and when Lady Emily didn't come back at all, I went looking for her, fearing the worst."

"And you were right."

"Yes. I found her in the shrubbery, hysterical. I knew he'd forced himself on some of the village girls, but . . . I never imagined he'd so forget himself as to do the same to a young gentlewoman. I helped her to her room; made her promise to let me come to her aid in the event she should find herself in trouble as a result of that night's work." Lady Seaton's gaze dropped to the grave beside them. "Obviously, it was a promise she didn't keep. But, my God, how I wish she had. You can have no notion of my joy the day his lordship's lifeless body was carried home." She looked up at him. "But you knew that, didn't you? Did you imagine I'd killed him?"

"Yes."

A strange smile played about her lips. "I used to lie awake at night and entertain myself concocting various ways in which I might murder him and get away with it. But I never would have found the courage to do it. Fortunately, someone else did it for me."

"Did you know, even then?"

"That someone had killed him? Oh, yes. But I didn't know who." She drew a deep, shaky breath. "I haven't told Crispin the truth—that Emma Chandler was his half sister, I mean."

"Will you?"

"I don't know. Sometimes I think it might make it easier for him, to know they could never have married, even if she had lived. But then I think, the woman he loved is already lost to him; what good would it serve for him to have to live with the horror of knowing he'd desired his own sister? Perhaps it would be best after all to leave him with the memory of his lost love intact."

"How well does Lord Seaton remember his father?"

"Hardly at all. He was very young when his father died. And Leopold never had any interest in what he used to call 'snotty-nosed nursery brats.'"

"Does he know what his father was like?"

"You mean, does he know Leopold had a nasty habit of slaking his lust on the village girls, willing or not? I don't believe so, no. But I must admit, I hadn't thought of what it would do to Crispin, to learn such an ugly truth about his father."

"He may eventually hear some of it anyway, from someone in the village."

"Yes." She searched his face, and he wondered if she saw there the traces of his own long-ago, secret anguish that their conversation had dredged up. "So what are you saying? That I should tell him?"

"You're the one who must bear the burden of keeping this a secret for the rest of your life."

"I would do it for Crispin, gladly. If only I could be certain it was right."

"There's no denying secrets can be dangerous. Yet some secrets . . . I believe some secrets are best left unknown. It would be different, had she lived."

"Yes. Yes, it would." She gave him a faint, tremulous smile. "Thank you, my lord."

He watched her walk away, her head held high, her back rigorously straight, her features carefully schooled into an expression that betrayed not a hint of the turmoil in her heart.

Or the admirable strength of her will.

Friday, 13 August

The next morning, Sebastian had two obligations to fulfill before he left the village.

First he climbed the lane to the vicarage, where Benedict Underwood was supervising two workmen repairing a gap in the orchard wall. Taking the vicar aside, he warned Underwood that if he ever laid a hand on his cousin Rachel Timms again, Sebastian would not only make certain he lost the living of Ayleswick, but see to it that he was never given another parish.

The Reverend's practiced benevolent smile remained firmly in place.

Sebastian said, "And if you think Rachel Timms is too afraid of losing Hill Cottage to be honest with me, then you should know that I've promised her a cottage on my own estate down in Hampshire, should that come to pass."

Underwood's smile slid away.

Sebastian touched a hand to his hat. "Good day to you, Reverend."

After that, he walked out to the little whitewashed cottage beside the stream.

He found Heddie Kincaid dozing on a bench in the warm sunshine. And there, hat in hand, he expressed his sorrow for the death of her son.

She lifted her blind face to him, showing him the ravages left by another unbearable loss. "I don't blame you for it," she said, her voice breaking. "Maybe if Jude'd had a better da, things would've turned out different. But . . ." She paused to draw a painful breath. "I was always afraid he'd end up being hanged. So in a sense I suppose you could say I'm grateful to you for sparing us that."

She asked him then to sit beside her, and he spoke to her of Jamie Knox and of the child the ex-rifleman had had by the barmaid, Pippa, and how much the boy resembled his dead father.

As he talked, he was aware of Jenny watching him through the window of the cottage. It wasn't until he rose to take his leave that she came to stand in the open doorway, her arms crossed at her chest. Her face was hard, her eyes red and swollen from her own grieving.

"I didn't send him after you," she said. "Jude, I mean. I wanted you to know that."

Sebastian paused beside her. "But you did speak to him after I left." It was more a statement than a question.

She stared across the stream to where Jude's three orphaned sons were playing with a puppy. "I was hoping Jude'd tell me I was wrong about him. But he didn't, and in the end all I did was warn him that you'd figured it out. For that, I am sorry."

Sebastian nodded, although he wasn't sure if she was sorry because she'd put his life and Hero's in danger, or because Jude had ended up dead.

She said, "His father, Daniel Lowe, was without a doubt the meanest man I've ever known, and even worse when he had the drink in him, which was often. I'm not sure who he beat more, Jude or Jamie. But after Jamie left, Jude was the only one he had to use his fists on."

"Daniel Lowe died in 'ninety-seven?"

Jenny nodded. "Fell off a haystack onto a pitchfork. I always figured Jude did for him, although Jude never admitted it. I think maybe he was the first person Jude killed."

Sebastian wasn't so certain of that. But all he said was, "I'm surprised he didn't kill Eugene Weston long ago."

"He wanted to. But he and the major were in the free-trade business together. Weston always liked to claim he didn't take to smuggling until after old man Irving died, but it wasn't true; he and Jude had teamed up long before that—a good six months before Alex was hanged. Jude had the brains and the guts to organize and oversee everything, but Weston was the one with the money. Jude needed him."

"I guess Jude decided he didn't need him anymore," said Sebastian. Weston and the caretaker, Silas Madden, had been found in one of the bays of the carriage house, their deaths staged to look like a murder-suicide. Jude had set it up so well that if he hadn't decided to go after Sebastian, he might well have succeeded in blaming the long string of both recent and past killings on the major.

Jenny shifted her gaze to where her grandmother now sat quietly mourning another dead child. Sebastian saw a quiver of emotion pass over her features. "I know you won't believe it, but there was much that was good in Jude. He was so loving. Loving and funny and kind."

As long as you stayed on the right side of him, thought Sebastian. And he wondered if they'd ever know how many people the innkeeper had murdered over the years.

He turned to leave, but she stopped him by saying, "You asked about Jamie's and my father."

He paused to look back at her.

She said, "Before my mother died, she told Nana that she'd laid with three men: an English lord, a Welsh cavalryman, and a stable hand named Ian from out at Maplethorpe Hall. But Ian was killed when Jamie and me was only two years old." She tipped her head to one side, regarding him appraisingly. "I'm thirty-six now. How old're you?"

"I'll be thirty-one this October."

"So I guess that narrows it down a bit, doesn't it?" she said, her gaze meeting his as a tentative smile curled her lips.

Author's Note

*A*yleswick, its historic homes, and its ruined priory are my own creations. I envision the village as lying near the River Teme between Bromfield and Downton Gorge.

Lucien Bonaparte (1775–1840), one of Napoléon's troublesome younger brothers, did indeed spend years in England as a prisoner of war. A fervent revolutionary, he originally supported Robespierre during the Terror. But later, as president of the Council of Five Hundred, he was instrumental in assisting Napoléon's coup d'état of 18 Brumaire. As a result, he always credited himself with his brother's elevation to power.

Lucien's wealth came from a stint as ambassador to Spain, during which he amassed huge bribes in diamonds that he sold and invested in England and the United States. His relations with his brother were always rocky and eventually deteriorated to the point of a split when Napoléon tried to pressure Lucien into divorcing his wife and contracting a dynastic marriage. Lucien's flight from Italy is generally seen as an attempt to escape his brother's wrath. The British, however, were convinced that Lucien's "flight" to America in 1810 was a hoax, suspecting that his true intent was to fan the flames of what would eventually become the War of 1812.

Captured by the British navy, Lucien and his family (along with a huge retinue of servants and baggage) spent six months in Ludlow before purchasing the estate of Thorngrove in Worcestershire. During that time, they became quite friendly with several noble Catholic families in the area, one of which invited the Bonapartes to baptize their newborn child in their private chapel. Lucien did indeed publish both a novel and a heroic poem about Charlemagne, as well as his memoirs. Convinced that his brother had deliberately gone over to the British, Napoléon did send spies to watch Lucien—as did London, of course. And while Lucien was in Shropshire and Worcestershire, he remained in close, secret contact with Paris; at one point his mother even passed money to him, using the smugglers that plied the Channel.

Allowed to leave England and return to Italy after Napoléon's banishment to Elba, Lucien rallied to his brother's cause when the Emperor returned for his Hundred Days—a fact that suggests the break between the brothers was not exactly as it appeared. Despite the bizarre instability exhibited by so many of its members, the Bonaparte family remained extraordinarily close, something to remember when analyzing Lucien's behavior, movements, and motivations.

For my portrayal of Lucien, I have relied mainly on Lucien's own memoirs; Pietromarchi's *Lucien Bonaparte: le frère insoumis;* and Desmond Seward's *Napoleon's Family: The Notorious Bonapartes and Their Ascent to the Thrones of Europe.*

Lucien did indeed have a son, Charles (1803–1857), who became a biologist and ornithologist of some renown. A friend of James Audubon, he discovered the mustached warbler and a new species of storm petrel, and created the genus *Zenaida,* named after the mother of his twelve children.

For the Enclosure Acts of the eighteenth and nineteenth centuries, see, amongst many others, J. M. Neeson, *Commoners: Common Right, Enclosure, and Social Change in England,* 1700–1820; J. L. and Barbara Hammond's landmark 1911 study, *The Village Labourer,* 1760–1832; Oliver Goldsmith's haunting poem "The Deserted Village"; and Joseph Stromberg, *English Enclosures and Soviet Collectivization.*

Regency inquests were indeed held in taverns and inns. I have relied mainly on Joseph Baker Grindon's *A Compendium of the Laws of Coroners, with Forms and Practical Instructions*, which provides a detailed and highly informative look at the practices of nineteenth-century coroners. The deodand was little used after the beginning of the nineteenth century, and formally abolished by Parliament in 1848 when people attempted to use the age-old tradition to hold the railroads financially responsible for those they killed.

The technique of smothering combined with chest compression used on Emma is today called "burking," after its use by the infamous body snatchers William Burke and William Hare in 1828. Burke and Hare quickly realized it was much easier to obtain fresh bodies for medical schools via murder, rather than going through all the trouble of digging up the already dead. By sitting on their victims' chests and putting a hand over their mouths and noses, they discovered they could kill without leaving any visible injuries.

The Corresponding Societies of Great Britain, founded in the early 1790s, were dedicated to parliamentary reform and drew their membership largely from the artisan classes. They were violently opposed by the government and their members driven underground by the end of the decade. For the history of Edward Despard, see Mike Jay's *The Unfortunate Colonel Despard*.

Tenbury Wells was known simply as Tenbury until the middle of the nineteenth century.

For a fascinating look at the villages and historic houses of Shropshire in the late nineteenth century, see *Nooks and Corners of Shropshire*, by H. Thornhill Timmins. I am grateful to Jim Almond for his beautiful and informative Web site and blog on Shropshire birds, http://shropshirebirder.co.uk/index.html and http://shropshirebirder.blogspot.com, and to Katherine Swift for her lovely books on her Shropshire garden, *The Morville Hours* and *The Morville Year*.